Single Books
Lost in LA
The Devil in the Deep South

Sun Valley Mafia
Syndicate Rising

Sun Valley Mafia

SYNDICATE RISING

AMY CRAIG

Syndicate Rising
ISBN # 978-1-80250-985-4
©Copyright Amy Craig 2022
Cover Art by Erin Dameron-Hill ©Copyright September 2022
Interior text design by Claire Siemaszkiewicz
Totally Bound Publishing

SYNDICATE RISING

Dedication

To Victor, who tried to bite me a time or two,
but we made peace.

Chapter One

Nina backed into the high-rise's smudged glass door and sacrificed her favorite red suit to the city's germs. The skirt displayed her ass to an advantage, so her immune system had better appreciate the tradeoff. Half of New York had left their handprints on the panel, and the other half would visit tomorrow. After the year she'd had, the limited contact approach made sense. Since Nan's death, she had wondered what she wanted out of life, but influenza wasn't the answer.

Free of the law office where she worked as a legal mediator, she adjusted her leather tote and inhaled a mix of freesia, exhaust and hot-dog fumes. Summer humidity hovered over the sunbaked sidewalks.

In a few hours, the concrete would cool, and the city's professional class would congregate in packed restaurants, dim bars and quiet subway stations. She would be home with the dog she'd recently adopted, Victor, a few journal articles and a chilled salad.

The red suit would go to the dry cleaners.

Most Fridays, she treated herself to a car, but her favorite driver had left town for a funeral. She headed for the subway station, but she missed the light. Standing on the street corner, she watched the cars jostle for position. The city felt impossibly big, but she carved out a place for herself and the achievement satisfied her.

An unkempt man rattled a cup full of change. "Heya."

Keeping her expression neutral, she focused on the opposite street corner. Her career trained her to avoid conflict, but she snuck a glance. Arms wrapped around his knees, he held the cup. A large, purple birthmark covered one cheek and his nearly black bare feet tapped to a private beat.

"Can you spare a dollar?" he asked.

She often gave money to people on the street, but she tried not to let their plights ruin her day. An unfolded newspaper lay next to this man, and the lead story detailed overcrowding at area homeless shelters. If she had a few million dollars to spare, she would do more than give him a dollar. Fishing in her tote, she pulled out a bill and offered it. Too late, she realized she held a twenty.

His face lit up, and he snatched the bill. "What's your name?"

"I don't think so." Shifting her stance, she eyed his bare feet. She'd spent more than twenty dollars on Victor's collar. If she couldn't afford the same generosity for another human, she might need to reevaluate her priorities. "If I give you another twenty, will you buy shoes?"

"Nope."

She frowned. "Why not?"

"Never needed them." He stretched out his legs. "I do need a hamburger."

"Okay then."

The light changed.

Striding across the intersection, she glanced over her shoulder. The unkempt man chatted with another suit-clad commuter, and she released the tension in her shoulders. Checking the time, she wondered if she would make her train, quickened her pace and descended the subway stairs.

On the last step, her red heel quivered.

Grabbing for the railing, she held fast.

The crowd rushed past.

If she had fallen, would someone have stopped to help her? Shaking her head, she continued into the station and lingered near the platform's back wall.

The train roared to a stop.

Gauging the flow of passengers, she squeezed into the cramped train and stood elbow to elbow with her fellow New Yorkers. More than anything else, the subway normalized the city's population. In a rocking and rolling subway car, everyone widened their stance, gripped the handlebars and hung on for dear life. She did the same, but she did it better than most.

After a few stops, the train's shaking rhythm lulled her, and she closed her eyes. She didn't really need a day off work. She needed a way to unwind. As a legal mediator, she helped opposing parties feel in control, but she could halt the discussions at any time. Some people were selfish morons and some were lovesick fools, but she stayed calm.

The first year in law school, she'd worn black. By graduation, she'd secured her place on the honors list and had turned red into her signature color. When people asked about the color, she told them she liked to put out fires, and they paid her good money to do it. The sense of achievement brought a smile to her lips, but in a city this big, her compensation bought her little luxuries, and she remembered her grandmother's admonishment to savor them.

"You look happy," a woman said.

She opened her eyes. An older woman held a cane between her knees. She nodded with the train's rhythm, but her pale blue eyes looked clear. "I am."

"But tired." The woman pointed a crooked, arthritic finger. "You should take better care of yourself."

"Great advice. You, too." Clearing her throat, she checked the train's progress toward Murray Hill. The borough's tree-lined streets were quintessential old New York City. Apple orchards, windswept daisies and benevolent livestock were an ideal childhood setting, but she craved museums, restaurants and the city's vibrant, diverse flavors. If Nan had decided to haunt her, she could go straight back to the countryside.

The rider dug in her purse. "I have a tea you could try."

"Oh. Um…" She tamped down her horror. If she wanted to land on *Page Six,* she could have a lot more fun before accepting drugs from a stranger. Rows of white subway tiles came into view and the train lumbered into the stop at 33rd Street. She pushed her way toward the train door. "Maybe next time!"

The woman snapped her purse closed.

Emerging from the station into fading late-afternoon light, Nina adjusted her skirt and turned toward the pre-war Park Avenue condo building she loved.

José, her building's doorman, spotted her and waved.

She waved back. His stomach stretched his black doorman's jacket, but he wore his hair like Elvis. When she smuggled Victor out of the back of the building for walks, she often heard him singing in the service hallways. More than once, she wondered if the songs served as an audible warning. She doted on her new dog, but she hadn't finished her pet application. Stopping at José's side where she could chat without interrupting his work, she adjusted her tote. "Anything good today?"

"Couple of packages," he said. "A new guy moved onto the twelfth floor."

"Oh?"

Pulling open the door, he winked. "The man's eighty."

"Good for him." She needed a way to unwind, but she could do better than eighty. Maybe she could make friends with the man and set him up with the lady on the train. Smiling, she slipped past José and made her way to the elevator. "Thanks for the heads-up."

She rode the elevator to her floor.

After typing her access code into her door's security panel, she dropped her tote on the hardwood floor and circled the leather couch. Victor pawed at the crate door, but the clever animal made no sounds. Lifting the crate's door release, she stepped back.

He bounded out, play-bowed and wagged his tail.

She held out her arms for the silly white animal.

Acting coy, he cocked his head.

"Come here, you little stinker."

He growled.

Crouching, she scooped him into her arms and buried her nose in his soft fur. "I missed you."

He licked her cheek.

After she'd checked her houseplants and emptied her tote, she lowered him into the leather purse and eased closed her condo's door. Looking both ways down the hallway, she found it empty and exhaled. "Quiet or some snooty neighbor will bust us, and we'll have to find you a new home."

He whimpered.

"Don't worry. They're all good people at heart." Stroking his head, she ferried him to the small park behind the building. She would present him to the condo board, but she needed time to complete the board's lengthy pet application. *Who wouldn't love this dog?*

* * * *

Two hours later, Nina and Victor lay sprawled across her bed. He licked the tamarind vinaigrette dressing from a discarded salad container, and she pretended not to notice the transgression.

Wandering around Murray Hill one night, she'd stumbled on a little restaurant that advertised Burmese Tea Leaf Salads. The mix of tofu, noodles, fried garlic, fried onions, chickpeas and green papaya tasted delicious, but the Myanmar immigrants' warm smiles made the sale. She stayed to chat and made a habit of stocking up on the salads. One day she would travel, but that dream would have to wait.

A knock sounded on the door.

Padding across the living room floor, she checked the peephole and smiled. Martha, her forty-five-year-old neighbor, stood in the hallway. The woman's hipbones jutted above the waistline of her jeans and made her look like a wrinkled teenager who had overindulged on self-tanner. Above her jeans, she wore a zip-up hoodie, a lacy camisole and diamond stud earrings. Well, Nina assumed they were diamonds. She opened the door. "How are you?"

Martha shook her blonde bob away from her face. "Fantastic."

Am I supposed to take a picture?

"If I texted, I knew you'd ignore me." She spread wide her arms. "So here I am."

"Here you are."

Martha narrowed her gaze. "Where have you been?"

She cleared her throat. Hiding a dog sounded like a terrible reason to ghost a friend. "Sometimes I don't see your texts."

Dropping her arms, Martha tilted her head. "Lame."

She smiled. "Do you want to come in for a drink?" She opened the door wider, but she knew Martha would decline. The woman's long, thin legs carried her through Manhattan's steamy streets, but she had a killer smile. Tourists bought her drinks to hear her stories and street artists drew her caricature to pass the time. When she winked and slid her rail-thin body past the subway stile, tollbooth operators looked the other way. She didn't need Nina to grab a drink.

Martha picked at her nails. "Come over and watch a show with me."

Nina looked over her shoulder and spotted Victor's raised head on the bed. "I can't."

"Bring the dog with you," Martha said.

Swallowing, she adopted the neutral expression she used for mediation. "What dog?"

"The one you sneak in and out of the building like a fraternity pledge." Martha raised an eyebrow. "I know you have a dog." She whistled.

Victor jumped off the bed and scampered across the wood floor.

His little nails made soft taps. Nina would have to trim them. "Traitor," she said. "Sit."

He sat.

"Impressive." Martha covered a yawn. "Now, come on. I miss you. Ever since Atlantic City, you're no fun."

Six weeks ago, she and Martha had taken a girls' trip to Atlantic City. Martha had brought home an arcade toy. She'd brought home a long-haired, tatted-up drummer with bulging biceps. At two in the morning, she'd lost her bearings in a casino and fallen into his arms. The relationship had lasted two weeks. Fearing an encore performance, she'd adopted Victor.

"Fine, but I get to pick the show." Scooping up the dog, she padded barefoot across the hall and walked into Martha's condo like she owned the place.

Martha worked at an art gallery and had an artist's eye for color and design. Large, abstract paintings brightened white walls, and sheer curtains billowed in front of an open window. A dip-dyed throw pooled on a jute rug and an ocean's breath candle fought the city's miasma. Despite the décor, Nina listened for the muffled traffic jams and pedestrian shouts that lulled her to sleep. A candle couldn't disguise the city she loved. She looked for a place to settle Victor.

Martha dropped onto her cream-colored sofa. "Wine?"

An opened bottle sat on Martha's reclaimed wood coffee table next to a sweating, half-empty goblet and a fresh glass. "Sure."

Filling the second glass, Martha offered it, settled back on the sofa and waved her hand toward the dog. "Oh, he's fine. Let him be."

Sipping the wine, Nina set it back on the table and perched on the sofa. She stroked Victor's silky, white fur, but she kept him on her lap. When a strand of fur drifted from her fingers, she made a fist and tried to catch it. Stray dog fur could alienate friends faster than recounting case files. "So, what's up?"

"Nothing." Martha reached for the remote. "Same old."

"I haven't seen you in a month." Maybe friendship could help her unwind. She had Martha, coworkers who pretended to set aside their cases over lunch and holdovers from college. Victor had the softest ears. "How's the gallery?"

"It closed," Martha said.

She stilled her hand. "What?"

"The owner wants to invest in non-fungible tokens." Martha drained her wineglass and channel surfed. "I told him he'd be broke in a year."

"Maybe." She had a client who paid big money for cat clip art. His wife had filed for divorce, but she was claiming the NFT. "It's gaining momentum."

"A fad." Martha shifted on the sofa.

She looked at the abstract art. "Maybe."

Turned from the television, Martha cocked her head. "What's he called?"

She considered how much to reveal. Her pet shared her pillow, and she refused to abandon him to an animal shelter. "His name's Victor."

Martha tapped her foot. "No, what's the breed?"

"Havanese." He looked like a Bichon, but his curled-over tail gave him charm. At thirteen pounds, he topped the charts, but he revealed himself as a curious, sociable pet that needed weekly grooming and slightly warmed dog food. "Do you want to hold him?"

Martha shook her head.

Other than racing around the condo and keeping her on edge, Victor was overall delightful. His tiny teeth looked like saw blades and the vet told her to brush them daily. The first time she tried, she feared her laughter would give away her secret.

"I would have guessed Pomeranian," Martha said. "Aren't they interchangeable?"

Victor lifted his head and growled.

Nina smoothed his fur. "Shush."

Martha stood and paced the condo. "Well, my ex-husband left me a pile of debt." She lifted a bleached seashell. "At least you were smart and chose the dog."

"True."

Martha plopped down next to her and leaned toward the screen. "I just love this show."

"Really? Why?" She tried to pay attention, but Martha kept checking her watch. "Are you expecting someone?"

Martha startled. "No."

Leaping from her lap, Victor claimed a sleek, tight back armchair and presided over the room's corner.

"Okay." Exhausted, she leaned against the sofa back and watched the show. If she wanted sleep, she could have stayed across the hall. After the show ended, she stood and moved to scoop up Victor. "This was great, but I have an early morning at work."

Martha jumped up and moved in front of the door. "Wait!"

She frowned. "Why?"

"I, uh"—Martha picked up a book—"want your opinion."

The intercom buzzed.

"Ms. Martha, your visitor's here." José's voice filled the room.

Victor barked.

Tapping the dog's nose, she scooped him into her arms and shushed him before a nosy neighbor ratted out his presence. "I'll leave you to it."

"No, stay."

"I don't have time."

Martha tilted her head. "You have time to watch shit television shows. You have time to sneak that leashed cotton ball onto the subway."

"Uhh…"

Reaching for Victor, Martha raised him in the air and examined him. "Trust me, you have plenty of time for visitors. Let Auntie Martha take care of you." Martha spoke to Victor in a singsong, baby voice. "We could be friends."

Victor peed on Martha's chest.

"Shit!" Martha laughed and shook her head. "I knew he didn't like me."

Reclaiming Victor, Nina settled him on her hip and accepted her past transgressions had paved the road to hell.

Stripping off her clothes, Martha darted into her bedroom.

"Who's the visitor?" Nina asked.

"My high school pen pal. His plane just landed." Drawers opened and closed.

"Oh, come on." Nina rolled her eyes. "I thought you met someone at the gallery."

"The gallery closed!" Walking out of her bedroom wearing a low-cut top, Martha cocked one hip forward and lifted her chin. "Alessio Chen is someone. How do I look?"

"Sassy. Is he an artist?"

Martha widened her eyes. "Oh, come on."

Striking a pose, she wondered how much time she had before Alessio Chen arrived at Martha's door. She didn't want to leave Martha in poor spirits. If another month passed before they saw each other, their friendship might fade away. "I could be his muse."

Martha laughed.

A knock sounded on the door.

Dropping her hand from her head, Nina straightened. "Really, Martha, tell me something about the man. I'm a little gun-shy after Atlantic City."

Rubbing her hands, Martha advanced on the door. "He's an insurance salesman. He's a little older than you, but he's fierce and loyal to the people he loves. I always fancied him a bit, but he's too smart for me."

The glimpse of vulnerability fascinated her. "You had a crush on him?"

Pausing, Martha looked over her shoulder. "Not a crush, per se, but an admiration. Sometimes, you meet people in the city, and you know they're going somewhere. You'll like Alessio. I hoped you'd be here when he arrived."

"You could have told me."

"I figured you might be a little... What did you say? Gun-shy? Let him take you on a date. He's rarely in the city."

"Wait! He knows I'm here?"

"No, but he'll want to take you out." Martha appraised her. "Anybody would."

Nina cleared her throat and prepared for the worst. Martha's family lived in Newark. Despite her dreamy-eyed praise, her pen pal could be anyone from a Florida cousin to a Sicilian convict.

A second knock sounded.

Exhaling, Nina penciled in 'meatballs and spaghetti'. If Martha pledged her loyalty to Alessio's character, she would make room in her schedule for one date with the potentially affable, overweight and balding man. Lowering Victor to the sofa, she smoothed out her loungewear. "I wish you'd warned me."

"So you could avoid me?"

"I don't avoid you…"

Martha opened the door.

Shy of six feet tall, the man's parted, wavy, black hair brushed his suit collar, and his full lips teased a smile. A slight bump on his nose hinted at past trauma, but she appreciated the character.

"I wondered if I had the right apartment," he said.

Leaning forward, Martha kissed his cheek. "You're in the right place, and you smell divine!"

Alessio laughed and returned the kiss. "It's good to see you, too."

Divine? Nina bit her tongue. She'd come across the hall to relax, but Alessio looked like a banker crossed with a wide receiver. Standing beyond the door, he filled out his suit jacket, and shifted with an athlete's easy grace. If age intensified his features, she wanted to be there when he reached full maturity. Stepping forward, she forgave Martha's shenanigans and vowed to buy her a case of wine. Subterfuge rubbed her the wrong way, but Martha was right about her recalcitrance. Since Atlantic City, she had shied away from people, but Martha had provided the world's best way to unwind.

Chapter Two

Alessio stepped into the condo and ignored Martha's beautiful houseguest and the curious dog occupying the chair. Martha had said she wanted to meet for a drink, but he'd assumed she needed money. As long as he'd known her, she'd never showed a shred of interest in animals. The dog must belong to the woman wearing red leggings and a tight, white shirt. He'd had his share of beautiful women. Keeping his hands in his pockets, he faced his friend. "You ready?"

Martha grabbed the woman's arm and pulled her forward. "This is Nina Levoy."

He extended a hand. "Alessio. Nice to meet you."

She tucked her blonde-streaked brown hair behind her ear and straightened her shoulders. Taking his hand, she shook it with quiet efficiency. "Nine to meet you, too. I didn't know Martha expected company."

"No?" He pulled free his hand. "I didn't know she had it."

Nina laughed.

None of the women he knew laughed like Nina. Her appreciation sounded like a soft release held back by good manners. He wanted to hear the real deal.

Cupping Nina's elbow, Martha pulled her toward the door. "You should join us."

"I can't."

He cocked his head. Martha's invitation and Nina's refusal surprised him. If Martha didn't need money, why did she call? He kept an old shoebox full of her letters in the Swiss house where he'd grown up. Eager to refine his English, he'd inflated his age and corresponded with the American teenager who knew everything about John Gotti's trial, The Mall of America and the Great Chicago Flood. The day after he'd arrived in America to establish the American arm of ADC Industries, he had called up his old pen pal and asked her to dinner. She had shown up wearing a dress with a thigh-high slit.

The dog barked.

He shook off the memory of the awkward meal and what had followed.

Turning, Nina pulled free of Martha and scooped up the dog. "Really, I can't."

"Can't or won't?" Martha asked.

The pair squared off, and he wondered if Nina could out-maneuver the cagey, older woman.

"Can't," Nina said. "Victor needs a walk, and I need sleep."

Blowing out her lips, Martha sighed. "You don't know what's good for you."

"Hmm. Maybe I do." Nina turned to him. "Martha said you're rarely in town. Would you like to grab dinner one night?"

He liked her forthright interest. Most women offered him drinks, but he doubted he could unpack her motivations over two martinis. Martha appeared to have told Nina little about him. With most people, 'billionaire investor' conjured a distinctive reaction. Some people stared, some people stammered and some people went for the gold. Nina held her dog like she had all the time in the world to get to know him. "Dinner sounds good."

Martha beamed.

"Great." Walking past him, Nina stilled. "What's your last name?"

She smelled like a rainy day in the woods. Up close, gold flecked her hazel eyes and a soft, sweet smell surrounded her. He cleared his throat before he got ahead of himself. Why shouldn't she research him? She would find very little information. In the business word, he went by his middle name and few people reconciled Alessio and Donato Chen. The anonymity suited him, but her interest suited him more. "Chen."

"Nice to meet you, Alessio Chen. I'll get your number from Martha." She walked out of the door without a backward glance.

Her generous hips swayed, and he considered transferring fifty thousand dollars to Martha's account and following Nina next door. "Nice to meet you, too."

* * * *

In the middle of the boxing ring, Alessio bounced on the balls of his feet. Perspiration dripped down his back and blurred his vision, but he had the upper hand.

His opponent had a bleeding cut above one eye.

Reading the other man's body language, Alessio tried to anticipate his opponent's next move. Forty years of survival had honed his instincts, and he refused to let down his guard for a cocky asshole with a jacked-up grin. If the fight played out how he expected, he would walk away without shedding his own blood. Arms up, he held his ground and waited for an error.

His opponent tried a kick and struggled to regain his balance.

Unimpressed, Alessio stepped forward and released a vicious left hook.

The blow snapped back the man's head.

Spitting out blood, the man put up his hands, guarded his face and danced from foot to foot. "Cheap shot."

"But effective," he said. "Yield."

The man spat. "They warned me you was a tough one."

If he could remember the man's name, he could talk sense into him, but he understood pride. ADC Industries owned several insurance companies, a boutique investment firm and a portfolio of casinos. He gave paid talks on corporate pride, and people wanted to beat him up. He wanted to conquer them. A boxing ring's ropes didn't change the rules.

His opponent went on the defensive, threw weak punches and skirted his strike range.

He bided his time, marked the man's weaknesses and waited for an opening. Faking a right hook, he raised his left leg and kicked the man square in the stomach.

The blow sent the man flying into the ropes.

"Fuck!" The man recovered and came out swinging, but he stumbled and shook the sweat from his head. "Lucky blow."

"Luck had nothing to do with it."

They danced.

His opponent's movements grew sluggish. He drew deep breaths, flared his nostrils and held his hands too low to block his face. Shifting his weight, Alessio waited for an opening. He never struck a defenseless man, but this man refused to yield. He circled his opponent, kept his stance light and let the man's weak shots expend his energy. Soon, he would go in for the kill.

The man tried a punch.

He turned his cheek and cut up with his left hand. Catching the man off guard, he spun him toward the ropes.

The man teetered on exhaustion's edge, but he pushed himself into the ring's center.

Admiring his determination, Alessio readied himself for a new onslaught.

It never came.

His opponent's feet dragged, his arms slumped and his jabs lacked precision. Alessio backed him into a corner, landed a final blow and gave him enough room to stumble off the ropes.

"You think you's better" — the man wiped sweat from his brow — "than me."

"I know I am." He planted a light kick square in the middle of the man's chest and watched him hit the floor. The dull thud never grew old. Unwrapping his hands, he removed his mouth guard and cleared the spit from his throat. "Good fight. For a while, you kept me on my toes."

Gym trainers helped the man off the floor, but he spit out his mouth guard. "You're nothing but a rich asshole."

"True." Picking up a towel, Alessio moved his damp hair off his forehead and climbed out of the ring. "When you're looking for a job, don't bother calling."

"What'd you say?"

Raising his hand in farewell, he let the exchange die. Antagonizing his opponent wouldn't change the fight's outcome. These open-call sparring sessions were a combination of multiple techniques, but they kept him in shape and kept his reputation intact.

Muay Thai relied on striking opponents. Krav Maga borrowed self-defense techniques from martial arts. Judo and Jiu-Jitsu had their benefits. The media sensationalized Tyson taking a chunk out of Holyfield's right ear, but they hadn't covered enough street fights. He fought to win, and ruthlessness kept him on top in business and in the gym.

To fight off the kids who'd cornered him in Zürich's back alleys, he'd honed speed, strength and a stoic commitment to win. As his holdings grew, he traded physical pain for business intelligence, but he remained in fighting shape. His team of associates knew little of his past, but they respected his pitiless business dealings. If their billionaire boss liked to spar or attended meetings with the odd black eye, they knew better than to ask questions.

He knew better than to care what his competitors thought about his behavior. Every business relationship boiled down to a transaction, and clear expectations mattered. He enriched his associates, and they pledged their working lives to him. The day his pilot or boat captain showed up late and asked for slack, he fired their ass.

Josh jogged up to his side and handed him a cold towel. "Mr. Chen, towel?"

"Thanks, buddy." He scanned the crowded gym and looked for Josh's mother.

Alyssa leaned against the railing on her observation platform and inclined her head.

He returned the gesture. For close to twenty years, he'd known and respected her. When he'd come off the European fighting circuit flush with cash, he'd taken a fight he should have turned down. One hand tied behind his back, he'd fought her bare knuckled. She'd taken several hits before she'd yielded. After the fight, she'd wiped sweat from her forehead and walked toward him. Instead of shaking his hand, she'd asked him to invest in a network of global, high-end gyms.

He'd gone all in.

Over the next two decades, her gyms had become a social hub for angst-ridden, high-net-worth individuals who wanted to let off steam in a press-free environment. Experts coached on a rotating basis, and local champions tested their mettle. For him, sparring did more than relieve stress. His peers knew he could hold his own in a dark alley, and he slept better after a fight. Hopefully, Josh felt proud of his mom.

Leaving the gym, he stopped and chatted with the men and women he knew.

An overweight man put down his weights. "When's your birthday party?"

"Next week," he said. "Idaho."

"Big crowd this year?"

He laughed. The celebrations had nothing to do with him, but they grew more elaborate every year. "No more than usual. You coming?"

The man shook his head. "Wife's planning to renew our vows. I thought she spent enough on the first wedding. Right?"

He slapped the man's back and kept walking. His father, Eitan, had taught him the value of personal attention and how to acclimate to a new culture. Family came first, and circumstantial loyalty meant as much as blood ties. In Zürich, Eitan embraced refugees, and he spent much of his time attending Jewish community celebrations. When the family had extra money, he left behind a thick envelope of cash.

So many times, Alessio had wanted to fit in with his Swiss peers. Watching Eitan hand out money at a Bar Mitzvah, he'd asked him why he prioritized other people over his family's needs.

"Money can't buy loyalty," Eitan had said.

He had disagreed.

The next week, Eitan had pulled him aside on the street and pointed out a bookmaker. *"That man's skimming money off the top, and each theft digs his grave. You know the story of the Jewish boy who refused to travel on the Sabbath. You must be the lion and enforce the rules."* Resting a hand on his shoulder, he had turned him away from the bookkeeper's theft. *"In the wild, pride members know their place. The leader provides protection and guidance. As long as the weaker members follow the leader, they thrive. That man across the street is not a leader."*

"I don't want to be a lion. I want new shoes," he'd said.

Eitan had laughed and clapped him on the back. *"One day, you'll understand. Presence in a community is everything. When people know you, they think twice before cheating you and they know you're paying attention."*

The whole world knew Donato Chen.

By the time he'd reached thirty, he had integrity and enough shoes to fill a house. He was the boss of ADC Industries, and his people followed his orders because they benefitted from his success. Loyalty followed suit. Through trial and error, his associates trusted his instincts or they left. The ones who cheated him left in duress.

In the gym's changing room, he showered and wrapped a towel around his waist. Running his hands through his hair, he shook out the excess water and stared at his reflection. Age was catching up. Retirement seemed too far off, but he considered settling down in one location.

For the last few months, he'd fought an uncharacteristic lethargy. Today's fight reassured him, but he lacked an explanation for the weariness shortening his attention span.

People dreamed of retiring at forty.

He dreamed of retiring on his deathbed, and he planned to be ninety when he did it.

Considering Nina's confident smile, he shook off thoughts of old age. Tomorrow, he'd let down his guard for the beautiful woman with the feisty dog, but he doubted anything would come of the date.

After shaving his face, he slipped into clean slacks, shrugged on a button-up and clasped his watch on his left wrist. Lewy body dementia had stolen Eitan's gregarious smile. When a famous watchmaker had created a one-of-a-kind watch to benefit research into the disease, Alessio had snapped up the piece. The watch had twenty complications, but if he removed the face, a button would transmit his location to Charon and those he trusted. He hoped he never had to use the alert.

He headed toward the exit, stepped from the changing room and powered up his phone. A dozen notifications crowded the screen.

Charon caught up to him in the hall. "Boss."

Sweat dripped down his bodyguard's temples, and heat left a red stain on his cheeks. He'd told the fool to use the plunge pool after the sauna, but Charon had his ways. "What is it?"

"We need to talk." Charon held a large manila envelope under one arm. "In private."

"Can it wait?"

Charon shook his head.

He slipped his phone into his pocket. Alyssa guaranteed the privacy of the upstairs conference rooms, and he trusted her judgment and Charon's scanning devices. "Let's get food."

Nodding, Charon started up the stairs. "I heard you beat the shit out of Jonny Germaine."

Pausing, he smacked his forehead. "That was his name!"

Charon laughed.

The sound echoed in the stairwell. Beyond acting as a bodyguard, his best friend and second-in-command carried a gun and a loaded sense of humor. "I knew it sounded like a porn star's name."

"What do you know about porn? The minute you blink, a woman falls into your lap."

"And you drag her out of it."

Charon smiled. "It's a tough job. Someone has to keep you focused on the present."

"Funny, I thought your job was to police my vices."

Turning his head, Charon worked his jaw. "My job is to keep you from flying off the handle so we all continue to get rich."

"Fair enough." He took a step and wondered how long he could keep ADC Industries on top. The conglomerate made money hand over fist, but it steered clear of life's baser pursuits. If his customers wanted to empty their pockets at a roulette table, he would gladly take their money, but he cut their losses before they ended up broke and helpless. Shaking off the possibility of ending there himself, he trusted Charon's calming, lethal influence and replayed his fight with Jonny Germaine. "Maybe we should get into the entertainment industry. I hear it's good money."

Charon cleared his throat. "Um?"

"You ready to take the top billing?"

Skin paling, Charon missed a step.

He shook his head and tried not to laugh. "Don't test the waters unless you're ready to put on a show." Pushing open a conference room door, he chose a spot at a large walnut table with views of the Hudson River. Boats traveled the water and determined runners battled the early evening wind. Pulling his phone from his pocket, he opened the gym's app. "What are you eating?"

"Steak," Charon said.

"Steak it is." Setting aside his phone, he waited. Charon had a mind like a steel trap and what little paper passed between ADC's top associates immediately went into the shredder. Homeland Security, search warrants and lawyers bent on discovery would slow down his acquisitions. "What do you have?"

Charon withdrew a picture from the envelope and slid it toward him.

He picked up the color print and stared at a man in a trench coat trying to look inconspicuous on a summer street corner. The best coders in the world encrypted ADC's digital files, brilliant hackers claimed bounties for identifying ADC system flaws and FBI agents took lessons from the business analyst responsible for keeping his appointments on track. He wondered what would possess Charon to print out a picture of a man when digital files could disappear. "Who is it?"

"Jack Santana. He's twenty-nine, has a petty rap sheet and he's the youngest son of Michael Sanna." Charon leaned back in his chair. "He also tails you every time you're in New York."

He stared at the image and waited for a shred of recognition. Nothing came. In the last decade, only one foolish man had pressed Charon to act, and Michael Sanna was long gone. "For how long has Jack tailed me?"

"A few years."

Looking up, he frowned. "A few *years*?"

"He's never been a threat, but he started lingering in the hotel bar, chatting up people you know and asking questions."

Alessio knew many people, and he refused to put them at risk. Charon had his back, but ADC restricted security to the company's top associates. He slid the printout across the table. "Make him disappear."

"Permanently?"

"No, just scare the shit out of him. I don't have time to worry about Michael Sanna's perturbed, illegitimate offspring, Jack Santana." He rolled his eyes. "Who the fuck does he think he is? Owning his family's name is the least he could do."

"Are you sure?"

He leaned back in his chair. Michael Sanna had been the former top executive of PIN Networks, a nearly defunct telecommunications company. After Alessio investigated the company's financial sheets, accused the CEO of hiding PIN's deteriorating financial condition and blacklisted the company, The New York Stock Exchange delisted the company's stock. Without insurance, PIN's creditors withdrew, and the company contracted. In 2011, Michael showed up at his Miami Beach house, brandished a gun and vowed revenge.

He laughed.

When Charon pulled his weapon, Michael fired, but Charon's bullet found its mark. The sixty-year-old executive tumbled from the exterior balcony and landed on the *Herald's* front page. By the time the first copies hit newsstands, Alessio and Charon had flown over the Atlantic. "Honestly, I didn't know Michael had a son."

"A bastard," Charon said.

"Like it matters." He glanced at the photograph. "Where'd you get this shot?"

"Emily said someone fishy was loitering around your building. I put a guy on the street, but I told him not to get involved."

"Good." Emily, his housekeeper, had an overactive imagination, but she couldn't manifest a man wearing a trench coat. "I won't forget his face."

"That's it?" Charon asked.

"You do your job and I'll do mine." Pulling open a drawer, he pulled the photograph back across the table and shredded it. "Should I put him in touch with Jonny Germaine? Are you planning to stop covering my ass?"

Charon picked something from his teeth. "Dick. I should let him come for you."

"He can try."

Charon dropped his hand and stared.

The door opened and a gym employee wheeled in a cart with two steaks, two liters of water and a plate of steamed vegetables. A basket held fresh, hot bread.

As soon as the server placed the basket on the table, Alessio flipped back the white napkin, grabbed a piece of bread and shoved it in his mouth. The garlic and butter soothed the hunger roiling his stomach, but the server refused to meet his eyes. "Problem?"

"The sommelier didn't have the wine you ordered," the server said.

He frowned.

The server backed up a step. "I uh"—he lifted a bottle from the cart—"picked out this vintage instead."

Charon bridged his hands over his stomach. "Ballsy."

Alessio swallowed the last bite of bread and crossed his arms over his chest. "Well, open up the bottle."

"You sure? I could, uh, ask the wine steward to pick out a selection."

"Is this one good?" he asked.

The server dipped his chin, and his cheeks went pink. "I heard you like the best, but it's nine hundred and fifty dollars."

Charon choked back a laugh. "You should see his dry-cleaning bill."

Alessio held up his hand and kept his gaze on the server. The man's nerves endeared him and reminded him what life felt like the moment before you stepped into the ring. Also, he loved the luxuries life offered, and he needed a break from Charon's familiar lip. "What's your name?"

"Ted," the server said.

"You like wine?"

"I'm studying at the International Culinary Center."

Alessio jerked his chin toward the bottle. "Open the wine."

Swallowing, Ted cut the foil, popped the cork and filled his glass.

Raising the wine to his lips, he inhaled the rich cabernet's aroma, took a sip and smiled. "Ted, you can spend your twenties serving rich assholes fine wine, but you can't piss your pants while you do it. I'll get you a job at my favorite Italian restaurant. Tell Alyssa I'm promoting you."

Ted's mouth twitched, and he returned Alessio's smile. "I don't think she's going to like that promotion."

He raised his glass to the light. The wine shone brilliant red, and zero sediment polluted its allure. Ted could go far. He met the server's gaze. "Too bad. She owes me."

Grinning and backing out of the room, Ted took the cart with him.

"Nice kid," Charon said.

Alessio unrolled the napkin holding his cutlery.

"What are you going to do about Jack?"

"Keep him the fuck out of my way." Cutting into his steak, he rationalized that he had no time for broken dreams and disgruntled boys. If he wanted to worry about night school and extramarital affairs, he'd go back to his old neighborhood. Then he thought of Alyssa's son and blushing Ted. Without Eitan, he'd be as untethered as the pair. "Did Jack know his father?"

Charon sipped his wine. "I don't know."

He put down his fork and knife. "Before you scare the shit out of him, find out. Answers might be the only things he wants."

"I doubt it."

He noted the beads of sweat still rolling down Charon's temples. "You're not eating."

"I need to cool down."

Giving his friend room to breathe, he tried to quiet his mind, but company financials and unanswered questions kept his thoughts churning. Only in the ring could he abandon the outside world and focus on one opponent.

Charon picked up his fork. "I heard Jonny Germaine was a loser."

"And you're not?"

Charon saluted him with his fork. "One day, I'll let you find out."

He grinned. He and Charon hadn't sparred in twenty years, but the moment they set foot in the ring, all hell would break loose. Until that day, they shared meals, ruled a conglomerate and plotted their moves.

His phone rang.

Seeing Martha's number, he ignored the call. When her first marriage had imploded, he'd invited her to a few cocktail parties. He hoped she would settle down with a tech entrepreneur, christen a yacht and sail away into the sunset. Instead, she appraised the room like a jewel thief. Some things never changed. After drinks the other night, he'd wired her fifty thousand and settled his conscience. It was a small price to pay for Nina's phone number.

"Who's that?" Charon asked.

"An old friend."

"You don't have old friends."

He shrugged. "I have a few."

"Liar."

He needed to get back to work before he took up golf, but Charon deserved more than a brush-off. When he'd made his first million dollars, they'd painted southern Italy red, but neither man felt like they belonged on the sun-dappled coast. After his hangover subsided, he hatched plans for the next million dollars. "I have a date tomorrow."

"With a hooker?"

Escorts bored him, and the women who tumbled into his lap bypassed his eyes and went straight for his wallet. Sharing a meal with the beautiful woman from Martha's apartment held a sweet-natured, innocent appeal, but in her red leggings, Nina looked far from innocent. "No, with a legal mediator."

"Come again?"

"I met her at my friend's apartment. She's pretty and confident. I like her."

Choking, Charon slapped his chest.

A piece of meat flew from his mouth and landed on the table.

Shaking his head, Alessio placed his napkin over the projectile and took another bite. "I can't take you anywhere."

"Dude..."

Ignoring his friend's stupefied expression, he chewed his steak and grinned. Nina had already outsmarted half the women in New York City. She'd rendered Charon speechless, and he couldn't wait to see what else she could do.

Chapter Three

"Red," Martha said. "When else can you wear a halter bow, crepe mermaid gown?"

Nina eyed the dress. "It's not a gown. It flares at my knees and the halter tie is the only thing keeping it from looking like a 1990s throwback."

Martha cackled. "You're right. Wear it!"

Victor yawned and nosed a crumb on the floor.

After work, she'd taken him for a five-mile walk to 'burn off energy' and abate the loneliness he might feel with her out on a date. After the walk, he kept his belly on the cool, wooden floor. The chill posture might be the only thing he could manage.

Exhaling, she held up a parade of jewel-colored dresses.

Martha shook her head at each one, reached in the closet and pulled out a lacy, black dress. "Oh, what about this one?"

"I'm saving that one for the Met Gala."

Martha rolled her eyes. "You with the high-powered clients and thriving career. Why don't they let starving artists into the Met Gala?"

"Because you would mock the stars. What time is it?" She took the red dress off the hanger and slipped it over her head. The smooth satin lining settled over her hips, and when she looked in the mirror, she looked lovely. "It still fits."

"Of course it fits." Martha sat on the bed. "You look amazing."

"Thank you." She smoothed her hands over her hips.

Victor moaned and rolled onto his back.

Stepping back from the mirror, she bent and rubbed his exposed, pink belly. "How's my little man?"

Martha hip-checked her and scooped Victor into her arms. "Leave him to me. You'll get fur all over your dress."

He licked her neck.

"Oh, he likes me!" Martha kissed his nose.

Nina tried not to be jealous, but she wanted an amusing night out on the town, and Victor was a taciturn companion. Well, he barked enough to make his presence known, but his enthusiasm for chasing pigeons made for lackluster conversation. "I wish I knew more about Alessio."

Cradling Victor like a baby, Martha rubbed his belly. "He's an insurance salesman. What else do you want to know?"

"Does he have hobbies? If I'd met him online, I'd know his entire backstory."

Martha shrugged.

Nina curled her hair. "He came across so reserved. Handsome as sin, but" — she lowered the curling iron — "aloof."

"He grew up in Switzerland, so he speaks a few languages. Sometimes idioms don't translate. He did well for himself and made the US his home. If you two hit it off, I'll get to hover like a fairy godmother."

She loosened a curl. "What happens when the clock strikes midnight?"

Toting Victor to the door, Martha paused. "I guess we'll find out. Bring me home a piece of tiramisu?"

"I will." Nina turned from the mirror. "Thanks for looking out for me. I haven't been out in a while."

Martha smiled. "I know. Sometimes we all make mistakes."

Nina shrugged off her neighbor's reflective comment. Martha had an artist's eye, but her temperament matched her career. Nobody survived life without making a few mistakes. If they did, she and every other professional mediator would be out of a job. She tried for levity. "Did you open my packages again?"

"No, but don't let past mistakes get into your head. If you have fun with Alessio, make the most of the evening. You never know where the night might take you." She winked. "And if it's a bust, Victor and I will be right here when you get back."

She glanced at Victor balanced on Martha's bony hip. He seemed happy enough. "Yesterday, you didn't know the dog's name."

Martha kissed his furry white head. "Since when has that stopped me from loving a man?"

Locking gazes, she and Martha burst into laughter. There were some things about her neighbor she preferred not to know.

* * * *

39

Afraid to mess up her dress, Nina called a car, held tight to her clutch and fidgeted her way to the Upper East Side restaurant Alessio had picked out. For a man visiting New York, he had firm opinions about the city's restaurants. Stepping from the car, she greeted the valet and walked up to the host. "I'm meeting Mr. Chen."

"Ahh." The host straightened. "Yes, of course you are. Please, follow me."

He led her through the crowded dining room and opened a set of partitioned, glass doors. Beyond the doors, a candlelit courtyard waited, but the space looked deserted. Given the restaurant's location and packed bar, she expected to see more couples arguing over lemony veal scaloppini and tiny grappa glasses. Shrugging off the good fortune, she sat at the table he indicated.

"Would you care for a glass of wine?"

She unfolded her napkin. "A cabernet?"

A few moments later, he returned and handed her a glass. "I hope you enjoy your evening."

"Thank you, I will."

He bowed and reentered the building.

For a woman bent on relaxation, she couldn't shake her nerves. Sipping her wine, she surveyed the courtyard. Hidden speakers played instrumental music and white candles sat in thick, glass jugs along the base of an old, brick wall. Despite the shelter, the candles flickered in a slight breeze. Terra cotta pots held mock orange trees and the sweet, citrus scent matched the romantic candles. She wondered who from the restaurant tended the plants, lit the candles and swept up the fallen leaves.

She also wondered how long she should wait for her date. If Alessio didn't show in the next five minutes, she knew a classic burger spot with green-checkered tablecloths. The guy behind the cash register would get a kick out of her dress. She also knew a deli serving the city's finest pastrami sandwiches. Martha and Victor were a phone call away and the ghosts haunting the Met would love Victor. She tapped her foot.

A server walked up to the table and offered to fill her glass. "More wine?"

Reclaiming her seat, she set down her empty glass in front of the server.

He filled her wineglass. "I'm sure Mr. Chen will be along soon."

"Is his plan to get me drunk?"

The bottle wobbled, and a drop of wine rolled down the glass.

He wiped it clean. "I'm so sorry."

Shrugging off the mistake, she looked up. "It's okay, Ted." As she held her smile, the lines creasing his forehead eased. Half her success came from putting people at ease. "The evening is too beautiful to worry about innocent mistakes."

"I'm kinda new here." He draped the white serving cloth over his arm, looked toward the restaurant's interior and straightened his shoulders.

When he made eye contact, the frown lines had returned. She sipped her wine. A woman could only do so much.

"Can I get you anything?" he asked.

She toasted him. "You're doing an excellent job."

He blushed.

The kid was the cutest thing she'd seen since adopting Victor.

Five minutes later, the courtyard doors opened, and Alessio stepped onto the bricks.

Amid the candlelight, he looked even more handsome than he had in Martha's apartment. His hair was wet and combed back from his face, but his sharp features and tanned skin lent him an air of confidence. In a crowd of relaxed professionals, his navy, three-piece suit and polished shoes would stick out, but he wore them well. Standing, she forgave him for being late.

He paused a few feet from the table and put his hands in his pockets. "Nina."

"Alessio Chen." She smiled. "You're late."

Returning her smile, he walked forward and kissed her cheek. "My apologies."

Feeling his lips brush her cheek, she inhaled his crisp, clean aftershave and forgot to return the kiss. He smelled of sunshine and cedar wood, and the thought of him prepping for the date thrilled her. Pulling away before she lost her cool, she tilted her head. "Forgiven."

He gestured for her to sit, walked around the table and claimed the open seat.

If he'd been five minutes later, she would have chosen the checkered tablecloths. Instead, she replaced the napkin in her lap and tapped her foot beneath the tablecloth to distract her nerves.

Ted walked into the courtyard and filled his wineglass. "Mr. Chen."

He nodded, raised the glass to his lips and drank deeply.

She wondered what gave him such thirst.

Ted cleared his throat. "Tonight, we feature fried baby artichokes, mezzaluna filled with prosciutto and mozzarella, focaccia and berries with cream. We also have a seven-course tasting menu."

She looked at Alessio. "Have you eaten here before?"

"Once or twice," he said.

Ted coughed.

She caught the response and hoped Alessio's family didn't own the place. One night of cheese-filled pasta felt like an indulgence, but her thighs couldn't stand a lifetime of treats. Then again, if she had to choose between Alessio and her thighs, she might rethink her decision. Clearing her throat, she reminded herself that unwinding was her goal for the night, and if he didn't like her thighs, he could shove it up his mezzaluna. She smiled. "What do you recommend?"

He rubbed the corner of his lips. "The chef's from the Emilia-Romagna region. He relies on generous seasonings, olives, meats, fish, salumi and cheeses. If you like Italian food, you're in for a treat."

Listening to him pronounce the words, she pulled at her earring. The words sounded so exotic coming from his lips, but he spoke English as well as a native. Martha's idiom explanation fell flat. If she wanted to get the man naked, she would have to keep him talking. "I love trying new foods. I haven't traveled, but every time I taste something new, I feel like I'm one step closer to going somewhere."

"Why haven't you traveled?"

"Time." She shrugged. "Finishing law school felt like a prize worth a few sacrifices."

"You'll have to make a list."

"What about you?" she asked. "Do you like to travel?"

"For pleasure?"

"Of course."

"I haven't had time to see the sights." He set aside his empty water glass. "Would you prefer the tasting menu?"

She laughed. "I'm not sure where I would put seven courses."

He inclined his head. "You look lovely."

She felt her cheeks warm. "Thank you."

The server stepped into place.

Looking away from her handsome date and his honey-brown eyes, she smiled at Ted. "Let's keep it simple. The artichokes and pasta sound delicious."

He dipped his chin and looked at Alessio.

"The same," Alessio said. "Also, a salad."

Ted refilled Alessio's wineglass and left the courtyard.

She stretched out her legs and crossed her heels. "Martha said you grew up in Switzerland. Do you speak Italian?"

"Some," he said. "Zürich's official language is German, but I picked up Italian from my mother, Hebrew from my father and English from my school. My mother and father met in Italy. She sold him summer fruit, and he sold her a life in Israel."

Finally, a shred of information! The man would be a brilliant negotiator. She tamped down her enthusiasm. "How romantic."

He shrugged. "Neither parent won their homeland."

After hearing the wistfulness in his remark, she wanted to ask what conditions kept his family in Zürich. Instead, she tabled her question and sipped her wine. Psychoanalyzing her date wasn't a prerequisite for getting into his pants.

Picking up his water glass, he found it empty and looked up.

Ted rushed to the table, tripped over a brick paver and righted himself.

A second later and he would have emptied a pitcher of icy water on Alessio's suit and ended the evening.

Biting back a smile, she realized how much she wanted the date to continue.

"My apologies." Ted filled the water glass and backed away. "It won't happen again."

Alessio sipped from the glass and looked toward her. "Do you speak any languages?"

She laughed. "I'm a lawyer. The only foreign languages I speak are Latin maxims."

He inclined his head.

Most of the time, that joke earned her a little laugh. "I've picked up the same phrases and proverbs every lawyer uses to make their jobs easier and their briefs longer, but once I took up mediation, I learned to choose my words. Martha said you sell insurance."

"I do."

He looked more like a swarthy pirate than a buttoned-down insurance salesman, but she needed him to talk before she decided whether to crawl into his lap. "Really?"

He nodded.

Great...

Ted returned with the salads. "I took the liberty of bringing two."

He backed away from the table like he feared Alessio. She wondered why, but she speared a piece of Romaine and put the lettuce in her mouth. The tangy, garlic dressing piqued her interest, but she glanced at Alessio's cold caprese salad and wondered if she should rein in her garlic consumption. She took another bite. Reining herself in never led to success. "Tell me how you landed in the insurance industry. I assumed the big, online companies cut out the small-time salesmen."

His gaze narrowed. "Who said I'm small?"

She laughed and waved her fork. "I'm sorry. I tried to Google your name and your work profile, but I couldn't get past some Italian footballer. Is it a big company?"

"Alessio Chen's a good center-back who sometimes functions as a left-sided full-back."

"Excuse me?"

He leaned forward and cocked his head. "Do you know anything about football?"

She tucked her legs beneath the chair and matched his posture. If the date collapsed over football, she'd collapse on her bed with a vibrator. "Does it matter?"

A smile warmed his face. "No, I guess not."

Leaning back, she sipped her wine. "Good. Have you ever been married?"

"Straight to the point?"

"No, but how am I supposed to know what you do for fun? You barely talk about yourself. Martha said she didn't know your hobbies." Considering his shoulders, she wondered how he kept in shape. "Are you beer and football, museums and shows, or snack sign-ups and soccer cleats?"

He laughed. "Those are my options?"

She stared. "Well, fill in the blank is always an option."

He stared back. "No, I've never married. You?"

"Never." She took another bite of salad. "My career seems to destroy my relationships."

He raised his glass. "Their loss."

She bit back a smile. The man was more than good looks and a nice suit. As his hair dried, it framed his head with the same wiry, springy intensity of the man who dodged her questions. If the evening went well, she would assess his dimensions. Her appraisal would have nothing to do with his profession, but it would certainly help her unwind. "Martha said you're rarely in the city."

"True," he said.

She had subpoenaed witnesses who were more forthcoming. "Tell me a more about your company."

He narrowed his gaze.

"Or would you rather talk about divorce mediation?"

He laughed and spread his fingers against the tablecloth. "The insurance industry has over seven thousand companies. You probably have renter's insurance or a separate policy for your antique ring."

She twisted the ring on her finger. The filigreed ring had belonged to Nan, and the connection warmed her heart. "I don't."

"Really?"

"It belonged to my grandmother. The resale value is meaningless." Her grandmother also left her more than a pretty ring. The School of Law at New York University had one of the best legal programs in the country, but the eighty-thousand-dollar tuition scared off applicants. Nan's savings had helped pay her tuition. As long as she maintained her billable rate, she'd be debt free in five years. "Do you think I should insure it?"

He shrugged. "Collectively, insurance companies collect over one trillion dollars in annual premiums. Much of that intake comes from risk-averse, sentimental people."

She slapped her chest. "That's massive."

He grinned. "Don't insure things you can afford to replace."

"Free advice?" she asked.

"On the house." He finished his salad. "The industry's size leads to competition, but it also leads to illegal activities. The bigger the prize, the greater the number of opportunities for insurance fraud."

She considered skipping the rest of the meal and spending the night ogling him. "I think of tiny, talking lizards."

He leaned back in his chair. "A brilliant marketing tactic."

The man spoke like a businessman, not a salesman. "Does your company have a mascot?"

He stroked the stem of his empty glass. "We don't handle small, consumer claims. Sometimes, consumer companies want the same protection they afford their customers. My company offers reinsurance. Think of it as insurance against loss for other insurance companies."

She rubbed the condensation from her glass. "When shit gets bad?"

His cheek twitched into a reluctant smile. "Catastrophic risks. Hurricanes, the global financial crisis" — he exhaled — "big-rig drivers who go without sleep or can't put down their cell phones."

She widened her eyes "Wow, that's awful. People think my job's depressing."

Laughing, he tugged his ear and looked toward the restaurant.

Ted scrambled to his side. "Sorry, um, someone's out sick, and I'm covering more tables than usual." He filled Alessio's wineglass. "Your meal's almost ready."

Alessio frowned.

Ted removed their salad plates. In their place, he left fresh plates and fried artichoke hearts. Without pausing, he turned back to the restaurant.

"Go easy on the kid," she said.

Alessio looked at her. "Why?"

"He's trying his best. Nobody's perfect."

He exhaled, and a faint smile lifted his face. "True."

Sitting on the patio with Alessio, she had a feeling she wouldn't sleep alone tonight, but she only knew enough about him to calm her nerves. Surrounded by candlelight, she played with an earring and considered her next question. Mediation required subtlety, but her libido urged her to jump on him.

"*Il dolce far niente*," he said.

She dropped her hand into her lap. "What does that mean?"

He draped his arms over both armrests and smiled. "The sweetness of doing nothing. At the end of a long day, my mother kicked off her shoes and relaxed."

When he let go, his smile positively lit up his face, and she wanted to see him shine. This strange ritual society called dating had its drawbacks, but she appreciated the give and take of a slow mediation. More often than not, the outcome superseded all parties' expectations.

Ted stumbled back to the patio.

She considered tripping the server and sending him to the urgent care clinic. Instead, she drew a breath and realized he'd asked about more wine. "What do you recommend?"

"Uh" — Ted loosened his collar — "artichokes are tricky. They have a compound called cynarin that tricks your tongue into ignoring sweet tastes. As you sip your wine, the cynarin dissipates, and your wine suddenly tastes sweeter than normal. I recommend serving artichokes with highly acidic wines, such as Sauvignon Blanc, Grüner Veltliner or Albariño."

She blinked. "You surprise me."

Alessio stretched out his legs, and she felt his muscled heat pressed against her calves. Looking at him, she caught the possession in his narrowed gaze and smiled. He surprised her, too. The aloof, handsome man she had met in the condo had depth and the possibilities intrigued her. "Grüner Veltliner or Albariño?"

"Albariño," he said.

Ted lifted their red wineglasses and backed away.

"The server seems nice."

Alessio worked his jaw. "He has potential."

She toyed with her water glass and let his legs and his possessive stare embolden her. As much as she wanted to unbutton his shirt, she wanted to understand what kind of man sipped wine in a candlelit courtyard. "Why's your hair wet?"

"I was at the gym." He stroked his clean-shaven chin. "Boxing. Tell me about your law practice."

The subject change caught her off guard, but his revelation intrigued her. Amid New York's towering skyscrapers, he willingly pitted his strength and speed against another man's power. The hint of violence intrigued her, but she barely knew where to start. "What do you want to know?"

He portioned the artichokes and slid a serving onto her plate. "Which cases give you the most trouble?"

"Trouble?"

He looked up. "Difficulties?"

She frowned. "None."

"None?"

"I'm good at my job." Shrugging, she cut her appetizer and let the savory lemon excite her tongue. Her boss cautioned her against arrogance, but she was an excellent and intuitive attorney. "What do you mean you were boxing? In a ring?"

"It's a sport."

"So is fishing. Most people in New York don't fish."

He laughed. "I like to keep in shape."

"I'm sure."

Ted set down the new wine.

She offered him a smile. "Thanks."

Alessio waited until the server left. "Don't change the subject, Nina. Tell me about your career."

She wondered how much he cared to hear. "Patents protect novel inventions or discoveries like pharmaceuticals, machinery or sophisticated software. Lawyers can spend years arguing over which inventions are useful and non-obvious. I can bring parties together and solves disputes in an afternoon."

"Handy."

The main course came and went with shaved cheese, amiable smiles and a lively discussion of her caseload. Stripping out the details, she told him about her most recent clients.

He relayed absurd claims stories.

She relaxed into the evening's warmth and his good company. If his insurance firm went belly-up, he could teach a course on effective listening skills. He faced her, maintained eye contact, attended to her stories and kept his 'solutions' to himself. Really, for that last fact alone, she would sleep with him.

Setting down his knife and fork, he formed his hands into a steeple across his stomach. "You're impressive, Nina. The stakes and egos don't faze you."

She shrugged.

"I like you."

She smiled. His hands mimicked a church steeple, but the glint in his eyes looked far from a choirboy's smile. "Well, that's good to hear. I like you, too."

"Dessert?" he asked.

She placed her napkin on the table. "I can think of other activities."

He opened his mouth, closed it and considered his words. "I have a hotel."

Relief rushed through her system. If he had suggested crème brûlée, she would have demurred, feigned an important call and reassessed her sex appeal. At this point in the evening, she wanted another glass of wine, a good orgasm and a dreamless night's sleep. Talk of caseloads could wait until the morning. If she wasn't *unwound* by midnight, she'd start drunk dialing ex-boyfriends. "Excellent."

Standing, he walked around the table and offered her his arm. "Shall we?"

She frowned. "What about the check?"

"I took care of it."

"Really?" Hesitation kept her from standing and taking his arm. "Will you let me buy drinks at the hotel?"

He smiled. "If you insist."

She took his arm, and the contact thrilled her. Beneath his jacket sleeve, his solidly muscled arm flexed and shifted beneath her touch. She wanted to peel off his jacket, unbutton his shirt and confirm the happy trail and six-pack abs she suspected. He smelled of olive oil, cedar, cypress trees and sunbaked dirt. "I insist."

A server left the kitchen carrying two steaming dishes, saw Alessio and backed into his coworker.

"Does the staff seem a little jumpy?" she asked.

He smiled. "No more than usual."

"Do you come here often?"

"Only when I'm in town." Leaning down, he dropped his voice. "If you'd started with that line, we could have saved the chit chat."

She paused and looked into his eyes. "What if I enjoy the chit chat?"

"Do you?" he asked.

She wet her lips. "Only if it leads to superior results."

Cupping her elbow, he urged her toward the door. "It will."

Chapter Four

A black sedan waited outside the restaurant's valet stand.

Walking toward the passenger side, Alessio opened the rear door and stepped back.

Nina looked over her shoulder at the subdued, brick restaurant and wondered if she should text Martha her intended location. Then again, she could tell Martha she was boarding a plane to Fiji with a deranged movie star and the woman would probably egg her on.

The sedan's driver glanced in the rearview mirror.

Above his reddish-brown beard, curious blue eyes met her gaze. If the man dared her to make her move, she would do it gracefully. Settling onto the plush leather seat, she slid toward the street-side window and made room for Alessio. The meal, the conversation and the wine enforced her first impression, and her body begged her to choose release.

Shutting the door, Alessio spread his legs and nodded.

The shade shuddered into place and the driver pulled away from the valet stand.

She plumbed her reservoir of small talk.

Alessio pulled her onto his lap.

Laughing, she braced her hands against his chest. "Shouldn't you tell the driver where to take us?"

"He knows."

She tipped her head to the side. "Do this often?"

"No." Pulling down her chin, he dropped his voice to a guttural whisper. "But we can go as many times as you want."

She raised her arms to his shoulders, leaned forward and pressed her lips against his. Waiting for him to take the lead, she felt his hands grip her hips. His erection pressed into her thigh, but he held himself still. She inhaled, leaned back and wondered if she'd misread the situation.

"Kiss me, Nina," he said.

The command sent a thrill through her system. The entire meal, she'd wanted to undress him, and the thought of denial physically hurt. Shifting her position, she angled her head and claimed his full, bottom lip. His warm, sensual mouth felt like coming home. Feeling him relax, she deepened the kiss. He met her thrust for thrust, and she tasted the crisp, clear control keeping his hands anchored on her hips.

He flexed his fingers.

Raising her hands, she gripped the back of his head where his dark hair had teased her throughout the night. If one kiss left her aching and wet, she couldn't wait to get to his hotel room and indulge satisfaction's perfect ache, but she needed more than a willing victim. Pulling back, she exhaled. Passing streetlights brought his warm, brown eyes in and out of focus. "Why aren't you kissing me back?"

He offered her a slow smile. "You enjoy being in control."

She dropped her hand from his head. "I enjoy a partner."

Spreading his hands at her lower back, he lifted her until she straddled him, cupped her ass and seated her over his erection. "I promise, I'm with you. Lead on." He stroked her butt cheek with his thumb and stilled. "No panties?"

"They always get in the way."

His grip tightened.

She glanced over her shoulder and confirmed the privacy screen. The driver might not be able to see them, but he was about to hear more than chatter. Truthfully, the thought of having an audience thrilled her.

Unfastening Alessio's belt buckle, she slid her hand into his slacks and released his cock. He glistened beneath her touch, and she stroked his length. She wasn't about to go down on him in the sedan's confined backseat, but testing his rhythm seemed like a prudent trial. If he couldn't match her pace, she'd bid him adieu and call a car to take her home.

He pulled a condom from his jacket pocket, ripped open the foil and sheathed his cock. "You're very direct."

"You've very erect."

He laughed.

Raising her hips, she centered herself over him and eased down until he filled her. The pressure and friction stole her breath. Any other night, she'd tease a date and swap banter until he threatened to rip off her panties or throw her over his shoulder. She had a feeling Alessio would never lower himself to such base tactics.

She barely knew him, but he didn't seem like the type of man who tolerated a tease. She could be direct. If he wanted to buy her dinner, let her use his glorious body and say goodnight, she was down for his kinks. Grinning, she reached behind her, grabbed one of his hands and centered his thumb at her clit. "Nobody eats for free."

He stroked her bare flesh. "I paid."

She rose to the tip of his cock and hovered. "I waxed."

He rubbed her clit, clenched his other hand and pulled her down on his cock. "You did."

His terse, guttural response made her wonder how much he held back. Setting a rhythm that pleased her, she arched her back until she looked past his shoulder at the flowing traffic. Anyone could see them, yet nobody would.

Closing her eyes, she rode him while the city's lights flickered against her eyelids. His heady scent surrounded her, his pulsing cock filled her and his firm hand anchored her back. Within minutes, she felt whispers of release teasing her senses and pulled back before she left him hanging.

"Vixen, come for me. I have you."

She grinned, increased her pace and leaned into his touch. Within seconds, her muscles clenched, her world shattered and she buried her face in his neck to smother her release.

Pumping his hips like a piston, he followed, dropped his hand from her back and leaned against the back of the seat. "Fuck."

She moved to climb off his lap.

"Wait." He gripped her hips and exhaled.

Swallowing, she leaned against his chest, relaxed in the afterglow and let her mind drift. He came into town, but she had no idea if work or pleasure brought him to the city. For a one-night stand, he topped the charts, but she wondered if she would see him again.

The driver slowed for a light.

Alessio lifted her, set her aside and pulled off the condom.

Given the ride, she wanted to grip it and test his endurance, but she untwisted her dress and looked out of the window to see a tree-lined street on the Upper East Side. Beyond the streetlights, a historic, brick hotel with narrow windows and uniformed staff waited at attention. She recognized the hotel and bit back a sigh of admiration. Located a block from Central Park, celebrities frequented the location, and travel magazines raved over its amenities. "The insurance business must be good."

"Good enough," he said. "Unless you'd rather go somewhere else."

She glanced at him. "Maybe we should spend all night riding around in this car."

He laughed. "I'd rather buy you a drink and fuck you on a bed."

"I thought I was buying the drinks."

He inclined his head and looked past her shoulder.

She followed his gaze. A valet approached the car.

"Nina," he said.

"Hmm?" She fixed her hair and looked at him.

"Never stifle your pleasure with me."

Her cheeks warmed.

He stoked her cheek. "Next time, I want to hear you scream."

Her core clenched.

The valet opened the door. "Good evening, Mr. Chen."

Alessio dropped his hand.

Caught between the two men, she considered signing over her 401(k) to close the door and take Alessio up on his offer. Instead, she stepped out of the car, walked past the valet and pretended she owned the place. Admiring the hotel's simple black and white moniker took little effort. The hotel oozed a gilded, edgy sophistication that scared curious tourists and kept pigeons from roosting on its sign. Well, maybe a spike strip took care of that aspect.

A doorman opened the glass-paneled door.

She stepped inside the wide lobby. Striped marble floors, oversized geometric art and warm gilded sconces greeted her. A candle glowed on the receptionist's desk and the warm, alluring scent of citrus, lavender and magnolia pervaded the space.

Alessio cupped her elbow. "I forgot my room key. Pick up two glasses of wine while I secure a replacement?"

Ready to get her bearings, she headed toward the hotel's bar. Dinner, a lusty car ride and a drink seemed like harmless, easy-bail activities, but the minute she stepped into the elevator, she knew the night belonged to him. Perhaps she would claim it first.

She approached the bar and scanned the drinks crowd.

Couples and business associates lounged on plush velvet-upholstered armchairs and a cow-print sofa. Sharp, metallic accents kept the scene from a stodgy

Victorian diorama, and the mix of refined sophistication and pop culture amused her. Beyond the luxury, the hotel staff smiled and offered hits of familiarity. A boy and an older woman huddled over a handheld game. A coiffed labradoodle drooled at its owner's feet. She thought of Victor and wondered if he and Martha had made nice over a pint of ice cream and a nature documentary.

Looking toward reception, she saw Alessio speak.

The receptionist pursed her painted lips.

Nina wondered if the hotel had declined his credit card.

"Yes, ma'am?" the bartender asked.

Turning, she channeled Martha's flirtatious confidence. The man's golden curls looked cherubic, and if she weren't fantasizing about dark-haired lovers, she'd ask to see his license and pair him up with her closest girlfriend. "Two glasses of cabernet."

The bartender reached for two wineglasses. "Mr. Chen's tab?"

She slid her credit card across the silver-topped bar. At a hotel this intimate, the staff must know every guest. She wondered how long Alessio planned to stay in town. "Mine."

"Of course." The bartender poured two glasses, scanned her credit card and handed her the ticket. The total amounted to fourteen dollars.

"That's it?" She raised a glass to her lips. "Maybe I'll have the entire bottle."

He slid the bottle across the bar. "It's on the house."

She held up her hand and shook her head. "I was kidding."

He shrugged. "Nobody else will order cabernet."

Scanning the bar's patrons, she counted multiple glasses of red wine. Were they drinking Malbec? How could an entire grape vintage go out of style while she toiled in an office building?

Alessio walked up to her side and skimmed his hand along her lower back. "Problem?"

"Not at all," she said.

The bartender inclined his head. "Mr. Chen, we'll send up the bottle."

She turned to Alessio. "I ordered two glasses of wine, but my taste in wine must be terrible. He gave me the bottle."

Alessio lifted a glass to his lips and drank. "Your taste is excellent."

"So why is he comp'ing us the bottle?"

He frowned and urged her from the bar. "People can be strange."

She followed him to the elevator. "Really?"

"Indeed." He pushed the button and trailed his hand along her spice.

She forgot about the glass. Inside the elevator, she watched him press the button for a mid-level floor, hesitated and drank deeply. She wanted to savor the evening, and coming apart in his hands would reveal how much time passed since Atlantic City and her last encounter.

"Having second thoughts?" he asked.

She toyed with his shirt's buttons. "Debating my next move."

He pulled her to his side.

Relaxing against his bulk, she remembered the glass he carried and decided not to jump him in the elevator.

The doors opened and revealed a long line of identical doors. He looked at the key in his hand. "Seventy-Seven King room."

"You said you lost your key."

He looked up. "I did."

Narrowing her gaze, she wondered why the artful hallway suddenly felt narrower. "Then why don't you know your room number? Is this where you're staying?"

He pressed a kiss against her temple. "It's where I'm staying tonight."

His honesty comforted her. She wanted a few mind-blowing orgasms and a peek into someone else's life, but honesty reigned high on her list. Taking the key from his hand, she opened the door and set her clutch on the console table.

The room looked out over the hotel's namesake street and the city skyline. In a town known for tiny spaces, a long, wide foyer led to an enormous bedroom and a spacious bathroom. Ebony accents picked up the lobby's color-popping severity, but warm, sycamore furniture, fine fabric and smooth bedding anchored the room. Turning, she drained her glass. "So..."

He lifted it from her fingertips. "Nervous?"

"No." She stroked his navy jacket's smooth lapel. "But I'm curious to strip off that suit."

He set aside his wineglass and shrugged out of his jacket, laying it across a gold-framed chair upholstered with gold-dotted horsehair.

His wide shoulders pressed against his shirt seams, but the fine fabric draped over his beautiful muscles like flowing marble. Spying how haphazardly he'd tucked in his shirt after their car ride, she acknowledged his polish, but his humanity pleased her more. "Off with the shirt."

He unbuttoned the first button and maintained eye contact. "Lose the dress."

Reaching for the halter bow, she dropped the dress and stepped out of the pooled fabric. "Try to keep up."

Grinning, he released his shirt cuffs, unbuttoned the remainder of his shirt and draped it over the chair. "I aim to please."

Strong, vibrant tattoos covered his biceps and his upper chest. She wanted everything his body offered, but the ink gave her pause. The Atlantic City hook-up sported ink, and every design came with a sob story. She could squeeze water from a rock faster than she could collect Alessio's stories, but she wanted everything he offered.

They hadn't left the foyer.

Walking toward him wearing a lacy bra and high heels, she ran her hand along his skin and traced the dark tattoos. Below his nipples, his chest hair disappeared into his briefs, and she grinned. "I didn't expect the ink."

He stepped out of his shoes. "You don't like it?"

She looked up. "Do I have to listen to the origin stories?"

"Words are overrated." He cupped her head and pulled her into a kiss.

The change in momentum thrilled her. No longer driving the connection, she submitted to his lips, his grip and his experience. His rhythm confirmed every fantasy spawned by their clandestine, backseat encounter. Pulling free, she tried to look him in the eye. "Alessio…"

He picked her up off the ground and buried his face between her lace-covered breasts.

She could take a hint. Anchoring her legs around his waist, she felt so kiss-drunk that she wanted to write down the cabernet's vintage and order an entire case. She gripped his hair. "We have all night."

He carried her toward the bedroom, turned her chin and plundered her mouth.

The kiss heated her blood, but if he disappeared tomorrow, she wanted him to remember her. Wiggling out of his arms, she scanned the room and spied a mirror. She walked toward a velvet-upholstered chair, dragged it toward the mirror and planted one leg on the chair. "I'm so over beds."

"Are you?" He unbuckled his belt and stepped from his pants.

His briefs separated their bodies, and she wanted nothing but skin. Unclasping her bra, she let it fall to the ground, lifted her breasts and rubbed her tender nipples.

He inhaled.

She glanced over her shoulder and watched herself in the mirror. She wasn't sure how much the room cost, but she'd book it for her next summer fling. In the cool light, her heels lifted her ass, but it never looked hotter. "Look at me. I want you to slide into me and..."

Striding closer, he gripped her hips.

His grip raced along her skin. "You like what you see?"

"I like you." He turned her and lowered his mouth.

Raising her hand, she blocked him and hooked one heel-clad leg around his waist. "You like what you feel?"

He tightened his grip.

"Get a condom," she whispered.

Exhaling, he strode across the room, ripped his jacket from the chair and pulled out a condom. Turning, he brandished the package. "Anything else?"

She could spend a decade unwinding this man. His proud cock jutted from a nest of dark curls. Every long, lean inch of muscled frustration thrilled her, but she focused on his bedeviled smile. Before he could close the distance and claim her, she glanced at the mirror, struck a pose and grinned. "I want to watch as you slide into me."

He inhaled again.

His reaction exhilarated her. Turning from the mirror, she took the condom from his hands, unwrapped it, tossed the foil wrapper to the floor and sheathed him. He burned hot and rigid in her hands. When they had all night, forgoing the pleasure of a bed felt like a minor delay. She pressed her body against his and claimed his lips. Kissing him until he moaned, she pulled back and looked in the mirror. "Look at us." She might be a country girl, but hotel sex burned hotter than she'd ever imagined. Wrapping her leg around his waist, she held tight and guided him inside her.

He maneuvered them to the chair, lowered her leg to the upholstery and grabbed her hips.

Joined, she rocked and let his hands grip her hips and the chair bear her weight. Each thrust and retreat sent her closer to release. In the mirror's reflection, their bodies met and slid against a posh backdrop, but she focused on the naked, panting man gripping her ass. She felt sexier than ever before, and she surrendered to the pleasure of watching their bodies merge in the silver-backed glass.

He hiked up her leg and changed the angle.

The pressure intensified, and she slammed her hand against the wall.

An artistic light fixture slipped off its anchor and hung from the ceiling.

"Sorry," she said.

"For what?"

Lost in the pleasure, she blinked and wondered how she could still form words. His steady thrusts drover her higher. Losing her grip on reality, she clung to his shoulders, closed her eyes and enjoyed the ride.

Chapter Five

"Your phone's ringing," Alessio said.

Nina stirred from the soft, carpeted floor. "Excuse me?"

"Your phone."

Clearing her throat, she climbed to all fours, stood and ran her hand through her hair. "Right." Her muscles ached in all the right places, but she straightened her spine to walk back to the foyer.

Of course, he watched.

Reaching for her clutch, she extracted her phone and wondered when room service would bring up the rest of the wine. She'd taken Alessio's advice and untethered her release, but the entire floor knew how Seventy-Seven King room's occupants planned to spend their night. "Hello?"

"Hello, is this Nina Levoy?" the caller asked.

"Speaking."

"Ma'am, a break-in occurred at your condo building. We'd like you to answer a few questions."

She frowned. "Was anybody hurt?"

"You'd better come home," the caller said.

"I'll be right there." She ended the call and rubbed her face. Two orgasms in one night made it a beautiful evening, but she had to go. "Alessio, something came up."

He rose from the floor. "Something is wrong?"

She picked up her dress. "I don't know. A break-in occurred at my building. The officer asked me to come home."

"The officer?"

She searched for a fallen earring, found it on the plush carpet and slid the post into place. "I'm sure they're contacting all the neighbors."

"I'll come with you." He picked up his shirt.

Shaking her head, she shrugged into her dress. "I'll handle it."

"But..."

Tying her dress, she strode across the room and pressed a kiss against his swollen lips. "I'm sure it's nothing, but I have a few trinkets the burglar might have lifted. I'll call you."

He cocked his head. "You'll call me?"

"Sure." Glancing in the mirror, she lamented she wouldn't spend the night exploring his body. The hotel claimed a prime spot in one of Manhattan's most elegant neighborhoods, but plush carpet and modern art couldn't erase the wine-fueled lust that propelled her into Alessio's lap. If the officer hadn't called, she would have summoned the energy for round three and hoped he could do the same. Instead, she had a life that required attention. "When are you leaving town?"

"Nina..."

As much as she wanted to stay, momentum carried her toward the door. "I know. I had a good time, too."

Opening the hotel room door, she found the bartender with his hand raised to knock. She strode past the cherubic man and let the door close behind her. "Give him a minute."

"Excuse me?"

She smiled. Alessio's confidence and amusement encouraged her to take on risks. "Suit yourself and ring the bell. I would."

The bartender stared.

Walking down the hall, she pushed the elevator call button and waited for the elevator cab to open its doors. Stepping inside her ride to the ground floor, she stared down the long hallway leading toward Alessio's room. Her date had turned into more than she'd expected, but he didn't live in Manhattan, and she doubted she would see him again.

In the lobby, she scanned her phone for directions to the subway and backed into the valet. "Gosh, I'm so sorry."

He brushed off his jacket and shook his head. "Don't worry about it. Where are you headed?"

"The 77th Street station," she said. "I'm catching the six train."

The valet frowned. "Use the hotel's private car."

She laughed and brushed past him. "I'm fine." Outside the hotel, she felt better than fine. Her night with Alessio had been an unexpected surprise, and she would find a way to thank Martha for the introduction. Hurrying down the subway steps to wait for the train, she felt her phone buzz.

Let me know when you get home. You should have taken the car.

Thanks...Grown Woman.

You're as stubborn as you are beautiful.

Forgiven.

The train approached, and the wind whipped her hair in front of her face. If the other passengers questioned her tousled look, she would blame the mid-summer heat and humidity. Martha wouldn't question her grin.

Outside her building, police cars blocked the curb. Their flashing lights threw disco patterns on the surrounding buildings. Yellow tape cordoned off the entrance where José held court and a posted officer glared at pedestrians who slowed to gawk.

She slipped under the yellow tape and approached the officer. "This is my building."

"You'll have to wait, ma'am."

She looked up. Condo lights shone on every floor. "Your peer called me back from a date. He told me to come home."

"Your name?" the officer asked.

She rubbed her arms and wished her dress had sleeves. "Nina Levoy."

The officer radioed her name into the ether.

"Send her up with Scottie," another officer said over the radio.

A short, fat man whose shirt bulged at his belt stepped out of the building. "You Ms. Levoy?"

She scanned the flashing lights and parked first responders. "All this for a break-in?"

The two officers looked at each other.

Officer Scottie held open the door.

She stepped into the air-conditioned, tiled lobby and looked for José.

He held the phone to his ear, looked at her and drew a deep breath. "No, absolutely no press. You know I can't do that. C'mon, Mikey. Lay off."

Goosebumps raced across her exposed arms. José did more than open doors, screen visitors and accept deliveries. He weighed luggage, hailed taxis, remembered birthdays and kept mints in his pockets. Most importantly, he gauged the residents' moods and tried to lift them. "Bad?"

He covered the receiver. "Terrible."

She squeezed shut her eyes.

Officer Scottie pushed the button for the elevator, and the signal dinged.

Opening her eyes, she faced reality. "When did the break-in occur?"

The officer shook his head.

"What did they take?"

He frowned.

"Why aren't you answering me?" Her voice bounced off the tile. "All this drama for pretty cash and electronics?"

"Wait," he said.

The elevator doors opened.

She stepped into the lift, braced her hands along the support bar and stared at Officer Scottie. Impersonating the devil in her red dress had merit, but she would have applied new lipstick.

He stepped into the space, hit the button for her floor and faced her.

The door closed and the elevator rose.

"Martha Phosphole is dead," he said. "Your neighbor died at approximately ten o'clock. I understand you two were close."

She clasped her hand over her mouth and sank to her heels.

Officer Scottie hit the stop button.

The elevator shuddered to a halt.

Tears poured down her cheeks. She squeezed shut her eyes and hoped the officer had made a mistake about the victim. "Are you sure?"

"When we step off the elevator, you can go straight to your condo. Someone from the force will be right there to talk to you. You have someone you can call?"

Struggling to her feet, she gripped the bar and nodded.

He handed her a tissue. "I'm sorry for your loss."

Pressing the tissue against her eyes, she wiped away her black mascara. "Thank you."

He called her floor, turned away and crossed his arms behind his back.

She appreciated the moment of privacy. In twenty years, Martha deserved to run laps around a Florida retirement community. Who could have harmed such a fun-loving, vivacious woman?

When the elevator doors opened, she stepped into the hallway and blinked. Uniformed officers from multiple divisions strode in and out of Martha's condo. The hallway looked like a *Primetime* scene, not the place she called home. Her phone vibrated.

Are you home?

Yes.

I wish you'd stayed.

She couldn't answer Alessio. Shoving her phone in her clutch, she let her tears flow, followed the carpet pattern and headed straight for her condo. Positive memories of Martha felt too bittersweet. She laughed over bralettes, chain-smoked on her balcony and cat-called construction workers with brazen aplomb. Men in dresses amused her to no end. Why shouldn't they be free to feel the wind? Some nights, she left open her sheer curtains and gave every person with a pair of binoculars a reason to enjoy the show, and now she was gone.

Approaching Martha's door, Nina realized how much she wanted to emulate the woman's carefree attitude. She closed her eyes out of respect, but years of flashing lights and turnpike traffic accidents pulled her gaze toward the open door.

A white sheet was draped over a slumped form. The sheet shielded her view, but nothing could disguise Martha's garishly pink toenails or the blood splattering the mirror. She wondered if the killer had seen his or her reflection before they'd taken her friend's life. Had they looked away or smirked? She closed her eyes, pulled in a deep breath and trudged toward her condo.

Every step felt profoundly selfish. The mistakes she'd made over the last thirty years dragged her shoulders toward the ground. Integrity mattered, but she questioned how many times she'd tiptoed past the truth, rooted for a client or tipped a server fifteen percent.

Once, she'd lingered over the elementary water fountain, and a brat had told her to save some water for the whales. Startled, she'd looked up and glared at the kid. His parents had rented out the entire community center for his and his twin sister's *b'nei mitzvah*, but he was another kid waiting to drink from a water fountain. Damn the whales, she drank the water, but she could have done better. If Martha had paid the price for her transgressions, she would spend the rest of her life mourning her friend.

"Ms. Levoy," Officer Scottie said.

She blinked and looked at the man. His job couldn't be easy. As she wallowed, he had a case to solve. Shaking her head, she stole a last glance at Martha's condo and wondered who would clean up the mess. "I'm sorry."

"It wasn't your fault," Officer Scottie said.

"Still, I'm sorry. She was a good friend."

He linked his hands below his stomach. "You had any trouble at this building in the last few days? Packages gone missing? Loitering?"

She shook her head. "I've been too busy at work to give the building a second thought."

She tried to focus on her door, but the hallway commotion tugged at her awareness and Martha's redemption hovered at the edge of her consciousness like a blinking warning light. She struggled to replay her last hours with her friend. *The red dress or the blue? Heels or flats?* Martha had told her to go all out, scooped Victor into her arms and ushered her out of the door.

"Victor!"

"Ma'am?"

"Where's my dog?" She rushed toward her condo. Tapping in her code, she flung open the door and headed toward the crate. Every throw pillow on the sofa remained perfectly in place, but tiny, white teeth failed to meet her with diminutive growls. Martha had carried him across the hall, but the pair barely knew each other. The first time Victor had scratched at the door, Martha had probably carried him home, yet he wasn't in his crate.

Rushing back out of the door, she headed straight for Martha's condo. "Victor? Victor!" She slammed into Officer Scottie's shoulder, knocked his hand from her doorframe and spun him into the hall. "Victor!"

Officer Scottie grabbed her elbow. "You can't go in there! It's a crime scene."

Pivoting, she tensed.

Officer Scottie tilted his head.

She adopted her professional resting bitch face. "Martha took care of my dog, Victor. Where is my dog?"

Scrunching his nose, he scanned the hallway and lifted his radio. "Anyone seen a dog?"

Silence answered him.

She tugged free of his grip. "I have to find my dog."

He scratched his scalp. "You got a picture?"

Pulling her phone from her clutch, she unlocked the screen and scrolled through her photos. She had a hundred pictures of Victor, but she wanted the first one she took when he looked scared and alone. Instead, she stumbled on a vivid shot of Martha practicing yoga on her jute rug. Light streamed through the condo's windows and the vivid paintings or the room's walls popped. She turned the picture toward Office Scottie and watched his skin pale. *Good.* If he'd seen Martha's lifeless form, now he'd also seen her alive. Swiping left, she revealed Victor. "Please help me find my dog."

Chapter Six

The morning after his date with Nina, Alessio couldn't get her out of his mind. Lawyers and claims aggregators waited for his signature, but he struggled to complete his tasks.

She didn't know a thing about his empire, but she made him laugh, and she looked like sin wrapped around his cock. In another life, he understood how a man could pick a woman, invest in a partnership and toil away at family life. He'd chosen a different path.

Shaking off regret, he pushed aside his work and considered his seldom-used penthouse. The office at the top of the Upper East Side hotel evoked the architectural classicism of the early 1900s. In the middle of the room, a slab of a desk rested on hand-carved fluted cornices, corbels and dentil detailing. For a split second in history, the city's designers had produced high-minded pieces of furniture. The moment hadn't lasted. Gilded nostalgia collapsed into an efficient rat pile, and the twentieth century had dumped garbage in

Times Square. A few decades later, the twenty-first century rolled into view. He doubted he would live to see the next century, but the desk would persevere.

On the desk's surface, two bookends supported a stack of art books. A sleek laptop waited in the center. If he opened the screen, economic dashboards, insider trading reports and whistleblower payouts confirmed his suspicions — the city was full of rats. Most nights, he ignored technology, went with his instincts and read books. Incorporation documents bound his empire, but his memory kept score.

Turning in his desk chair, he surveyed the wall of books behind his desk and pulled down a book on Israeli art. He thumbed through the glossy pages. Images spanned the period from nineteenth-century folk art to kaleidoscopic postmodern patterns, but none of the images caught his eye. His father said books had saved more than one nation from destruction. If Alessio's empire went to shit, he had a hell of a reference section. Giving in to his desire, he picked up his phone.

I'd like to see you again.

You're amazing.

Pick the date, and I'll clear my schedule.

An hour separated each text, but she ignored each one.

He was certain she had absolutely no idea of his wealth. Most people recognized his power and bowed their heads. She spoke of her work with artistic grace and enthusiasm and her confidence fascinated him.

Then they'd fucked and her tight pussy cemented his attention. If she didn't respond to his missives, he'd send Charon to retrieve her or beg for mediation.

Exhaling, he replayed the night in front of the mirror. He'd never watched himself slide into a woman with voyeuristic curiosity. The sight magnified the physical sensation. Every dumb blonde, cat-eyed redhead and mixed-up pink punk rocker he'd taken to a lower floor hotel room had dropped to her knees or stripped to please him. Nina came to him as an equal, and he'd enjoyed the show.

Watching himself slide in and out of her, gripping her firm ass and letting her soft, brunette waves cascade over his arm, he'd known she was present in the moment. For the first time in a long time, he understood the unabashed freedom of voyeurism and exhibitionism. If he could get a hold of the damn woman, he'd please her until he fulfilled her fantasies and returned the favor.

Did I wear you out?

Did you drop your phone down a manhole?

Woman…

Annoyed at being denied anything he wanted, he stood, pushed in his chair and strode to the door. "Emily! Bring me lunch!"

His housekeeper, a college dropout who fancied herself an exotic dancer, scampered down a seventeenth-century antique Persian runner in bargain basement shoes. The twelve-thousand-square-foot penthouse had five bedrooms, six baths, two powder rooms, a library, a kitchen, a dining room, a living room the size of a ballroom and a grand terrace overlooking Central Park. If he wanted to ice skate on the terrace, the hotel staff would pipe enough water to the roof to stress the building's foundation and make his request happen. Despite the opulence, Emily wore a French maid's costume that belonged in a pop-up Halloween store. She might be the sole reason he avoided the city.

"Yes, Mr. Chen? What would you like? A lap dance?" She wiggled her fingers.

The old joke tugged a smile from his lips. "A sandwich."

She pouted.

"Has the cleaning crew been in?" he asked. "I see dust on the bookshelves."

"Maybe you shouldn't have painted them black."

"Emily…"

Covering a yawn, she waved her hand in the air. "One sandwich, coming right up." She sauntered down the hallway, paused in the middle of the runner and looked over her shoulder. "Unless you'd like something else?"

"Just a sandwich." If the woman had anyone else to keep her out of trouble, he'd gladly discharge her. Her father and brother had died in the span of a year, and he couldn't figure out how to offload her. Judging by the lace thongs he found stuffed in his closet, her interest extended past her employment contract, but he held the line.

He recognized talent and rewarded it, but Emily's future remained an enigma. When he asked about her college classes, she'd bemoaned seven-thirty start times. *"Schedule a later class."*

"You don't understand, Mr. Chen. I'm an artist."

Exasperation stole his interest. The only art he'd seen Emily create came with a pickle.

Dropping back into his chair, he shelved the Israeli art book and drummed his fingers.

What was the point of all his wealth and power if he couldn't have what he wanted? Outside the hotel, world-class shopping, gourmet restaurants and wealthy residents existed to amuse him, but he'd tried their charms and found them lacking. Beyond the au pairs, dog-walkers, nannies and blacked-out town cars cruising the block, he found the Upper East Side neighborhood as stimulating as a sauna.

His phone glowed.

Finally! Picking up the device, he held it to his face and waited for facial recognition to unlock the device.

Didn't you hear?

Wait, never mind. I'll call you.

She made good on her offer. "Alessio."

"Nina," he said.

"I'm so sorry!" She sniffled. "This is so unexpected."

During the decade he'd spent undercutting his competitors, women had either changed or he'd lost his mind. Alyssa's rational business plan made sense, and he trusted Emily's flighty act would resolve itself, but Nina needed more than a lame sob story to put him off. She could have ghosted him.

"Oh, Alessio, I'm so sorry." She drew a deep breath and adjusted the phone. The clatter sounded like static. "The break-in didn't make the news, but I should have called you sooner."

"Nina, what are you talking about?"

The silence stretched.

"Nina?"

"Martha's dead, and Victor's gone. Oh my God, I'm so sorry!"

He swallowed the grief constricting his throat. He counted Martha as a friend, but her intense smile should have followed him to the senior citizen's home. When the restriction in his throat remained, he slapped his chest and cleared his throat. "Come again?"

"Someone broke into Martha's condo" — she lowered her voice — "and slashed her."

The gruesome detail left him with little time for irregular heartbeats or solemn remembrances. Later tonight, he would pour himself a glass, unpack her letters and see where he'd gone wrong. "Do the police have a lead?"

"No. I mean, nobody in the building feels safe."

"Come to the hotel." He would apply his resources to the case. In the meantime, he would keep Nina safe and under his roof.

"I can't," she said. "I have to find Victor. In the chaos, he must have run out of Martha's condo and made his way outside. Or some well-intentioned neighbor picked him up. Or" — her voice caught — "I can't lose him, too."

"Let me help you find your dog."

"What?" she asked.

"It's the least I can do." He could do a hell of a lot more.

She waited. The beat stretched into two beats. "Okay. Sure."

"Great."

"Call me when you're here," she said. "I'm going outside to hand out flyers."

Staring out of the window, he waited for grief, but regret came first. If Martha had tangled herself in something unsavory, she knew she could come to him. He would find time to grieve her, but he wouldn't find time to recapture his connection with Nina.

How many animal shelters could there be on the island? If they couldn't locate the precious pouch, he'd woo Nina with a replacement, sweep her off her feet and work her out of his system until he could go back to his fucking work. Standing, he recalled the indistinct fur ball in Martha's chair. Nina loved the little bastard, and she wouldn't accept a generic replacement. For the first time in his life, he gave the species its due. Rolling his shoulders, he strode out of the office. "Charon!"

His second-in-command emerged from the kitchen holding a sandwich. "Yeah, Don?"

"We're going out." He stared at the sandwich. "Is that my lunch?"

Charon rubbed crumbs from his beard, shrugged and returned to the kitchen.

He exhaled. If he found Nina's mutt before sunset, he could end the day over dinner, tell her stories about Martha's wayward youth and move on with his life. Remembering her keen fascination with the hotel mirror, he fought off a grin. Whatever happened to Martha had nothing to do with him. Nina's grief mattered, but they would both move on.

A minute later, Charon returned carrying a wide-mouth water bottle and a set of keys.

He looked like a rough, unkempt Athenian seaman, but he drove like a street racer and accomplished shit. "After you drop me off at Forty-Two Park Avenue, I want you to find out what happened to Martha

Phosphole. She lived in Condo 10F. Last night, someone killed her. Find out."

Charon worked his jaw. "That's your old friend."

He walked out of study. "We weren't close."

Emily intercepted him and waved cookies in a plastic bag. "Don't forget your snacks."

Taking the bag, Charon kissed her cheek, slapped her ass and sent her back to the kitchen.

"You wouldn't last a day in another man's house," Alessio said.

"This is a hotel." Offering a cookie, Charon shrugged. "And your house suits me fine." When Alessio declined the offer, he bit into the cookie. "God, she makes the best damn snacks."

Shaking his head, he turned a corner and headed toward the elevator. "Don't let the cookies over-impress you. The recipe came from the *New York Times*."

Charon tripped on the carpet and grabbed at the wall. "When did Emily learn to read?"

"You're ridiculous. If you keep encouraging her, you'll have a gaggle of brats to manage."

Closing the plastic bag, Charon tossed it on a gilt side table and pulled out his gun. "Children are out of the question." He spun the handgun around his index finger, checked the ammunition and slid the piece back into his shoulder holster. "She's barely twenty, and I don't do kids."

"Thank God." He stepped into the elevator.

Charon followed.

Asking Charon to investigate Martha's death was like sic'ing a bootstrap hunting dog on a hot trail. The stubborn asshole wouldn't give up, and he wouldn't obey the rules. When he and Charon set up base in the

US, he'd sent Charon to gun safety school. Neither the school's instructors nor the state's licensers cured Charon of his cowboy ways.

When he aimed for a target, he hit his mark and holstered his gun with smooth familiarity.

The instructors had preached gun safety, but Charon aced the test for a concealed carry permit, walked out of the exam room and kept his gun loaded.

With Charon at his side, he knew he would never have to lift a finger in defense, but power dynamics complicated their friendship. Time and time again, he tried to pull Charon into a business role. The Greek idiot resisted the upgrade.

The elevator doors opened to the service floor.

He jogged down the stairs to a private garage.

Charon followed. "Where are we going?"

"I gave you the address."

"But why are you going? You don't have business in Murray Hill."

He paused at foot of the stairs and looked over his shoulder. "Do I need a reason?"

Charon jostled the keys. "Can we stop for curry?"

"You just ate."

Charon frowned. "Spoilsport."

"You have no idea."

Shaking his head, Charon flipped on the garage lights.

A line of black cars shone beneath the overhead spots. The vehicles ranged from sports cars to an armored van, but he inclined his head toward the rusted, blue sedan parked near the entrance. "We'll take Emily's car."

"The fuck?" Charon asked.

He headed for the passenger seat. "We're going low-profile."

"Like border smugglers." Slipping a key off the ring, Charon left it on the side table for Emily. "Maybe you should take off your watch."

Glancing at the steel timepiece, he shook his head and climbed into the passenger seat. Nina thought he was a well-to-do insurance salesman. He would bet most salesmen still owned watches. The timepiece sat heavy against his wrist and reminded him of his father's edict. He had plenty of time to play lion, but protection and guidance left him feeling hollow. How long could he convince Nina to see only what he wanted her to see?

* * * *

Charon drove through Murray Hill's tree-lined streets.

In the relative silence, Alessio used the time to process Martha's death. The lead investigator would ask questions about her financial windfall. He preferred not to entangle himself in the investigation, but she'd deserved more than a violent end.

Nearing the river, historic townhouses, modern condo buildings and small businesses anchored the neighborhood. The Murray Hill area was a popular home base for recent college graduates and young professionals who enjoyed frequenting bars along Lexington and Third Avenues. Finding a good time north of 14th Street perplexed most Boomers, but Martha could find a party blindfolded. He never knew why she remained in the neighborhood after her divorce, but he made sure the lease on her stately, pre-war Park Avenue rental remained in her name. As her building came into view, his throat constricted, and he swallowed his grief. "This one."

Charon put on his flashers and stopped in the right-hand lane.

"You could park."

Rubbing his beard, Charon scanned the sidewalk. "You sick?"

Shaking his head, he climbed from the sedan. The cloth interior smelled like cheap mall perfume, and he hoped Nina wouldn't catch a whiff of the cologne. Then again, maybe the smell would help his charade.

I'm here.

I'm at the corner hanging up flyers. Walk to the light and you'll see me.

After pulling sunglasses out of his pocket, he slid them into place, jerked his thumb toward the corner for Charon's benefit and slid his hands into his pockets. The traffic annoyed him, but he admitted the avenue's appeal. In another life, he could see himself whiling away an evening at a corner café with a beer. He snorted. If he wanted café beer, he'd fly to Amsterdam.

Scanning the corner, he saw Nina clutching a bundle of flyers to her chest. Despite her education and professional achievements, she could have passed for any impassioned activist campaigning for a cause. The early evening wind blew her highlighted hair across her face. Her red crop top left an inch of skin to show above her jeans and her wedge sandals increased her height. The minute she slipped off the shoes, she would lose the height, but the heels lifted her ass and balanced her generous hips. Remembering grabbing her hips, he grew hard.

Tucking her locks behind an ear, she passed out another flyer, looked up and waved.

He pulled a hand from his pocket, lifted it and strode toward her. Leaning forward, he pressed a kiss against her cheek. After a busy day, she smelled like sweat, faded deodorant and cinnamon gum. He'd spent the day moping in his office while she'd mourned Martha and fought to reclaim her dog. He was partial to her evening attire, but her perseverance said more about her character than her cologne could have. "It's good to see you. I'm sorry about Martha and your dog."

"Victor," she said.

Taking a paper from her stack, he examined the full-color printout. Victor, the errant white mutt, peeked from a mounded blanket. Above the picture, vivid red text advertised a reward. He handed the flyer to a stranger and turned back at Nina. "Wouldn't black and white have worked?"

"People respond to color," she said.

"How much is the reward?"

"Five hundred. Is that enough?"

"I have no idea." He rubbed his cheek and felt his five o'clock shadow. "Any leads?"

She shook her head and turned to a crowd of tourists toting smartphones.

He lifted a stack of flyers from her hands and mimicked a bookie's amiable smile. For some reason, nobody wanted the flyers he held, but the papers flew out of her grasp.

Looking over his shoulder, he found Charon parked on a bus stop bench. A laptop occupied his lap, and he held his phone to his ear. With any luck, he would identify Martha's killer before the week ended. Nina, on the other hand, could hand out a thousand flyers, but an awe-struck Midwesterner wasn't going to find Victor cowering under a dumpster. His decision-making skills kicked in. "How much is a new dog?"

She pushed him away like a sister telling her brother to shove off.

The gesture amused him, but he held up his hand to stop Charon from perceiving a threat.

Charon ignored the signal. Unfolding his frame from the bench, he tucked the laptop under his arm and walked up. "What's going on?"

Nina stared. "I've seen you before."

"Yeah, I was there when you fucked Don in the car."

The condo building's doorman stepped forward.

To avoid controversy, Alessio schooled his expression and remained still. If Martha was his liberal, estranged older cousin, Nina was the class pet. As much as he valued taking her home for the weekend, he couldn't put his life on hold to teach her the rudiments of his world. "Excuse his choice of words. He's my assistant, and he likes to drive."

Charon rolled his eyes.

Nina tilted her head. "Why did he call you Don?"

"We're also old friends. It's my middle name."

"Right." She handed out a wad of flyers. "And what's your name?"

"Charon," he said.

She scanned him. "Your name's Charon?"

Pronouncing the name with a softer 'S' like 'Sharon', she neutered Charon with a single blow. Alessio bit back his smile. "He also has his charms."

"I'm sure."

Charon walked off mumbling about hookers.

Alessio ignored the protest and considered how the evening would play out. The odds didn't look good. Forests were dying on Victor's behalf, but at this rate, he'd die before he enjoyed Nina's company. He eased the flyers from her arms. "Is this working?"

She yanked back the flyers. "You know what? I'll find Victor myself. You're visiting the city, and you lost your friend. You don't need my problems, too."

He crossed his arms. "We both lost Martha."

Her lip quivered.

After pulling off his sunglasses, he hung them from his shirt's neckline. "What do you need?"

She hesitated. "I don't know. I didn't sleep last night. Every odd noise kept me awake."

The admission slayed him. Taking her arm, he guided her toward the condo building.

The doorman cocked his head.

"You have no idea who broke into the building?" he asked. "Did the officers say anything? Security footage? Visitors you don't recognize?"

The doorman stepped forward. "Can I help you, Ms. Nina?"

She smiled a sad smile. "I'm okay, José. He's a friend. He knew Martha."

José shook his head. "She was a rare one." Stepping back, he opened the door, admitted them to the foyer and held out his hand for the flyers. "Why don't you give me the handouts? I'll hold on to them until you're ready to distribute more. Maybe the maintenance crew will pass out a few at the end of their shift. Nobody can resist the sight of a crying *hombre*."

"Your *hombres* don't cry," Nina said.

José stacked her printouts under the house phone. "For Martha and Victor, the tears will come."

Alessio considered hiring the man for his hotel. "Did you see anything?"

José narrowed his gaze.

Lifting his chin, he waited.

José looked out of the glass windows. "No. I wish I had. I really got a kick out of that woman."

Some loyalties weren't for sale.

He scanned the foyer. He'd been inside the building, but death had a habit of sharpening contrasts. He checked the ceiling corners for cameras and noted each red, blinking light. On the backside of the building, he would bet another set of doors segregated the pristine tile floors from the oil-stained parking spaces. Someone saw the assailant enter the building. Whether he, Charon or the police found the lead mattered little, but he itched to canvass the building. The veins on top of his hands bulged and the familiar adrenaline rush of a fight beckoned, but he lacked an opponent.

Nina sniffled and folded her arms across her chest. The elevator chimed, and she jumped.

She had nothing to fear from him, but his callousness risked alienating her. He let years of practiced small talk settle into place and followed her into the elevator. "Have you spoken to her family? When's the service?"

She paled. "She's not coming back, is she?"

"La speranza e l'ultima a morire."

"What does that mean?" she asked.

He thought of his family and wished he'd spent more time with them. After his father passed, his mother went in short order. *"Hope is the last thing to die."*

"She" — Nina wet her lips — "didn't want a service. She left a will. It's pen and paper, but it's legible. Her parents don't know she's gone. They can't." She swallowed. "They're in a memory care unit, and they're too old for the shock and confusion."

He should have known that fact. "We should try to contact them."

Her eyes brimmed with tears.

Abandoning his plans for dinner and foreplay, he exhaled. "I'll call them."

"Thank you." She gripped his arm. "I can't be the person to deliver the news."

Her voice shook, and he pulled her to his chest. Last night, she'd fallen apart in his arms, but if he walked away, she would continue to stand. "We'll get you settled."

"Alessio, I didn't sleep well last night. I'm not sure I'm up for another date…"

Pressing a kiss against her forehead, he rubbed her back. He wanted to play, but she needed comfort, and he wanted to comfort her. "I know."

She relaxed against him.

To the East Coast elite, he was Alessio Donato Chen, billionaire tycoon. To Nina, he was a fuck-toy and Martha's distant friend. Depending on Nina's needs for the evening, either role would suffice. Tomorrow, Charon would make his report, and Alessio would decide how to act.

Chapter Seven

Slipping from the elevator, Nina felt her heart rate spike, and she scanned the hallway. No officers or crime scene tape marked the scene. She exhaled. Last night, she'd tossed in bed and listened to New York's finest completing their investigation. The commotion assured her the officers would find the criminal, but heavy footfalls at four o'clock gave her pause. She waited for an ominous knock, but it never came. Uneasiness settled in. If she'd stayed home from her date with Alessio, the officers might have found her dead. Now Alessio stood by her side and the hallway's silence stretched. She paused in front of Martha's door. "Do you want to go inside? I know the code."

He slid his hands in his pants pockets and cleared her throat. "No. The police have their investigation." He toed a loose piece of carpet. "Seeing the site of her death won't bring her back to life. I prefer to remember her smiling. Charon will look into it."

"Right. 'Pseudo-Karen'."

He pulled one hand from his slacks and urged her down the hall. "What's wrong with the name Charon?"

"It's a chick's name." Nerves made her words run together. Hilarity obscured Martha's death. "Like, from the sixties. People have 'Aunt Sharons'."

"I'm sure Charon appreciates the competition. The name has historical, masculine roots. In Israel, both genders still use it."

"Fascinating." She forced a smile. "Does Charon question his gender?"

He released her arm and rubbed his temples. "Should we stand outside and discuss Charon for the rest of the evening? Do you have a crush?"

"I don't get crushes." The lie burned her lips. "Why do you need an assistant?"

He shrugged. "Good question."

Forcing the joke about Charon's name pained her, but getting out of bed this morning had pained her, too. Near dawn, she'd replayed her evening. While Martha drew her last breath, she'd laughed on a patio with a man who'd looked delicious in a suit and rubbed her clit until her world had shattered. Then he'd showed up to hand out dog flyers. She cleared her throat. Martha would understand her attraction. "He should stick to the Greek pronunciation."

He dropped the hand at the small of her back. "How do you know he's Greek?"

Outside her door, she shrugged, picked up her hair and piled it on top of her head. Pulling a hair tie from her pocket, she made a messy bun and shook her head to judge the topknot's resiliency. "Lucky guess. I'd change my name, too. Who wants to be the butt of every drunk Karen joke?"

"You'd look terrible with short hair."

She laughed and dropped her hands. "Well, aren't you full of compliments? How on earth did you and Martha ever get along?"

He paled.

"I'm sorry. I shouldn't have mentioned her."

"Don't be sorry," he said. "I miss her, too."

"I recently lost my grandmother." She twisted Nan's ring. "I'm tired of losing people."

He rocked back on his heels. "Me, too."

Her limbs felt so heavy that she wondered how she could stand, but people lived their lives with heavier burdens. Here she was, simpering in front of a man who'd known Martha ten times longer than she did. He easily bore the weight of her loss, but she could regain her balance. "You're right. Loss makes life feel poignant. Let's celebrate life and toast Martha. I'll make you a drink."

"Okay."

"Okay?" How could he be so nonchalant?

"It's going to be okay. You're safe, and whoever committed this crime will reap the consequences. Let's get you squared away."

At least one of them could be sensible. Turning, she smoothed her crop top and tapped her entrance code into the condo's lock. The tumblers clicked. Opening the door, she stepped inside and beckoned him to follow. "I have wine."

He hesitated in the doorway. "Someone tried to get inside."

Turning, she found him rubbing the door's exterior frame. She peered at the trim and shook her head. "Movers probably knocked it loose."

"The chipped paint's fresh." He peeled off a piece. "Wood softens with humidity and subtle grime. This exposed wood's pristine."

She shrugged. If the people who went bump in the night had come for her, she would know. "I'll ask José."

He pocketed the paint chip, followed her inside and threw the deadbolt. "You're sure you haven't seen anything strange? Martha didn't mention any personal issues?"

She ignored his paranoia and surveyed the condo from a visitor's perspective. In the early evening light, her walnut furniture glowed, and the condo looked more welcoming than his fancy hotel room. She tried to be more critical. Pillows littered the floor, and her empty ice cream bowl sat on the coffee table. Maybe she should have tidied up. Scooping up the debris, she dropped the pillow in place and ferried her dishes to the sink. She would pick the condo over the hotel, but maid service would be a nice touch.

"Nice place." He walked up to her towering fiddle-leaf fig. "You live alone?"

"Except for Victor" — she rubbed dust from the fig's wide, glossy leaves — "and my plants."

An outgoing tenant had abandoned the plant, so José had brought it to her. She kept the plant out of the morning light, but the damn thing kept growing, and its gigantic leaves collected dust. She knew she should wipe down the foliage more often, but who kept a fiddle leaf in a post-war condo?

She ran water in the bowl and wiped her hands on a dishtowel. "I do live alone. Space is my one indulgence."

"Must be nice," he said.

Rounding the couch, she sat, drew up her leg and rested her chin. "Don't you live alone? You're too old for roommates."

He sat on a chair's edge. "I do, but my housekeeper thinks she owns the place. The minute she leaves, I loosen my tie and exhale."

"You have a housekeeper?"

"Emily. She's mostly a charity case."

Huh. Standing, she pulled down two wineglasses, opened a bottle of red blend and filled the glasses. Her fingers left prints on the dust-coated bottle. The condo definitely needed help. She wondered if Alessio's housekeeper came once a week. Most people called their cleaners 'maids', but politically correct terms changed so often. Maybe she should call her cleaning lady, Angelica, her 'condo steward'. Well, first she should call Angelica to clean more often. Handing Alessio a glass, she reclaimed her spot on the sofa, pulled up her legs and crossed them. Victor should be there to scramble into her lap. She tried not to think about his fear. "Get a new housekeeper."

Sipping the wine, he picked up a law book and tested its weight. "I feel responsible for her."

"Has she been with you a while?"

He looked up. "Long enough."

Without music and candlelight, she struggled to place herself in his life. "Where do you live, anyway?"

"When?" he asked.

She frowned. "What do you mean, when?"

"I live wherever work takes me." He set down the book. "Nina, I haven't been entirely honest with you."

Jumping up, she slapped her hand over her mouth. "I knew it! You and Martha hooked up!"

"Um." He cleared his throat. "That's not what I planned to say."

She worked her jaw and wondered what on earth he planned to confess. If he had a wife in another city, all bets were off.

Her phone chimed.

Picking up the device, she opened a text from an unknown number. The image showed a green, slatted trashcan overflowing with food wrappers, discarded wattle bottles and crumbled papers. A hairy hand held a wrinkled copy of her flyer.

Who do you think cares about your missing dog? If you want protection, get something that can win a dog fight. What use is a guard dog that can't defend himself?

She dropped the phone like it burned her hand.

"What's wrong?" Alessio asked.

Looking up, she made eye contact, but she felt so helpless she could cry. "What do you mean?"

"You're pale."

Touching her cheek, she looked at the floor. Victor's hairs formed sweet, little balls of fluff. She wasn't about to knit a sweater, but she missed the crazy little ball of fur. "Am I?"

Standing, he walked over. "Can I see?"

She moved a pillow over the phone. "It's not your problem."

He held out his hand. "Maybe I can help."

Making eye contact, she swallowed, gripped the pillow to her chest and showed him the text. "People are rude."

"People are emotional." He forwarded the message apparently to himself. "Something doesn't add up."

"What? You have ESP?"

He handed back the phone. "I don't believe in coincidences. Besides living in this building, what else connected you and Martha?"

"Nothing." Standing, she paced the living room. Victor's crate took up space, but she made room for him in her life as easily as Martha made room for her. "We grabbed drinks once a week. She invited me to gallery events. Outside of the condo building, we rarely spent time together."

Staring at the wall as if she could see into the hallway, she wondered what would happen to Martha's things. If the household goods needed new homes, she would make sure the items went to people who needed them. Shaking her head, she scooped up her law books and a pamphlet from the veterinarian. "Don't worry about the text. I gave my phone number to a few hundred strangers. One of them is bound to have a bad sense of humor."

He adjusted his watch. "Maybe."

Looking at the room from a stranger's perspective, she tried to discipline her emotions. She didn't have a housekeeper come every week, but she did her best. If Alessio questioned her housekeeping, he could find his way to the door instead of her bedroom. She rubbed a houseplant's smooth leaf of and sighed. "As soon as I find Victor, I'll take off time from work and scatter Martha's ashes. You should come with me."

"Is that my cue to leave?"

She looked up. "No, that's not what I meant, but you're grieving, too. Martha doesn't have to be the thing that keeps us in contact."

He rounded the couch, but he stopped short of approaching her. "If Martha lived, would you have answered my texts for a second date? Would you have let me take you out and spoil you?"

"Yes, but I can spoil myself." She gripped the books and papers to her chest.

He caught her hand and pried the stack from her fingers. "Can you?"

"Alessio…"

"Nina." He set down the stack and tipped up her chin. "The moment you left the hotel room, I wanted to see you again. That fact hasn't changed. I would do everything in my power to prevent Martha's death, but it's done. Whoever committed the crime will pay."

She swallowed. "I can't. I mean, I can't ignore what happened."

"And I can't ignore that damn crop top." He pulled her into his arms and held her fast against his erection. "We all have our weaknesses. Some things are harder than others to conquer."

She closed her eyes.

"Kiss me, Nina. Pretend everything's okay."

One taste. She grabbed the hair at his collar, angled her lips and kissed him as if her life depended on it. One taste turned into two, and she reached for his shirt's buttons.

"Yes, but no. I want you, but I don't want you to kick me out in the morning." Pulling away, he brought her hand to his lips, kissed her fingers and smiled. "Let me take care of you."

Sex trumped death, and she was so close to a win. "You're a tease."

He laughed.

Mischief tightened the corners of his eyes, and any man who could flip the switch between lust and mischief shouldn't be trusted. She narrowed her gaze.

Bending his knees, he grabbed her thighs and hoisted her over his shoulder.

Unceremoniously draped across his fine, thick shoulder, she considered biting him, but she couldn't quite reach his ass. "Put me down!"

"Where's your bedroom?"

She pressed together her lips and refused to answer.

"No matter, I'll find it. What is this place? Twelve hundred square feet? You only have two doors."

For the first time in her life, she wished she had a bigger condo. Screaming for help would bring the neighbors running to her aide, but Alessio had plenty of opportunities to harm her. Wasn't she his alibi? She imagined her deposition and giggled. Screw whoever killed Martha. She hoped the authorities threw him in jail, but she had a life to live.

He strode toward the bedroom door and opened it. "Wouldn't you know?"

She laughed. "Lucky guess."

He tossed her onto the queen-sized bed.

The foam mattress absorbed her weight, and she propped herself on her elbows. The spider plants crowding her windowsill wafted in the disturbed air. Like her, they were hardy and resilient. To kill the striped beauties, you'd have to get creative. "Was that really necessary?"

Crossing his arms, he worked his jaw. "I've never seen you in a bed. The view's nice."

She tilted her head. "You could have asked."

He kicked off his shoes, settled against the headboard and pulled her against his shoulder.

"This doesn't feel like sex."

"We'll get to the sex, but you're too nervous for pleasure. Tell me about Martha. I haven't seen her in ages. When she called about drinks, I knew she needed money."

Pulling away from his shoulder, she frowned. "You gave her money?"

He nodded.

"She *pimped* me!"

Laughing, he tugged her back into place. "Hardly, although she did offer me Victor."

The thought amused her, and the combination of humor, heat and easy acceptance let her relax her fears. "Martha always needed money. Most of the time, I paid for drinks."

"I'm sure."

Weighted by the somber subject, her desire simmered on a low flame, but if she trusted him naked, she could trust him clothed. "We watched stupid shows together. The characters were so predictable. She kept track of the costuming and the set pieces. I kept track of the plot."

"Did you ever see her paint?"

She turned her head. "Once. It was the skyline from her window. She said she hated the piece."

He stared into the living room like he could see clear across the hall.

"She was too hard on herself. All those days staring at other artists' work eroded her self-confidence. Henri Matisse said, '*Creativity takes courage,*' but it also takes strength. Martha never had the strength to represent her skills."

Turning on her side, she settled her hand over his heartbeat. "And you?"

He lifted her palm and kissed it. "You don't want to see me paint."

"But you have courage. Insurance takes a fair amount of risk."

Exhaling, he shifted his weight. "What do I have to lose?"

"Insurance premiums?"

He swatted her ass. "True."

The quick pain reminded her what her body missed. Wiggling out of his comfortable embrace, she wrapped her arms around her legs and rested her chin on her knees. "We should order dinner or have sex."

He raised his eyebrows. "Is that an ultimatum?"

"I only have energy for one." She yawned.

He tugged free a leg and kneaded her calf muscle. "You do look beat."

Lifting her chin from her other knee, she smiled. "I told you, I didn't sleep."

His hand stilled. "Are you still afraid of the dark?"

She looked past the potted plants and the curtained window. "I was alone. Since I moved into the city, Martha's been across the hall, steady and full of life. If she laughed her way to cocktails, so could I. Even Victor liked her...mostly. She had that way with people. Once you were in, you were in all the way."

"How long have you had Victor?" he asked.

"A few weeks."

His shoulder twitched. "Come again?"

She turned. "I love that dog."

"How can you love something you've known a few weeks?" He rubbed his hand over his face. "I'm sorry, but I thought this was your treasured pet."

"He needs me!" Picking up a pillow, she tossed it in his face. As soon as she'd adopted Victor, she'd run to the pet store. She'd never had a dog, and there he was, wide-eyed and eager for comfort. The thought of leaving him paralyzed her, but the thought of him peeing on her floor had goaded her into action.

Alessio set aside the pillow.

His disciplined expression cracked, and no amount of wild, black, collar-skimming hair would soften the intensity of his gaze. Apparently, the grief processing had ended.

"Nina..."

Her ultimatum wobbled toward naked, sweaty skin, but death deepened her one-night stand into troubling intimacy. After tonight, how many times would he pick up the phone and text her for company? The quick thrill of an orgasm beckoned, and she liked the way he smelled, but if she pared down the relationship to sex, the pleasure and novelty-laced comfort faded. The next time his plane landed, she'd be another buttoned-up professional with no time to cultivate a connection. She would set aside his texts with a regretful sigh and caution herself not to get too attached to a dream. "We should order food."

He released her calf. "What kind of food?"

She scrambled to the bed's edge. "We already had Italian. What did your father cook in Zürich?"

"You paid attention."

Standing, she stretched her arms over her head. "Of course I did."

He stared at her abdomen.

Once her nerves calmed, they'd get back to the sex.

He swung his legs off the bed. "Meat and vegetables. He didn't have time for Middle Eastern spices and Mediterranean preparations. My mother ran an Italian restaurant. When my mother left for the evening, he fired up the grill and blasted everything we needed. Jews have lived in Switzerland for a thousand years, but most Israelis immigrants follow Ashkenazi customs."

"I know little about religion."

He smiled. "Let's say our neighbors looked down on my father's grilling technique. They expected brisket, latkes, matzo ball soup and tzimmes."

She tilted her head. "Do you practice?"

He shook his head and stood. "Growing up with two vibrant, religious individuals nets a cynical asshole."

"You're not cynical."

Looking over his shoulder, he smiled. "But I am an asshole?"

"That remains to be seen." She rubbed her upper arm. "Will you let me buy dinner?"

"No."

She smiled. "Asshole."

He walked around the bed and stopped three feet away. "Most people enjoy a free meal."

Shaking her head, she walked toward the kitchen and opened a drawer. "If you won't let me buy dinner, I'll cook. If you think your father was a good cook, wait until you see what I can do with a bag of cabbage slaw, a red pepper and a box of bone broth." She choked on a laugh and shook her head. "You'll think of me all week."

"Or not." He cracked his knuckles. "I'll wait while you get dressed. Pick any restaurant in the city."

She looked up. "You're in my house, Alessio. Let me order food or eat what I serve."

A smile teased his lips. "I look forward to eating you."

Her cheeks warmed and the carnal acknowledgement shot straight to her core. She reveled in the promise he offered, but she looked away to maintain her plan. "That's not what I meant."

"You said I had a choice." Walking into the kitchen, he stroked her arm. "I'm choosing sex. By the time I'm done with you, you'll be too tired to care who pays for the takeout."

She smiled. "That option expired."

He dropped his hand and swatted her ass.

"Really?" She raised her eyebrows. "You think that felt good?"

"Isn't that why you're flushed?" Walking into the bedroom, he dropped back to the bed and picked up a pillow. "We can negotiate on pillow talk. Serve me, woman."

She raised an eyebrow. "Why, so you can lie around and doom-scroll on your phone?"

He chucked a pillow.

The soft, linen case hit her with more force than she'd expected. Grasping the pillow against her middle, she examined him reclining in her bed as if he had every right to be there. She had a perfectly good leather couch, but he'd hauled her into the bedroom like a prize, and despite her protestations, she kind of liked his attitude. Hell, she liked it a lot, but the condo remained her turf. "Cabbage?"

Cocking his head, he sighed. "Take mercy on me. Please order food."

Watching his curls fall across his forehead would be her undoing. She crossed her arms. "I get to pay for the food."

Closing his eyes, he flopped back on the remaining pillows. "I hope they overcharge you."

Laughing, she walked into the kitchen and rifled through her takeout menus. Every restaurant in town wanted her to download an app or like their mobile storefront, but nothing beat sauce stains and ballpoint pen circles. She liked Alessio, but she knew next to nothing about the insurance or reinsurance industry. As soon as she had time to breathe, she'd research Alessio Chen, filter out football stars and find out what kind of fish dangled from her line. Looking over her shoulder, she smiled. Sprawled across her bed, the fish looked comfortable as hell.

Phoning the southern Indian restaurant, she ordered skewers and pastry dough-topped *biryani*. Returning to the bedroom, she found Alessio on his phone and leaned against the door jamb. "Work?"

He looked up. "A few emails."

"I'm headed to the shower."

He rubbed his thumb along the side of his lip. "Is that so?"

She smiled. "Alone." Watching his expression fall, she almost felt bad for teasing him. "I left my card by the door. If you don't use it to pay for dinner, I'll give your portion to José and tell him you're *persona non grata*."

"*A mali estremi, estremi rimedi,*" he said.

"What does that mean?"

"*Desperate times call for desperate measures.*" He glanced at her midriff. "Put on flannel pajamas. Don't tempt me."

She licked her lips. Beneath his suit, his muscles bulged, and she had every intention of temping him. After their date, she respected his success as a self-man made, but she didn't expect candlelight, wine and drivers. The sooner he started treating her like an equal, the sooner she'd be able to figure out what the hell to do with him and his confident, sexy, European attitude. "The card, Alessio."

He closed his eyes. "Yep."

Stepping out of her shoes, she stripped off her top and jeans, turned on the hot water and looked over her shoulder. His phone remained on the bed, but his gaze remained on her. Unbuckling her bra, she let it fall to the floor and stepped out of her panties.

His eyes narrowed and his nostrils flared.

Encouraged by his reaction, she moved toward the steaming shower and swayed her hips. She wondered if he would heed her directions or follow her into the shower.

"Nina," he said.

She looked over her shoulder.

"I'm not a houseplant or a pet. You can't set me aside and take me out when you want to play. I respect your loss, but you're playing with fire."

She hesitated. The date had gone so well. She'd dived in headfirst and reveled in the wine-fueled laughter and courtyard lights. Climbing in his lap had made her feel like a brave woman, but watching their bodies join in the mirror had sent her over the edge. She had to catch herself. In a few days, he'd fly to another part of the world and her life would carry on. His reminder hit home. She didn't have time for pen pals, long-distance relationships, sugarcoated lies or prickly house pets. "Alessio, I only meant to tease." Her voice cracked.

"You're running on fumes."

Standing naked in the swirling steam, she weighed her choices. "Do you want to join me?"

"More than you can imagine, but I'll respect your wishes."

Regret tugged a sigh from her lips. "Will you?"

"Yes, but if you don't get in the fucking shower, I'll revisit my decision."

She pondered his words, stepped into the shower stall and reached for the soap bar. Knowing he could see every shadowed move, she slowly washed her skin. "As soon as you start treating me as an equal, we'll both win."

"Is that so?"

The intercom buzzed.

He shut the bathroom door.

Alone, she exhaled and wondered how much longer she could play. Exhaustion pulled at her muscles, and she let her head hang beneath the brutal spray. She would have welcomed him into the shower, but after dinner and a satisfying tumble, she would also have shoved him out of the door. On some level, his fortitude worried her more than his desire. He cared for Martha, handed out reward flyers for Victor and resisted her strip tease. If he had a flaw, she feared its magnitude.

Chapter Eight

The delivery person held out the paper bags, scrolled his phone and waited.

Alessio handed Nina's card to the bored teen and added a cash tip.

"Thanks, man." The teen toggled between screens. "Later."

He closed the door in the kid's face and carried the waxed cartons into her kitchen. More plants lined the countertop. The woman cultivated a garden where most people stored food, but the quirk fascinated him. Her ability to nurture wilted plants, small dogs and lonely women said something about her personality. He wanted to explore her depths, but first he needed her to eat. If her cabbage and broth threat summarized her cooking skills, he would give her a grand tour of New York's restaurant scene.

In the wake of Martha's death, excitement and curiosity seemed like the wrong response, but he liked Nina. He couldn't tell if sex had hooked him or if he'd stayed to protect her but curiosity had pinned him to her side. It had also upended his life. Taking off a few days would set back his deals, but her allure would wear off. He scented the fragrant steam rising from the cartons and his stomach rumbled. Dismissing thoughts of the future, he rummaged through her cabinets, looking for plates.

"What are you doing?" she asked.

He turned and found her standing in the living room. She held a towel beneath her breasts, but her skin shone, and she no longer looked ten minutes from collapse. He wasn't a gawking youth who would come at the first sight of breasts, but he was close. He looked away and opened the next drawer. "Looking for plates."

"We can eat out of the cartons."

He shut a drawer full of takeout menus. "You do own plates, don't you?"

She walked past him and reached for an overhead cabinet he'd missed.

When her towel slipped, a peppery, rosemary scent reached him, and he discarded his pretenses. Abandoning all interest in food, he hooked an arm around her waist and pulled her back against his chest. Her wet hair soaked his shirt, but he didn't care. Since he'd met her, he'd teetered between desire and concern, and his control finally slipped. Dropping his head, he kissed her neck and held the towel beneath her breasts. "You smell much better than dinner."

Leaning her head against his shoulder, she turned and gave him easier access. "Shampoo."

"Hmm." He turned her in his arms, lifted her to the counter and caged her with his arms. "Fascinating."

A slow smile lifted her lips.

"Plates sound nice, but I have a better idea."

She shifted her hips. "You're full of ideas."

Running his hand up her smooth thighs, he paused short of her towel. If she were one of the women who used his credit limit and his dick, he would yank down the towel and finger-fuck her until she screamed his name. She wasn't. He closed his eyes and considered pitching the suggestion. "You're right."

She cupped his jaw. "Try me."

Choosing finesse over satisfaction, he claimed a soft kiss. The moment her laughter turned to a sigh, he pulled back. This wasn't a charity gala. Beneath her eyes, dark shadows marked her skin, and he refused to burn the association so quickly. *Pace. Moderation.* He swallowed. *Control.*

In the fading light, she blinked and chewed her lip.

"The night's young." Stepping back from temptation, he opened the nearest carton. Steam escaped the pasty-topped dish of lamb and rice. In India, goat often replaced tender lamb, and clay pots filled the role played by flaky dough. One day, he could show her the world. The thought caught him off guard, and he cleared his throat. He wondered if her adventurous tastes extended past Murray Hill.

"Does everything look okay?" she asked.

Pulling a spoon off the counter, he scooped up a bite, blew on the mixture and offered it.

"That's my coffee spoon." She opened her mouth.

"You only have one spoon?" He wiggled the bite.

She grabbed the spoon, claimed the food and swallowed. "I only wash one spoon."

Shaking his head, he offered her the carton. "Then we'll share."

"How diplomatic."

He bit his cheek. The only times people referred to him as 'diplomatic' were the times they hoped to negotiate a new deal without realizing how badly they'd already fucked up.

Lifting a bite, she held it out.

Instead of trading flatware back and forth, he opened his mouth and obediently claimed her offering. A heady mixture of spices, onions and yogurt seasoned the lamb. Aromatic star anise, bay leaves and cloves kept the basmati rice bright. Despite the dish's warmth and flavor, he moved closer to her legs and the dish he truly wanted. In the tiny kitchen, her damp skin lured him like a siren's song, and he itched to stroke her. For the last hour, he'd fought an erection and thirty more minutes wouldn't kill him. Pulling the spoon from his mouth, he refilled it and offered it. "Your turn."

She blinked. "Do you want to feed me?"

"Among other things." He set down the spoon.

She tilted her head. "I'm not into…"

He traced her lips. "What? Submission?"

Wetting her lips, she inhaled. "Waiting for instructions."

"I gathered that fact." He set down the spoon and spread her thighs. Her sweet, musky desire inflamed his senses, and he knew his thirty-minute estimate had been overly optimistic. He would take her on the counter and pay homage in her bed.

Even as her stomach rumbled, she held his gaze. Grabbing the spoon from the counter, she took the bite and dropped the flatware. "Okay, now we go."

The spoon clattered like an alarm bell. He imagined her cross-examining a witness and pitied the person on the stand. "I'll make you a deal."

She chewed her bottom lip.

"You let me feed you, we fuck and I'll get breakfast in the morning." He scanned the kitchen. "I take you for a coffee person. Croissants?"

"Tomorrow's Sunday," she said.

He frowned. "What does the day of the week have to do with anything?"

"Sunday brunch."

He narrowed his gaze and reconsidered how much he knew about the woman derailing his thoughts and his productivity. "You're an eleven o'clock, eggs and mimosa kind of woman?"

"Bacon." Picking up the spoon, she dipped it into the carton and took a healthy bite. "I want hot coffee and hot bacon."

He cleared his throat. "For bacon, I can stay the night?"

She smiled. "For hot coffee and bacon, you can stay all week."

Despite his desire, the gulf between what he wanted and what he could promise loomed like an inland sea. As much as we wanted her, he couldn't commit to more than one night. The marks on her doorframe and the insulting text worried him, but Charon would uncover the murderer. He could ensure Nina's safety, but he couldn't guard her heart. "Nina, I can't…"

Loading up a spoon, she shoved it in his mouth.

He choked back a laugh and swallowed.

"I know you're passing through," she said. "Humor me."

"And Monday?" he asked.

She reached for a glass, filled it and let her towel drop. Bare-chested and sitting on the counter, she swung her legs and dug into the remainder of the *biryani*. "Monday doesn't matter."

He stared at her perfect breasts. "Doesn't it?"

"Alessio."

His name sounded like a shared secret.

She shifted on the thin granite. "Touch me."

He stroked her thigh. "I am touching you." His hand shook with the impulse to do more.

"Are you?" she asked.

He inhaled. Every one of her barbs and teasing glances came with the same intelligent, delicious amusement that had caught his attention in Martha's condo. Making promises beyond a one-night stand worried him, but so far, Nina wanted bacon, physical comfort and his dick.

Stilling his hand on her thigh, he cursed his restraint and molded her slim waist. Her shallow, expectant breaths were the only things keeping him from closing his eyes and treating her like every other woman who pretended to please him. For the first time in a long time, he felt a clever woman's admiration and knew she wanted him above what he could give her. He swallowed. "Listen closely."

She scooted to the counter's edge. "I'm having difficulty focusing."

"Good." He raised his hand and cupped her breast. His other hand fisted at his side, and he resisted the urge to turn her over the counter and claim her before she asked too many questions. He made eye contact. "Nina, you don't really know me, but as long as we're together, I will give you every fantasy your clever mind can conjure. In return, you'll tell me what feels good, what intrigues you and what you're ashamed to admit."

She frowned. "Don't make promises you can't keep."

He thumbed her nipple. "I'll keep them."

Exhaling, she melted into his touch and her thigh muscles shook.

"Also, you'll eat."

She gripped the countertop.

He could carry her into the bedroom, fuck her until she screamed his name and walk away, but he wanted more than a second night. "Why are you shaking? Are you scared of me?"

She raised her head. "I'm scared you'll deliver."

Closing his eyes, he exhaled. "I'll make you come, Nina, then I'll tuck you into bed and let you recover. If you're very good, coffee and bacon are yours."

"If I'm very bad?"

He opened his eyes.

She blinked.

"I'll spank you," he said.

She chewed her lips. "Really? I said I wasn't into submission."

He pinched her nipple and watched her jump. "Submission and pleasure go hand in hand."

"I'm a lawyer."

"And I'm an insurance salesman." He buried the truth beneath a simple fact. He sold insurance to multinational corporations, and when their bets went south, he collected. Somewhere in Nina's kitchen, forgotten skewers grew cold, but the only dish he wanted sat topless and flushed on the kitchen counter. He pulled her to the floor, turned her and pulled her back against his chest.

She shifted her hips. "Alessio."

Cupping her pussy, he stroked her, found her wet and wanting, and he listened to her moan. He dropped his head. "You wondered if I would follow you into the shower." His rough cheek teased her soft skin, and he whispered to focus her attention. "You wanted me to follow you."

She sighed and arched into his touch. "I did."

"I don't lose control." He stroked her slowly because the alternative was to push her against the counter, spread her cheeks and fuck her until she screamed. "You enjoy putting on a show."

Her body shuddered.

He worked two fingers into her and listened to her starving whimpers. Last night, she had been heat and impulsive fire, but tonight, she needed comfort and release. He would give it to her. Keeping one arm anchored across her middle, he explored her depths and searched for her pleasure.

She hooked her arm around his neck, drew down his head and claimed his lips.

Content to savor her embrace, he matched his finger to her lips' pace.

Within minutes, her fevered kisses eclipsed the previous night's curious playfulness. If she wanted to feel alive, he wanted to meet her demand. Shifting his stance, he spread her legs and rubbed slow circles against her clit. With her arm anchored around her his neck, she clung to him and gave him free rein to work her pleasure.

"Alessio…"

He pressed his cock against her ass and stilled. "Tomorrow, you won't feel exhausted. Tomorrow, you won't wonder who I am. Eyes wide open, you'll come to me, and we'll test the limits of what we started."

She drew a deep breath. "Yes."

"Will your neighbors hear you scream?" He rolled the bud between his fingers and traced his nail along her lips. "Will they know you're coming undone in my arms?" The urge to claim her reverberated in his system. He couldn't help but drag his teeth along her shoulder and work her until she teetered. With his desire threatening to outrun his mind, he recognized how quickly she'd made an impression and how firmly he intended to hold her. "Will you scream my name?"

Her hips bucked against his touch. "Alessio, please."

"Will you?" The harsh question escaped his lips. He marked her shoulder, felt her pulse skyrocket and pushed her over the edge. As she chased her satisfaction, he memorized every pleasurable cry. When she moaned, he captured her lips. She tasted like damp desire and bright life. Feeling his control slip, he pressed the heel of his hand against her clit and increased the pressure and friction. If she didn't come soon, he'd lose control and deal with the consequences.

Moaning, she tried to turn in his arms.

He tightened his grip, held her fast and felt her slick muscles clench around his fingers. He changed the pace. "Let me take care of you."

She buried her face against his neck.

Refusing to release her, he held her while she shook. Her muscles clamped around his fingers, and he rode her pleasure as if it were his own.

"*Alessio!*"

His name had never sounded sweeter. He could replay her release a thousand times and still get off, but he promised to care for her. Holding her while she fell, he waited until she sighed, scooped her into his arms and carried her toward the bed. Somewhere, her towel fell to the floor, a neighbor tentatively knocked on the door and neither he nor Nina cared.

Within minutes, she lay limp against his shoulder.

He wanted release as much as he wanted those meat skewers in the kitchen, but her even breathing satisfied him in a way he'd never considered. When his phone lit up the tangle of covers, he considered abandoning it until dawn.

His watch vibrated.

Closing his eyes, he reached for the phone, turned down the volume and lifted it to his outside ear.

"Jack Santana," Charon said. "Surveillance video from the corner bodega shows him carrying a grocery bag flush against his chest. He came out of the back side of the building and threw back his hoodie the moment the street looked clear."

Proximity mattered and his connection to the Sanna family felt too close for comfort. "He targeted Martha to get to me, but why did he kill her?"

"Fuck if I know," Charon said.

Nina shifted against his side.

"I pulled phone logs. He met Martha more than once at the hotel. They may have had something going on the side. The whole thing could be domestic violence."

Turning from the phone, he looked at the peaceful woman sleeping at his side. "I doubt it. I don't think she would put up with his sycophantic shit."

"Is everything about you?" Charon asked.

"Yes. Find him."

"On it," Charon said.

He ended the call. He had to tell Nina about his connection to Jack, but her presence felt like an unexpected gift. If she thought she was in danger, she would run. He would keep her safe.

Unless she had something going on the side, too.

Closing his eyes, he inhaled deeply and sorted fact from fiction. Despite the red wardrobe, she looked as innocent as Victor. She grieved Martha, and she came to the restaurant brimming with curiosity, intelligence and fun. Her devotion to Martha, Victor and every stick of chlorophyll in the building seemed consistent, but coincidences killed men—and he intended to live. He stirred her against his shoulder. "Nina."

She raised her head. "Bacon."

A dull laugh rumbled in his chest, but he refused to detour from his line of inquiry. "Did Martha have a boyfriend? Any dates?"

Lowering her head, she sighed. "Tomorrow."

"Where did you get Victor? Maybe he found his way home."

She shook her head. "Rescue agency. I haven't seen Martha in a month."

He traced her thigh. "Why?"

Rolling to her back, she lifted her head on her elbow and frowned. "I had a brief, bad relationship and swore off men for a while. I have no idea what she did last month. Let the police sort it out."

"Okay."

"Okay?" she asked.

He pulled her close and stroked her arm. "Okay."

She draped an arm across his abdomen and inhaled. "Okay."

Closing his eyes, he listened for movement in the hall. Nothing stirred. He believed her and her reaction to Martha's death. As soon as Charon verified who killed Martha, Alessio would counterstrike, the game would collapse and he would hold the prize. Nina asked him if a five-hundred-dollar reward would be enough to return Victor to her arms, but he had little interest in the dog. Every fiber of his body compelled him to protect her and keep her safe from men like Jack.

He had a hunch the man wanted millions and wouldn't rest until he had it.

* * * *

"Bacon," a woman said.

Alessio inhaled and scanned the unfamiliar bedroom. Plants and feminine shit lined the walls. A woman with sun-streaked brown hair straddled him, and as soon as he put together the pieces, he remembered how much he wanted to fuck her. "Pardon?"

She leaned over him. Her hair teased his chest. "You promised me coffee and bacon."

He rose on his elbows. "What time is it?"

"Nine."

"Impossible." He never slept past six.

She climbed off his chest.

He tried to grab her ankle. Coming up short, he flopped back on the bed. "Did you drug me?"

"Huh? What kind of person are you?" She picked up her phone. "I guess I'll have to order breakfast."

Rubbing his face, he sat up, reached for his phone and opened a text to Charon. If he didn't stay a step ahead of this woman, his entire diet would arrive by courier. He texted Charon.

I need hot coffee and bacon.

Diva.

If you get the food here in the next thirty minutes, I won't dock your pay for scratching the car I bought in Kissimmee.

You don't know it was me.

Was it?

Bacon in thirty.

Pressed between a rock and a hard space, Charon never lied.

Alessio dropped the phone and reconnected the neurons that led to coherent thoughts. He reached for Nina and hoped a morning tumble would untangle his thoughts and affirm his motivations.

She danced out of range and opened a drawer. Purple, lace underwear dangled from her fingers.

His motivations remained intact.

Her phone vibrated on the dresser.

Picking up the device, she used two fingers to zoom. "Shit."

Propping himself on one elbow, he frowned. "What's wrong?"

She turned and held up her phone. A man's fingers dangled a small, white dog by its back leg. "I thought the last text was junk, but someone has Victor, and they want more than the reward I'm offering. The text asks, 'How much is a life worth?'"

He knew it! Coincidences belonged in fairy tales. Whoever killed Martha took Nina's dog for a reason. He put his money on Jack and desperation. If the game ended this easily, he'd laugh all the way to the meet point. Then he'd fuck up Jack-The-Wannabe and make sure the man stayed the hell away from him, Nina and whomever else he cared about. Who ransomed a dog? He tamped down his emotions. "How much does he want?"

"I don't know." She tossed him the phone. "Is this real? Maybe it's a meme."

He picked up the phone and looked at the image. The dog could be Victor or any other toy breed, but Nina recognized her pet. In the picture's background, the Hudson River glimmered. He scratched his chest. Jack's life was worth a blue-collar job and an early heart attack. "I don't think that's a filter. Whoever has your dog is still on the island."

She pulled the phone from his hands. "Where is this? The east docks?"

He folded his hands beneath his head and flopped back on a pillow. "It doesn't matter. He'll reveal himself, and he won't harm Victor."

She pinched the screen and zoomed into the image. "Are you sure?"

"Positive. Send me a screenshot of the messages." He preferred her practical, flirtatious, pre-date texts, but if Victor's absence dictated his weekend, he would return the little terrier to her arms. When the text arrived, he sent it to Charon with explicit instructions to locate Jack.

"*How much is a life worth?*' What does that even mean? Should I call PETA? Victor's such a sweet boy." Her thumbs flew over the screen. "He must be so scared."

"What are you doing?" he asked.

"Telling Victor's captor he's a sick asshole. Also, that he prefers liver and beef kibble."

"The captor?"

Nina looked up. "The dog."

He bit back a smile. "Did the captor answer?"

She dropped her shoulders and sighed. "No. I don't know who would take a dog when so many need homes. Maybe someone nabbed a flyer, threw together the image and tried to mess with me."

"Is it working?"

She set down her phone. "Yes. I love that dog. I hope he's okay."

He couldn't imagine loving anything as soft and earnest as a dog. "People use burner phones to stay anonymous. Do you have any enemies? Any clients who feel wronged? What about your last relationship?"

Shaking her head, she stared at her phone. "Clients get impatient with the justice system, but not with counsel or pretty mediators who get them what they want." She looked up. "I thought he'd escaped. Why would someone take him?"

He had a million-dollar hunch.

The doorbell rang.

Swinging his feet over the edge of the bed, he stood and rubbed his face. "Your coffee and bacon are here."

"Already? I haven't placed the order."

"I took care of it." He cracked his knuckles and prepared to level with her before life's demands outstripped his patience. "Nina, we have to discuss some shit."

She waved him off, grabbed a robe and waltzed toward the front door. "Casual hookups, Alessio. I'm not asking you for more."

"But I am." Watching her ass sway, he considered abandoning Jack's game, barricading Nina in the condo and living out his life with takeout cartons, an altar to Victor and a satisfied grin.

Opening the door, she scooped down and picked up a white paper bag and a cardboard tray bearing two coffee cups. Her ass peeked out of the robe.

He groaned and put on his briefs.

Prying a coffee cup from the tray, she took a sip and closed her eyes. "Which café did you pick?"

"Café Charon."

She frowned. "Are you sure he's just your assistant?"

He reached for his shirt. "Something like that."

Shaking her head, she walked to the leather couch and curled into a corner with both hands wrapped around her coffee cup. "Most people don't pay for friendship."

"Of course they do." Sitting on the other side of the couch, he leaned back and looked at the ceiling's plaster details. "It's called fraternities, tithing and country club dues."

"How cynical."

He turned his head and stared at her relaxed, awakening form. She would fit into all three establishments, but she had a thriving career, and he pitied her opponents. He wondered if she would take on his merciless, rough and tumble negotiations. "Friendship is a ruse for profit. You have no idea how many friends have used me."

She tilted her head. "Enlighten me."

Her legs peeked from beneath the robe, and he envied the smooth leather. Faced with a nearly naked, willing woman, he wanted to pull her into his lap and make good on his morning wood. Yet, as soon as he surfaced for air, the situation would remain, and his desire kept him balanced on a knife's edge. As soon as she had Victor, she'd chock up their fling to a brilliant memory, buy the dog a crate of squeaky toys and tell him to call her the next time he came through town. Case closed. "I don't have a lot of friends. The traveling gets in the way. Sometimes, I think I know someone, but I find out they're playing the long game."

"What's worse?" she asked. "Disappointment or loneliness?"

He opened his mouth to answer.

"Martha never picked up the tab. She showed up late. She ate most of my appetizers. But she was there when I needed her. Even when I didn't think I needed her, she had a second sight. She pulled me out of my funk."

"What if she was using you?"

"For what?" she asked.

"Free food."

She digested the idea for a moment and looked out of the window. "That's not the kind of person I am. If you're hungry, I'll find a way to feed you."

Dumfounded, he stared. He could take Nina to Idaho and protect her, but he could also work her out of his system. This level of empathy floored him. Enmeshed in his world, he could protect her until his organization reestablished the equilibrium in Murray Hill. When the dust settled, she could return to her houseplants and her noble gestures. "You and Martha were neighbors. You might be in danger."

She frowned.

"Serial killers."

She paled.

"Why Martha?" he asked.

She stood and paced. "Come on!"

"I can take care of you." He felt like an ass for stoking her fears, but the pledge to protect her slipped past his lips before he thought about it.

She peered at him over her steaming coffee cup. "What?"

"I meant, I can take care of the details, but I want to take you on a trip."

"To where? Coney Island?"

"Farther west. Idaho. I have plans there next week. While we wait for Victor to turn up at a local shelter, we can scatter Martha's ashes and climb a few mountains." If a week didn't satisfy his itch and give Charon time to act, he'd convince her to stay for two. As soon as she bored him, he'd return to his regularly scheduled agenda of superb wine, satisfying fucks and quick goodbyes.

She shook her head. "The police said cremation would take a week or more."

"Fine, Martha can wait, but come away with me. Getting out of town will do you good."

"No." She looked at the rug. A small, red, rubber toy rested near the coffee table. "I'll wait until I find Victor. The flyers might work, but I haven't looked hard enough."

He ran his hands through his hair. "Victor will be fine." If Jack had the dog, he wouldn't endanger his leverage.

"How do you know?" She picked up her phone and stared at the screen. "People don't kidnap dogs."

"Or kill women."

She swallowed.

Why are women so difficult? He reached across the couch, pulled the coffee from her hands and downed the sallow American shit. Charon knew better than to bring him drip brew. As soon as he sorted out his reaction toward Nina, he'd sit down his right-hand man and reestablish the pecking order that had served him well for the last twenty years. "What's in the paper bag?"

She opened the paper sack. "Parfaits."

He rubbed his brow. "Fuck him."

Looking up from the fruit salads, she stared. "Are you okay?"

"Yes." Lying through his teeth, he walked into the kitchen, poured the second coffee down the drain and braced his hands on the counter. Insubordination stung, but calling Charon and asking the man if he'd lost his mind would halt his progress with Nina. Torn between two interpersonal issues, he considered going back to the ring and working out his frustrations on a willing opponent. Instead, he inhaled and surveyed the sunlit kitchen. "Have you checked the animal shelters?"

She moved around the small living room. "I called and emailed a picture."

He refused to turn around and admire her ass while she stacked books, fluffed pillows or did whatever charming domestic tasks he ignored and outsourced to Emily. Shorting the stock of multinational corporations required capital and patience, and he held both assets in spades. Wooing Nina required a fresh skill set, and he wondered if he might be too old to learn new tricks.

He looked at the kitchen counter, thought about the prior night and wet his lips.

If searching for Victor bought him time to explore his attraction to Nina, he'd call the little dude's name from one end of the island to the other. Whether his efforts worked remained entirely out of his control, but they would give Charon enough time to locate Jack and settle the little fuck's involvement in this mess once and for all. He straightened. "Of course you did. You're a responsible pet owner."

"But we can check out the facilities in person. New York's full of small dogs. How could the shelter staff tell one dog from another?"

He turned and cocked his head. "He's not microchipped?"

"No, I ugh"—she swallowed—"didn't have time, and the chips are kind of scam. Why do I need to pay an annual fee to keep a series of numbers in a database? I can't imagine how much money the company makes off worry and fear."

Her heart and her intellect captivated him over candlelight. Crossing the room, he tucked her hair behind her ear. "Plenty. It's my specialty."

She tilted her head. "Is it?"

"Scared people overreact." He pulled her between his legs for a kiss that would clear the cobwebs from his mind and give him time to formulate a strategy. "They show their cards, reveal their weaknesses and fold."

She ruffled his hair. "Remind me not to take you to a Christmas party."

He skimmed her soft arm. Sleep-crusted and full of dopey-eyed wonder, she fascinated him, but she deserved the truth. "I should tell you more about myself, but I don't know where to start."

"What's your favorite book?" she asked.

"Not that kind of stuff." He swallowed. "These circumstances suck, but I, ugh, might like to spend more time with you."

She laughed and pressed a kiss against his shoulder. "I like you, too."

His declaration came out so fumbled and uncertain that he wished he could start over, declare his interest and carry the burgeoning relationship into the future. Smooth, confident public speaking earned him six figure speaking engagements in front of a room full of investors. He cleared his throat and decided to try again. "I like you, Nina."

She blinked. "I feel a 'but' coming on."

"Let's go to Idaho."

"Victor."

He didn't know how to move forward without scaring her. His ruthless, high-stakes world demanded confidence, and he came with too much baggage. She would never be content to lounge poolside while he cut deals. Then again, why did she have to lounge? Her carefree laugher, urban curiosity and professional pride shone, but if she accepted his life, it would change her. Then again, Martha's killer had broken her naïve bubble, not him. He needed more time to decide how much to reveal, and a day chasing Victor's shadows would buy him time. "Never mind the trip. We'll go when you're ready. Let's head to the animal shelters."

Gripping his shirt, she bunched the fabric in her hand. "Don't 'Never mind' me. Say what you mean to say."

He swallowed. Omissions weren't lies. "You're hot."

She released her hold. "Is that all?"

Raising his hands, he cupped her face. "I don't understand women. I thought I figured out your gender, but you're unique..." He exhaled and scowled. A billion dollars insulated him from most social gaffes, but without a plan, he knew he would put his foot in his mouth. The tiny kitchen amplified his breathing, and his heartbeat and the sounds echoed in his subconscious. He wondered if Nina's neighbors would hear his desperation and call emergency services. "And you care."

Pulling back, she wound her hair around her fist, secured it on top of her head and laughed.

He frowned. "Why are you laughing?"

As she reclaimed the space between his legs, her pupils dilated, and she wet her lips. If the woman looked at him any harder, he'd feel like a beetle pinned to a museum board. No wonder she excelled in her field. One minute, she looked like a summer breeze, the next minute she looked like she could summon thunder. "Nina?"

"I don't know." She toyed with his chest hair. "You're flustered. It's adorable."

"Adorable." He bore her inspection. "Like your dog."

She looked up. "Not like my dog."

"Good." His throat ached. He wondered if he screwed up things so badly that she wanted to send him packing. Fearing a chance encounter, he doubted he would find peace in the city, but other cities remained free of her infectious grin. "I'm not your dog."

"Why don't we break for the day and get together over dinner?"

He knew a brush-off when he heard it. Relegation to her contact list would end in failure. She'd lose track of time, follow a lead to Harlem or run through her phone battery. When he couldn't reach her, he'd chuck his phone against the wall, pretend she didn't matter and yell at Charon.

Then Jack would strike.

He would see her picture on the newspaper's front page and know he could have done better. The possibility cauterized his insecurities, and he drew a deep breath. He wanted more. "No."

She smiled. "No?"

He bent down and pressed his lips against her sweet, surprised smile. Her confusion lasted a minute, but she angled her head and sighed. Then she kissed him back, open-mouthed, soft-lipped and generous. He deepened the kiss and reminded her how they ended up in an anonymous hotel room. Heat pulsed between his body and hers. He put his hand on the back of her head, stroked her head and pulled her weight against him.

Leaning against his frame, she angled her hips.

Lust brought him back to solid ground. Groaning, he felt her open to his kiss like a sun-warmed flower. He raised his head and stared. Her lips, red and swollen, remained parted.

"You're right." She touched her lips. "Let's skip the never-minds."

He crouched to throw her over his shoulder. "Back to bed?"

She laughed, turned away and looked over her shoulder. "Victor, Alessio. We're going to find Victor."

Adjusting his pants, he cleared his throat. "Game on."

Chapter Nine

Outside her Park Avenue rental building, Nina slid on her sunglasses and adjusted her tote. Sneakers, jeans and a peasant blouse seemed appropriate for a day of canvassing the island's pet shelters. "The shelter's on FDR Drive. We can walk through St. Vartan Park and be there in twenty minutes. Victor loves the park."

Alessio adjusted his collar and donned his sunglasses. "Walk?"

The wind off the river teased his hair and drew admiring looks from strangers. *Fate wasted that hair on a man.* Shaking her head, she sipped her coffee, wound her errant strands into a bun and moved toward the park.

"We're walking," he said.

She looked over her shoulder. "You don't like to walk?"

"Fucking love it." He lengthened his stride and matched her steps. "I can walk."

She considered taking his hand, but public displays of affection felt too established. A few days into their acquaintance, his generosity and wry amusement shouldn't matter, but they did. This morning, she'd woken with a smile. The realization startled her. Missing a step, she faltered and grabbed his arm for support.

"You okay?" he asked.

Forcing a smile, she withdrew her hand. "Never better." She had a law degree, a solid professional reputation, a kick-ass body and a plan to recover her dog. If she played her cards right, she could also have Alessio in her bed. Relationships could wait.

"How long have you lived in Murray Hill?" he asked.

"A few years. I can't imagine living anywhere else." Passing the historic townhouses, modern condo buildings and small businesses anchoring the neighborhood, she crossed the boundary into St. Vartan Park. "Where do you like to spend time?"

"Places."

She let the evasion rest. Seducing a man didn't entitle her to his secrets.

In the park, a perimeter of mature trees provided shade for kids to play and adults to unwind. The park's western half contained a few asphalt fields, but Victor always pulled her straight toward the grass, playground and abandoned snacks—not that she ever let him snatch up the junk food. He was beautiful, but he'd probably mistake a plastic ring for a cookie and set her back several hundred dollars at the vet.

Nearby, St. Vartan Cathedral's conical gold roof presided over the corner of 2nd Avenue and 34th Street. The towering building looked a little like a prison playing dress up. Its smooth walls were too austere for joyous song, but she knew little about the faith or Armenia. Once, while had Victor rubbed noses with a Shih Tzu, she'd looked up the country on her phone. Now, she looked for a trashcan to discard her coffee cup. "My news show said Armenia and Azerbaijan are at odds."

He stared at the cathedral. "Two former Soviet republics fighting over disputed territory isn't odd. Ceasefires have failed." He shook his head and looked at her. "You care about international conflicts?"

"I don't want anyone to get hurt. I care about people." She scanned the park. Kids ran around the grassy area in swimsuits. Within the hour, the sprinkler would start and pickup games on the sports field would dissolve into laughter and shrieks. Jungle gyms, swings and happy children seemed ubiquitous, but she wondered if Armenia's children had the same freedoms. "I don't know enough about the conflict to choose sides. Do you?"

He looked toward the river. "I sell insurance."

She tilted her head. "But you box." The word tasted gritty. "You understand why people fight."

Skewing his mouth, he nodded.

She wished she could read his expression behind his sunglasses.

"Bombs, bullets and brutality produce threats," he said. "If I had a ceasefire in front of me, I would do everything in my power to honor it."

"And if that failed?"

He took her hand and pulled her toward the river. "Then I'd go to war."

His declaration brought a shiver down her spine, but his hand felt sturdy and warm. She let her arm swing with the walk's momentum and tried not to read too much into the gesture. Geopolitics could wait for the third date. "So what are your plans for next week?"

"Idaho. Power players and their private jets will converge on Sun Valley for a week of tennis, long hikes, whitewater rafting, foursomes and business deals."

She watched a pair of boys playing tag. "Sounds boring."

"Hardly," he said. "The excitement comes from the details."

A kid on a scooter raced across the hard surface and nearly buzzed them.

Alessio stopped short and released her hand.

The absence of connection felt like an exposed wound. She wondered if he felt it, too.

He rubbed together his fingers and dropped his hand. "The power players can make deals in their boardrooms. They come to the conference to relax and network. Why else would they come to a lodge in Idaho?"

She frowned. "Nude yoga?"

He choked out a laugh and scanned the kids. "Nude yoga... Maybe."

Pulling up her phone, she looked at the image of the white dog dangling over the Hudson River. "Maybe I should rent a car and expand my search."

"Why? Do you have any reason to believe he's not in Manhattan?"

She dropped the phone in her tote. "No."

"Nina, he's been gone for two days. I don't think you need to rent a car and go traipsing across the Northeast on a wild goose chase. Let's stay on this trajectory and exhaust the local possibilities."

She looked up. "Coming from the man who sent his buddy to circumvent a police investigation, your advice sounds ironic. What would you do? Hire a private investigator?"

Lifting his sunglasses, he settled them on his head. "You're doing all the right things."

She looked away. "I'm still worried."

He pulled her into a hug and rubbed her back. "I know. We're going to find him."

Despite his welcome embrace, his promise sounded too comfortable. A week ago, she, Martha and Victor existed in a neat suspension. Every morning, she left for work and every evening, she came home to soft leather, lazy-dog snores and Martha's incessant television noise. Even when the woman went out, she left on the set. Why hadn't a neighbor heard something?

"Coming home to an empty condo destroys the soul," Martha had said. *"You might as well come home to a laugh track."*

Shaking off the memory, Nina pulled back and rubbed her arms. "Thanks for your confidence."

"My pleasure."

Judging by his smile, he meant it. She turned toward the park.

A young teenager riding a shiny, new bike stopped beneath the shade of an elm tree. He couldn't be over thirteen or fourteen years old. His apple-red bike looked straight from the store. If she leaned close, she could find bits of foam clinging to the paint and giving off the astringent odor of packing beads.

Three other teenagers stepped away from a bench and approached the kid. Fist bumps, back slaps and slow whistles made the group look fit for a special about coming of age in the big city.

Watching their hijinks, she smiled. Life didn't have to be doom and gloom. If Victor waited at the shelter, she would reclaim him and decide what to do next with her caseload, her lease renewal and her sudden interest in Italian-Israeli insurance salesmen.

Circling the bike, the biggest teenager rubbed his chin. His muscles flexed beneath a cutoff T-shirt. Locking eyes with a member of the trio, he jerked his thumb over his shoulder.

The second teenager pulled the handlebars from the owner's grip, threw his leg over the frame and pumped the petals.

The bike owner lunged. "No! Dude, *no!*"

Waiting until their coconspirator created distance, the two remaining teenagers held the bike owner's shoulders and shoved him to the ground.

Breaking into a run, she rushed toward the teenagers to intervene. "Hey! Hey, you!" She waved her arms and tried to draw attention to the scuffle. "Get off him!"

The pair pivoted and fled.

Rising to his feet, the bike's owner braced his hands on his knees and hung his head. "Shit, my mamma's going to kill me."

She stopped short of touching him. "Are you okay? You need help?"

The teenager looked up and shook his head. Then his eyes went wide, and he burst into a grin. Pushing past her, he jogged in the direction the bike thief fled. "Yo, man, you got my bike back!"

Turning, she found Alessio gripping the thief's arm with one hand. The red bike hung over his shoulder. Lowering the bike, he handed it off to the owner and turned his attention to the thief. "You risked your future for a bike?" He brushed his hair out of his eyes with his free hand. "You're worth more than a bike. Bus tables, break down boxes at the bodega or get a fucking babysitting certificate."

She clapped a hand over her mouth.

The teenager spit. "You don't know nothing."

Alessio discharged the teenager. "I know I could have been you."

The thief bolted.

Surging ahead, Alessio grabbed his shirt. His sunglasses fell to the path, but he gripped the kid's shirt. "I'm not done with you."

The teenager went limp.

Alessio released him. He crossed his arms and jerked his head toward the red bike. "That yours?"

Looking around, the teenager sighed. "Nah."

"Then you're a thief." He glanced over to her. "What do we do to thieves?"

Tough love wasn't her thing. If she misbehaved, Nan had given her the silent treatment until she corrected her actions. In a house with two occupants, the treatment didn't take long. She made a face. "Call the police?"

"You gotta be fucking kidding me!" The teenager scanned the park. "You a cop?"

Alessio rubbed his face. "Risk and reward, idiot. The sooner you learn about consequences, the sooner you'll learn to succeed. People don't trust thieves. Without trust, you'll get nowhere in life." He pointed his finger. "Nowhere."

The teenager glared.

"Right." Alessio waved off his hand. "Get the hell out of here."

Looking from side to side, the teenager pivoted and ran.

Alessio looked over his shoulder at the teenager inspecting his bike. "And you. What're you doing showing off what you have? Next time, put a sign on it. Free bike. You want to come to the park and put on a show? Bring a goddamn friend!"

His voice rose, and Nina struggled not to laugh. She bit her lip and imagined him berating a fleet of insurance salesmen. She doubted he handled his firm's incoming phone calls. Judging by the cut of his suit, his willingness to pick up the tab and the hotel room he rented, he did fine without that duty. "So you're good with the mentoring stuff."

He glared.

Letting loose the laugh, she shook her head. "After we find Victor, we'll sign you up for after-school programs and the middle-school circuit. No wonder you don't have friends."

The bike owner peddled off, glanced over his shoulder and waved.

"Idiot," Alessio said.

She linked her arm with his arm. "You're cute."

He frowned.

"Ferocious."

"Right." Picking his sunglasses off the path, he settled them back into place. "I'm not your dog."

A thought nibbled at her subconscious. Possibilities and permutations scrolled through her mind's eye. Planting her feet, she dropped his arm and jabbed his chest. "Wait! Did *you* take my dog? Of all the sick, twisted tactics to secure another date…"

A man wearing a thick, wool blazer dropped his newspaper to the bench and stood.

Alessio lowered her arm, pulled her close and dropped his head. "If I wanted another date, I'd send a case of champagne and a bouquet so big you could plant your ass in the middle of it. I would fuck you until the blooms fell off."

She swallowed. "Interesting tactic."

He looked toward the stranger and shook his head.

The formally dressed man sat down.

"Where's Charon?" she asked.

"Why?"

"People in New York don't intervene. If the muscle wants to cover your ass, you're paying him. Geez, it's a walk in the park. You're paranoid."

"I'm busy."

"Right." If he wanted to pay people to watch his ass, he could go right ahead. She focused on the man in front of her. "Has that flower thing worked before?"

Leaning back, he cocked his head. "I've never tried it. Does it interest you?"

Heat blossomed in her core. "Many things interest me, but please tell me you didn't take my dog as part of some sick" — she frowned and searched for the right world — "damsel in distress pickup technique." Pulling an extra flyer from her tote, she presented the sweet, wide-eyed pup. "Victor's innocent. He doesn't deserve your abuse."

"You think I'm the type of man who'd kidnap a dog?" Crumpling the flyer in his hand, he tossed it toward a trashcan. "Find someone else to help you canvass Manhattan."

Watching the flyer sail through the air, she reorganized her thoughts. "I wanted to post that flyer. He's just a dog, Alessio. He needs our help. He matters."

"Why?" He crossed his arms. "Without that damn dog, we could be on a tropical island toasting Martha and picking sand out of our ass cracks. Fuck Victor."

Hearing the frustration in his voice, she admitted he wouldn't snatch a dog. Where would he keep it? His suitcase? She fished the flyer from the trashcan, smoothed out the paper and bit back a smile. "I didn't know dogs were on your kink list."

He growled. "You're insufferable."

Planting her hands on her hips, she forgot about the flyer. "Did you call me insufferable? Because unless you don't know the difference between sufferable and suffragette, this day is over."

"The fuck? When did I start hitting on brains? You vex me." He rubbed his temples. "I don't know what to do with you. I didn't have sisters. The women I know have agendas."

"Trust me, sisters have agendas, too."

His frown wrinkled his face.

He looked so miserable that she dropped her indignation like a thirty-pound weight. 'Vex' sounded like a power play she could embrace. Aside from a very satisfying hook-up, a bedtime routine she appreciated and a willingness to summon coffee, he checked all her boxes. She would add boxes for the aforementioned items, but really, he intrigued her. "I'm sorry, Alessio. Let's find my dog."

With a curt nod, he walked toward the park's edge.

Trailing, she realized she had done nothing but dump problems at his feet, question his help and mope about as if she were the only person who knew Martha. Stubborn independence had carried her through law school, but if she wanted to succeed, she needed to connect with people whose IQs matched her own.

Unless she was mistaken, Alessio had depths, and she wanted to plumb them. She'd be happy to sport a nautical hat doing it.

Maybe they could escape to the Hamptons, spend a few days drinking white wine and pretend their relationship had started under typical conditions. She cleared her throat. "I'm sorry for lashing out at you. I'm on edge." She rolled her lip. "Did you want sisters?"

He skewed his jaw. "Not if they're as much trouble as you."

Slapping the flyer against his chest, she passed him and walked toward the shelter. "Animal."

When he failed to catch up, she turned and caught him handing the flyer to an old woman sitting on a bench. His muscled ass shifted, and she almost tabled her search for Victor in favor of sand. Frowning, she thought of the teenagers and their silly altercation. Her first impulse had been to comfort the teenager, but watching Alessio take down the thief had landed him in superhero territory. She shook her head. The poor kid was probably fourteen years old. He'd never had a chance — and neither had Victor.

* * * *

The animal shelter on FDR Drive was a low-ceilinged warehouse along the river, but dogs played behind a fence, and every time the front door opened, a New Yorker emerged toting a pet carrier. Nina quickened her pace and grabbed the door from a woman juggling two cat carriers. "New pets?"

The woman smiled, but she shook her head. "Fosters."

"Oh! Good for you."

A cat's plaintive meow begged to differ.

The other cat hissed.

Nina swallowed and reached for a bottle of hand sanitizer.

"Are you allergic?" Alessio asked.

She frowned.

"The gel?"

Glancing at her hands, she shrugged. "Habit, I guess." Inside the shelter's front room, a perky twenty-year-old woman with bouncing curls staffed the reception desk. Looking around, Nina hoped signs would give her a clue about where to proceed. "Why is it so quiet?"

"Soundproofing," Alessio said.

"Hi! Can I help you?"

The receptionist's high-pitched question ricocheted between framed photographs of pets and their happy owners. Flinging wide her hands, her curls bobbed and a cluster of inked stars peeked from her collared shirt.

Nina pulled her phone from her tote and presented Victor's picture. "Hi, I'm looking for my dog. I hoped I could walk through your facility and see if I recognize him."

The receptionist took the phone and grinned. "He's a cutie."

The door behind the receptionist opened.

A sound wave of barks and excited yips filled the room, and a man carrying cardboard boxes dropped supplies behind the desk. "More intake forms."

The receptionist grinned. "Thanks, Chuck." She handed back Nina's phone and beamed. "Sorry about the noise. It's feeding time. You can't imagine how much food we go through in a week."

Nina swallowed and wondered how many animals waited in the facility.

Alessio rubbed her back. "You okay?"

She smiled. "Yeah, I just want to find him, you know?"

He nodded.

The receptionist came around the desk and offered a second bottle of hand sanitizer. "Don't touch the animals, for your safety and theirs. The surrendered dogs and cats might be runaways, but most of them come from struggling, stressed households. Animals feel stress, too." She opened the door and stepped into the wave. "You don't want to add illness to their troubles."

Nina and Alessio followed.

The receptionist walked past the large dogs and headed for a row of smaller wire cages.

Nina looked at every dog. The standing dogs had large, chocolate brown eyes pleading for attention. She hoped the staff had resources for a quick pet or a comforting word. Some animals remained at the back of their cages. They paced or tucked their heads beneath their tails. A third group slept through the noise, resigned to their fate. She wanted to take home every single one of them. "Where do they all come from?"

The receptionist waved at a passing staff member. "People lose their jobs, deal with evictions or struggle with unemployment. In most cases, they love their pets and surrendering them feels like a really hard choice. When they drop off the animals, I can tell where they stand. Some people look as miserable as their pets do. Adopt and foster. I can't say it enough."

Nina couldn't imagine the pain of surrendering a pet. She stopped outside a cage housing two matched dogs. The short-coated dogs sported a bewitching mix of spots and color variations. Looking close, she realized each animal had different color eyes. "What are they?"

"That's Randy and Rex. They're Catahoula Leopard Dogs." The receptionist tilted her head. "Do you want to meet them?"

"Absolutely."

Alessio took her hand and pulled her away from the pair. "Let's find Victor."

She looked over her shoulder and swore the dogs winked.

"They'll find a home," the receptionist said. "We offer outreach options for struggling pet owners who need a little breathing room. Free pet food and low-cost veterinary care can lift a ton of worries. Don't worry about those cuties."

She wanted to surrender her wallet and her PIN code. "I'm sure they'd be happier in the country."

The receptionist grinned. "Oh, I bet they're city dogs. If a pet owner tells me they need help with landlord-tenant disputes involving pets, I'm all in."

"I bet you are," Alessio said.

Twenty minutes later, she had peered into every cage, but Victor had never peered back. Defeated, she leaned against the building and dropped back her head. Heat radiated from the sidewalk and the warming day compelled her to find air conditioning and a quiet lunch.

Alessio rubbed her arm. "You okay?"

She turned her head. "Just, so many, you know? I'm worried about Victor, but a dozen shelters and non-profits serve Manhattan. How can so many animals be without homes? And their owners?" She straightened and stared at the entryway. "I should volunteer."

Throwing an arm over her shoulder, he led her away from the front doors. "That would be nice. Let's get lunch and strategize."

She ducked under his embrace. "I'm going to check a few more shelters."

Furrowing his brow, he opened his mouth, closed it, and settled on a direct observation. "That visit wrecked you."

He wasn't wrong, but Victor deserved everything she had. Straightening her shoulders, she pulled up the list of shelters on the island. "Wrecked isn't the right word. It gave me perspective, maybe. Those animals have possibilities. They're in transit."

"In transit." He looked at the building.

"Just like us." Turning, she aimed for the city's biggest shelter north of Central Park. If she walked to Penn Station, she could catch a train to Central Park North and make her way into East Harlem. The Lexington Avenue bus would take as long as the train ride, but she preferred the subway's predictable jolts. "We'll pick up a sandwich on the way."

"Nina, wait," he said. "You can't go all day."

She paused and considered his assistance. "You don't have to come, you know. I can call you in a few days." She exhaled. "You were right. I have to stay the course. I'll find him."

"It's not that." He walked up and cupped her elbow. "You'll wear out yourself. Let's get a car."

Shaking her head, she smiled. "You're right. You didn't have sisters. We're made of sterner stuff..."

"Sterner?" he asked.

She kept her gaze on the crosswalk signal, but a smile teased her mouth. "… than men."

"Cute," he said.

The light changed and released the bullpen of walkers ready to brave the intersection.

Accustomed to the city's pace, she joined the throng. "Don't worry, Alessio. You'll catch up. We're all in transit."

* * * *

At three o'clock, Nina's feet ached, her stomach rumbled and Victor's absence felt like a personal failure. Despite her best efforts, he remained missing, and she felt responsible. Opening the message over the Hudson River, she assumed the worst and typed.

Why do you have my dog?

You're sick.

Please return him and collect the reward.

The messages failed to send. She dropped her phone in her tote.

"No luck?" Alessio asked.

"Nope." She chose a bench at the edge of Central Park. A few times, she walked from 59th Street to 110th Street, but she never walked home. The north side of the park felt different. Ducks plied the Harlem Meer and the buildings on the park's south side softened into an indistinct mountain range. Her neighborhood beckoned like a homing beacon, but she couldn't move.

Alessio sat on the bench. "Let's get an ice cream."

She shook her head.

"You barely ate your wrap."

Wrinkling her nose, she regretted her few bites of greasy gyros and wilted lettuce. After tossing it into the trash, she'd felt bad. The wrap would probably give trash-savvy squirrels indigestion. "I've had better."

Instead of worrying about rats with tails, she looked at Alessio. In profile, he looked as handsome as a classical statue. His hair defied the mid-summer humidity and his sunglasses made him look aloof and mysterious. No wonder she enjoyed getting him naked. "I'm sorry. I'm dragging you all over town, and you don't have to be here."

He smiled. "The day's been an adventure. Let me buy you an ice cream."

"Am I twelve?"

He removed his glasses. "No."

She laughed and shook out her hair. "So, no ice cream."

He sighed. "Fine. Let's catch a cab and head back to your condo. After a shower, you'll feel better."

"And if you join me?"

He laughed. "I promise you'll feel better."

Banter felt like a balm on her raw emotions. She wanted to take him up on the offer, but cabs existed for lost tourists, wobbling drunks and over-burdened shoppers. "Walking clears my head. The park's two and a half miles, but the paths meander." Standing, she stretched. "You can call a cab and head back to your hotel."

"You have to be kidding."

She jerked her thumb over her shoulder toward the park. "Come with me. I'll buy you an ice cream."

Staring up, he stretched his jaw. "What an offer."

"Fine, an iced coffee."

He stood and crossed his arms. "Bike rental? Pedicab?"

She laughed.

"Horse-drawn carriage?"

"Oh my God, no!" Scanning the park, she made sure no drivers could overhear her. To be safe, she dropped her voice. "Seeing Manhattan by carriage is a unique opportunity, but it's not the 1800s. We have engines and motors! Missing the city's hustle and bustle is a shame. Torturing a horse is a crime."

He stared at her chest and raised his gaze. "I can summon enthusiasm for select bustles."

Heat flooded her cheeks. "Wrong end, Alessio. The bustle covers the derriere." Nan's penchant for historical romances had finally paid out. She cleared her throat. "I mean, a few years ago, a carriage horse collapsed and died in the heat. The city passed a measure forcing the drivers to abide by the heat index and give the animals a break, but I couldn't relax in a carriage. I'd spend the whole ride worried about heat suspensions for the horse."

He slid his glasses into place. "You would have made a crappy queen."

She lifted her chin. "Or a great one."

"True." He crouched, picked her up off the ground and tossed her over his shoulder. "I'll carry you back to Murray Hill."

"Is this your thing?"

"It seems like the easiest way to handle you."

She laughed. Upended, she let her hair hang over her face and admired his ass. It definitely beat the equine variety. "Don't fart." His laughter rumbled against her chest. Except for the indignity of being carried, the view and the passing joggers' expressions made up for the ride.

He strode across a roadway.

Sill striped for automobiles, the wide, slate-gray path wound through the park. Walkers, runners and cyclists followed the shaded causeway. Traffic signals no longer tempered drivers' enthusiasm, but they failed to inspire obedience from pedestrians and cyclists, either. She watched the erratic dance of people and wondered how the city's residents would adapt to the next hundred years. "How long can you keep this up?"

"At least three miles."

Based on his confident stride, she believed him. "Don't be ridiculous."

"I offered you a perfectly good car."

"I told you, you don't have to come with me."

He adjusted his grip. "What if I want to come with you?"

She pushed against his back, felt him loosen his grip and slid down his chest. With her feet now firmly on the ground, she tilted her head. "I want you to come, too, but this is who I am. People tug at my heartstrings, but I love plants and animals. I've never left America, but I like exotic food. New York is an amazing city, but I like to walk."

Opening and closing his mouth, he stared. "You're a brilliant lawyer, but you're stubborn as fuck."

"That quality makes me a brilliant layer. Also, for a businessman, you have a sailor's vocabulary."

"You don't know how I grew up."

She pressed a kiss against his mouth. His lips felt warm and pliant, and the salty tang of sweat reminded her exactly how he spent his day. She pulled back.

"We'll split the difference fifty-fifty. Walk with me a while then we'll do things your way."

He nodded.

Taking his hand, she pulled him into the park. "Tell me more about the fighting." Exercise classes focused on core strength, but expensive black pants wouldn't get him out of bed, and she wasn't to find out what made him tick. "Where do you find opponents?"

"I belong to a club."

She imagined a cinderblock building, dingy mats and rusted lockers. "That's helpful."

He cleared his throat. "How much do you want to know?"

"How much do you want to tell me?" She glanced at him.

"Everything."

"Good answer."

He took her hand. "When I was younger, I fought for respect. The fights eventually drew an audience and the bookies followed. When the fights moved into warehouse spaces, profits started moving into my pockets. I thought I could send myself to university and skip debt in favor of a busted nose."

"And?" She glanced at the bump on his nose. "The fights paid off?"

"One day, an organizer asked me to throw the fight. Given enough money, people lose their moorings. I said no, and shit got serious. That's the thing about cheats. They forget who has the power. I knocked the guy flat on his ass and told my opponent about the rig. She and I agreed to a fair fight. She backed me into a corner, but what happens between start and finish doesn't matter. I won, and the bookie lost his bet."

"Are you, like, a triple black belt?"

He wet his lips. "When I was younger, fewer than ten people in the world fought at my level. If I looked at organized fight disciplines, I'd call myself a fourth degree black belt."

"How high do the belts go?" she asked.

"Sixth degree."

She turned and winked. "Amateur."

Laughing, he scanned the path. "You may be right. I've been busy selling insurance and other things."

She tried to imagine him dancing in place, ready to go hand-to-hand with an opponent. Subbing in a female opponent threw her for a loop, but she understood how the bookie had sought to capitalize on the audience's expectations. What kind of woman put herself up against men in the first place? She didn't care if the woman could bench press a compact car. Pound for pound, Alessio must have had a muscled advantage. Maybe Nina would watch him spar. On the edge of East Drive, she checked the light, stepped off the sidewalk and entered the intersection.

He yanked her to the pavement.

Chapter Ten

Alessio saw the accident unfold in slow motion. A cyclist on an e-bike blew through an intersection, struck a pedestrian and landed on his head. He yanked Nina to the pavement and shielded her.

Arms flailing, the struck pedestrian flew backward.

As the cyclist skidded along his trajectory, the helmet tied to his e-bike rubbed the pavement like a foam bumper. He came to a stop and moaned. Blood dripped from his road rash.

The crowd waited, breathless, for the cyclist to stand.

He remained down.

"Oh my God!" Nina struggled in Alessio's arms. "That poor man."

He gripped her hand.

A woman reported the collision on her phone. Converging traffic from the south and east came to a sudden halt. The western flow backed up, scanned the accident and skirted the mess.

The pedestrian winced and leaned on one arm. "I knew I should have taken a cab."

Judging by the cyclist's trajectory, the impact had caused fatal harm. New York's medical professionals might alleviate the damage, but he gave the man two days tops.

Sirens roared to life, and the crowd shifted in expectation.

"Let me help them," Nina said.

He tightened his grip. "You're not a medial professional."

She tugged on his hand. "So?"

A woman eased closer to the bleeding cyclist and murmured. She kept her hands to herself.

"Wait for the first responders," he said.

"What if he dies and nobody lays a hand on him? What is he dies alone?" Nina struggled against his grip. "Would you want that fate for a person you loved?"

Her question had merit, but he kept her by his side. Keeping her from entangling herself in the ensuing lawsuit felt more imperative than helping a random, dying man. "No, I wouldn't wish a lonely death on anyone."

"Then let me help!"

"Nina" — he swallowed — "emotions are high. I know you want to help, but the minute you lay hands on that man, you open up yourself to liability. Think with your head instead of your heart."

Her hand went limp. "Why do I have to choose?"

"Because you have to protect your assets." Trusting her not to bolt, he released her hand and waited for the first responders. If no one stayed to give testimony, he would. The traffic light and crosswalk sat in a trough and the road angled upward. Coming off the hill, the cyclist had to hit the brakes to stop for the crowded light. Fate waited for a second of distraction. Whether the cyclist missed his chance to stop or missed the light hardly mattered.

Scanning the road, Alessio looked for pavement markings and signage to alert oncoming traffic. He felt for the moaning cyclist, but he understood his mistake, too, and he bore no responsibility for it.

The park cut out unofficial traffic, but emergency vehicles, maintenance workers, vendors servicing concessions and private cars for on-duty officers traveled the roads. He shook his head. The next collision might not lead to one fatality, but two. Vigilance remained the best offense, and if he could keep Nina out of the mess, he'd be content.

Lights and sirens blazing, an ambulance parted the crowd.

"All right, let's go." He reached for her hand. Finding nothing but thin air, he looked to the side.

She crouched next to the pedestrian. Pulling the man's water bottle from his backpack, she handed it to him and made eye contact.

Alessio glared.

Holding up her hands, she lifted her chin.

Her selfish defiance angered him, but he accepted her decision. Seeing her oversized purse lying on the pavement, he strode toward the bag.

A man wearing a sweatshirt scooped up the purse and strolled through the crowd.

"Hey!" He raised his voice. "Thief!"

Heads turned.

Nina stood.

The thief made eye contact and bolted.

He looked for the bodyguard he paid to protect him from annoyances.

The man hiked up his pants and gave chase.

Watching his gait, he sighed. The bodyguard's job was to deter unwelcomed attention and media requests, but at this rate, the thief would escape with Nina's purse. "I don't know why I bother." He joined the pursuit. Sprinting wasn't really his game, but he lengthened his stride and wondered if replacing the damn bag would be easier than reclaiming it.

Going up the hill, the thief lost ground.

Pedicab drivers, cyclists, joggers and bikers formed a scrum. Feet planted on the pavement, they waited for the intersection to clear and the drama to resolve. At the top of the rise, scooter riders and in-line skaters did figure eights. A horse-drawn carriage held up the rear.

The thief sprinted toward a gap near the animal.

Rearing on his hind legs, the horse kicked out his forelegs.

"Watch out!" the carriage driver shouted.

Covering his head, the thief fell to the pavement, rolled and came up staring at Alessio.

Bracing his hands on his knees, he took deep breaths. "Give me the purse!" He roared the gravely command. "Now!"

The thief rolled and scrambled to his feet. "Fuck off!"

"Wrong move." Heart thudding and blood pumping, he caught the thief, pinned his shoulder to the ground and drew back his fist. The audacious fool stole from him, and the impulse to fight and defeat an opponent coursed through his system. A thousand adrenaline highs conditioned his muscled to clench and ready for battle. So many people underestimated him, and he refused to give them satisfaction.

"Alessio!"

Nina's voice, clear and precise, punctured his blood lust. Lowering his fist, he exhaled and worked through his rage. The men and women he fought in the gym knew the rules. Pinned by his strength, the idiot below him shook with fear and had acted out of greed. A heartbeat later and he could have toppled his empire.

Holding out her hand, Nina waited.

He handed her the purse, but he kept his gaze on the thief and unpinned him. "If I ever see you again..."

The thief scrambled to standing and ran.

"You caught him!" Nina threw her arms around his neck. "Amazing!"

Her admiration slid off him like a cold shower. Gripping her around the waist to keep her safe, he closed his eyes and questioned why he'd overreacted. For years, he had vetted his opponents and held himself in check, but one sentimental thought sent him running up a hill. Senescence spared his reflexes, but if age eroded his decision-making skills, he needed to stop while he was ahead.

The next time he careened over restraint's edge, he might keep falling.

Swallowing, he released his grip on her and wondered if wealth had corrupted his ability to be normal. Stepping back from decision-making at ADC Industries would leave him adrift, but he could regroup. If Nina contributed to his impulsiveness, he needed to step back from her, too. "You might be trouble."

Laughing, she slung her purse over her shoulder. "You might be right."

Her flushed cheeks and wet lips drew his gaze, but he looked away.

The panting bodyguard arrived.

"You're fired," Alessio said.

"What a shameful thing." Opening her purse, Nina riffled the contents. "Can you imagine taking advantage of another person's tragedy?"

He exhaled. "I do it every day."

She looked up. "Say *what*?"

"You don't know me. Our lives smashed together." He rubbed his temple. "Nina, next time, the idiot won't be a common thief. It might be someone dangerous. When you're beside me, you could get hurt. Look what happened to Martha."

Checking her extremities, she shrugged. "I'm fine! Why do you think you're responsible for Martha's death?"

"I don't believe in coincidences." He shook his head. "Let's get you home."

"My boss won't believe the weekend I've had." She swung her arms and laughed. "Maybe I should request hardship pay." Covering her mouth, she looked toward the intersection where first responders assisted the crash victims. "I shouldn't joke about the accident. Those victims have actual problems."

"So do I." He mumbled his response.

Looking away from the scene, she tilted her head. "Huh?"

The bodyguard uncapped a bottle of water and poured it over his sweat-streaked face.

Alessio rolled his eyes.

She took his hand and pulled him toward the nearest major street.

He didn't give a shit whether she reserved cabs for geriatrics or expectant mothers. She would get in the vehicle, and he would go back to the hotel to regroup. "I need a break."

"I'm sure."

"Let's meet up later." He gauged her reaction.

"Sure." She smiled. "Dinner?"

Completely unfazed. Relieved, he exhaled. "First Martha, then Victor and this shit with your carryall. Shouldn't you be afraid of the city?"

She scanned the busy park. "Three bad people can't ruin a city. What about the good people who stepped in to help?" Swinging her bag over her shoulder, she reached for his hand. "What about you?"

He hesitated. He had helped. He'd helped because he cared about her feelings. Now, he needed to decide what to do with his feelings. Protecting her would be easy. Keeping her from undermining his life would be a nightmare. If he went home with her, dinner would lead to sex, and sex would lead to complications. "I don't live in New York."

He spent most of his life screening out complications. Taking Martha's houseguest on a date hadn't been a mistake, but it hadn't been the most straightforward decision he'd ever made, either. Sending Nina a case of champagne would have made more sense, but he wouldn't have seen her come apart in his hands. He closed his eyes and raised his hand.

A cab stopped.

Holding open the door, he relayed Nina's address.

She ducked into the backseat.

Relieved he didn't have to tuck her head into the backseat and plant a swift kick on her stubborn ass, he bracing his arms on the frame and considered shutting the door. "Well, aren't you compliant?"

"You're the person playing cops and robbers." She patted the seat. "Maybe you need a break."

"I'm fine."

Hand clasped to her chest, she traced her collarbone. "Are you?"

The day's excitement smothered her objections to metered transportation, but it couldn't keep her safe. He'd take the opening and see her home. Following her into the cab, he leaned back his head and closed his eyes.

"The park's a small city," she said. "It needs infrastructure to keep it safe. Right now, bikers speed race the trails during peak traffic hours. The loops and signals are out of date. Of course a crash occurred."

Her critical assessment made sense.

"Maybe the Parks Department should take over the park roadways instead of the Department of Transportation. I'm going to talk to my friend who's running for council. Without car traffic, the pavement is no longer a city street. I bet when the DOT repaves the streets, they update markings, but they should regularly meet with Parks and the Conservancy. Prioritizing bikers, pedestrians and dog-walkers has to be a priority."

He let her ramble.

"Still, why don't they have flashing yellow signals at night?"

Opening his eyes, he cocked his head. "What the hell are you doing in the park at night?"

She shrugged. "I get bored."

"Get a pet."

She gasped.

Too late, he registered his mistake and reached for her hand. "I'm sorry."

Letting her take his hand, she stared out of the window, but she didn't return his caress.

He shifted in the stale backseat. "Nina, that was a crap thing to say."

She lifted her palm to the glass. "What else can I do?"

He kept his mouth closed. If Jack had her dog, he had a personal vendetta, but he didn't understand the extent of what he'd done. That kind of 'fuck you' negative energy led to mistakes, and Jack lurked. Keeping Nina from Martha's fate remained his driving goal.

"Is anything I'm doing helping?" She wiped away a tear.

In the shadowed cab, she looked as innocent as her pet. Except, she wasn't a ten-pound, over-brushed plaything. Using her legal degree and a solid record of accomplishment, she thrived. Victor should take notes before scampering off with the next asshole who offered him a rawhide. Pulling her under his arm, he pressed a kiss to her hair. "You're doing a good job. We're going to find Victor."

Somewhere in Manhattan, Charon sat holed up with an Internet connection. The sooner Jack sat behind bars, the better. "You're doing everything you know how to do."

She nodded and turned her face into his chest.

Relieved, he let his shoulders relax. Pummeling the thief would have satisfied him, but Nina's intervention and common sense prevailed. As soon as he regrouped, he would figure out how one woman knocked him off kilter when so many others had tried.

"My mother loved Italy." The statement slipped out before he considered the implications, but he wanted to share something of himself.

"Why didn't she return without your father?"

He rubbed his brows. Without thinking too much about the words, he told her about his parents' love story. His grandfather had run a small cocaine smuggling operation. He'd left his wife and daughter to tend a coastal farm, but pulling fish from the sea hadn't been his main objective. More than once, the motorists stopping at the fruit stand had tried to lure Alessio's mother, Maria, toward an uncertain fate. His father, Eitan, had had a fresh approach. He'd stayed, polished melons and hawked the fruit until he'd won her love.

"That's the sweetest story," she said.

"Not really."

"Come again?"

"She feared her neighbors. Their drug-smuggling connections kept the town on high alert." Starting in the late 1960s and lasting over three decades, almost seven hundred people in Italy fell prey to abduction. Southern Italy's feared mafia orchestrated most of the abductions, but its sister groups noticed the trend and unleashed reigns of terror in their territories. The groups bartered wealthy, middle-class men, women and children for ransom. After a lengthy imprisonment, the victims returned to their families and the abductors invested the ransom money in villas or cocaine trafficking. The brutal start-up loans fueled decades of discord, but stories of the victims' scars moved from town to town in whispers and outraged protests.

"I see," she said.

The simple, non-judgmental statement let Eitan and Maria's love story shine. He could bury her in details and counter arguments, but he understood what made her a successful mediator. He tore through fronts to uncover facts. She prompted honesty. "My grandfather was a petty mobster."

"But your parents raised you." Tracing the scars along his hands, she looked up. "I'm sure you're tired after a long day. I thought about a bubble bath and a back rub, but I don't have a tub."

He frowned. "You want a back rub?"

"I want to give you a back rub."

His dick twitched. He had three bathtubs in his New York penthouse. If she wanted to rub him down with soap and water, she could have her pick.

"Except I don't have a tub," she said.

He bit his lip.

She tilted her head. "Your hotel room has a tub."

Scrambling to remember the number of the anonymous hotel room he'd booked, he realized the truth would set him free—or it could backfire miserably. Revealing his wealth and holdings might overwhelm Nina or send her off the deep end. Every other woman he'd dated who glimpsed his assets acted the same fucking way. "Going back to that hotel room isn't a good idea."

She looked away.

Expect none of the women he'd dated quoted legal terms and offered to rub his back. He skewed his jaw and prepared for her reaction. "Look, Nina... I haven't been completely..."

His phone vibrated.

Pulling the device from his pocket, he accepted the call. "Where the hell have you been?"

Nina winced.

"Making waves," Charon said. "Our boy, Jack, has a penchant for dramatics."

He snorted. "I told you to find him."

"Easier said than done." Charon cleared his throat. "Our crew can't locate him from the first messages he sent. Wait for another text message and keep him going long enough for a Global Positioning Systems signal or a decent triangulation."

Alessio rubbed his face. Cell phone towers maintained bi-directional communication with nearby wireless phones. Overlapping service coverage allowed network analysis software to estimate a phone's geographic position, but triangulation wasn't an exact science and software programs couldn't pinpoint a phone's exact location. GPS worked better. The only person who could keep Jack talking sat beside him, and he didn't want to endanger her. "Find another way."

"*Si*, Don Pedro. I'm just a simple, self-satisfied night constable." Charon bumbled an acceptance. "Technology but ties my hands."

Alessio ended the call and slid the phone back into his pocket. If he wanted a reference to a Shakespearian comedy, he'd go to a theater. "Fucking telecommunications companies."

He adjusted his seat and decided to lay out Nina's options. She could embrace his life, or she could look for another friend with benefits and a security detail. He cringed. Shakespeare could teach him a thing or two about tragedies. "Look, Nina. I meant to say I want to spend more time with you, but life's complicated."

She kept her face averted. "Don't worry about it."

"You want a bathtub?" If a bathtub would smooth out the forthcoming conversation, he would fill the vessel with roses. Billions of dollars made some people swoon, but collecting prizefight winnings, cashing out casino takes and exercising contract clauses made other people wince. Finding a woman who could stand the conditions of his wealth eluded him, but he would take the risk. He leaned forward and redirected the cab driver to the Upper East Side hotel. "I have a bathtub."

She took a twenty-dollar bill from her purse and handed it over the seat. "Pay no attention to him. Take me to the first address. I'll pay your fare."

The driver slid the note into his shirt pocket.

"You're mad," he said.

She shrugged. "You're opaque. One minute, you're my ally, and the next minute, you're pinning me into a tidy corner. I don't need a keeper."

He exhaled. "I'm trying to take care of you!"

"Just because you ran up a hill doesn't mean you're a superhero! That idiot you straddled could have pulled a gun and shot you...for a tote! Does the insurance industry have temporary credit card deactivations? Because the rest of the world does. I can freeze my spending power with a phone call. Your life isn't worth a hundred dollars of cash!"

As she raged, her doe eyes dropped their wounded appeal. Instead of a beautiful woman looking for comfort, she morphed into a beautiful woman looking for answers and atonement. For the last two decades, he'd thought he preferred dependency, but watching her temper flare in the tiny, stale space changed his world. He would never ride in a cab without thinking of her.

She looked like she wanted to kill him.

If she left him with the smell of sour upholstery for the rest of his life, he would make the memory count.

Leaning forward, he cupped the back of her head and claimed a last kiss.

She wiggled free and slapped him.

He rubbed his cheek. "What the fuck was that for?"

She crossed her arms and leaned back. "You can't kiss me into silence."

"Who said anything about silence? You're worried some street thug will beat me?" Dropping his hand, he reveled at the tingling sensation on his cheek. Idiots around the world punched and kicked him, but he couldn't remember the last time someone tried a slap. She had excellent technique. He wondered if she wanted to slap any other features of his body. If he could send blood rushing around her body, too, quid pro quo might not be so bad. He grinned. "You're worried about me?"

She rolled her eyes. "I was. Obviously, you're mad."

The cab driver stopped in front of her condo building.

José walked out and opened the backseat door. "Miss Nina!"

She graced him with a smile. "Any news of Victor?"

The doorman shook his head.

Her shoulders slumped.

"We'll find him." José offered her his arm. "Only two days have passed. He could still be under a dumpster reenacting *Ratatouille*."

She laughed and took his arm. "Thanks."

Alessio climbed from the cab and made a split decision. "You really only carry a hundred dollars in cash?"

She frowned. "So? Most people carry none."

"Come back to my hotel." He exhaled. "Please? Let me order in dinner. I'll give you the back rub."

Her cheeks blushed.

José cleared his throat.

"If anyone finds Victor on the street, José will be the first to know. The flyers. The shelter visits. You can take a break, Nina. We'll find your dog." He left out his determination to take her west. Some adjustments went down better over champagne. "Let me take care of you for the evening. We'll celebrate Martha. I know where to find one of her paintings."

She widened her eyes. "Really?"

He slid his hands into his pockets. "A big one."

Looking over her shoulder, she smiled at José. "If you hear anything, you'll call me?"

The big doorman narrowed his gaze and worked a kink out of his meaty neck.

Recognizing the message, he nodded.

José adopted a reassuring smile and patted her shoulder. "Have a good time, Mrs. Nina. Send me a picture of the painting."

The doorman's voice almost sounded wishful.

She gripped the doorman's forearm. "You miss her."

Alessio scrambled to up his ante. "What's your favorite restaurant?"

José laughed and stepped out of the way.

Blinking, she moved toward the building's entrance. "Come upstairs, and I'll tell you." She looked back at the doorman. "After dinner, I'll come down and chat with you."

"I'm always here," José said.

The man looked as dedicated as a minor league baseball player hoping for his break in the majors. If he managed the building's door, Martha's killer passed him or slipped out the back. Charon said he'd slipped out the back, but how many times did he waltz through the front door first? "Did Martha have a lot of visitors?"

"No, she always went out." José narrowed his gaze. "You were the first."

"Huh." He shifted his stance.

José stared.

Nina stepped between them. "Alessio? Dinner?"

Turning away from the doorman, he offered her his arm. "What is it, some strange delicacy you picked up at the corner store? Fermented Baltic herring? Live octopus?"

She stared. "Who are you?"

Pushing the elevator's call button, he drew a deep breath. "You're about to find out."

* * * *

The elevator to Nina's floor rattled on its cables.

Alessio checked the safety certificate mounted on the wall.

"Fear of heights?" she asked.

Straightening, he shook his head and pulled her close for a kiss. If everything went to shit in her condo, he wanted a final taste before he drowned his sorrows in the penthouse wine room.

She braced her hands against his chest.

He looked down. "Are you going to slap me again?"

She tilted her head. "Do you deserve it?"

"Probably." Changing his angle, he skimmed his lips along her jaw. Grass buried deep in her hair smelled of sunshine and crisp corners. After the day they had, he couldn't imagine how she kept her cool. Then again, she wasn't the person yanking teenagers off bikes and sprinting up a hill.

Amy Craig

Tightening her arms around his neck, she wet her lips. "People have surrounded us all day."

"Most of them thugs."

She grinned. "The shelter volunteers are wonderful, but you probably have more interesting tattoos. One day, will you tell me what they mean?"

"I thought you didn't want to know."

"I thought you were a one-night stand," she said.

Long sentences surpassed his abilities. Wrapping his hands around her waist, he hitched her against his thigh, bent to her mouth and teased her lips.

On a sigh, she opened.

Deepening the kiss, he let her fresh energy wash over him. When he nipped her bottom lip, she arched against him, and he wondered if the elevator would stop on a dime. An emergency stop might bring New York's finest rushing toward the building and those fuckwits hadn't caught Martha's killer. Charon would...

Nina curled her fingers into his hair and tugged.

Called back to order, he changed his angle, met her thrusts and released the low, guttural groan building in his chest. Cupping her ass, he lifted her and felt her heat against his abdomen. "Fuck the police and the fire department."

Pulling back, she swallowed. "Huh?"

The elevator doors opened.

He slid her down his thigh and stepped in front of her to give her time to compose herself.

Looking back, he found her holding her phone. A tear slid down her cheek.

"Nina," he said.

She looked up.

He held out his hand. "Come here."

Shaking her head, she looked down at the phone. "It's Victor. I want to imagine him romping in a park with a herd of slow, fat squirrels. The alternatives hurt too much."

"I know. I'm going to take care of it. We're going to find him."

She stepped from the elevator and the doors closed behind her. "How?"

Her whispered uncertainty scraped raw his ego. He spent so much time delegating work and issuing orders that he forgot the quiet satisfaction of accomplishing goals. Without expending sweat equity, money piled up, and he cared for the riches as much as he cared for Nina's dog. The cash was an end to a means, and right now, he wanted to avenge Martha, but he wanted Nina more. He extended a hand. "Trust me."

She took his hand. "What choices do I have?"

"Wait," he said. "Get a new dog. Get a new zip code."

Looking up, she frowned. "What?"

He pulled her down the hallway. "Victor didn't run away. A stranger didn't scoop him from the hall. The person who took your dog did it to hurt you. Who feels that way about you? Who have you disappointed?"

She frowned. "Nobody."

He stopped outside her door. "Someone felt that way about Martha."

"No way" — she exhaled — "everyone loved Martha."

"Did you love her?"

She frowned. "Like a friend."

"I'll save myself before I'll save my friends. I don't love them, and they know it. Whoever killed Martha felt strongly enough about her to hate her." *Or to hate me*. He suppressed the possibility. Keeping Nina at his side would keep her safe.

Entering the code, she shook her head. "How can you hate a person?"

He thought of the billions of dollars sitting in his bank account. The money stemmed from someone else's dreams gone wrong. Plenty of people spanning the globe hated him, but he hadn't given her a reason to join their ranks. But after admitting what he suspected, she might lead the charge.

Walking into the condo, he headed for the sunlit kitchen. Thriving plants kept Nina company, but they all needed second chances. He needed one, too.

Chapter Eleven

Nina walked into the kitchen, wrapped her hands around Alessio's torso and slowly unbuttoned his shirt. Dropping it to the floor, she laid her head against his skin and pressed a cheek to his heated muscles. After accepting Martha's death, his shoulders remained tense, and she wondered if his reserve cracked. Instead of dragging him around the city investigating Victor's disappearance and burying her grief, she should have sent him back to his hotel and given him time to process his loss. "Tell me what's wrong."

"I haven't been completely honest with you," he said.

She lifted her head. Paying off her law school debt, stockpiling a 401(k) and finding time to build a family felt like worthwhile goals. She'd slept with a few men along the way, but she chocked up her freewheeling experiences to an unwillingness to settle. Alessio had started as a one-night stand, but he'd appeared on the street like a white knight, ready to rescue her pooch,

172

and she struggled to reorient her expectations. If he weren't honest, what was he? Releasing her hold, she stepped back and tightened her robe. "You know who took Victor?"

He braced his hands on the counter's edge. "Yes and no."

Faced with his bare chest and his tattoos, she struggled to keep her mind focused on her tasks. Last night's indulgence had let her sleep like a rock, but if she had her lips wrapped around a man's cock, she'd prefer to trust the man. She stepped back.

He reached forward, grabbed her hips and settled her between his legs.

His cock pressed against her thigh, and she thanked biology a man's body couldn't lie. Maybe she had a thing for deceitful men.

"I think I know who killed Martha and took your dog."

She stiffened.

"Charon saw a man named Jack Santana on the building's video feed. Does the name ring a bell? Did he have reason to be in the building?"

Rubbing her jaw, she thought hard. "Why does Charon have access to the building's security cameras?"

"My business interests don't end with insurance." He took a deep breath. "I have a few other assets, and gathering data helps me close deals."

She struggled to wrap her mind around Alessio's involvement. He deployed Charon and fired bodyguards like a man picking up his dry cleaning, but he boxed and fought his way to the top. The top of what? She scanned the condo. Law books and plants covered every available space. The only framed photographs included Nan. Her romantic tracks record might be headed for a ravine. "How did Charon identify the man? Social media?"

"He's good."

She snorted. "Remind me to hire him the next time I have a recalcitrant client."

"You couldn't afford him."

Twisting out of his grip, she moved to the other side of the kitchen and crossed her arms. "What's your other business? Do you sell that branded shit insurance reps give away on street corners? That plastic crap's a waste of energy. You might as well throw it down the gutter with abandoned Mardi Gras beads."

"More like casinos," he said.

She shook her head. "Most of the time, casinos give you free food tickets and stuff. I'm sure the same people who like slot machines like buffets, too."

He crossed the kitchen and stroked her cheek. "No, I own the casinos."

She frowned.

"And a boutique investment firm. I move a lot of money."

Shaking her head, she turned away and pulled faded leaves from a plant.

He braced his hands on either side of her. "Nina, look at me."

His presence at her back felt warm and encompassing. She wanted to back into his touch and rewrite history, but after losing Martha, life seemed like more than a series of harried workdays and languid hookups. She kept her gaze focused on the plant. "How much money?"

"Billions."

She yelped.

"The money's not a big deal." Dropping his head, he pressed a kiss along her exposed neck. "I'm still the same person."

His soft touch curtailed her reaction. If she reached up, she could play with the hair skimming his collar and pretend this conversation had never happened. Martha would go back to being a good-time friend, and Alessio would go back to being an insurance salesman. "You're messing with me."

He sighed.

She turned and assessed his sanity.

Running a hand through his hair, he shook his head. "You thought the server was a little jumpy. Did you see the bodyguard? Did you wonder why Charon's at my beck and call?"

She wet her lips. "You have dependency issues."

He laughed and dropped his hand. "Maybe."

"Prove it," she said.

He stared. "What?"

"You're a billionaire, and I'm a genius. One claim is much easier to prove."

"What do you want, a letter of credit from the bank?" He narrowed his gaze. "Most people just believe me."

"Those people probably don't spot lies for a living." Slipping past him, she walked to the refrigerator and removed a pitcher of water. Either the man had lost his mind, and she needed to escape, or he had a few assets tucked away, and she needed to replay their conversations. Had he laughed at her attempts to split the bill? Filling a glass, she downed the water and filled it again. He behaved and carried himself in a confident, unassuming manner, but half of New York's male population thought they owned the room.

"Nina…"

She set down her glass.

He held out his phone.

If he handed her a bank statement, she would probably drop the phone down the garbage disposal. She didn't need this photoshopped drama. She wanted to unwind, not upend her world. If Martha lived, she could ask for help. That woman could spot money a mile away.

Taking the phone, she swallowed and looked at a news article. Alessio stood in a suit on a slate step. The wind lifted his hair, and it shone in the golden hour's light.

"*Swiss billionaire A. Donato Chen announced a $150 million gift through his private foundation to Zürich's main university, according to a statement by the institution. The gift will go to the Chen Institute for Advanced Gaming and Economics, which the university established following a $125 million gift Chen made in 2010. Altogether Chen, whose charitable foundations have assets of more than $2 billion, will have given $300 million to the institute and the university. The pledged gift will be paid out over several years.*"

She swallowed and handed back the phone. "I liked our fling better when we were equals."

He left it on the counter. "So did I."

She stared at the floor. Nan had money, but not endowment money. "So Charon's your…"

"Right-hand man."

"Of course. Not your assistant."

He picked up his shirt, slipped it over his shoulders and stepped closer.

She exhaled and buttoned the panels back into place. "You think I'm ridiculous."

Taking her hand, he shook his head and held it. "You're exactly what I needed, but you scare the shit out of me. This thing between us grew too fast, and I'm not sure how to unwind it. I owe Martha a debt I can never repay."

"Because she's dead." She looked up. Stating the facts carried her through so many cases. She needed time to regroup. She needed time to answer Alessio's earnest emotion, because she felt it, too. "Martha's dead."

He pulled her into his arms and held her close. "I know. I'm going to figure out what's happening. In the meantime, I want you to stop traipsing all over the city looking for Victor. I can't put my life on hold to help you, and I don't trust hired men to do it. Stay with me for a few days. I have a trip scheduled to Idaho. Come along. Let me protect and spoil you."

"I want to go to Italy, not Idaho."

He laughed. "Start small."

She skewed her jaw. "I'm not sleeping with you for free passage to the wild west."

He laughed, hitched up her leg and waited until she found her balance. "No, you're fucking me because we have fun together. Consider the money icing on the cake."

She draped her arms over his shoulders. "This trip sounds like a three-scoop sundae."

Holding her gaze, he inclined his head.

"I'm more of a sugar cone and a single scoop kind of girl."

"Have you ever tried a sundae?" he asked.

"Apparently I've been trying it and need to dig myself out of a binge."

He laughed. "Most women don't have this reaction. They come up with wish lists."

"Most women haven't lost their friend, their dog and their privacy."

Straightening, he nodded. "You want me to go."

She ran a hand through her tangled hair and turned to face the kitchen window. The window caught their reflection and turned it back on them. A man and a woman held each other, and all was right in the world. She pondered the implications of his wealth. "What am I supposed to do with a billionaire? I shop at chain stores."

He laughed. "We're still equals, but while we're together, let me pick up the tab. Other than ordering whatever rando foods strike your interest, ignore that aspect of my life. You might not even notice it."

"And when we're not together?" she asked.

He surveyed the kitchen. "Your plants will wait for you. What do you have to lose?"

His shot hit home, and she looked around the kitchen. If her life shrank to case law, plants and an empty dog cage, she would disappear into the corporate abyss. Her peers indulged on the weekends, but she chose sex over whiskey, and so far, her choice had worked out. Without her bohemian fairy godmother across the hall, she needed an outlet, and a billionaire's trumped-up sex romp suited her fine. In some ways, his wealth fit his curtailed answers and evasive gestures. If she didn't have to report to the office every Monday, she might roam the world, too. "You should have told me sooner."

"Why?"

She frowned. "So I would have understood you better."

"Now you know."

She exhaled. Victor still needed her help. If Alessio's claims fell flat, she had enough resources to turn her plump ass around, board the next plane leaving Idaho and return to her fiddle-leaf fig. The damn plant probably wouldn't even miss her, and she would find her dog. If she needed to direct Officer Scottie's attention toward Jack Santana, she would throw the man under the bus and out Charon's surveillance hacking. "Are we flying out of Newark, LaGuardia or Kennedy?"

"Neither." Alessio ran his hand beneath the edge of her blouse.

His touch brought a flush to her skin. She enjoyed his honed presence. If he came with a Malibu dream house, all the better. If she climbed into the convertible and waved farewell to return to Murray Hill, it would be there when she returned.

"We'll fly out of Teterboro, but we have a few stops to make."

She blinked. "Stops?"

He turned her, pointed her toward the bedroom and set her in motion. "The first stop is my hotel. Go pack a bag. You'll need cocktail dresses, jeans and lounge wear."

She looked over her shoulder. "No underwear?"

"Spend the entire trip bare-assed and see where it gets you."

She smiled and felt the stability of solid ground. "In your lap?"

He wet his lips. "Exactly. You're taking this rather well."

"Am I?" she asked. "You've promised me cowboy chaps, Victor and Jack Santana's head on a pole."

"I did no such thing."

She raised her eyebrows. "Alessio? I want the chaps and the dog."

He huffed out a smile. "I thought you'd be mad that I lied to you about my wealth. Defending Jack would come next" — he shook his head — "then hysterics. Most women hate lies of omission."

Drawing back her chin, she reconsidered her approach to billionaire management. "Hysterics?"

"I don't know. Functionally unlimited wealth scares people. They don't know how to cope. I'm a man."

"With a chiseled chest, magnificent hair and a talented dick."

He stared. "A talented dick?"

"Why do you think I'm spending the weekend with you?" She shrugged. "The foundation helps."

He walked toward the bedroom with a feline's lazy grace. "Does it?"

She slammed the door in his face, pivoted and wished she had more than bitch-ass boss suits to pack. He'd already seen the red trumpet gown. She had a sleek black cocktail number and a silver sheath, but she didn't know what billionaires and their friends wore. Jewelry? She twisted her grandmother's ring. The crowd would laugh at her achievements and her jewels, but she'd done it all with Nan's help.

Twenty minutes later, she heard the front door open.

"Oh, Don! Your lackey awaits!" Charon said.

"You can drop the Don-shit," Alessio said. "I told her."

"Fuck, how'd she take it?"

"Like a champ. I mean, relatively."

Charon laughed.

She poked her head out of the bedroom and found Charon and Alessio engaged in a round of backslapping and mutual affection. Assuming the men could handle themselves, she shoved a pile of lace into her suitcase. She maintained her game face in front of Alessio, but in her bedroom, her bravado slipped. Maybe she should demand to see his bank statements. Imposter syndrome existed. How many zeros did she require before she suspended civilian rules? Her grandmother taught her to work hard, but she also teased the possibility of loving a rich man instead of a poor one. Having tried her luck with Atlantic City, Nina was more than ready to enjoy Alessio's body, sip champagne and prove her nan's adage, but she wondered if she could hang with the platinum crowd.

Zipping up the suitcase, she pulled it out of the bedroom, planted her hands on her hips and waited in an ass-skimming two-piece that exposed her legs and covered very few inches of her ass.

Both men turned and stared.

Charon looked away.

Alessio held her gaze. "You look lovely."

She paraded the flowered skirt. "Very D&G?"

"Very you," he said.

"You've only seen me in a halter dress and a pair of jeans."

He smiled. "I've seen what you wear beneath the clothes."

"Bras are your things?"

"You're my thing," he said.

She grinned. If he knew she wore nothing beneath the sundress, he might not let her leave the condo building. "All right, let's go."

Charon took her bag and carried it down the hallway.

"It has wheels," she said.

Alessio laughed. Linking his hand with hers, he pulled her toward the elevator. "If I'm wrong and someone else returns Victor, where will you send him?"

"José," she said.

He nodded.

"Alessio" — she paused and checked her front door — "if you're full of shit, tell me now."

He tipped up her chin and pressed a kiss against her lips. "Nina, if you're faking, leave me in the dark."

She exhaled. "I have three discretionary days. As soon as we burn out, I'm coming home. The next time you're in Manhattan, call me."

"I will." Reaching down, he lifted her skirt and gripped her upper thigh.

His thumb rubbed the curve of her ass where her underwear should be. She leaned into his touch, wished he'd move his hand a few inches farther north and pulled away before her impetuous adventure had a delayed start. "How did you know?"

Laughing, he pulled her down the hallway. "We may have more in common than you expect."

"And if you'd been wrong?" she asked.

He tightened his grip. "When's the last time that happened?"

Charon loaded her suitcase and her laptop bag. He drove her and Alessio to the Upper East Side hotel. Given Alessio's wealth, his nomadic presence made sense, but she sensed his watchful observation. The entire trip across the city, she sat pressed against his side, but her gaze remained fixed out of the window.

She felt like Alice tumbling down the rabbit hole, but every somersault gave her a handhold and a chance to say no.

At the valet stand, Charon stopped the car and left the engine idling. "How long?"

"Twenty minutes," Alessio said. "Wheels up in two hours."

Charon pulled out his phone.

She reached for the door handle.

The valet beat her to the door.

Stepping out of the car, she straightened and felt Alessio's hand at her back. Beneath the midmorning sun, the tree-lined street softened the hotel's narrow windows and modern formality, but the uniformed staff no longer met her gaze. As the evening's entertainment, they smiled and eased her way, but now they stepped back and deferred to Alessio. She considered rewinding the clock and telling Martha to take her date and shove it.

Whistling, Charon preceded them through the lobby.

"Are you hungry?" Alessio asked.

"I ate the top of the parfait and a few bites of the gyros."

"That's hardly breakfast."

She looked up and met his warm, brown eyes. "What did you eat?"

He rubbed his nascent beard. "When we're on the flight, I plan to remedy that oversight."

"First class food must be better than I've heard."

Smiling, he led her to the elevator and pressed the button for the top floor.

"Did you switch rooms?" she asked.

He turned and loosened his collar. "So, I get a pass for the last few days?"

Charon barked out a laugh.

Alessio's day-old, wrinkled shirt looked out of place in the posh hotel, but she enjoyed his creased familiarity, and she wondered if she preferred it over his new, polished demeanor. "The first room?"

"I thought it matched the evening," he said. "Salesman in town for a business meeting."

She rolled her eyes. "No wonder I couldn't find your toothbrush."

"You didn't have time to look. You bailed on me like I'd admitted to loving origami."

Making a noncommittal sound, she wondered about his hobbies, but the elevator doors opened. For a man to fear revealing his wealth, he must question whether he deserved it. She couldn't relate to billions, but he did nothing but try to please her. When the elevator door opened on the top floor, she took a deep breath and walked into a black and white receiving space. A large format art piece showed a woman smelling a flower. Striped fabric upholstered a gilt bench and a red vase of flowers picked up the art's accents. "You need to pack?"

"Yes. It won't take a minute." He opened the door and walked inside the penthouse.

Looking over her shoulder, she locked eyes with Charon. "Is this working?"

"I thought you were a one-night stand," he said.

"So did I." She took a deep breath and followed Alessio into the living room. While he packed, she could look at art books, set up Out of Office replies and remind José to check on her plants. She sat on the edge of a small divan and tucked her feet beneath the seat.

The room dwarfed her, and she wasn't a small woman.

On the opposite wall, a large painting presided over a console table and two chairs. The painting's scale dwarfed individual brushstrokes, but its lushness held the eye. The colorful slashes and twisted geometries jumped off the wall and avoided the brittle impersonality popular in today's galleries. Beckoned by formal melodrama, she stood, moved across the room and raised her hand toward the textured paint.

"That's Martha's painting," Alessio said.

She dropped her hand. "No."

"She painted it a decade ago, after her divorce. For a month, she wouldn't leave her condo, and she wouldn't let anyone inside."

"Smart woman." She lifted her hand and followed the lines. Beneath her shadow touch, the lines unfolded into organic leaves and buds ready to bloom. Each shape hovered between abstraction and representation. From across the room, she hadn't seen the life. Up close, she couldn't deny it. Dropping her hand, she remembered the paintings in Martha's condo. Those canvases belonged to her, too. "She never talked about her work."

He shook his head. "Nobody bought it. To her, that was failure."

"Why? It's beautiful and alive."

He stood at her side. "Sometimes, the story matters more than the work. You said you'd seen her paint. Did the work look anything like this one?"

She shook her head. "I didn't know her in this headspace. Laughing women and cocktail glasses filled the canvas I saw. Maybe that's what she wanted me to see."

"I'm sure both pieces meant something."

She sighed and wondered how she could claim a painting from Martha's estate. She had the condo code, but stealing from her friend made her a terrible person, and she strived to stay legal. "Maybe."

"Make yourself comfortable. I'm going to pack." He turned down a hallway.

A woman wearing a French maid costume sauntered into the living room and struck a pose.

If the woman leaned forward, Nina would view her tits, and she felt more than a little jealousy. She hoped the maid chose boy shorts beneath her skirt. Acknowledging her double standard, she adjusted her dress.

"Oh la!" The woman fanned her face. "Monsieur Chen finally brings home a friend."

She extended her hand. "Nice to meet you. I'm Nina."

Dodging the gesture, the woman lifted her leg to a wooden ladder on rails, reached for a tall vase and lifted down the object. "Please excuse me. I have so much work to do."

She swore the woman gripped the wooden ladder rail like a stripper pole. If Alessio kept a harem, she would be the first to flip the tables and introduce him to reverse ratios. She could handle billions. Sharing remained off limits.

Charon dropped into a chair and kicked up his feet. "Lay off, Emily. She's staying."

"*Oui.*"

Charon's flip attitude did nothing for her, but if warranted, she could find his lips and make a scene. Charon would push her off or Alessio would push her out of a window, but her point would stand. She focused on the dollar-store maid. "You work for Alessio or the hotel?"

The woman laughed. "What is the difference?"

The sound bubbled out of the woman's throat like an animatronic doll, and she exhaled. People came with a range of physical and mental capabilities, but most knew the difference between costumes and everyday clothes. She remembered Alessio mentioning a housekeeper. If this woman fit the bill, Nina would have to pay more attention to specifics.

"Emily! Where are my bags?"

Alessio's voice boomed through the penthouse. Having hosted him in her dusty condo, she had no qualms about navigating his suite, and she walked toward his voice.

"Oh, no, Miss! You can't go back there," Emily said.

Nina ignored her and strode down the carpeted hall. The farther she went from the front door, the more the modern art transitioned to oil paintings, bronze statues and delicate objects suspended in light. If the Met lost an art gallery, they should check Alessio's house, but he probably had many homes. Seeing an open door, she leaned against the jamb. "Finding skilled help is so difficult these days."

He peered out of a massive walk-in closet. "Where's Emily?"

"Fucking a candlestick," she said.

He laughed and pulled down a rack of ties. "I don't know what that woman does all day."

She walked into the opulent room and picked up an olive-green tie that would bring out the highlights in his eyes. "Why do you employ her?"

"She needs me." Taking the tie, he added it to a pile of two suits and two sets of daywear.

She eyed the very European swimsuit resting on the bed and wondered what she needed. Victor's safe return reigned supreme, but a grande coffee and a croissant no longer felt like Monday thrills. "Is she coming with us to Idaho?"

He shook his head and ferried a pair of shoes to the bed. "She prefers New York."

"A housekeeper in every city?"

Dropping the shoes, he looked up. "Jealous?"

She traced his jaw. "You shaved."

"You prefer the stubble?"

Moving closer, she stroked his smooth cheek and inhaled. When he wrapped a hand around her back, she leaned against his strength and let their breaths mingle. "Alessio, what am I getting into?"

He tucked her hair behind her ear. "I don't know, but I have you." Pressing a kiss against her forehead, he unwound her arms, stepped back and bellowed. "Emily!"

The woman careened into the bedroom, lost her footing on the polished floors and grabbed a statue's arm for balance. "Yes, Alessio?"

"Pack up this shit and my toiletries. Give it to Charon and change out of that ridiculous outfit."

Emily pouted. "How long will you leave this time?"

"Long enough for you to dust."

Nina covered her mouth, avoided Emily's glare and followed him out of the room. Whatever history existed between the pair had nothing to do with her, but she enjoyed the show.

In the hallway, Charon handed Alessio a small, steaming cup of dark coffee.

Alessio took the cup and tipped back the liquid. "Finally, we can start our day."

"It's five o'clock," she said. "The day's almost done."

He took her hand and pulled her toward the main door. "The private jet will wait."

"For the two of us?"

He glanced at his phone. "Plus Charon and the pilot."

The man was so nonchalant about the jet that she wanted to laugh and ask him if his feet hurt from traipsing across the city. "In that case, let's party."

He nodded. "Good girl."

She pulled free her hand and pushed the elevator button.

Looking up from his phone, he caught her expression and linked hands. "Women."

His grip steadied her nerves. "You learn fast."

"I hope so." Squeezing her hand, he stared at the elevator doors while the indicator light descended the floors.

At the valet stand, Charon loaded Alessio's suitcase next to her bag and climbed into the driver's seat. She slid into the backseat and Alessio settled next to her.

Thigh to thigh with him, she felt miles away from their sun-streaked morning. He tapped out messages on his phone, dictated instructions she barely understood and traded quips with Charon.

All day, she'd caught him tapping at his phone while she'd chatted up shelter staff and made nice with the public. His efforts finally made sense. Her work required precision and jurisprudence. His work required — she watched his leg twitch — perseverance.

She wondered how a confident, lazy and indulgent man had shown up to their dinner date. If he needed sparring to come down from his nervous productivity, she would find a way to spar on her grounds.

Thirty minutes and twelve miles from New York City, Charon stopped at Teterboro Airport's gates.

The guard checked his identification, Alessio's passport and her driver's license.

For a wannabe flight attendant, the guard looked remarkably comfortable in his swivel chair.

"Welcome to the region's premier private jet airport. Have a pleasant flight."

She knew about the jet facility, but she'd never been there. Located in New Jersey, the airport weeded out smaller, slower aircraft from regional flight patterns and reduced congestion at the city's three commercial hubs.

Charon navigated toward the terminal doors.

Alessio set down his phone.

"So, you own a jet?" she asked. "Isn't that complicated?"

He cleared his throat. "When someone flies in or out of a facility like this one, they go through one of a few fixed base operators. The FBO handles passengers, baggage, fueling, maintenance, de-icing, parking and the facilities. Consider it a glorified truck stop. If you get the jet to Teterboro, the FBO takes care of the rest."

"Can Charon fly the jet?"

He laughed. "Do you want to make it to Idaho?"

Parking the car, Charon gave his boss the finger and climbed from the driver's seat.

She looked out of the window at the modern, gray buildings. "I don't know."

Taking her hand, Alessio brought it to his lips. "You want to go back to Manhattan?"

His breath tickled the fine hairs on the back of her hand, but excitement and apprehension warred within her stomach. Emily was a joke. The jets gleamed. "My life's pretty straightforward, but the last two days have turned it on its end. I'm not sure which way is up or down. Maybe you're right. I should stay here where I belong."

He lowered her hand. "Unless you try new things, how can you know where you belong?"

Lost in his warm, brown eyes, she focused on his long, black lashes and the flecks of gold dotting his irises. "I'm glad I met you."

He smiled and squeezed her hand. "We're just getting started."

She looked over her shoulder at Manhattan's familiar skyline. She wanted to be breezy, but if he were right, a killer lurked in the shadows. Maybe she would be safer in her condo with her doorman, NYPD on speed dial and daily check-ins from her paper-pushing boss. "Are we?"

Chapter Twelve

Charon opened the door, flooded the car with light and offered his hand.

"Oh, now you're a gentleman," Nina said.

He laughed.

The glimmer of rapport soothed her. Taking the hand, she stepped out of the car and stood in a wide, asphalt parking lot. Fading evening light cast long shadows. Holding her hand against her skirt to keep the wind from blowing up the fabric, she inhaled the smell of sunbaked pavement. How different could Alessio's world possibly be?

He opened his door, climbed out of the car and buttoned his suit jacket. Coming around the rear bumper, he nodded at Charon and took her hand. "Ready?"

She swallowed. "Of course."

Leading her toward the building's wide, glass doorway, he breezed into the lobby and approached the receptionist. "Hello, Cindy."

"Mr. Chen! Always a pleasure," the receptionist said.

Nina looked around the spacious, airy lobby. High ceilings and walls of glass let in copious later-afternoon light, and several large plants grew straight and tall. She struggled to imagine her condo-bound plants reaching such heights, but given the right environment, they could.

Instead of lingering in the terminal's plush seating or stocked lounge, he walked straight toward the aircraft.

She followed. "When do we take off?"

"Thirty minutes," he said.

She quickened her step.

Uniformed workers serviced, repaired and cleaned neighboring aircraft. Rubbing elbows with celebrities seemed like a fun addition to her one-night stand, but the passengers disembarking looked like a management team girding their loins for corporate battle. She took home a mediator's salary. All she wanted to do was climb aboard a jet with Alessio, regain her footing and chase another mind-blowing orgasm. If Victor turned up in the next twenty-four hours and the police booked a suspect in Martha's killing, she would label this weekend the most exciting adventure of her life.

He stopped in front of a jet parked outside the terminal.

She checked for propellers, but sure enough, the gleaming machine looked made for speed.

An employee stationed at the jet stairway smiled. "Welcome aboard."

Walking right past the woman, he climbed the steps.

She stalled. So many people passed through her experience, and most of them were good. She didn't need Idaho and Alessio's money. She needed time for the justice system to prevail. Alessio said he didn't believe in coincidences, but he'd arrived in her life at the same time Martha had met her end. "I can't."

Turning, he looked down. "What do you mean, you can't?"

She gestured to the busy jet ways and shrugged. "You're right. This isn't my space. You don't owe Martha or me anything. I can take care of myself."

Charon coughed.

Descending the stairs, Alessio stood in front of her. "What changed your mind?"

She struggled to articulate her uncertainties. The rush from her condo to his penthouse felt surreal, but the jet would carry her farther from New York City. Gooseflesh raced up her arms, and she crossed them. "If Martha's killer took Victor, he'll grow bored with the dog and abandon him somewhere. When he returns, I should be there."

Alessio took her hand. "José is there."

"But he's my dog." She swallowed. "He trusted me."

"Nina..."

She pulled free and walked past Charon to the terminal building. Too many changes in too short a time led to trouble.

"Fifty thousand," Alessio said.

She continued walking.

"Five hundred thousand."

She rolled her eyes. "I'm not for sale!"

"The money's for the animal shelters, not for you."

Slowing her pace, she knew what the facilities could do with an infusion of cash. Instead of drumming up food donations and old towels, they could spend more time with the animals. "If you want to write a check and clear your conscious, do it for yourself." Head high, she reached for the terminal door.

"A million."

She turned. "You're ridiculous."

He stood at the base of the jet way. "You came this far. What's keeping you from getting on the plane? I didn't kill Martha. I didn't take Victor. What have I done to skew your trust?"

"You lied."

"I never lied to you," he said.

"Well, you obscured the facts. Who throws around millions of dollars?"

"It's a tax write-off." He cocked his head. "Don't you claim deductions?"

Shaking her head, she eyed the sleek aircraft. Why hadn't she boarded any international flights? Bouncing from coasts to coast for business meetings felt like a waste of airtime, but she did it to connect with her clients. *Idaho* — she exhaled — *would be for me*. No matter how she pitched her decision, she understood the selfishness of getting on the jet. Then again, if she risked her life for the unknown, nobody but Victor would care. "Why are you taking me with you?"

"Jack Santana unnerves me. Knives are tools of passion, but I can't find a passionate connection between him and Martha. Someone gashed your door frame. I don't know why. I do know I can keep you safe."

She swallowed.

"I'd rather have you by my side than leave you exposed," he said.

She looked away from the jet and made eye contact. "Why couldn't this be about sex?"

He smiled. "It can be."

"Give me the park guy in the suit," she said, "or leave Charon with me."

"Wait a minute," Charon said.

Alessio held up his hand. "A million dollars in Victor's name."

She exhaled. "You can't throw around that kind of money. Coercion isn't sexy."

He crossed his arms. "Take it or leave it."

"What? Will you pick me up and throw me over your shoulder?"

Cocking his head, he worked his jaw. "The thought occurred."

"Stupid Italian-Israeli billionaires and their bloated checkbooks." Walking past him, she grabbed the handrail and climbed the steps to the waiting jet. "If you back out, I'll take you to court—and make it two million."

"Done," he said.

She swallowed back a gasp.

Inside the cabin, chairs faced each other in sets of two, cabinets housed sparkling glassware above a polished wood bar and a small banquet circled a table. On top of the table, a tray held water bottles and bagged snacks. She walked toward the table, uncapped a water bottle and downed the contents.

Alessio stepped into the shadowed interior. "Why did you really balk? Nervous to fly?"

She wasn't about to name her uncertainties. The implications scared her as much as Martha's death.

Wiping her mouth with the back of her hand, she recapped the empty bottle. "How fast does this thing go?"

"About five hundred miles an hour."

She swallowed. Commercial airlines had so many checkpoints and corporate rules. She trusted their track record. Alessio's record stretched less than a weekend, and she refused to let him faze her. Searching for a wastebasket, she dropped the water bottle in the bin and sat in the nearest leather chair. "I'm a little disappointed. Where are the gold inlay and the scantily clad attendants?"

He claimed the chair opposite her. "The luxury is saving time. If you want gold and exotic inlays, we can stay in Manhattan."

Charon pulled shut the cockpit door.

Shouldn't one flight attendant staff be onboard? The men and women staffing commercial airlines did more than serve drinks and peanuts. They conducted safety checks, looked after the wellbeing of passengers and possessed untold powers to stop planes halfway over the breadbasket. "I guess I can take care of myself."

Charon walked straight to the bar. "You want anything to drink?"

She shook her head.

Alessio did the same.

"Good. I'm riding with the pilot," Charon said.

She started. "Isn't that illegal?"

Charon shrugged, cracked open the cockpit door and exchanged pleasantries with the pilot, Kathy. A moment later, he slid into the co-pilot's seat.

"I guess that answer's that question." At a minimum, she thought Alessio's champion would play chaperone. Looking across the divide, she faced her choice. Alessio was as handsome and self-assured as the day she'd met him, but that had been Friday, and she would prefer more time to process and research her decision before she found herself metaphorically fucked.

He put down his phone and stared.

She tapped her fingers on the armrest. "Did I say something wrong?"

"You're cute when you're nervous."

"Thanks." Taking a deep breath, she extended her legs into the aisle and listened to Captain Kathy's pre-flight instructions. She hadn't felt nervous, she'd realized what she'd wanted out of life and worked her way through college to achieve it.

Her high-strung professors acknowledged her grades, her first employer praised her results and her clients sought her services. Before mediating any cases, she meticulously researched prior opinions, asked peers for feedback and honed her strategy. Packing a suitcase hadn't prepared her for this trip. She buckled her seatbelt. "For the record, I'm not nervous."

"Good."

The jet's engines fired to life and the aircraft surged down the runway.

Gravity pulled her against the plush leather. She gripped the chair's armrests and closed her eyes.

"I'm sure Charon's not flying," he said.

Eyes wide, she stared.

He smiled. "Relax, Nina."

The jet gained elevation and leveled off. When Captain Kathy announced cruising altitude, Nina unbuckled her seatbelt and stood. "I think I will have that drink."

He looked up from his phone. "You'll find champagne in the fridge."

Following his instructions, she pulled open the fridge door and found rows of mini splits. "Are you joining me?"

"If you'd like," he said.

She reached for the full-sized bottle, straightened and deciphered the Italian label. *Metodo classico* conjured up a thousand questions. "Do Italians export a lot of champagne?"

"Italians specialize in ingenuity, and they love wine. You'll find sparking variations in almost every one of the country's twenty regions. The Veneto, Tuscany and Piedmont regions house the most famous champagne producers."

His capacity for facts amazed her.

So did the sunset beyond the jet's windows.

She popped off the champagne cage, pulled out the cork and filled two glasses. Scooping ice into a bucket, she set the chilled bottle in the bucket, left it on the bar and carried both glasses toward the seats.

He took a glass from her and sipped the sparkling wine. "You do that well."

"Pour champagne?" she asked.

"Ask questions. You've very casual. It's either practiced, or you're genuinely curious."

Sitting in the opposite chair, she tucked up her legs and sipped from her glass. "Curious. I know very little about you. I went to dinner with one man and woke up next to another."

He set aside his glass and leaned back. "Ask me your questions."

"The fighting," she said. "Before our date, you were at the gym."

He cocked his head. "Why would you start there?"

"I don't understand it."

Looking out of the window, he settled into his seat. "It gives me peace of mind."

"How?" she asked. "It would terrify me."

"My parents loved their homelands, but neither parent conceded defeat and moved back to their spouse's country. I grew up in Switzerland hearing tales that made Zürich's storybook streets look placid, but shadows always hide danger. In school, I was an easy, foreign target for bullies. When my father taught me what he'd learned from his national military service, my classmates stopped picking on me. Other boys took their place. I was fast, but I turned up with black eyes and fractured bones."

She stretched her legs and reached across the aisle. Letting her calves press against his slacks, she relaxed into the story and hoped the gentle proximity encouraged him. No matter his wealth, swapping stories with him felt natural.

Looking at the place where their limbs met, he exhaled. "As I grew and claimed the upper hand, the fights drew more attention. By the time I reached maturity, I made more money beating up Swiss brats than I did working at my mother's restaurant."

She laughed.

"The thrill of physical combat satisfied me. It's a comfortable, controlled tension. In the ring, I don't have to choose my words or risk alienating my peers."

"Who do you fight?" she asked. "Charon? He probably lets you win."

He scratched the side of his mouth. "Not quite. Charon was a year behind me in school. When the bullies needed an ego boost, they came after him. He didn't win every fight, but he fought back. I've never fought him for money, but we've gone a few rounds over personal disagreements." Picking up his drink, he drained it and set it aside. "I spar with gym members or the people who think an aging international billionaire might be a fun mark."

She laughed. "And you win?"

He nodded. "I also know when to concede defeat. It's an outlet and a challenge. I wouldn't be successful without the sport."

"So why are we going to Idaho?" she asked. "You have plenty."

He frowned. "Business never ends."

She covered a yawn. "Hobnobbing with tech entrepreneurs sounds like torture. I'd rather go to Atlantic City and laugh my way through free drinks."

He smiled. "What better way to gamble than the stock market?"

"But your friends…"

Clearing his throat, he looked out of the window. "I don't really have friends."

"Charon?"

"Complicated," he said.

"Maybe you should step back from the gym and take up bowling."

He laughed. "Maybe."

Flying west, the sun's rays filled the jet with light. Racing across the country, they would land before summer stars filled the sky. She considered her next question. "Are you a pessimist or an optimist?"

He leaned back and settled his hands across his stomach. "I'm rich."

"Right." Standing, she pulled the champagne from the ice bucket, carried it to the seats and looked at his sunlit face. A few laugh lines fanned out from his eyes, but his smooth skin and neat clothes fit a wealthy businessman's profile. Based on the scars crisscrossing his knuckles, she believed his story, but a stranger would never notice the marks. Beneath his ironed dress shirt, his muscles and tattoos waited, but she wondered which side of him ruled his personal life. She filled his glass. "Which came first, the casinos or the insurance?"

"I'll answer your questions sober."

She dropped into her chair. "I'm perfecting a new cross-examination technique. Indulge me."

He stretched out his legs.

The moment she felt contact, she relaxed and set aside her drink.

"One day, a man in Germany asked me to throw a match. If I lost, he'd pay me more than my usual take-home. I did the math, realized how much money exchanged hands and bet everything I had that I'd come out ahead. The bet paid off."

"Winning a bet doesn't buy you a casino."

He examined the wine in his glass. Bubbles caught the light and raced up the flute's interior. "No, but a developer in Atlantic City bit off more than he could chew."

She sipped her wine. "I know the feeling."

"Pardon?"

Waving her hand, she urged him to continue.

"When the Atlantic City Revelry closed, I leveraged my connections and bought the property out of bankruptcy court for $82 million. I hired the right people to renovate it, added an indoor golf facility and revamped the extensive sports betting facilities. The original floor plan was a maze. When my team and I re-opened the doors, we welcomed gamblers of all playing levels, allowed smoking and placed a premium on customer service. The visitors came back."

She knew the place, and she swallowed. No wonder he'd laughed off her comments on glitz and glamour. The casino he described existed somewhere between riverboats and Las Vegas towers, but it had cache and the rooms went for a premium. "You know sports betting can be corrupt. If you're taking money from people who can't afford to lose it, how do you sleep at night?"

He leaned forward and braced his arms on his knees. "Money doesn't pass judgment. People do. As long as my facilities operate legitimately, I let people weigh the odds and roll the dice. If I see something shady, I remove the threat from the premises. Nobody crosses me."

His statement rang true. The light reflected in his eyes and obscured the fine lines and full lips that softened his image. She'd met him in Martha's apartment, but if she'd met him on the street, she might have run. "Doesn't the government have enforcement agencies and gaming commissions?"

He rolled his head. "The laws are ineffective. Most people would risk a year of prison against a lifetime of ease. The control boards keep quaint Black Books, but the conviction entries hardly make a dent in the crime. Cagey accomplices pull the next heist." Working his shoulders into the seat, he looked up. "Taking preemptive action saved me in the past. I'm not depriving criminals of library access. I'm depriving them of a game of chance. Everyone else is free to come and play."

"As long as you win," she said.

He lowered his head and smiled. "The house always wins."

His voice deepened, and she feared she'd touched a nerve. Skipping her underwear, flying over Middle America and sipping Italian champagne on a near-empty stomach weren't everyday occurrences, but she excelled at everything she took on...except rehabilitating men. She met his stare. "Until it overextends and folds."

He formed his hands into a steeple across his stomach. "What's my biggest challenge?"

She considered the question. "A jackpot you can't afford?"

He shook his head. "Fraud."

"But you must have security and cameras on every floor."

"And everybody knows it," he said. "The fraud comes from within the organization. You think Charon's amusing..."

"I didn't say that!"

"...but I don't question his loyalty. The rest of my associates weigh their decisions and pledge their loyalties. I trust them. The people on the floors"—he shrugged—"they spend their lives trying to defy the odds. A desperate person will bet everything he or she has and try to come out ahead. They might try to defraud an insurance copy, use an investment firm to prop up a failing company or do more than count cards. I'm waiting."

She shook her head. "I've been to plenty of casinos. Counting cards can't be that easy."

Leaning to the side, he propped his hand in his head and smiled. "Would you like to make a bet?"

"On your casinos?"

He smiled. "On me."

The temptation to move across the opening, climb into his lap and table the conversation gave her a moment to wet her lips and nod.

"While we're in Idaho, people will know you're with me. To thrive, you have to respect the stakes."

She swallowed.

"If I tell you about past frauds, will you guess the magnitude of the loss?"

Scooting to the edge of the seat, she felt her skirt ride up. "Your losses?"

"I don't lose."

She frowned. "And if I guess correctly? Order of magnitude?"

He leaned forward and tucked a strand of hair behind her ear. "I'll let you pick our leisure activities. You can schedule as many spa days, horseback riding trips and meditative yoga sessions as you please."

"Wait! Are we headed to a resort?"

He sighed. "Nina..."

She held up her hand. "Deal. And if I lose?"

"You'll remove an article of clothing."

A quick mental inventory told her she had little to bet and even less to lose. "How about I get naked, and we settle my nerves the old-fashioned way?"

"The pilot has a cabin feed. She can see everything that goes on back here. So can Charon."

Looking toward the cabin door, she frowned. "He drove us home from dinner, didn't he? He's probably already seen my ass." She faced Alessio. "Unless you get off on sharing?"

He narrowed his eyes. "I don't."

"Me neither." Leaning forward, she rested her hand on her chin. "What's the annual revenue?"

"Fishing for Christmas presents?" he asked.

"Fishing for perspective!"

He laughed. "About four hundred million. Add in sports betting and horse racing to make it a cool five hundred million."

Her billable rate didn't seem as impressive. "All right, hit me."

"You're sure? I doubt you're wearing panties."

She raised an eyebrow, settled back and mimicked his steeple pose. "I'm not, but I hope Charon and Kathy enjoy the show."

He laughed. "Okay. Over two decades ago, a guy devised ways to trick slot machines into paying out. He would insert a wire through the machine's payout chute, trip the micro-switch and trick the machine into releasing a jackpot."

"I'll buy you better security cameras."

He tipped his glass to her. "It wasn't my casino. As slot machine technology improved, the guy invented tools that could blind machine sensors and trick machines into spitting out coins. The FBI convicted him on federal charges, sentencing him and his crew to a year in prison and made fun of the industry's lax attitude. If I'd found the guy cheating at my casinos, the agency wouldn't have found him or his friends."

She exhaled. "One million."

"Close," he said. "They targeted five-dollar slots. Loose the shirt."

"I knew I should have asked more questions!" Sighing, she pulled her shirt over her head and kept her back to the cockpit door. A smarter woman would have picked a cardigan set. She'd picked a tank with a shelf-bra.

He grinned. "I like his game."

She rubbed her nipple until it peaked. "Do you?"

"Better yet, let's stop." He moved toward her. "I like your idea better."

Shaking her head, she dropped her hand and grinned. "I want to try again."

He exhaled and leaned back in his chair. "The spa's overrated."

"Winning isn't."

Inclining his head, he narrowed his gaze. "For about two decades, an ivy league card counting team used…"

She laughed. "I've seen the movie."

"I wanted to give you a shot." He shifted in his seat. "Okay. A software designer coded slot machines to pay out huge jackpots to his accomplices."

"How did he do it?"

"The machines recognized a certain sequence of coins." He rubbed together his fingers like he could feel the coins slip through his hands. "Those little plastic cards?" He smiled. "Nobody plays with coins anymore."

"Interesting. You can't trust anyone, can you?" She sipped her champagne. For the casinos to catch the software engineer, the losses must have been significant. She chose ten million as her starting point, but a ten-million-dollar loss boggled her mind. The mediation cases she dealt with tipped into the millions, but selling products felt more tangible than selling dreams. "How'd they catch him?"

"In exchange for a shorter sentence on a side hustle, one of his accomplices revealed the scheme."

She dialed back her estimate. People with a take in a ten-million-dollar scheme didn't need side hustles. "One million."

"One hundred thousand," he said.

"C'mon! Is that even worth your time?"

"It's not my time, but as soon as someone walks away with one hundred thousand, the next person's eyeing a million."

She stood, shimmied out of her skirt and flounced onto the seat. "How much for the shoes?"

He smiled. "The shoes can stay."

Raising an eyebrow, she waited to see his next move.

"Don't beat yourself up. Criminals have tried past posting, counterfeit tokens, international money laundering, seduction and outright theft. Some people come to casinos to beat others, others come to beat the house." He stood, dropped to his knees in front of her and spread her legs. "The best players know how to lose gracefully."

Exposed to his stare, she wanted more than stories, but she refused to back down from his big, bad casino schemes or his warm hands. Despite the strange surroundings and voyeurs, she focused on his levity since leaving the condo. Free of his secret, he seemed more relaxed, and his ruthless approach to business made sense. As long as he abided by the law, she respected his achievement. She faced down hamstrung corporate attorneys, but she could handle him. "Is this how you win bets?"

He spread her legs wider and smiled. "This is how I collect my winnings."

His hands gripping her calves and running up her legs made his intent perfectly clear.

"You love an audience," he said. "First Charon and now this exhibitionism. Where will you go next?"

"I don't know." Her whispered confession left her feeling exposed. She wanted the intimacy his posture promised, but she'd received so much pleasure from him in the preceding days, she knew she would pay her dues. "Alessio, what are we doing?"

He lowered his mouth and kissed her inner thigh. The lingering caress and proximity to her heat drove her questions from her mind. His licks mesmerized her, and she dropped her head back. Staring at the cabin ceiling, she wondered if the oxygen masks would drop. He cupped her ass and teased sweet sensations from her pussy. At this rate, they could fly to Hawaii, and she wouldn't care. When he slid two fingers into her, found the spot that ached and moved his mouth to her clit, she grabbed his hair and held on tight. Pleasure coursed through her system, and she closed her eyes. "Alessio…"

Rocking back on his heels, he gripped her thighs and grinned. "No clever puns?"

"I'd like to cash in my chips."

He laughed. "That's the plan."

The intercom system chimed.

"Don, fuck her already. We're about to land," Charon said.

Alessio raised his middle finger toward the front of the jet, gripped her hand and pulled her to standing.

Limp against his chest, she held on and hoped ground control knew better than to take pictures before she found her clothes.

Dropping his head, he pressed a kiss against her cheek. "You taste good."

Even in the chilled cabin, he smelled of sunshine and cedar wood. Maybe the dry cleaners steamed the scent into his clothes. Musk rose like a promise. The only way she could match his scent would be to wake up on a sunbaked hillside, straddle him and ride him until the chirping birds dropped dead of boredom. She bit back a smile. "You can't keep smoothing over rough patches with oral sex."

His eyes darkened. "Watch me." Running his hand up her spine, he lowered his head. "Don't worry…"

His whisper teased her neck.

"The cameras face the cabin's rear."

Pulling free from the intensity in his gaze, she looked him in the eye and shook her hair out of her face. Her clothes littered the cabin floor, but on a longer flight, his clothes would have joined them. He'd thrown her for a loop, but she excelled at regrouping. Scooping up her skirt and top, she held them over her arm and smiled. "I'll remember that tip for the flight home."

Chapter Thirteen

Nina pulled her top over her head and slipped on her skirt.

Watching her curves disappear, Alessio shook his head. Her taste lingered on his lips, and if the flight had lasted longer, he would have whetted his appetite with more than her throaty moans.

Charon emerged from the cockpit and settled into the first row of seats.

The shit-eating grin on his face told him his right-hand man had watched every second of the game, and he'd loved the outcome. Alessio wasn't shy about sex, but he wasn't about to share Nina. Her sharp mind and playful laughter lured him from weightier matters and sodden grief, and she came alive in his arms. "Everything in place?"

Charon nodded.

Tapping her foot against the carpet, Nina took a deep breath. "So, what are we really doing all day in Idaho? Shooting buffalo?"

"Hardly." Charon snorted then looked up. "Wait! Can we do that?"

Alessio rolled his eyes. He'd dodged the question since leaving her condo. The moment he saw her handing out those ridiculous flyers, he'd understood her innocence, but he refused to scare her with Jack's family history. Keeping her safe had become his priority, but keeping her innocent hovered in second place. Safe, naked and in his bed would be even better. "My investment firm's hosting a small conference. Consider it an off-season meet and greet for people interested in forging connections."

She frowned and stared out of the window.

On Bald Mountain, light green ribbons tumbled down the mountain face where winter's ski runs cut through the evergreens. The summer grass thrived in the sunshine. Nearby, rapid-filled rivers tumbled past Dollar Mountain, breweries turned out award-winning beer and half the world's dealmakers argued over rooftop bars and seasonal menus.

"Can you gamble in Idaho?" she asked. "Are we going to a casino?"

The rural Friedman Memorial Airport came into view. Within minutes, Captain Kathy would land the jet. The small town knew him by reputation, and their plaid austerity welcomed his investment, but they almost feared him. Nina's view of him would change in an instant. "There will be a few parties. The facility's an off-season ski resort."

She turned from the window. "Do you own it?"

Charon laughed.

Alessio made eye contact and raised his eyebrows.

Turning on his phone, Charon looked busy.

"No," he said, "I don't own the facility."

She exhaled. "So is this conference cold banquet falls, shit ballpoint pens and bland chicken?"

He thought of the tech moguls, international investors and CEOs swarming the town. "Not exactly. Did you bring sunglasses?"

She reached into her purse and brandished a pair. "Are we going incognito?"

"I doubt that will be possible. Stay close to Charon or me. As soon as we get to the resort, put on sunscreen. Up in the mountains, we're closer to the sun. If you're not careful, you'll burn."

"Alessio, the sun's ninety-three million miles away," she said.

The jet's wheels hit the runway and the aircraft skidded to a halt.

He ignored the landing. "The elevation change makes a difference, and the locals wear sunscreen year-round. They keep it in their bags, their cars and their houses. If you want to launch a sunscreen brand, get a mountain town to embrace the product. Most businesses have free samples on the counters. Take the hint and protect yourself."

She wrinkled her nose. "I didn't bring sunscreen."

"I'll get you everything you need." He stood behind his pledge. If he couldn't remain close, Charon would stand in his place. As long as Charon understood not to get too close, the week would pass smoothly. He and Nina would out Jack, recover Victor and bridge the gulf separating their lives. If traipsing around Manhattan had taught him one thing, it had taught him that he wanted more time.

"Right now, I need dinner," she said.

Charon stood, reached into the top cabinet and pulled out a basket of meal replacement bars. Setting the basket on the table near the snacks, he dropped onto the banquet bench and crossed his arms over the table. "Take one of these." He looked at Alessio. "A conference?"

Determined to pay better attention to Nina's needs, he raised his eyebrows. The description seemed apt. What was he supposed to call the meet and greet? Summer camp for billionaires? As soon as the drinks flowed, dealmakers would do what they did at every business conference. They would network and make deals, but these players negotiated for billions.

Whether the deals covered engineering bids, newspaper acquisitions or IPOs mattered little. He cultivated relationships, paid attention to stress points and exploited opportunities. The vain social media honchos and twig-necked hedge-fund managers could stick to their shiny, media-blessed partnerships. He didn't have time for their posturing press releases. "Call it a gathering."

"Is there a program?" she asked.

"Yes," he said. "Mostly short, powerful talks from subject-matter experts. Some economic forums focus on the principles, policies and partnerships needed for a better society. Our aspirations aren't so lofty." He toyed with his hair's blunt ends. He couldn't change his stripes. "The people who attend this event have something to sell or they thirst for profit."

Charon whistled. "Wait until the lights go down and the sharks smell blood."

She frowned. "What does that mean?"

The jet slowed to a stop and the ground crew rolled the stairway into place.

Charon unlatched the exit door. "What does what mean?"

Amy Craig

Alessio stood, brushed off his knees and donned his sunglasses. "Charon means the conference often runs late. When you get tired, sleep. I'll find you." He caught the flicker of uncertainty in her eyes and wondered if he should have done more to prepare her for the event. He could blend into her world, but could she blend into his?

She slid on her glasses. "Got it."

Charon stood and crossed his arms. "Like he'll let you out of his sight. Domineering dick." Brushing past Alessio and Nina, he descended the stairs.

"What's wrong with him?" Nina asked. "I thought we were going to be friends."

He took her hand and pulled her toward the sunlit opening. "He's possessive."

"Of what?"

He smiled. "Me."

She blinked. "Is that why he called you a dick?"

The woman was as innocent as a raptor. Pulling a hand to his lips, he kissed her fingertips. Word traveled fast, and everyone in attendance would know she belonged with him for the week. Smiling, he kept his grip on her. "More or less."

Outside the cabin, wind blew off the mountains. At high elevations, summer days alternated between blinding sunshine and sudden storms. As a boy in Switzerland out hiking, he'd prayed for clouds. The reprieves reminded him grades would change and paths would end. Ever since he'd left Zürich, he'd questioned his destination. "We're on the edge of a desert climate. The weather's hot during the day, but the nights are cold."

She squeezed his hand. "You can warm me up in bed."

215

The jet had a bed. Turning around and getting back on the aircraft seemed like a reasonable proposition. Instead, he led her down the stairway and paused on the tarmac.

Most of the airport's employees went about their business.

A young man held up a phone.

Charon walked up and took the phone from his hand. Peeling off a few bills, he pressed them into the youth's hand, turned his shoulder and shoved him away from the activity.

Biting back a smile, Alessio turned toward Nina.

She pressed her hand against her thigh. "Everyone's staring. Is the wind picking up my skirt?"

"No, they think you're beautiful."

She smiled.

A driver stepped out of a black sedan and walked toward the terminal.

Charon tossed the crushed phone into a nearby trashcan and climbed into the driver's seat.

Opening the door for Nina, he watched her tuck in her legs, meet his gaze and grin. If he left the door standing open, she might spread her legs and give Idaho's blue-collar workers a mischievous show.

The press would never shut up.

He would never let her go.

Charon navigated the car past the airport's chain-link fence and turned toward the lodge. Beyond a gas station and clusters of older dwellings, enormous mountains loomed above the horizon, swollen rivers raced through canyons and rolling plains sported a rainbow of wildflowers.

"The landscape's beautiful." She turned from the window. "Why don't more people live here?"

He took her hand. "It's big sky country, but the winters can be brutal and long."

"Why did you pick this place for your conference?"

Running his thumb along her knuckle, he let nature's rugged beauty hold the spotlight. "I like it. The freedom of the landscape seems fleeting. One day, it will vanish, and I want to remember the emptiness."

"You don't like people?"

"I do." He frowned. "But sometimes, I like space, too."

She shifted on the seat. "I know what you mean. New York thrills me, but I can't wait to walk into my condo and let down my guard."

"Move somewhere less crowded," he said.

She shook her head. "I couldn't give up the possibilities."

The car climbed the foothills toward the resort. Trees grew denser until they parted and the building's looming, stone edifice came into view. Built by a gaudy, French aristocrat, the main house unfolded like a palatial residence crushing on cowboy culture. Stonewalls, split-rail fences and manicured switchgrasses kept the wilds from a landscaped circle driveway.

After the Frenchman had lost his fortune in the Great Depression, a local entrepreneur had opened the house as a resort. Subsequent management added blocks of modern hotel suites and a portfolio of rustic, luxury amenities. Behind the main building, a great lawn hosted croquet courts and outdoor fire pits. On the backside of the clearing, a spa building, pool, fitness center and business center erased boredom. Three restaurants served five-star cuisines and polished wood, natural stone and roaring fireplaces kept the Idaho ambiance.

Charon saluted the gate attendant and pulled up at the front door.

Before he could turn off the engine, a valet rushed to the door. "Mr. Chen! We've been expecting you. Your rooms are ready, and your guests have arrived."

The man's mouth opened and closed like a bobble-head doll, but Alessio tuned out his commentary. Taking a deep breath, he offered Nina a hand out of the car.

Straightening, she looked up. "It's big."

He laughed.

The valet wet his lips. "Ah, but so beautiful. Come, Miss..."

"Levoy." She held his grip, but she smiled at the valet.

Before she set foot in the atrium, every staff member would know her name. Alessio pulled her toward the front door and let Charon deal with logistics.

"Alessio," she said.

He turned his head.

"They're staring."

He scanned the room. The conference's casual, outdoorsy dress code kept lunch relations light, but when attendees came in from their tennis matches, golf games, hikes and rafting trips, they shed their fleece vests, slipped into button-down shirts and rolled up their sleeves. By nightfall, wool jackets held back the biting wind and jewelry flashed. He pulled her toward the elevator bank tucked near the lobby's rear. Every person in the lobby looked busy with a newspaper, cocktail or phone, but he spied several curious glances.

She stalled in front of the pub. "I'm starving."

He scanned the rear lawn where caterers erected tents and infrastructure for tomorrow evening's festivities. He thought they would be farther along. "We'll get food sent up."

She looked wistfully over her shoulder.

The elevator doors opened.

Holding his hand to the scan pad, he told the lift to take him to the top floor. When the door opened on his floor, an oversized chair and a simple, black door greeted visitors. He opened the door and revealed the pared-down luxury he maintained. Nina asked if he owned the resort, but he'd only bought the top floor. Once the servant's quarters, he'd knocked out the back wall facing the mountains, installed floor-to-ceiling glass and created an effective aviary. A fire simmered in the middle of the room, books lined an adjacent wall and clean minimalism balanced the rugged view.

She walked straight toward the glass. "Breathtaking."

He wanted to throw her over his shoulder and finish what he'd started on the jet. Instead, he walked up behind her, slipped an arm around her waist and pressed a kiss to her temple. "So are you."

She turned and smiled.

He recognized that smile. The first night they'd met, she'd extended her legs during dinner and confirmed their mutual attraction. He had been a well-to-do insurance salesman, and she had been a legal mediator. If he closed his eyes, nothing had changed. "You like it?"

"You keep surprising me, but you have consistently good taste. I like you."

He closed his eyes and wondered if she'd rehearsed the line. Instead of picking apart her motivations, he let his heart crack open. When life reformed into a fight he understood, he would pick up the pieces.

"Even when you're keeping things from me, I like you—and I shouldn't." She sighed. "Maybe I have a problem."

He stared at the mountains' cool, purple glow. "I can solve your problems."

Turning, she walked her fingers up his chest. "I don't want you to." She pressed a kiss against his lips.

For a moment, he resisted. Then he threw his concerns to the wind. The kiss devolved into a frenzied, torrid, tangle of need. He dropped his hands to her ass, grabbed it and pulling her toward his cock. His altruistic kisses on the plane had banked his fire, but he intended to claim his reward.

She ground her hips into his length.

Her response was like crashing into the sun's surface.

Heat and need ripped through him. He slid one hand under her blouse, over her skin's silky softness and cupped her breast.

She moaned and arched to his touch.

His cock strained against his slacks. Each time she rocked into him, her heat stole his focus. People made mistakes when they lost focus. He wasn't people, but he would lose himself in her.

She reached between them and pulled at his slacks.

Stepping free, he waited.

She undid his shirt buttons, tugged the smooth fabric from his chest and dropped it to the floor. "Cold?"

He shuddered. "No."

Pulling his briefs away from his jutting arousal, she wrapped her hand around his cock, stroked his length and encircled him. Dropping to her knees, she wrapped her lips around him and sucked. The hot, wet embrace nearly undid his control. He could taste her memory on his tongue, and the only thing keeping him from releasing down her mouth was the promise of holding her in his arms. Gripping her head, he flexed his fingers at the pleasure and pulled her to her feet.

She wiped the corner of her lips. "Do you have a condom in that gigantic pile of sunscreen bottles you keep on hand?"

"Nina, I don't…"

Cupping his balls, she pulled a condom from her skirt pocket. "Don't worry, I came prepared."

He closed his eyes and almost died. *Pockets.* The entire day, she had carried around that foil packet. He took the condom from her, ripped open the packet and unfurled it down his length. The sky outside darkened and the wind blew, but he wanted to feel her heat.

Laying her down on the sofa, he exhaled a long, tense breath. "You're so fucking beautiful, Nina."

She pulled him to her, spread her legs and angled her hips. "I know."

Laughing, he settled between her legs, cradled her head and teased open her mouth. Expecting her to crumble in his worlds had been a mistake. He would shatter her. Stroking his fingers along her opening, he felt her wetness, shifted his hips and pushed home. With every stroke, he pressed deeper, and she lifted her hips to meet his thrusts.

Beneath him, she arched.

He braced his hands on either side of her head and captured her lips.

After scoring his back, she clenched his ass and slapped him hard.

He tore his lips from hers and loomed over her, panting. "Fuck! Nina?" His arms shook, and he waited for the censure following her reprimand.

A slow smile warmed her face. "Faster."

Laughter joined with the effort of holding back. He seated himself dead within her, pulled back and set a punishing pace. Lost in her cries, he drew shallow breaths into her neck, fisted his hands against the cushions and plunged deep.

She cried out, gripped his torso and brought up her hips to meet him. "More!"

The command struck home. Growling into her neck, he nipped at her shoulder and thrust harder. Each time he sank his cock deep, she gasped, and her response inflamed his senses. When holding back no longer became an option, he shifted, reached between their bodies and stroked her wet clit. Hissing through gritted teeth, he closed his eyes. "Fuck, I don't want to hold on."

"You don't have to." She bucked up her hips, clenched her muscles around him and she fell.

He followed her and roared her name. The orgasm scoured his system, and he pumped deep within her until the last echo of pleasure simmered to a steady heartbeat. He collapsed on top of her, fighting for breath, and he raised himself on shaking arms.

She kept her eyes closed. "Stay."

"Nina?"

Trailing her fingers along his back, she sighed. "I want you to stay."

"I'm heavy."

She smiled. "I know, but the pressure feels good."

Chapter Fourteen

Condensing steam dripped down the bathroom's luxurious white, marble walls. Alessio flipped on the fan, stepped out of the bathroom and considered the master bedroom from Nina's perspective. The bedroom's leather-clad walls were as rich as her hair, and he'd never slept better in his life. Each time he'd stirred, she'd met his energy and pushed him to give more. When room service carted off dinner, he found her holding a plate of strawberries and a dish of whipped cream. She looked so pleased with herself that he didn't dare ask how she'd ordered it without him noticing. This morning, he hoped she found the space relaxing. Rubbing his freshly shaven cheek, he donned a navy-blue suit and thought about whistling.

She nuzzled the pillow. "No cords?"

"I thought you weren't into submission."

Throwing her arm over her eyes, she smiled. "I'm not."

He sat on the edge of the bed and traced the valley between her breasts. "Order breakfast. Poke around the grounds and meet me for lunch at the pub."

Nodding, she inhaled. "You smell good. I should have joined you in the shower. My laptop?"

"In the living room." He stood and adjusted his jacket. "If you need anything, pick up the phone."

* * * *

At one o'clock, he stood in the lobby with his hands in his pockets. A man claiming to have developed the future of interactive sports betting ran through his elevator speech. The smell of grilled meat wafted from the pub's kitchen. Alessio watched the elevator.

When the door opened, Nina stepped out wearing jeans and a long, cotton tunic. Her feet peeked out of metallic sandals, and the glimpse of skin brought a smile to his face. Promising to take care of her was one thing, but he'd never defined the terms. Tonight, she would have her pick of dresses. Walking away from the entrepreneur, he held out his arm. "You're sure you want a burger?"

She kissed his cheek and pulled him toward the greeter. "A table for two."

The woman bit her lip, scanned the room and swallowed.

"A seat by the window?" Nina asked.

He scowled at the greeter and memorized her nametag. Customer service mattered.

The greeter forced a wide-eyed smile, picked up two menus and led them toward a table in front of the picture window. "Of course! Adam will be right with you."

Nina dropped into her chair. "Why is everyone scared of you? The server at the Italian restaurant? Bartenders don't comp bottles of wine for fun. Now...this chick."

He loosened his collar. "I may have a reputation."

She rested her chin on her hand. "A reputation?"

Leaning back, he watched her curious expression for signs of judgment. "I didn't become a billionaire by playing nice and making friends."

She snorted and picked up her menu. "For the right price, Martha would put up with anyone."

He skewed his jaw. "Even you?"

Looking over the top of the menu, she grinned. "I've had a rough morning. First, you left."

"I had business."

"Then Charon growled."

He set down his menu. "Literally?"

She laughed. "He said he didn't have time to take me sightseeing."

Shaking his head, he excused Charon's surliness. He'd served as a stand-in, but he'd received none of the perks that came from Nina's soft smiles and warm embraces. *He'd better not be receiving any of the perks...*

She sipped her water. "So anyway, be nice."

"I'm trying." He loosened his collar. "It feels strange."

She leaned across the table. "When we're alone, you knock it out of the park."

He exhaled and debated his next question. He spent the morning chasing down leads, but every spare thought had gone to her. If he'd known she would have been this much of a distraction, he might have hired a team of security specialists and left her in Manhattan. "No regrets?"

She set down the menu. "Did you want me to get my own room?"

"Hell, no."

Laughing, she sipped her water. "The lazy morning was delightful, but I didn't fly across the country with a strange man to get a pedicure."

Surrounded by luxury and picturesque beauty, he only had eyes for her. "Why did you come?"

She bit her lip. "Victor's not coming home."

He stared.

"He slept on my pillow and learned commands, but he should have come with a warning label." Her voice wavered. "I didn't mean to get so attached to a pet."

Searching for her leg beneath the table, he made contact. "Why not?"

She exhaled. "Time? I don't know. My job keeps me at the office until late at night. I grew up with my grandmother and excelled at school. When my parents died and I moved it with Nan, I knew I'd used up my second chance. Who knows if I'll get a third?"

"You were lonely," he said. "I'm sure you did your best for Victor."

She looked at the floor.

His throat felt tight, but pubs catered to boisterous laughter. Every person in the room monitored their presence, and vulnerability was the last thing he needed. "You're wrong, Nina. We'll find Jack, and we'll find your dog."

"Okay."

"Okay?" he asked.

"You can't keep that promise" — she smiled — "but I don't want to ruin the trip by holding you to it."

He could damn well keep it.

An hour later, he sent his compliments to the chef, conceded that the local beer had improved and wanted to shuck his responsibilities in favor of an afternoon in Nina's arms. Instead, he cleared his throat. "I have appointments to keep."

The server approached the table and hovered near his elbow.

Alessio turned and faced him. "What's wrong?"

"You have company," the server said.

Frowning, he followed the man's gaze. His associates, whom he'd left in a conference room with two hundred slides and a catered lunch, waltzed into the pub holding a birthday cake. "Shit." He looked at Nina.

She frowned.

His associates converged on the table and sang *Happy Birthday* so off key that half the diners in the pub winced or averted their gazes. He'd punish every last one of them. Only Dante, who he'd dispatched to Miami, would avoid his wrath.

Driver set the cake in front of him. "Happy Birthday, Boss."

He kept his gaze trained on Nina.

"It's your birthday?" she asked.

He nodded.

"Blow out the candles," she said.

Swallowing, he extinguished the flames and waited for the backlash. They'd shared so much in the last forty-eight hours that omitting this personal detail might feel like a distancing betrayal.

Standing, she walked around the table and dropped her head. "You said you don't have friends, but these men proved you wrong."

He wanted to lean into her heady warmth, but his held himself resolute and prepared for the worst. "The cake has nothing to do with me. They wanted a glimpse of you."

She laughed. "Well, I hope they enjoy the view."

Raising a hand, he cupped her elbow. "I do."

She pulled free, straightened and smiled at the men. "What a lovely surprise. I'm on one of those low-carb regimes" — she stepped away from the table — "but you guys enjoy your cake."

Closing his eyes, he wondered whether to dock his associates' compensation or deck them all. Dante was in Miami closing a deal, so the asshole remained in his good graces, but the rest of them would rethink their clever antics. Standing, he made eye contact and ensured that they understood how much their little stunt cost them. "Not funny. If I wanted a fucking birthday cake, I would have ordered one."

Stefano dropped into Nina's seat, dragged his finger through the cake's icing and licked clean his finger. "Well, we heard you were in the mood for something sweet."

The shortest of his associates, Stefano had left *Sapienza Università di Roma* with an electrical engineering degree and never looked back. He drifted through low-level software engineering and technical director positions before the Bay Area's techno-verse swallowed his aspirations. One night, he'd climbed over the Golden Gate Bridge's railing and paused before jumping.

Alessio had halted his midnight walk and took a chance on *la lingua madre*.

Surprised, Stefano had leaned back.

Grabbing his shirt, Alessio had hauled him over the barrier and planted a foot on his chest.

Stefano knew he could always return to the bridge.

Today, Alessio was pissed enough to mention the option. Instead, he stood, walked from the pub and left the assholes to their cake. A casual lunch and afternoon delight no longer sat on the table. Riding up the elevator, he considered his approach. Birthday celebrations belonged squarely in a family environment, but Nina was right. ADC Industries functioned like his family, but he remained firmly at the table's head.

Opening the penthouse door, he found her sitting at her laptop.

She kept her gaze on the screen.

"I should have told you," he said.

Pecking a key, she shrugged. "Why? We're not dating."

He walked across the room and pulled her to standing. "What are we doing?"

"Playing cops and robbers," she said. "You do you. I'll run up your tab and be out of your hair before you can blink. Thanks for the shelter donation."

"It's not like that." He cupped her elbow. "I'm too old for games."

"But not birthdays," she said.

He couldn't undo the last hour, but he could improve the next ones. "Nina, I have obligations, but tonight I'll be all yours. Humor me. I would have told you before the party tonight."

"The birthday party." She pulled out of his arms and settled in behind the computer. "You're running an empire. What should I this afternoon? Fly fishing?" She tapped the keyboard. "Right... Don't forget the sunscreen."

He didn't know how to apologize or shake her mood. Physical intimacy smoothed over life's rough edges, but he read her posture and decided to preserve his extremities. A packed agenda waited downstairs, and he didn't have time to tease her into forgiving his mistake. "I'm sorry."

She looked away.

Shaking his head, he hoped time would diminish her frustration. "After the afternoon meetings, we'll have a carnival on the back lawn. At some point, a cake will appear, and everyone will remember why they're sipping my champagne and ogling the performers."

"A carnival?" She tilted her head. "Funnel cakes?"

"More Venetian," he said. "The concierge will bring up costumes and masks. Choose whatever you want to wear. I know you didn't come to Idaho to get your nails done, but spend the afternoon unwinding."

"What's the alternative?"

He smiled. "Spend the afternoon with Charon."

"I like Charon."

Crossing his arms, he stared.

She cracked a smile. "If he stays on the opposite side of the door, I like him better."

"He'll stay close by. I'll text you his number, but if you need anything at all, pick up the house phone."

"Who will protect you?" She closed the laptop.

"From what?" He cracked his knuckles. "The conference attendees are shrewd men and women, but they're here to have a good time. I can protect myself."

Standing, she walked up, pressed her body against his chest and cupped his balls. "Can you?"

In an instant, he hardened and hitched her against his erection. "You forgive too easily."

She squeezed harder. "I have forgiven nothing."

Pain shot through his core.

He cleared his throat. "Noted."

Releasing him, she moved toward the wide windows overlooking the mountains. "You're keeping me at arm's length? Fine. I can take care of myself."

He reached for a bottle of water, uncapped it and finished the drink. After his balls dropped and his meetings concluded, he would hit the gym to work off this nervous energy. "I'll be back by seven. Cocktails start at eight."

"Why so late?" she asked.

"Last night, the sun stayed up until nine."

She looked toward the mountains. "I didn't notice."

"Nina…"

Holding up her hand, she shook her head. "I'll be ready at seven."

He wondered if she would run.

Closing the front door, he faced the elevator, took a deep breath and pressed the call button. One floor down, his administration waited for his reaction, but he refused to acknowledge their stunt.

Each man ran a crew skilled in economic assessment, data analytics and information gathering. Their subject-matter expertise covered unique industries and their legal staff kept them a razor's edge away from insider trading. To rile him, Charon called him 'Don', but Alessio ran his investment firm with an iron fist. Half the profits went to him, and the other half went to his men and their organizations. Given the size of the take, his administration's loyalty remained solid, even if their sense of humor did not.

He opened the door to the conference room, met six pairs of eyes and claimed his seat at the head of the table. "Where's Charon?" He'd been notably absent from the cake stunt.

"Kissing the president of Argentina's ass," Jason said.

He debated scolding the man, but he appreciated the intelligence. The president's entourage attracted considerable attention at the conference. After Nina's arrival, Charon need a getaway to Patagonia. He deserved an all-access pass to South America's arid steppes, lush grasslands and bewitching deserts, but Alessio needed him to keep an eye on Nina until Jack's threat dissipated.

Stefano leaned back in his chair. "So, who's the friend?"

Leave it to the IT guru to shuck discretion. He had accumulated these men on his rise from street fighter to casino owner and diversified billionaire. Once a person accumulated wealth, keeping it became the trick. He placed his palms on the polished table, took a deep breath and picked the first contestant. "Driver, where do we stand?"

Looking up from his phone, Driver frowned. "Who is she, Alessio?"

"Her name is Nina," he said. "Like Stefano said, she's a friend."

Driver popped his cheek.

The six men exchanged looks.

Alessio bore their exchange. Calling Nina a hooker, mistress or arranged match would have signaled a financial arrangement. ADC's leadership executed deals, raked in profits and maintained a united front. As far as they knew, he didn't have friends outside his business interests. He took a deep breath. Martha's death weighed on him, Jack's involvement perplexed him and Nina's presence distracted him. He didn't need six intelligent men questioning his leadership and ratcheting up the stakes of the conference. "Questions?"

"Electric aviation," Jason said.

"Most investors think it's fifty years too soon."

Stefano reclined in his chair and braced his hands behind his head. "Most investors think they're successful day traders, too."

The group laughed.

He let the group's banter calm his jitters. He'd come a long way from the Swiss lakeside town, but honed relationships kept him sane. At some point, those relationships had morphed into friendship, and he had Nina to thank for the observation. One floor above, she had her pick of designer gowns, jewels and a hairstylist willing to pamper every strand of her sun-flecked hair. She had to forgive his birthday omission. By the end of the night, he'd peel the clothing off her body, wrap her hair in his fist and claim her. Her taste had distracted him and lingered far too long.

Chapter Fifteen

After a hard workout in the resort gym, Nina showered and stepped into the leather-accented bedroom. The chilled air pebbled her nipples. Her billionaire buddy maintained hard lines between life segments, and she would remember where she stood.

She opened the wardrobe where a housekeeper had unpacked her clothes. Sundresses, athletic leisure wear and a pair of worn jeans would carry her through the daylight hours, but nothing matched Alessio's suits and the prospect of a Venetian carnival. Pulling back the curtains, she peered over the clamor on the back lawn. She could have laughed her way through a church fair, but the scurry on the lawn suggested brocade, silk and — she swallowed — wigs?

Finger combing her hair, she wondered if she could fashion a dress from the penthouse's towels, three friendly mice and a flat sheet. She smiled and shook off the impulse. If Alessio wanted to see her dressed up in Venetian lace, he should have given her fair warning.

Actually, any warning at all would have helped her prepare for this trip. Pasta and wine should lead to glowing skin, but a transcontinental flight and a spare, modern penthouse left her feeling adrift. She rubbed the towel across her skin. The bath products gave her a residual, moisturizing glow, but nothing held a candle to Alessio's warmth...except that stupid cake. She hated playing the fool.

A knock sounded on the door.

Reaching for a robe, she belted the fine fabric and paraded through the living room. Peering through the peephole, she found Charon's clipped smile. She opened the door, cocked a hip and raised an eyebrow. "I'm surprised you knocked."

He shrugged and stepped back.

Behind him, a line of sumptuous, full-length gowns hung from a garment rack, and a redhead woman gripped a second rack. Nina reached for the nearest gleaming strip of silk, but she pulled back her damp hand before she stained the fabric. "I guess I won't have to make a dress out of curtains."

He frowned. "Is that a thing?"

"Only for Julie Andrews."

A woman cleared her throat. "Can we come in?"

The woman held a black duffel bag on her shoulder. Her clear, pale skin suggested she spent her life indoors or adhered to the town's sunscreen obsession. Too many of Nina's redhead acquaintances spent their teenage years worshiping the sun's rays and their thirties trying staving off the damage. If Charon's conscripted helper took the long view, Nina liked her already. "Really, two racks of clothes? Does Alessio own a costume shop?"

Charon wheeled in the first rack of brocade and starched lace. "Start with these outfits."

"Okay."

The redhead caught her gaze and shook her head. She fingered a pleated, gold lamé maxi skirt with a wide, black waistband. A three-quarter sleeve, black, crop top hung from a second hanger. The combination of glamour and subtle sexiness eclipsed the costume ball gowns Charon had put forth. Nina accepted playing dress up, but she wanted to shine on her terms. "No, I'll take the second rack."

"You don't understand the importance of this event," Charon said.

To catch Jack, Alessio might offer to let her go undercover as a server, lead bottle trains or claim a position at his side. She knew which choice she'd make. The stubborn ass shut her out but watching him from a distance hurt. As long as they shared a bedroom, she would make the evening work. She made eye contact with the redhead and stepped back to make room for the second rack. "I do."

"Fine." Charon massaged his thigh, scanned the suite and wheeled in both garment racks. Finding it to his satisfaction, he retreated to the foyer and dropped into an oversized chair. "Gabby, she's all yours. I doubt you'll need me."

Gabby chucked her duffel bag onto a console table. "If we do, you'll be the first to know."

Charon tapped his foot and reached for a small sculpture.

He had a restless energy and often held something in his grasp. Nina wondered if the soothing technique hid a quirky need to occupy his hands. "Thanks, Charon."

He nodded.

"Ditto, Toots." Gabby shut the door on him. Turning, she planted her hands on her hips. "So you're the piece that has everyone talking."

Tightening her grip on the robe, Nina assessed her new acquaintance. She looked friendly enough, but she had the advantage of clothes. Nina tightened her robe. "And you are?"

Flicking her long, red hair over her shoulder, Gabby smiled. "Your hairstylist."

"Hmm. I usually wash and wear."

Gabby lifted a strand of hair and rubbed it between her fingers. "I can tell."

She duplicated the gesture. "What does that mean?"

Walking past her, Gabby stood in the middle of the light-filled room. "I always wondered what Mr. Chen built up here. You can't imagine the gossip five years ago when he rolled into town during the off-season, booked the entire resort and warned the regional airport to expect an influx of jets."

She tightened her robe. "Sun Valley isn't immune to A-list celebrities."

"True, but none of them looks like a brooding god in a suit."

Laughing, she picked up an apple and bit into it. "I like you."

"Good," Gabby said. "Right now, you need me, too."

She reached for the gold skirt. "This is beautiful."

Gabby twirled her hair. "Want to switch places?"

Raising her head, she smiled. "Fuck you,"

Laughing, Gabby reached for her duffel bag and hoisted it to the table. "Oh, don't worry, I have a type, and it doesn't come with bodyguards."

"Charon's not a bodyguard. He's…" She let the statement die. Alessio's soft pitch as a well-to-do insurance salesman ballooned into a billionaire's portfolio, but too many oddities remained. Charon hovered and the waitstaff acted like they might shit their pants. When his buddies presented the birthday cake, his jaw went so tight she wondered if he would crack. "So, what do you know about Alessio?"

"He's hot." Gabby pulled out a curling iron. "And he's rich."

Slumping into a chair, she kicked up her feet. "Well, aren't you a wealth of knowledge?"

"You're the one fucking him," Gabby said.

She laughed.

Gabby rolled a chair away from a large, wooden table. "Come over by the windows, so I can see what you have."

Transferring her pampered limbs from one chair to another, she soaked up the indulgence of having someone care for her. Life as a legal mediator demanded one part ego management and one part legal expertise, but she conceded Alessio's achievements. if he wanted to pamper her to atone for his birthday admission, she could ignore his exclusionary tendencies and chock up the trip to an extended date. "I'm bad with highlights," she said. "I keep one or two touch-up appointments then I get bored."

"Balayage hair went out of style."

She flinched. "Go figure." Pushing down her cuticles, she looked across the room at a wide mirror reflecting the mountains. The glass also reflected her and Gabby. Alessio had a thing for mirrors, but Gabby's alluring smile triggered a different reaction.

She'd hadn't had a same-sex encounter since college, but vacation life intrigued her. "Are you from here?"

Gabby sprayed a fine mist on her hair.

The particles landed on her nose, and she caught the subtle combination of roses and patchouli oil. Shaken from her thoughts, she tried not to sneeze.

"Mostly," Gabby said. "I moved here when I was twelve. My dad was a bartender and all-around mensch. He made drinks for a living. My mom took care of the kids and we all got along. After college, I came back to do graphic design, drink overpriced coffees, star in community theater productions, announce the Wagon Days parade"—she tugged free a tangle—"and I do what I can to get along."

"Like hair." She closed her eyes. The woman had hands like an angel.

"Like hair. Sun Valley's an interesting place. I doubt you want to go snowshoeing or downhill skiing in shorts, but the weather isn't as bad as people make it out. You can go for a walk every day of the year. Each morning, I walk up to the golf course on Sun Valley Road, pick up a sixteen-ounce latte at the local shop and come back to town to start my day. Nobody bothers me, asks me where I got my red hair or offers me a lift back."

"They let you be."

"Exactly," Gabby said.

Weaving together pieces of information, she understood why Alessio had picked the resort, but she wondered why he'd chosen her. Reaching for her phone, she checked the reception and found full coverage. Her flyers and social media posts had failed to rescue Victor. Closing her eyes, she tried to relax instead of letting her grief weigh down her emotions.

"Don't let the sunny days fool you," Gabby said. "My daddy said we live in a donut, and the weather's all around us. I can't tell you how many times I've walked a mile out of town, felt the chill and turned around for indoor heating. This region spits on predictability. I've been in the playhouse when the rain poured down one side of the building, but the sun shone on the other side."

"No way," Nina said.

Gabby tipped pointed her finger. "Stay prepared."

She shrugged off the warning. "I'm from New York. We get one inch of snow, and the MTA preemptively closes the subway tunnels. If you slip on ice, people either help you up or post your picture to social media. Treachery and bad weather abound."

Gabby laughed and finished combing her hair. "Maybe you should stay here."

She hesitated. "I don't belong here."

Lifting her hair off her shoulders, Gabby ran a hand along her collarbone. "Then what's so special about you?"

The question resonated as much as the unexpected caress. "I don't know." She turned her head and met the stylist's inquisitive stare. Before she went to dinner with Alessio, she led a predictable, boring life, but taking risks might be worth the gamble. "Why are you hitting on a woman you just met?"

Gabby dropped her hand, grinned and pulled out a volume spray. "Curiosity."

Surveying the suite and straightening in the chair, she recalled her gleaming condo, thriving plants and familiar books. "I won't be here long."

"Shame," Gabby said. "Gold and black will look wonderful on you."

* * * *

At seven, the door opened and Alessio walked into the room.

Turning from the windows where the crowd assembled on the lawn, Nina glanced over her shoulder. "Hey."

Hands in his pockets, he stared. "Hey."

His intensity alarmed her, and she turned back to the windows. Performers in gold leotards circulated between guests—blowing fire, posing for pictures and performing unthinkable contortions. Lights illuminated the trees, chandeliers hung from the branches and elaborate dinner tables glowed with flickering candelabras. "How do you control the wind?"

He walked up to her and looked down. "The wind?"

"I see the trees moving, but the candles remain lit."

"LEDs," he said.

"Of course." She exhaled and turned her head. His eyes looked tired, and his hair stood on end, but he smiled. "That's it?"

"What did you expect?"

"Magic." She whispered her response. "The party looks like magic."

He cupped her elbow and pulled her close. "Am I forgiven?"

She swallowed and looked at the carnival scene. Before she'd left, Gabby had revealed she would be one of the masked performers, but a shimmering, gold wig would hide her distinctive hair. No wonder Gabby had picked out the gold dress. If Nina could keep her foot out of her mouth, she might blend in with the crowd. "I don't know a single person down there except you, Charon and Gabby."

"Who's Gabby?" he asked.

"The hairstylist who helped me dress." Facing him, she pulled back and focused on the future. "How do I look?"

He rubbed the pleated gold lamé skirt between his fingers. Dropping the fabric, he leaned forward and kissed her cheek. "Lovely."

She wiped the gold bronzer from his lips. "Careful, the glitter and costuming don't come cheap. If you get too close, you'll end up looking like a bedazzled hero." She pulled away and spun until the full skirt twirled around her ankles. "I don't care if it's a costume. I couldn't resist the glow."

"It's gold thread."

Laughing, she walked toward a bar in the room's corner. She wanted a drink, but she refused to drink alone. Faced with rows of crystal decanters, she pulled a clear liquid from the shelf, opened the bottle and inhaled the woody, winter aroma of gin. "I'm sure Marilyn Monroe and Elvis Presley would approve."

He lifted the bottle from her hand and turned her to face him. "Nina, I'm sorry you felt left out earlier. I'm not good at shared decision-making, but I need you to trust me. The next time Jack texts you, keep him going. We're going to find Victor."

She smiled and knew she'd fly back to New York alone. "Of course."

"The guys at lunch put on a show, but the conference attendees"—he cleared his throat—"play for keeps. Stick by my side and don't forget who you are. If someone says something unkind, remember his or her name and tell me. Pretend they're a smarmy patent troll."

Scratching the edge of her lip, she left her lipstick intact. "Smarmy. I like that word, but the pep talk's not enough. How am I supposed to stick by your side *and* stay one step behind you? You should have told me today's your birthday." She pulled the bottle from his grip. "Also, I can make my drink."

Removing a single-serve glass bottle of tonic water, he set it on the counter.

"I'm making a negroni." She pulled the red vermouth and an herbal liquor down from the bar. "Give me some space."

"I'm trying."

"Really? The room's four thousand square feet and you're crowding me."

He rubbed his temples. "Why don't you trust me?" He turned, opened a drawer and pulled out a lighter. Flicking the tab, a flame sprang up. "If I tell you I'll take care of you, I mean it. When I tell you your dress is gold, I mean it. Saying you're beautiful..."

She held up her hand. "I get it! I'm beautiful."

Reaching down, he lifted the edge of her skirt and applied the flame.

Dancing out of reach, she stomped her feet and patted her thighs to smother the flame. Chest heaving, she stared. "What's the hell's wrong with you?" To be sure, she ripped off the skirt and stood in her heels, her chest heaving.

He tossed the lighter in the drawer, shut the drawer and crossed his arms. "Nice thong."

"Uncomfortable as hell, but the stylist insisted." Shaking her head, she picked up the skirt and hoped she could salvage the beautiful fabric. Running her fingers along the hem, she searched for scorch marks. A warm spot marked the lighter's touch, but the fabric shone. She looked up. "What if you'd been wrong? Do you know how much hairspray is in my hair?"

"The fabric's genuine lamé, Nina. You're wearing a skirt of long, golden strands, and you deserve it."

"No wonder it's so heavy!"

He laughed. "Modern lamé has a clear, plastic coating to increase strength and prevent aging, but your skirt is vintage. It has a slight tarnish." He rubbed the metallic fabric between his fingers. "I like it."

She swallowed. "Gabby said mid-twentieth century."

He dropped his hand. "The skirt suits you. Instead of arguing every point tonight, can you give me the benefit of the doubt? I don't care about my birthday. If the date mattered, I would have mentioned it. I have so much going on that a self-indulgent cake is about as exciting as a prostate exam."

She rolled her eyes. Balancing in her black heels, she stepped into the skirt and pulled the fabric to her waist. A single button held the black band in place, but her desperate disrobing had popped it out of place. Walking toward her purse, she pulled out a safety pin and presented her ass and the tool to him. "The next time you want to make a point, a slide deck will do."

His hand gripped her hip. "Is that what you want? Sterile printouts? Printing press degrees and prep school graduates?" Securing the skirt, he swatted her ass.

If she were stronger, she would give him a love pat to knock him on his ass. Instead, she shook out her hair. "I wanted a drink."

"Fine." He set an orange at her side and pulled a peeler from a drawer. "Tell me you'll trust me."

She scraped off a strip of orange peel, and the peel's oil misted and filled the bar area with a crisp, sweet scent. "Sure, when you get around to telling me the truth. Just like you mentioned you might have a lead on a murderer and a dog thief." She glanced at the edge of her skirt. "And you might be an arsonist with control issues."

He leaned against the counter. "Falling asleep with my dick buried in you was the best birthday present I can imagine."

The image shot through her core with blazing heat. Closing her eyes, she bit back a reciprocal smile, but sex couldn't solve every issue. She blinked and assembled the ingredients for her drink. "Yesterday doesn't count."

"It was after midnight."

Turning to argue, she brandished the peeler.

He pulled it from her hand. "Truly, you look beautiful. Enjoy your drink and give me another chance?" He leaned close and kissed her cheek. "If you want to celebrate my birthday, I have plenty of ideas."

Afraid to undo Gabby's work, she tilted her head to the side and let him skim his lips along her throat. The stylists' exploratory touch had surprised and flattered her, but Alessio's skimming caress heated her blood, and she would forgive his unintended transgressions to languish in his arms. "Okay."

Releasing her, he stepped back. "Good."

The inch of skin banding her waist felt cold. Inhaling, she tried to reset her expectations.

"Let me change clothes. As soon as I'm done, we'll go down." He walked into the bedroom.

She turned toward the bar. "Do you want a drink?"

"Do you want to leave the suite?"

His challenge echoed in the expansive room. "I'm not sure." Gripping the decanter, she made two drinks, changed her mind and made hers a double.

* * * *

As soon as the elevator doors opened, Nina forgot how handsome Alessio looked in his tuxedo and focused on the bass-thumping music. The carnival might have a Venetian theme, but the party planners melded modern opulence and with past flourishes. Mingling around dinner tables, guests waved their masks in the air, flung out lined capes and showed off their gemstones.

She fingered her simple ring.

Alessio offered her his arm. "Relax. You look beautiful. Rich people are just like you, but they don't take selfies. The spouses are here to let off steam in a press-free environment, gossip like *bubbes* and fuck like rabbits. Remember you're with me."

His description took the edge off her nerves. Taking his arm, she settled into the habits she formed at law school mixers. Smiling, repeating names and making polite conversation came as easily as criminal records searches. Her first year out of law school, she'd trailed her mentor around New York cocktail parties, but she'd worn a suit and knew the famous faces she encountered. Tonight, she would fake her enthusiasm until she found her groove.

He steered her past a group of serious techies snarking over the deregulation of the financial sector and the spread of global capitalism.

She leaned in to overhear the conversation.

Stopping in front of a couple, Alessio offered a hand to a man. "Damon, your foundation keeps making the news."

Damon laughed and shook his host's hand. "That's the point, man."

The man's pockmarked skin surprised her, but his red sneakers matched his laid-back vibe. Beside him, a woman wearing a sleeveless, white beaded gown cradled a baby bump. The woman's curled, blonde hair and immaculate red lipstick made her look like a knocked-up starlet from a 1950s Technicolor film. Nina fingered her gold skirt and offered her hand. "I'm Nina."

"Vivian."

A man dressed in a black T-shirt and jeans paraded through the crowd. A dozen tall, thin, beautiful women waving pink bottles of champagne followed in his wake.

Vivian rolled her eyes. "That's Branson. Don't mind him. Before every party, he ups the dosage on his ED prescription."

She laughed at the humility of billionaires medicating their erectile dysfunction, but every human deserved compassion, and she covered her mouth. "Really?"

Two shirtless, male servers followed Branson and carried bins of champagne and sparklers high above their heads. A pageant of stiletto-clad waitresses bearing shots and more sparklers fought the lawn's grassy pull.

Branson flirted between tables.

The bottle train followed.

Onlookers cheered, whispered behind their hands or held up their phones.

She leaned toward Alessio. "I thought the rich kids didn't take selfies."

"They don't. That's blackmail."

She wet her lips. "I thought your colleagues would be classy."

He laughed. "Where did you get that impression?"

Vivian stepped closer. "This is what happens when deregulation of the West's financial sector meets the spread of global capitalism. Yesterday's aristocrats and tight-fisted capitalists aren't nearly as much fun to watch."

She turned and reassessed the woman. "And you are?"

"I run a nimble Silicon Valley resource called Hoat Analytics. People come to me for business intelligence and big data analytics. What's your gig? I can see you thinking."

Feeling self-conscious, she stepped back. "A legal mediator."

Vivian smiled. "How convenient."

Unable to turn away from the show, she watched the leggy blondes and oiled bodybuilders surround Branson. The actors let him spray them with champagne, pinch their ass cheeks and mock their squeals. Alessio's presence condoned the scene, but his aloof silence said volumes. Vivian stood by her side, as elegant as a heavily pregnant woman could hope to be. "This party isn't what I expected," Nina said.

Taking Damon's hand, Vivian smiled. "Don't get hung up on expectations."

"Good advice."

"I told Martha the same thing, but she thought their sexual history mattered." Waving, Vivian pulled

Damon toward a server passing elaborate appetizers from a sun-shaped tray.

Nina swallowed. Alessio's skills pleased her, but she assumed he and Martha had a platonic relationship. She thought she was special. The tender, unfurling forgiveness in her soul withered and died. "Have you been with those women?"

He cocked his head. "Those particular women?"

She gripped his arm and felt his muscles tense. "No! Women like them."

He signaled a passing server. "Bring me a negroni and a glass of cabernet."

The server pivoted.

Alessio held her hand and stroked a thumb along the underside of her wrist. "Those women don't matter. The point of this party is to put my guests in the right mood to spend money."

"And celebrate your birthday."

He laughed. "I already had my cake. The mingling guests submit to the illusion of spontaneous fun. In the morning, I survey the information my team collects and I decide how to act. It's all an illusion."

She tried to focus, but Vivian and her crew dropped gossip like atomic bombs.

"I'll introduce you to my associates one on one, and you'll understand. Relationships founded at this party led to some of the biggest tech deals, media mergers and initial public offerings in the last twenty years. The aggregate wealth on this lawn exceeds one trillion dollars. Run-of-the-mill bankers, tech developers and high-earning professionals don't make waves in Sun Valley. My team knows the difference, and they know the stories and gossip, too."

"How convenient."

He looked at Branson's entourage draped over a small bandstand "Those models are here for a good time and a paycheck. When the conference ends, they'll go back to their day jobs, wait until Miami's season fires up and decamp to warmer climates. They're props."

"You promise you're not pimping out their services?"

The server returned and handed him both drinks.

He sipped the gin cocktail and handed it to her. "I don't sell people, drugs or guns."

"Just dreams and connections." She clutched the drink, but she feared she'd already had too much.

He leaned down. "Right now, you're my most important connection."

His whispered pledge soothed her nerves, but she twisted her grandmother's ring. She felt the damp heat of crowded bodies, the cloying smell of mismatched perfumes and the glancing brushes and accidental tugs of a crowd. Conversations swirled out of earshot.

"*Una buchona...*"

"*Donne dei boss...*" A woman wearing a red, strapless dress turned up her nose and walked away.

She tracked the speaker's dress through the crowd and wondered what she'd said.

Disappearing behind a fountain, the woman removed her chance to find out.

Her hand shook and the ice in her glass rattled. Pulling her arm free of Alessio, she wondered if sudden onset claustrophobia existed. "I need a minute." Arms on her hips, she made her way through the crowd and marveled at how quickly partygoers parted. As much as she'd enjoyed Martha's company, she didn't want to end up like the woman — and she and her neighbor had fucked the same man. Who did that make her?

Breaking free of the crowd, she let the clean, cold, mountain air wash over her face and neck. Solitude had never felt so good. If she abstained from more alcohol and dinner started before she passed out, she might make it through the evening.

Alessio strode to her side. "What's wrong?"

She avoided his gaze, but she heard the censure in his voice. "I needed air."

"Next time, tell me."

Spinning, she faced him. "What? That I'm not cut out for this type of party? That you slept with Martha, and I don't want to end up like her..." Her voice trailed off.

At the edge of the crowd, a man wearing the resort's uniform chatted with the woman in the red dress. He looked strangely familiar and yet completely out of place. His nose bulged and his ears looked too small for his face. She shifted closer to Alessio. "I've seen that man before."

"Which man?"

The man in the resort uniform didn't belong among the oligarchs, New York hedge-fund managers and Silicon Valley investors. If the conference were a polished club scene, he would never make it past the rope. "Jack's here."

Alessio gripped her elbow. "Where?"

His fierce grip immobilized her, and his terse, controlled expression summoned her fears. "Talking to the woman in red." She swallowed. "That's my color."

"Nina, let's go." He pulled her toward the resort.

She looked over her shoulder at the place where the strange man had stood.

He had vanished into the crowd.

Billionaire blind dates made charming cocktail conversation, casino ownership came with interesting perspectives and Charon, may the Greek gods bless him, was the best-looking bodyguard she'd ever seen. Yet, somewhere in New York, Martha's body lay in a morgue and Victor might need her. She had no reason to connect a familiar face from Murray Hill with a service member in Sun Valley, but she feared the connection and the narrowing scope.

Yanking free of Alessio's grasp, she planted her feet. "Let go of me!"

The crowd's noise diminished from a festival's tittering to a congregation's nervous coughs.

He unhanded her.

Walking as fast as her high heels allowed, she made her way toward the exit and feared she would be too late.

Chapter Sixteen

"Nina, wait!" Alessio jogged to Nina's side, cupped her elbow and escorted her to the white catering pavilion. He looked at the nearest server. "Leave us!"

The tent's captain cleared the space.

Power could be so convenient. Nina considered wrenching free her arm, but she would lose the fight. Instead, she waited for the servers and prep cooks to leave. "I'm done with this charade."

"I'll tell you when we're done," he said.

She laughed. "What a line."

He leaned in close. "Nina, who did you see?"

Scanning the silhouettes beyond the tent walls, she searched for the unnerving profile. "Someone who doesn't belong." Her voice wavered. "Why is he here serving drinks?"

He released her arm. "I don't know."

A server peered through the tent opening.

"Out!" Alessio roared.

She rubbed her ear and faced her lover. He divided the world into two hierarchies, those who mattered and those who served his needs. Her position wobbled, and she needed more than a hot shower to wash away Sun Valley's madness.

A million-dollar donation and requited lust shouldn't be enough to alter her life's trajectory. How had she boarded his jet? The last time she'd checked, handsome, Italian-Israeli businessmen had better things to do than guard her doorstep. "I should go after him. Maybe he's trying to contact me."

"Maybe he killed Martha and snatched your dog for fun. Maybe he's a sick fuck. I host this conference every year. If he knew where to find me and where to find you, he's out for revenge."

She frowned. "Who uses a dog for revenge?"

"He's not using a dog," Alessio said. "He's using you."

"No." She paced the tent. In Alessio's world, he saw a problem, dealt with it and kept communication to a minimum, but her world shared the same spinning planet. "He's not after me. I thought everyone here would wear fleece vests, jeans and vegan leather shoes. Instead, you're a bunch of type-A hotshots with too many lackeys. He's after you, isn't he?"

He shrugged. "Everyone wants to play spin the bottle at summer camp."

She ignored his misdirection and pointed her finger. "I told you, I'm not cut out for this shit. Didn't you vet me? What kind of millionaire…"

"Billionaire."

"Whatever!" She threw up her hands. "What kind of billionaire goes out with a total stranger?"

"For fuck's sake, Martha vouched for you."

Lowering her hands, she exhaled. "And you'd already fucked her, so why not move on to round two?"

"Come on, Nina! It wasn't like that between us." He stepped forward. "We went on one date and the celebrations got out of hand."

Holding up her hand, she stopped his progress. "That sounds familiar."

"It doesn't. I knew Martha from her letters, and I should have kept the relationship platonic. The next day, I woke up and immediately regretted my mistake. You're different. I woke up the next day and I wanted to get to know you."

She shook her head. "And I wanted to get to know you, but you won't let me in. I should have read the signs. You held me at bay over and over again. My mistake." She closed her eyes. "I thought everyone needed love."

He shifted his weight. "They do."

"Then why do you keep boxing me into a convenient space?" She whispered the question, but she clenched her fists at her side. "I thought we had something."

"The entire world is yours." He ran a hand through his hair. "You don't want me to dictate your days? Fine. You don't want any surprises? Ask me anything. Just find your dog, get back in my bed and help me enjoy life."

She stared and worked to release her hands. An impulse to swing twitched her arm's muscles, but she held it back. "Cute. Can't you pay someone to suck your cock?"

He smiled. "You do it better."

Picking up a bottle of water, she heaved it. Ice and water droplets flew, but he neatly dodged the missile. Rehabilitating men and quarrelsome billionaires was beyond her expertise. She wanted a connection, and he let her drift. Panting, she braced her hands on her hips. "I'm leaving."

Closing the distance, he stroked her cheek. "Don't."

She turned away from his worry lines and tight-lipped control.

He dropped his hand. "Do you know anything about the man you saw?"

She exhaled. "No."

"You recognized him, but you can't place him? Don't you know a single thing about him?"

She turned and lifted her chin. "I slept with you, didn't I?"

He cupped her arm and drew her close. "Good call."

"Was it?" Pulling free, she replayed her apprehension on the Teterboro runway. She chastised herself for subduing her suspicions, hiding her fears behind Alessio's million-dollar donation and allowing her greedy little mind to wonder how the other half lived. Storming out of the tent would suit her skirt, but she wanted reason to prevail. "Alessio, what's going on? What do you know about this man?"

He cleared his throat and crossed his arms. "Jack's the bastard son of a man I ruined. His father, Michael Sanna, was a top executive at a telecommunications company. I made sure everyone knew how mismanaged the company had become. After it collapsed, Michael showed up at my Miami Beach house, brandished a gun and vowed revenge. Charon killed him. The company never recovered."

She recoiled. "What?"

"The story's old news, but I don't know why he came after Martha."

"What do you mean the story's old news?"

He frowned. "It happened years ago."

"Not for Jack."

He nodded.

"Your parents are dead, and your bodyguard is an asshole. Of course he came after Martha. She's the only person you love."

Jerking back, he stared. "I don't love Martha."

"Of course you do!" She flung her hand over her eyes. "When the hell were you going to tell me about your connection to Jack? What's the one thing that connects him and Martha? You! I shouldn't be here." She dropped her hand. "I'm going home."

Alessio gripped her arm. "The night Martha died, Jack came in and out of your condo building. He may have overheard us together. When the menacing texts appeared on your phone, I couldn't leave you unprotected. If Jack tried to get into your condo, you might be next."

She jerked free and tapped her foot. "Maybe he found Victor terrified."

"And sent you a picture of him dangling over a river?"

The unmistakable challenge in his question raised the hairs on the back of her neck. He hadn't raised his voice with her, but all patience runs thin. Despite her bravado, her lip quivered, and she eyed the main building. "You should have told me about your history with Jack."

"Maybe." He ran his hand through his hair. "We can try to reclaim Victor, or we can turn over everything we know to the police."

She looked at the man who shared her bed. He mentioned his reach and ruthless business dealings, but she failed to comprehend the scope. If he caught

Jack, she doubted he would face trial. The man kept a mental tally sheet and only he knew the score. The whispers and reverence surrounding him suddenly made sense, and she feared the implications. "Police."

He raised his eyebrows. "Seriously?"

She swiped a stray hair out of her face. "New York's full of sickos. If I want Victor back, I'll reclaim him using the law. Who the hell steals a dog?"

"Martha let him in." He crossed his arms. "I question her taste in men."

"So do I!" She threw up her hands. Depending on how long Jack had spent planning his trap, it could linger like a sticky, sweet lure, or it could close with a snap. Either way, multiple people might wind up dead. She eyed two hundred plates waiting for dinner service. "Who the hell blows this kind of money entertaining their friends?"

"Someone with a reputation to uphold."

She laughed. "You should have stuck with the birthday candles. Those men are your friends. These people are using you, and you're using me like a piece of bait."

Closing his eyes, he exhaled. "Maybe you should go home. We live in two different worlds."

"You're right." The facts stung, but she wouldn't tolerate more death. She swished her skirt free of her legs and stared him down. "Fuck you, your reputation and your private jet."

He clenched and unclenched his hand. "So be it."

Turning away, she marched out of the catering tent and faced the crowd. Every person knew she'd entered the party on his arm. Power radiated from his persona, but she wouldn't let his power cow her. These people would remember how she left.

In the middle of the festivities, Gabby wrapped her leg around an elevated, gold, carousel pole. Holding on to the pole, she swung her body in time to the music.

Nina aimed for the stylist. The partygoers' silky limbs and glittering dresses crowded her, but Alessio reigned over the carnival, and nobody would touch her, not even Jack.

Climbing the steps leading to the circular platform, she tucked one side of the gold skirt into the thick, black waistband, grabbed the pole and extended her leg toward Gabby's waist. Her black heel pointed toward the catering tent where Alessio stood, and she hoped he had an excellent view of her thong.

Beneath the thumping bass, the crowd silenced.

Gabby's smile remained in place, but she raised an eyebrow and challenged her to make the next move.

Stroking her collarbone, she beckoned Gabby closer.

The dancer's smile bloomed. Holding onto the pole, she pulled Nina's leg closer, pressed together their cores, bent backward and presented her chest.

A man whistled.

Leaning forward, Nina pressed a kiss to Gabby's breast. She rained kisses along the woman's neck, cupped the back of her head and pulled her out of her backbend to claim her lips. Gabby tasted like spiked champagne and kissed like a ninja, but as much as she relished the power play, Gabby's flavor wasn't the one she craved. Pulling back, she smiled. "You're beautiful. Thank you."

Gabby laughed and her showgirl smile slipped into place. "You're screwed."

A second later, a muscular arm wrapped around her waist and pulled her down from the platform.

She wet her lips and turned in the man's grasp, but she found Charon's disapproving stare. "Not you."

"Who did you expect?" he asked.

"Alessio…"

"…doesn't like scenes." Charon crossed his arms.

She lifted her chin. "Why do you do his dirty work?"

He smiled. "So he doesn't have to."

She scanned the crowd until she found Alessio standing beneath a lit white pine. Head high, she stalked across the lawn and stopped in front of him. The party lighting charged his honey-brown eyes with fire and indignation, and the wind blew his hair across his face. She braced herself for a reprimand, but anything would be better than his aloof disapproval. "Did you enjoy the show?"

He yanked her forward, caught her waist against his hip and bent her over his palm.

The crushing kiss answered her question, but lightning cracked, and she smelled ozone. She didn't care. Caught in his steady rhythm, she remembered the pleasure of watching him slide in and out of her core. She wanted to purge the suspense from their attraction. She wanted to wrap her legs around his waist, drape her arms around over his shoulders and tell him to take her upstairs. Sunshine and cedar wood would always summon his memory, and she wanted to soak up the pleasure of his touch like the sunbaked earth, but he didn't like a show. Now he had one.

Pulling away, she drew a breath and reclaimed her indignation. "Stop trying to claim me." Her harsh, whispered demand hovered between their jagged breaths. "I know you think you can protect me, but you can't."

His wiry hair hung over one eye.

She fought the urge to fix it. "I don't want you to protect me. I want to go back to our dinner date and wonder when you'll call."

"What if I don't want to let you go?" he asked.

"You can't make that choice." Swallowing, she turned and found Gabby lost in her gilded sideshow. She wondered if choosing fun over collegiate achievements would have brought her to the same place. Facing Alessio's narrowed gaze, she had her answer. "How old are you today?"

"Forty-three," he said.

"And this?" She waved her hand toward the billionaire's masquerade. "How long has this spectacle gone on?"

He frowned. "Years?"

"Every year, do you bring a different dope? Am I a game for your friends' entertainment?"

He sighed. "Nina..."

"Don't 'Nina' me! You're right. We live in two different worlds, and I'm choosing mine." She strode toward the resort building. Somewhere on the main floor, she would find a telephone and a ride to the airport. If she had to walk to Boise, she would do it.

Her heel broke.

"For the love of God!" Pulling off her shoes, she flung them into the darkness. The cool grass soothed her feet, but her outrage burned.

"Nina..." Alessio's long stride carried him to her side. "This event pulls me in all directions, but you're safe at my side. It's an unorthodox business strategy, but the conference has been very good for ADC's bottom line."

"*Your* bottom line." She stepped on a rock and struggled to keep a straight face. If the man she'd recognized was Jack, she didn't have a few days. "Fuck your bottom line."

"You don't understand. These relationships yield major deals and pay big dividends. I expect to take a cut from any deals that emerge from the week. As soon as the event concludes, we can sort out this thing between us." He frowned. "I can't set it aside to spend unlimited time with you. I can't pivot on a whim."

Walking toward the resort, she hoped he came up before she walked into the lobby. "You can't arbitrate people's lives, either."

"Why not? People treated me like shit and gambled on my life," he said.

His admission slowed her exit, but the time for talking had passed. "Do better." Lengthening her stride, she drew a deep breath and felt as if she could take on the world. "Be better than those men."

A man walked up and tugged her arm. "Nice show. Come have a drink with me."

Alessio spun the man, punched him and knocked him to the ground. He looked at his hand and shook his head. "Shit."

The crowd cheered.

She met his stare. Every time they came together, she glimpsed his tethered violence, but he kept it reined, and it never scared her. Kudos to him for controlling his impulses and making something of himself, but she wouldn't live with the threat. "Not a big investor?"

He worked his jaw.

"You think knocking people around makes you look strong? It makes you look weak!" She stepped forward and dropped her voice. "Violence doesn't make me feel special. It makes me wonder if you'll lose your cool and hit me, or you'll hit someone who fights dirty."

His chest heaved, and he stared, but instead of answering her challenge, he gripped her hand and escorted her toward the building.

Losing her footing, she stumbled.

He pulled her upright.

"Alessio..."

Stopping outside the resort's doors, he released her and rubbed his hand over his face. "I'm sorry."

"For kissing me? For marking me? For assuming you could?"

"For making decisions about your life." He dropped his hand and straightened his lapel. "Nobody will bother you. You're free to leave whenever you wish. I'll deal with Jack, find the dog and send him to you as soon as possible."

She closed her eyes. Winning shouldn't feel like a profound, lonely loss. Throughout her life, people looked at her performance, respected her abilities and let her work out her issues. If she wanted to nurture plants, puppies and percussionists, her peers indulged her whims. Alessio called out her bullshit. Running into his wall of protectionism chafed, but she loved his ferocity. If he could meet her halfway and treat her like a partner, she could deal with his quirks.

He looked away.

Pissed off, she still found him handsome. She had to leave before she caved and ended up in his arms. "Thank you for the weekend."

He inclined his head. "Charon will see you home."

"I'm sure." She exhaled. "Goodbye."

Turning, he walked away.

She closed her eyes and said goodbye for him.

Chapter Seventeen

Charon stepped from the shadows.

His tuxedo fit beautifully and Nina felt relieved to see him, but he was another handsome man standing in a crowd of beautiful people—she frowned—with a gun under his jacket. "I can see myself home."

"Humor me."

She scowled.

He walked to her side. "When you pull that trick, you look like a fiend. Have you heard of Botox?"

An insult never sounded so sweet. "Really? For your health, stay clear."

He laughed. "Did you eat?"

Her stomach answered.

"That's what I thought. Let's get you tanked up before we hit the road." He opened the resort's door and stepped back. "I'm sure the pub's open."

"Really, I'm fine."

He scratched his beard. "Just so you know, I'm fresh out of granola bars, and airport food sucks."

Sighing, she stepped into the lobby. "I guess we're not taking the jet."

"Do you want to take the jet?"

She let his question dissipate. Employees lingered in the cavernous space, but they averted their gazes. While on Alessio's arm, she had felt like an admired object. Free from his aura, she felt like a pariah. If everyone feared the man, why weren't the people who knew him cheering her rebellion?

Charon walked toward the pub and tapped the glass. "Sorry. It's closed."

Her stomach clenched. "Fine. Wait down here and I'll go pack my things."

"I have a better idea." He gestured to a service hallway. "Follow me."

She frowned. "That's not a good idea."

He cocked his head.

The man acted so much like Alessio that she wondered if they shared a parent.

"Who's going to stop me?" he asked.

Rolling her eyes, she blazed past him, swept into the kitchen and spied a bowl of peaches sitting on the counter. Saliva pooled in her mouth. "They're probably under-ripe." Picking up a fuzzy orb, she squeezed the flesh and felt it give. Before she second-guessed herself, she bit into the peach and let the fruit's sweet, acidic juices coat her lips. "Screw granola bars."

He laughed and leaned on the large, stainless-steel island. "That good?"

"Delicious." She nudged him the bowl and grabbed a paper towel to stem the juice.

"Did you notice the catering tent outside? Caviar?"

She worked her jaw. "I'm not eating his food."

"Right." He cleared his throat. "My mother grows the best peaches."

Lowering the fruit and the paper towel, she stared. "You're a peach snob."

He laughed. "Greek peaches are incomparable. In the northern regions of Macedonia, near Naoussa, you can find twenty different varieties. My mother sliced them, baked them and grilled them. Truly, she could do no wrong. My favorite dish was grilled peaches drizzled with honey and served with buttery manouri. It's a semi-soft, fresh, white cheese. "

"Mah-NOOR-ree," she said.

"Your Greek is terrible."

She bit into the peach, chewed and swallowed. "My grandmother made cobbler. Every summer, flats of peaches hit the farmer's market, and she used them as fast as she could. With only two of us in the house, the remaining peaches landed in Sunday cobbler. She called it 'Lazy Girl Pie'."

He straightened and turned toward a baker's rack. "What goes in the pie?"

"Butter." She frowned. "Sugar, self-rising flour."

He opened a refrigerator and withdrew a block of butter.

"I'm not here to cook."

"Why are you here?" he asked.

Scraping the peach to its seed, she considered the question. "I came to have a good time. I came to run away from Martha's death." She scanned the kitchen for a trashcan. Tossing the pit, she turned back to the island and found him in front of a large tub of flour, a baking dish and a slender knife. "Idaho seemed like an escape."

"It can be." He slid the baking dish toward her. "Prove me wrong about the peaches."

Shaking her head, she eyed the door. "Cobbler takes like forty-five minutes to cook."

"We have time." He popped the top on the flour container. "The first flight out of Boise isn't until six in the morning. You don't want to fly out of that airport anyway. Spokane's a better jumping-off point. If you're desperate to leave, I can dump you at Friedman Memorial Airport." He grinned. "Trust me. You might as well bake."

"Or stop for a hamburger."

"True."

She braced her arms on the island. "You're stalling."

He shrugged. "To what end? I'm the lackey."

"Liar." She pushed the baking dish back across the counter. "Your job title doesn't matter. You two are as thick as thieves."

Turning, he flipped on the oven. "Three-fifty?"

"I'm not making you cobbler."

He turned. "Why not? Every life has sweet spots and sour ones. Let's make this one sweet."

She knew next to nothing about him, but if he thought she spent her twenties memorizing recipe books, he would drive hungry. "You make the cobbler!"

"Sure." He picked up a knife. "Tell me what to do."

Gripping the countertop's edge, she wiggled her bare toes. "If you think this dish will buy you enough time to convince me Alessio's a good man, I should give him another chance and everything's a misunderstanding, you're wrong."

Slicing into the peach, he cut away half the flesh, segmented it and dropped it into the bowl. "I'm guessing three peaches."

She shook her head. "Five."

"Easy enough."

"It's not easy," she said. "He should have told me about Jack sooner—like, before we got naked at the hotel."

"What about the car?"

She kept her game face in place. "Oh, did you like that?"

A smile tugged at his lips. "Not if I want to live."

Pointing at him, she raised her eyebrows. "Exactly! He controls you, too."

"Control isn't a bad thing." He picked up the next peach. His knife moved through the flesh with practiced ease. "As people shift toward smaller resorts and shorter lift lines, this valley struggles with exponential growth. Home sales are up seventy-five percent, locals are cashing out rental properties and service workers have nowhere to live."

She released the counter. "So?"

Looking up, he stilled his hand and withdrew the knife. "So, Alessio read the local government the riot act about affordable housing and sustainable expansion plans. His businesses flourish because he's not a cheat, he pays fair wages and he looks after details." He sliced off another section. "He thinks people are scared of him, but they're scared he'll call out their bullshit."

"I'm not a business."

"But you're unfamiliar territory, and he deserves a learning curve."

She opened the drawer, took out another knife and sliced off a chunk of butter. Tossing it into an industrial baking pan she found resting on an open shelf, she slid the pan into the warming oven. Leaning against the oven, she crossed her arms and considered how a forty-three-year-old man could need dating lessons.

"Alessio has a short list of enemies. Given the way Michael Sanna died, Jack hovered near the list's bottom, but until he went after Martha, he wasn't an explicit threat."

"Who's at the list's top?" she asked.

He stilled the knife and looked up from the fruit in his hand. "You want to know?"

She looked at the gleaming kitchen. "I want to know Alessio will be okay."

"He'll be okay," Charon said. "Will you?"

Hearing the concern in his voice, she scooped flour, salt and baking powder into a bowl. She thought she could entertain Alessio with rumpled sheets and a few candlelit dinners. Too bad Martha had forgotten to mention his control issues. Pulling the hot pan from the oven, she placed it on the stainless-steel counter. "Toss a quarter cup of sugar over the peaches and add three quarters cup more sugar to this flour."

He followed her instructions and passed her a bowl of lumpy batter.

Reaching for the row of industrial spice jars, she shook cinnamon and ginger over the peaches, picked up the batter bowl and poured the liquid into the dish. The edges puffed in the hot butter, and she smelled the rich promise of sugar, fat and carbs. In the last few days, the only times she'd eaten properly had been the times she and Alessio had lingered in bed—except the restaurant. She would die for that pasta right now.

"Drop in the peaches and bake the dish for forty-five minutes."

Tossing in handfuls of peaches, Charon frowned. "Forty-five minutes?"

She braced her hands on the counter. "You said we had time."

Shaking his head, he slid the cobbler into the oven, turned and leaned against the appliance. "I've known Alessio since we were eighteen. He beat the shit out of me."

"Charming story."

"A bookie tried to rig our fight. The minute we stepped into the ring, Alessio told me what was afoot. He said, 'As soon as we're done, the asshole's next.' Maybe I caved too soon, but the bookie didn't stand a chance against us."

"Delightful story." She opened her clutch and withdrew her lip-gloss. "I get it. You're both big, handsome, honorable men who can't stand cheaters."

"You think I'm handsome."

She looked up.

He winked. "Alessio likes rules. If the authorities won't act, he will. He maintains order, and his transparency has consequences."

"His wealth lets him get away with too much." She glossed her lips. Sheathing the wand, she pulled out her phone to check the time. A new text message waited in her inbox. Enlarging the image, she gasped. Victor, alone and obviously afraid, sat in a crate in a dilapidated shed. Rain poured over the rusty, corrugated roof and puddled on the dirt floor.

Is this Jack?

Are you enjoying your gilded cage?

Give me back my dog.

Maybe your rich boyfriend will buy you another.

She initiated a call.

It went to voicemail.

Hurling her phone across the kitchen seemed like a reasonable response. Instead, she dropped it in her bag and focused on her fury.

While she bided her time in a resort kitchen, poor Victor was afraid, and she felt like the world's biggest jerk. If a kind, old lady picked him up and fed him sausages on her floral couch, she could let him go. If a lonely kid trucked him home in a bike basket, he could warm the kid's heart. At the worst, Victor met his end beneath a taxi's wheels. But Jack? A testosterone-fueled, corporate pissing match? An existential crisis wasn't enough to contain her frustration. "That's it. I'm calling the police."

Pulling Officer Scottie's business card from her wallet, she wagered he still worked the night shift and typed his number into her phone. "Hello, Scottie?"

"Ma'am?" the officer asked.

Charon walked around the island.

She dropped her chin and stared down his interference. "This is Nina Levoy. My neighbor, Martha Phosphole, died on Friday night." She swallowed. "Someone killed her."

"Yes, ma'am. How can I help you?"

The short, fat man whose shirt bulged at his belt sounded remarkably alert. "I think Martha knew the man who killed her. A mutual friend mentioned he'd seen Jack Santana coming in and out of the condo building. I think Jack has my dog, too."

"Do you have any proof?" Officer Scottie asked.

"Isn't there a camera feed?"

"We can't make out everyone's faces."

"But I'm giving you a name. Jack Santana." Repeating herself undermined her credibility, but she trudged ahead. "Someone sent me two pictures of Victor in distress. I think he has my dog" — she swallowed — "in Idaho."

Officer Scottie sighed. "Ms. Levoy, I have a lot of cases, and Idaho's outside my jurisdiction. I'll run a background check on Mr. Santana, but I can't do much about your missing pet. Can you prove ownership? Animal Control could do a welfare inspection."

"The adoption was cash. I've paid all the vet bills. Isn't he mine?" She heard the uncertainty in her voice and straightened. "I want to file a police report. Pets are valuable property, and their theft is a felony."

"Misdemeanor," he said.

Feeling powerless wrecked her reserves. She always had legal precedents to reference, but Victor wasn't a case. He was her pet. Squeezing shut her eyes, she took a deep breath.

"Ms. Levoy, I can take down the dog's description and his microchip number. I can post the information in the stolen article category of the National Crime Information Center. If someone encounters your pet, you may have a chance of getting him back."

"Victor," she said. "And he's not microchipped."

"Victor." Officer Scottie cleared his throat. "Do you have any reason to believe Mr. Santana harbored a grudge against Ms. Phosphole?"

"I don't believe in coincidences"—borrowing Alessio's line barely stung—"but the connection must mean something."

"And who is your mutual friend?"

She swallowed. "Officer, check the security footage for a man who matches his profile. He had no reason to be in the building. José wouldn't have let him in. If you can get a DNA sample, it might match evidence from the crime scene."

"DNA isn't unicorn dust," Officer Scottie said, "but thanks for the tip. Good luck recovering your pet."

After ending the call, she set down the phone and bit her lip. Tears welled. Determined to escape the kitchen before she lost her composure over a few pounds of wet, matted fur, she turned toward the door. Her need to let loose undermined her career, her neighbor's life and poor Victor's happiness. The tears fell.

Charon pulled her into a hug.

He smelled entirely wrong, but she closed her eyes and leaned into his shoulder.

The kitchen door opened.

"What the hell is going on?" Alessio asked.

Charon stiffened and stepped back. "Nothing."

She lifted her chin and prepared to march past Alessio, call a car and make her way to the airport.

He stood in the doorframe and halted her progress. "Nina."

She swallowed. "Alessio, I can't."

"Can't what?" he asked.

Squeezing shut her eyes, she wished she and Martha had another evening to get tipsy over bad television. Overbooked schedules meant nothing against a laugh track and a box of takeout. She wanted more time with Nan and more memories with her parents. For the last few weeks, Victor, with his furry little paws and ridiculous pink tongue, had returned her love. As much as she wanted him back, she wanted Jack to pay for using then discarding her friend. "Alessio, I need your help."

He pulled her into his arms and settled her against his chest. "You have it."

His jagged inhalations echoed in her heart. She felt his arm around her waist and a shuddering kiss against her hair. She looked up. "Help me find him, Alessio."

"Victor?"

"Jack," she said. "He used me, and he used Martha. Don't let him play games with Victor. If we don't stand up for the weak, who are we?" Nan's admonishments echoed in her memories. Without her grandmother's love and support, her move to New York might have resulted in germaphobia, wobbling heels and little else. Instead, she'd thrived and a misogynistic drifter with bulging biceps couldn't discard her achievements. He would see her and know she played a part in bringing him down. "Make sure he knows I sent you."

Chapter Eighteen

The kitchen smelled like summer fruit and cinnamon, but Alessio understood blood, steel and revenge. Nina's remarks hit home, and instead of venting his rage on some two-bit broker, he should take her advice and let her bewitching eyes center his rage. Shifting her to his side, he focused on the idiot who had seen him at his workouts and taken plenty of blows. "I gave you a simple instruction."

Rubbing his beard, Charon nodded.

"Do you plan to second-guess all my instructions?" He struggled to keep the frustration from his voice. Nina was right, he could do better, but he needed time to digest her remarks. Finding Victor might mend the rift in their burgeoning relationship, but the emotions stealing his focus required introspection. Charon had been his rock, and doubting him would shake his confidence. "Did I speak clearly?"

Charon cracked a smile. "Your woman was hungry."

"Hungry," he said.

The oven timer went off.

Nina slipped from his grasp and walked across the room.

Her gold skirt swirled around her bare feet and the only things keeping him from throwing her over his shoulder were three hundred invited guests, a missing dog and whatever she and Charon had concocted. By now, his woman and his right-hand man should be twenty miles from Sun Valley. He crossed his arms.

Grabbing a silicone potholder, she opened the oven door, pulled a baking dish from the oven and set it on the stainless-steel counter. "Cobbler."

He stared at Charon. "You defied me for cobbler?"

Picking up a large, metal spoon, Charon scooped out a generous helping and dropped it in a white, ceramic bowl. "Peach cobbler." He examined the serving spoon and licked it. "You should keep her."

Nina slammed her hand on the table. "You can't keep people!"

He and Charon stared.

She took a deep breath. "It's good?"

"Almost as good as Greek peaches," Charon said.

Rolling her eyes, she turned to Alessio. "Tell him he's full of it."

He blinked. "Give me the spoon."

Charon complied.

Swiping his thumb along the metal scoop, he lifted a taste of cobbler to his mouth. Sweet spices and buttered cake outshone the delicate desserts awaiting his guests. His mother disappeared every night to man the restaurant, but as he grew older, he understood her pride and her regret. Without her skills, his family wouldn't have thrived in Zürich. He looked at Nina. "You cook?"

"Hardly," she said.

"Good."

"Good?" she asked.

He narrowed his eyes. "Perfect women are tricky."

She grinned. "I'm nowhere near perfect."

To make sure she understood the bargain, he pulled her to his side. The sense of belonging unnerved him, and he stared at her parted lips. "You're sure?"

She wet her lips and pressed a soft kiss against his cheek. "I'm sure."

Taking her hand, he pulled her toward the kitchen door.

She laughed. "Where are we going?"

"The Health Department frowns on kitchen island sex." He stopped in front of the elevator and called the car to take him to the top floor. "We're going back to the room."

She tugged free her hand.

"Would you like to go back to the room?" He adjusted his delivery.

Rubbing together her lips, she redistributed what little gloss remained. "Maybe."

If he looked in the mirror, he probably sparkled like a damn fairy. Taking a deep breath, he moderated his voice. "What would you like to do, Nina?"

"Get you naked," she said.

His dick twitched, and he almost accepted her offer then and there. When he'd walked into the kitchen and found her laughing with Charon, his breath had fled, his heart rate skyrocket and he'd almost blown a gasket. Their innocent explanation, too simple and guileless to ignore, kept him centered. As much as he trusted Charon, Nina remained an enigmatic temptress, and he half expected his right-hand man to cave. For Charon's health and safety, he was glad the guy had kept his cool.

The doors opened.

Deciding, he picked up Nina, threw her over his shoulder and walked into the elevator. As far as he knew, carrying her wasn't strictly off limits.

"Alessio! Put me down."

Complying, he smiled and looked forward to continuing their conversation in bed, in the shower and in every position she would let him try.

She cleared her throat. "Alessio, I don't want to play games. Admit you're running a mafia organization."

He cleared his throat. "Excuse me?"

"Charon calls you 'Don'."

"It's a joke."

"You keep a mental tally sheet, sell financial protection and circle like a shark sensing blood."

As the elevator rose, he loosened his collar. "We're the good guys."

"Are you sure about that?" she asked.

"Are you biased against foreigners?" His counter question bought him time. Major criminal organizations existed. The criminals carved out fiefdoms and dueled over drug trafficking, prostitution, loan sharking, gambling and other vices. Violence's shadowed communities like south Tel Aviv or the outskirts of Naples. He didn't want to mimic the mob. "I don't run drugs, traffic humans or exhort small businesses for protection."

She raised an eyebrow. "Be a shame if something happened to your business."

"Cute." He knew many of the veteran bosses who visited his casinos. One or two mingled on the back lawn. When authorities intervened, their organizations rebounded under new leadership and settled old scores. He never felt compelled to integrate into *La Familia*, but he leveraged fear like an asset. He wasn't above making a point in the boardroom, the gym or the bedroom. "You're free to examine my books."

Crossing her arms, she sighed. "Just consider your image. Victor matters. I'll figure out the rest" — she waved her hand in the air — "tomorrow."

If her hand gesture bought him time to figure out the subtleties of a partnership, he'd take it.

The elevator doors opened.

She walked into the foyer, turned and looked at him. "Alessio?"

He stepped out of the elevator and stalled. Poverty, social neglect and lawlessness allowed mobsters to take control of society, but he existed above the fray. Cocking his head, he listened to the revelry on the lawn. Charon's gun, his cadre of associates and the guests kowtowing to his favor suggested the fray had lined up at his backdoor. "Shit. Give me a minute."

In the late 1920s, every bootlegger in the country had converged on Atlantic City to streamline operations and maximize profit. The loosely connected confederation ran hooch, but new efficiencies gave rise to more powerful criminal organizations. The press dubbed the partnership The National Crime Syndicate, but the power already existed.

Today, syndicate bosses watched proceeds fill their coffers without lifting a finger. Guns, drugs and chattel created a pyramid of pain. He preferred more order and less murder, but farming out his business territories and letting his associates manage specialty interests could allow him to step back from daily operations and grudge accounting. "Can I run the Billionaire Mafia?"

She laughed. "The Sun Valley Mafia?"

The idea took root. His associates understood the value of data, strategy and market dominance. If they preferred to break a sweat and handle transgressions the old-fashioned way, he would look away. ADC Industries' organizational structure could thrive without his daily control.

"Alessio?" Reaching behind her back, she produced a safety pin. A moment later, her skirt pooled at her feet, and she stood in the foyer wearing a cropped, cashmere sweater and a lacy, black thong.

He strode forward. "Nina." Her coy smile drew him closer. If yielding promised this much pleasure, he would have laid down his gloves long ago. She belonged to him. If she ran back to her annotated past, he would patiently pursue her. In the meantime, he intended to spoil her and earn her trust. But first, he intended to fuck her.

"Alessio." His name escaped her lips on a sigh.

As much as she railed against his overbearing, jealous tendencies, she welcomed them into bed. Craving his cock didn't make her less of a strong and independent woman, but it made her his woman. "Drop your panties."

"Come again?" she asked.

"With pleasure." He walked into the suite. Lifting down a bottle of whiskey, he made two neat pours and handed her a glass. His hand itched to tease the pale flesh along her black thong, but rewards came to those who waited. Rewards came to him. "I said, drop your panties."

She sipped the whiskey, shifted her hips and pulled the black lace from her hips. Spinning the scrap of fabric around her ankle, she tossed it toward the seating area.

The cleaning staff would spread the word. He grinned.

Standing in her top, she sipped the whiskey. "You're overdressed."

He backed her against the edge of an overstuffed chair. Taking the glass from her hand, he set it beside his glass and dropped to untie his shoes. Instead of standing, he looked up from her feet and watched her lips part. He ran his hands up the backs of her legs and cupped her ass. This close to her pussy, he could smell her heady desire, and he wanted to bury his face in her dew-slicked skin. Instead, he scraped his chin along her public bone, left a chaste kiss on her stomach and lifted the black shirt from her back.

She gripped his hair and held him against her abdomen. "Don't even think of pulling that shit again."

"What shit?" he asked.

"The plane. My condo. I said I wanted to fuck."

Laughing, he stood, lifted her into his arms and carried her to the bedroom.

She wrapped her arms around her neck. "You're really not that scary."

"Try me," he said.

Smiling, she played with the hair at his collar. "That's the plan."

He lowered her to her feet and stripped off the shirt. Her black bra matched her panties and the teasing constraint stood in contrast to her beautiful form. "Are you cold?"

"A little," she said, "but you make me burn."

Stripping off his jacket and shirt, he wrapped his arms around her and blocked out everything but the heat they shared. She belonged with him. Given a chance to run, she lingered, and he understood the compulsion to hold the things he craved. Looking down, he traced his thumb along her jaw. "All this time, I thought I had everything I needed." His husky voice surprised him, but the desire and awe stemmed from her presence felt pure.

"Maybe you were looking at the wrong metrics."

Her soft correction elicited a laugh. "I have an opening for a talented lawyer."

"I specialize in mediation, not brute force."

"Details. Start your own firm." Holding her face in his hands, he slanted his lips over her lips. Desire, acceptance and something close to love wound its way through his system. Billion-dollar mergers waited for his guarantee, but he wanted to spend the night wrapped in her embrace.

She welcomed him, matching his rhythm with her hips. When he gave her room to breathe, she pulled him closer. "More of this."

He raised his head. "This?"

"This feeling of not knowing where you end and I begin. You're like a magnet, Alessio, and as much as I crave distance, I keep snapping into place. We're going to figure out the logistics, but now" — she swallowed — "I want to burn."

He tightened his grip.

She ran her hands down his chest, undid the button on his pants and cupped him.

His dick strained in response.

"No more foreplay. I want you to fuck me, Alessio. I want to sink into that stupid, oversized bed, find something to hold on to and go for the ride of my life."

He traced her bottom lip. "Your life?"

She bit his thumb. "How about we get through tonight?"

Lowering his hands, he gripped her shoulders and buried his face in her hair. Beneath the hairspray and perfume, he caught the fresh, tangy scent permeating his sheets. How much time did he need before that scent became part of his life? Claiming her mouth, he unhooked her bra and backed her onto the bed. Her skin shone, and she could have been a siren tempting him toward death. He didn't care. Covering her, he braced on one arm and traced his hand along her smooth curves.

She lifted her hips.

"Not yet," he said. "You'll think twice before you walk away from me again."

"Foolish decision."

He nipped her lower lip. "Do I need to exile that woman?"

"Which woman?" she asked.

Her panted question pulled a smile to his lips. "The one dancing on the pole like she wanted to fuck it and every man in the room."

"She prefers women."

"Good." He frowned. "And you?"

She drew a deep breath. "Why?"

"I don't share."

Grinning, she stroked a hand along his spine. "I'm with you. I want to be with you."

"For now," he said.

She jerked her hips. "For now...for the foreseeable future."

In the morning, he would amend the terms of the contract, but for now, he wanted to fuck. Cupping both of her breasts, he lowering his head, closed his mouth around a nipple and sucked. His other hand thumbed her breast and searched for a rhythm that made her hum.

"Alessio..." She arched her back.

He wanted to disappear into her moan. Pulling back, he licked and nipped his way down her body until she writhed. Trailing kisses across her stomach, he gripped her hips, dipped his tongue into her belly button and rubbed his chest along her mound. The friction and pressure connected with a gasp.

She wiggled between his hands. "Nobody's ever kissed my belly button."

Raising his head, he looked up. "Do you like it?"

She grinned.

Her breasts caught his attention, and he considered changing course. Unwilling to release her, he dropped his head between her legs and found her soaked. He'd never tasted so much sweetness and heady desire. Scraping his rough cheek against the soft skin of her thighs, he ran his tongue toward her center and stopped before he tasted her. "Nina?"

"Please..."

Her moan urged him to continue. He kissed the fold along her bikini line. "Please what?"

"Stop this infernal teasing and fuck me," she said.

Rolling her to the side, he slapped her ass.

She propped her head on her hand and looked over her shoulder. "Really?"

He raised his hand again. "Tell me what you want."

Desire simmered in her heated gaze. When she chewed her lips, the tension in the room hovered near a breaking point. She knew as much about him as any woman did, but she had to accept him for a relationship to work. He could ease his way into her life, but he couldn't reform.

Reaching for his hand, she pulled him over her, spread her legs and ground against him.

An inch closer and he could slide into her and forget his name. Grabbing her arm, he anchored it above her head.

She sighed and arched against him.

Lost to her desire, he released her hand and rained kisses between her breasts. "You're so beautiful. You don't know how much I want you—to be inside you."

Gripping his shoulder, she shifted and stroked him.

Sliding his fingers inside her heat, he worked her clit and watched her gaze, heavy with pleasure. When she gripped his hand, he stretched his fingers and teased her tight bud until she bucked her hips and withered beneath the onslaught.

"Soon." She chewed her bottom lip.

"That's right," he said. "Come for me, Nina. I want to feel you." Adding a finger, he hooked up and found the right spot.

She clenched around his fingers and collapsed against the sheets.

He coaxed forth every echo her body offered. Removing his fingers, he licked them and pulled on a condom.

Focusing her gaze, she grinned. "This is where you take a phone call."

"Not tonight." Desire snaked through his veins and experience kept him from driving into her and taking what he wanted while she lay pliant on the bed. He kissed his way up her body, captured her mouth and let her taste the sex on his tongue.

She reached for him and positioned him at her opening. "Alessio."

Braced on either side of her head, he smiled at her heavy lids and soft smile. "Nina."

Her smile blossomed into a grin. "I'm waiting for you."

"Are you?" He pushed into her the slightest bit, lost his willingness to go slow and sank to the hilt. "You're mine." His gruff pronouncement felt raw, but he met her gaze.

"Yours." She traced his jaw, wrapped her legs around his hips and lifted her pelvis.

Her viselike heat and eager response unleashed his control. As he plunged into her, she met his thrusts. She was so wet and tight that he wondered if she would be the indulgence that blunted his edge. Lust did funny things to a man, but her body's deepest recesses and keen acceptance fueled his strokes. "Nina, what are you doing to me?"

"Alessio." She gasped. "Harder."

He pumped into her, felt his release edging closer and reached to secure her pleasure. Drawing her leg over his shoulder, he reveled in the new angle, opened her farther and shifted his hips. If he did this right, every thrust would rub against her clit. Balanced on the edge of release, his body throbbed, and he pushed through to please her.

Her legs tightened around his waist. "Alessio! Yes!"

Her screams unleashed a reservoir of pleasure. Roaring in response, he poured into the condom and her wet, welcoming heat. Without that fucking piece of latex, he doubted he could have lasted as long as he had. Her eager thrusts and pleasure-fueled cries had eroded his reserves. Pulling out of her, he stripped off the condom and tossed it in a trashcan. Lowering his face to her stomach, he admired her breasts from a new angle and grinned.

She ran her fingers through his hair. "I can feel you laughing."

He raised his head, kissed her reddened lips and brushed her damp hair from her face. The compulsion to wrap her in his arms and protect her from the world pulsed like a second heartbeat. "I never expected you, Nina. Until tonight, I didn't know I could feel this way about another person. I've never loved anyone but my parents."

She took his face in her hands. "I've loved too many things. Maybe I didn't know the meaning of the word, but I know you. Do we have a future?"

He sat back and pulled her into his lap. "I'll make one."

Laying her head against his shoulder, she yawned. "I believe you. I thought New York and my law degree were my achievements. Now, I'm thinking bigger."

Exhaling, he traced her back. "That might be a problem. I've been thinking about retirement."

She propped her head on her hand. "Really? If your associates are capable, let them lead. You won't lose your grip. If they mess up, you'll be there." She smiled. "Like a really overbearing, terse, father figure."

"You say the sweetest things."

She yawned.

Shifting his weight, he pondered her advice and felt her slide into untroubled sleep. With her at his side, he felt less cynical about the world, and he wasn't about to give up his position for the golf course.

Chapter Nineteen

Sunlight streamed into the room and pulled Nina from a golden dream. Blinking, she replayed the night and reached for Alessio.

He pulled her hand to his lips. "Good morning, beautiful. I'm about to head to a meeting. Order room service." Biting her thumb, he smiled. "As long as it's not cobbler."

Pulling back her hand, she laughed and covered her eyes. "Fried chicken's my favorite food. You can take the girl out of the country, but" — she yawned — "some things stick. Maybe fried chicken and waffles."

"Of all the things." He ruffled her hair. "Order it."

The bed shifted, and she moaned the loss of his heat. Opening her eyes, she stared at the strong, vibrant tattoos lining his biceps and his chest. Last night, her mouth had traced the lines, but she'd found she needed the stories. Dragging herself to a sitting position, she let the sheet fall to her waist and scratched her scalp. "I will. Extra syrup."

"Modesty isn't your thing, is it?"

Stilling, she searched for censure in his comment.

He dropped back to the bed, pulled her to his side and anchored his arm over her shoulder. "Mine, either. Let's do waffles. The meeting can wait."

Skin-to-skin beneath the sheet, she watched him pick up a laptop from the bedside table. An array of small windows displayed tickers and multicolored symbols she vaguely recognized. "What is all that?"

He navigated the touchpad. "A scorecard for companies under my consideration."

Leaning against his shoulder, she followed his cursor. "Under consideration. What is that, like, talking before you date?"

"More like stalking." He kept his gaze on the screen. "This one needed commodity prices to fall on their main import." He rolled his lip and smiled. "The prices didn't fall."

"And you'll call in the chips." The cold, absolute statement felt true, but so did the man whose scent felt like coming home. The wry insurance salesmen she'd fucked in the hotel room had turned into the figurehead leading a powerful ship. Beneath his wool suits and confidence, he flexed his muscles and people acted. In the time it took her to shed her training bras and grasp a diploma, he'd accumulated an empire, but she could handle him.

"I will," he said.

She ducked under his arm and scooted away. "I'll leave you to your work."

He caught her ankle, but he kept his gaze on the screen. "If you keep running, I'll chase you, but each time I catch you, we'll be further and further apart."

Releasing his hold, he closed the screen and rubbed his face. "I don't run a charity."

She hesitated. "But you have a foundation."

"For tax purposes and workforce development." He stared. "I'm not anchoring you to my side, but I don't want you to shy away from me. Ask me anything."

She understood the hard-edged competition driving him, but she needed to understand its limits. "Bottom line."

He frowned.

"Have you ever killed a person?"

Setting aside the laptop, he leaned against the pillows and closed his eyes. "Not the question I expected you to ask."

She drew up her knees and rested her chin on top. "Because I'm thinking we might need to kill Jack."

He smiled and opened his eyes. "We'll find your dog."

"How?"

Reaching toward her, he wound her hair around his hand and rubbed a strand between two fingers. "Jack's a 'red collar' criminal. In another life, he would have been a paper pusher or an overpayed vice president. Instead, he has an axe to grind. Controlling situations and controlling people gets him off, but kidnapping your dog is a low opening bid."

She shuddered.

He released her hair.

Unfolding her legs, she reestablished contact amid the tangled linens.

He rested his hand on top of her thigh. "Murder is the ultimate form of control over others, and being able to control another person's destiny, even if it results in death, takes a lot of balls. Jack's a lingerer. I think he saw a crime of opportunity or lashed out. I don't think he planned to kill Martha."

"How do you know?"

Picking up her hand, he traced the lines marking her palm. "He used a knife."

She slipped her hand from his grip and stared at the antique ring she wore. After her parents' death, her grandparents had raised her, but her grandfather had succumbed to a heart attack. For so long, she and Nan had existed as a team. Climbing from the bed, she walked across the room, opened the closet and pulled a soft robe from a hook. "Losing a parent is hard. My grandmother always believed in me. Who did Jack have?"

Alessio frowned. "I don't know."

"Find out."

"Witchy woman."

She fussed with her hair. The robe slipped open.

He reached for her but stilled his hand and made eye contact. "The answer's yes, Nina, but I'm not proud of the fact."

Tightening the robe's belt, she pulled back and digested his confession. In her heart, she'd known the answer before he'd said it. She valued his honesty, but his presence had upended her life. "Thanks for being honest. I think people always have an opportunity to do better. Before you destroy Jack, ask him what he endured."

"Endurance doesn't justify murder," he said. "I acted in self-defense."

"Okay," she said.

"Okay?"

She nodded. Second-guessing Alessio's past led nowhere. Stripped of his obfuscations and omissions, he pledged transparency. She had to believe him. Picking up her tote bag, she dug out her phone.

Good morning, Asshole. I saw you at the party last night. Couldn't get an invite? How's my dog?

An incoming text revealed a picture of Victor. The sun shone and Victor slept with his head buried beneath his tail. For the moment, the dog was safe, and she exhaled. If she could settle Victor's return as efficiently as filing a brief, she didn't need to worry about life and death.

How much do you want to return him?

Tell your new, rich boyfriend a $100 million will do. Quite the upgrade.

Anyone's better than you.

Man's gotta eat.

Get a job.

Quaint.

Do you know any two-syllable words?

She tossed her phone on a side table.
"How much does he want?" Alessio asked.
"Too much." She bundled her hair on top of her head. "He's irrational."
Climbing from the bed, he strode across the room and wrapped her in his arms.

His weight and solidity calmed her. She had simple goals and an unwillingness to settle, but he tipped the scales toward possibilities she never considered.

"How much?" he asked.

She swallowed. "Would you believe $100 million?"

Pressing a kiss against her head, he pulled back. "I mean, five-year-olds would ask for the same amount, but the amount doesn't matter. We'll set a trap and get your dog back."

She smoothed her robe. "We're not paying a dime, right?" The thought of 'we' felt too tender. "I'm sorry I pulled you into this mess. Without me, you'd visit Martha's grave and continue on with our life."

"Hardly," he said. "Jack would find a new way to attack. I ruined his father's company."

"Like a decade ago." She frowned. "What does he want from you? An apology letter?"

He rubbed his face. "And a $100 million check. I miss Martha," he said. "I hate thinking of this mess as her legacy."

Her heart contracted. "Her art is her legacy."

"Among other things. Maybe they worked together? Maybe a partnership went wrong?"

If Martha and Jack had acted together, she would throw in the towel, hitchhike to some ragtag Idaho town and handle successions for the rest of her life. She couldn't think of an easier, more mindless career. Flopping into a chair, she crossed her arms across her chest. "He'll haunt you."

He laughed and sat at the foot of the bed. "Maybe. When are you going to eat?"

She extracted the throw pillow behind her back and hurled it at his head. For a man on the other side of forty, he moved like a cat, and she wondered how much time he spent in the gym. His muscles bulged past wiry, and some tattoos looked fresh and black. Soon, she would trace the lines and let whiskey lubricate his memories. Right now, she needed action. "When my last relationship bombed, Martha gave me space. I chalked up her silence to discretion."

"Martha couldn't spell 'discretion'."

She wished she had another pillow. "I have no idea what she did during that time. Maybe she met Jack. Maybe he targeted her to get to you."

"Why?"

"Some people are romantics," she said.

He shook his head.

"I don't understand why Martha would even talk to Jack. I mean, what did she have to gain?"

"Money," he said.

"What?"

"She never had money. Any time she failed to pay rent, I picked up the balance."

Standing, she walked toward him and tipped up his chin. "You are a softie."

He exhaled and pressed his forehead against hers. "I hate being the connection."

Breaking the repentant contact, she pressed a kiss against his lips. He tasted of coffee, and she considered abandoning the tender moment for her own caffeine. Instead, she toyed with the erratic curls behind his ear. "Martha might have met Jack at a bar, run her mouth about her rich, old pen pal and given him opportunistic ideas."

"Calling me 'old' undermines your argument," he said. "I'm not going anywhere."

"Don't be ridiculous." Stepping back, she slapped at his chest. Hitting a rock might have felt better. "The point is, we'll never know what happened between them unless we find Jack." She hated saying his name.

Alessio pressed her hand against his chest. "Nina, we'll get Victor back. If Jack killed Martha, we'll turn over the evidence to the police. I swear." He released her. "I'm definitely not relinquishing one hundred million for an overbred powder-puff."

"Victor heard you."

"Victor's ruining my vacation."

She licked her lips and pulled free. "Is that so?"

"If you keep looking at me like that," he said, "the dog can rot."

She frowned and dropped her hand. How many dogs needed a good home? Pleading brown eyes weren't fungible. Even though she couldn't help every shelter dog, she could help Victor. "So, how do you negotiate over text message?"

He shrugged into a faded rock concert T-shirt. "You make your opponent think they're winning."

Letting Jack win was the last thing on her mind. "Just like court. Lead the witness until the judge calls out your line of questioning."

He pulled on a pair of athletic shorts.

She licked her lips. A man's ass shouldn't look that good in fabric, and she doubted she could do her job with Alessio standing in the room.

"Can you string him along while I get someone to pinpoint his location?" he asked.

She tore her gaze from his glutes. "I'd rather not call him."

"Texts are fine."

She sighed and reached for her phone.

Let's try again. Good morning, dirtbag. Surrender my dog.

Waiting for a response felt like a miserable way to waste a perfectly good day. Siding up to Alessio, she watched him issue edicts by text and followed his minion's affirmative responses. She wished her firm's junior associates accepted her directions with so little pushback. "So, what's on the agenda for the day?"

He continued typing. "Kicking Charon's ass."

She recoiled. "Why?"

He stopped typing and stared. "Are you on a flight east?"

Resting a hand against her chest, she wondered if she misread the situation. "Do you want me to leave?"

He cupped her chin. "I want you chained to the bed, spread-eagled in the shower and on your knees sucking my cock."

Struggling to draw a deep breath, she swallowed. "Yes."

He dropped his hand. "In the meantime, Charon and I will reestablish our relationship boundaries."

"Have you heard of mediation?"

He worked his jaw.

"Therapy?"

Shaking his head, he jumped in place. "Don't worry. The fight will be over in a few rounds. Charon never hits right. Can you sit tight that long? Given your predilection for mischief, keeping you at my side might be the safest course of action."

Arching an eyebrow, she played along with his serious façade. "Mischief?"

He shook out his hands. "Not concerned over Charon's fate?"

She stretched her arms above her head and let her breasts peak from the robe. "He's a grown man."

He stopped the calisthenics and toward her. "Exactly — and he knows me."

Backing up, she teased how much freedom he allowed her. "What happened to dropping the violence?"

"Between the two of us, it's about respect. Charon understands the rules."

His voice resonated with sincerity, and if two grown men wanted to pummel each other in a boxing ring, she wasn't about to stop them. She walked toward the shower, let the robe slip from her shoulders and added a swing to her step. "I hope nothing distracts you during the fight. I'd hate to see something happen to your pretty face."

"I'll pretend you're not there."

Looking over her shoulder, she blew him a kiss and turned back toward the shower.

A throw pillow landed square on her ass.

Offering another shake to tempt him, she slammed the door.

* * * *

"Wouldn't a gym be more dignified?" Nina asked.

Charon laughed and dusted his hands. He unwound a length of tape and wrapped his wrist, thumb and mid-hand. "What's wrong with the lawn? Would you prefer a cage fight?"

She gasped. "People do that?"

Alessio looked up. "You really need to travel."

Throwing the chalk dust at him seemed like a satisfying reaction, but half the resort's guests surrounded the makeshift ring and would witness her infantile response. If the world's high net worth individuals wanted a once-in-a-lifetime show, they'd come to the right place. She leaned forward and blew against Alessio's neck. "You know, the cobbler was my idea."

"Liar," Charon said.

Looking over her shoulder, she winked. "Whose side are you on?"

Charon widened his stance. "What? You want me to lie."

Pulling away from her, Alessio cracking his knuckles and tossed Charon the tape. "I want you to follow orders."

"And when you're too old to boss me around?" Charon asked.

Alessio smiled. "I'll be dead."

Nina recognized the veiled threat behind his expression. Undoubtedly, Charon did, too. If he were a wise man, he would concede the fight and take whatever meatheaded punishment Alessio dealt. She moved to break the tension between the men with flattery and a promise to behave.

Alessio held up his hand. "If I step back, someone else will knock heads and keep the world's assholes from backing out of their agreements. In the corporate world, I use leverage and lawyers. With my friends, I use fists."

"Maybe friends are overrated." Shaking her head, she backed away from the pair.

Charon rolled his shoulders. "Maybe you should take up golf."

"You can be my caddy," Alessio said.

Lunging, Charon knocked him to the ground.

Someone rang the fight bell.

She climbed under the ropes. "So much for a referee."

Alessio rolled, jumped to his feet and kicked his best friend's legs out from under him.

The assembled crowd cheered.

Searching for stable ground, she stumbled in the grass and tripped over her feet.

A solicitous man helped her up, turned to his friend and handed over a wad of cash. "You were right. Alessio's slowing down."

She brushed the grass from her hands. "He'll win."

The man rubbed his chin and watched the fight. "Maybe."

Alessio and Charon circled each other on the mat.

She thought the two men would exchange blows, blacken a few eyes and settle with their arms hung over each other's shoulders. Instead, Alessio and Charon sparred with a ferocity she'd never expected. Each grunt and blow echoed in their chests, and she rooted for Alessio to pummel a man she liked and respected.

A brutal blow knocked out Alessio's breath, but he pivoted and swung a blind elbow into Charon's temple.

"This is ridiculous," she said.

"She's right," a second spectator said.

The gentleman shook his head. "It's something else entirely. Bare-knuckle boxing is brutal and deadly, but the fighters only strike with closed fists. This kicking, elbow, grappling shit" — he shook his head — "street fights draw crowds. Alessio made his first few millions kicking the shit out of his friends, and his peers remember it. Hell, I'd hand over a few million to avoid this kind of beat down."

"A few? I'd hand over ten. Assholes like you would bet on my downfall."

The two spectators laughed.

"You can see them pause and consider strategy. With gloves, they could hit each other as hard as they wanted, wherever they wanted. This style is slower and more methodical."

Alessio landed a solid blow.

The speaker flinched. "Without strategy, they'll break their hands."

The second man nodded. "Just like business, pick your shots and hope they land."

Both men grinned.

She watched Alessio and Charon with renewed interest. Their sweat-slicked, bloodied bodies looked savage and beautiful, but she wouldn't sanction a cockfight. Why would she cheer for this spectacle? What good would Alessio be at the end of the match? If the blows lasted more than ten minutes, he'd need electrolytes and a plastic surgeon to recover. She hoped door number two hid a hyperbaric chamber.

"Fuck, nobody is like him," the first spectator said.

"Thank God."

She backed away from the ring and second-guessed her presence at the resort. If someone took her to a street fight, she'd expect a secret warehouse location, boisterous crowds and illegal bookmakers. Beer and blood would stain the floor. Instead, the men and women crowding around the makeshift ring ran the world's most successful companies. They flinched and moaned, but they stood back and let two men pummel themselves for fun.

Glancing away, she found Vivian and Damon standing to the side sipping lemonade. Vivian cradled her pregnancy and Damon laughed aloud at an onlooker's joke. Didn't anyone sympathize with the pain Alessio and Charon endured? Nina backed deeper into the crowd.

Charon fell to all fours and hung his head.

Alessio stood nearby, shifting his weight and panting. "You yield?"

Raising his head, Charon took a deep breath and struggled to his feet. "Fuck you."

The crowd cheered.

The next blow landed hard enough that she turned away.

"Miss Nina," a woman said, "are you ready for the spa?"

Blinking, she focused on the gray-haired woman and her embroidered resort uniform. "The spa?"

"Mr. Chen booked you a treatment room for the rest of the afternoon."

Considering her options, she glanced at the crowd of bloodthirsty spectators and the smooth-skinned older woman offering her an afternoon of Zen. "Yeah, the spa sounds good." Turning her back on the fight, she walked toward the resort.

The woman stayed one step behind her. "Just through those doors on the left."

Pulling open a French door, she stepped into the building. The sound of moving water and soft, instrumental music surrounded her. A diffuser filled the room with lavender and bergamot. She closed her eyes. "How did he know I would need to escape?"

A sharp pain in her neck brought her to her knees and darkness closed in. She desperately tried to breathe through the lethargy and reach for her phone, but the world's weight pressed her toward the ground.

The older woman knocked her feet from under her. "What you need may surprise you."

Stumbling, she hit her head. As the darkness engulfed her, she hung onto the hope Alessio would come. He'd coerced her into the trip, but she'd let herself fall. Whoever knocked her to the floor had abandoned their qualms long ago. Her eyes felt too heavy to open and she moaned. She should have stayed to watch Alessio win.

Chapter Twenty

Pulling Charon to his feet, Alessio slapped his back and swung his arm over Charon's shoulders. "You put up a good fight."

Charon cleared his nose and spat on the grass, but he accepted the crutch. "You're an asshole."

"I know." Bearing Charon's weight, he pulled him toward the pair of chairs flanking a cooler of water. He took as much pleasure in the fight as he took in taking down a peer's company, but arbitrating contracts and meting out consequences kept his world turning on a predictable, trustworthy axis. The idiot would think twice about disobeying him for cobbler.

Transferring his weight to the chair, Charon winced, reached for a water bottle and downed the contents.

Alessio kept his mouth shut about recovery techniques.

Tossing the bottle to the grass, Charon pulled the cooler between his legs. He splashed his face clear of blood and plunged his hands into the icy bath.

Nodding, he turned and faced the crowd. He rolled through a few punches, but nobody in attendance would doubt his presence. As the adrenaline subsided, the effects of Charon's blows would remain. By mid-afternoon, he'd feel as aching, stiff and drained as a marathon runner completing a race. Severe headaches were common. So were IV infusions. Reaching for a towel, he wiped his face clean and stole a sports drink from Charon's ice bath. "Good show."

"Fuck you."

During the fight, nothing hurt. Charon knew the rules and had accepted the match. The moment Alessio had landed the first hit, he'd stopped thinking and started reacting. Through every deal and altercation, he trusted Charon's abilities. That's why the man's disobedience meant so much. "If you spent less time at the firing range, you'd remember how to fight."

Charon looked up. "If I spent less time guarding your ass, I wouldn't have to fight."

He adjusted his stance. "Ready to quit?"

"Hell no."

Smiling, he looked away. He put his body through a lot and now was the time to rest and heal. As soon as he found Nina, he'd take her upstairs and let her tend his wounds. Whether she interpreted the challenge with butterfly stitches or a well-deserved blow job depended entirely on her preferences.

Damon walked up. "I thought you might have been down and out."

He stretched his jaw. "Is that so?"

"Charon has a few pounds on you."

He snorted. "Charon should spend less time in the kitchen."

Damon laughed.

Turning from the good-natured ribbing, he scanned the crowd. Tomorrow would be the most painful day. Sparring, running, jumping rope, hitting the bag and ball work prepared his body and his mind for competition. If his day didn't end in the ring, it ended in a conference room. In his youth, imposing his will on people required strength and quick reflexes. Now, it required mental acuity, ironclad data and fearsome resources. He still liked to fight.

The ring felt like familiar ground. A willing opponent grounded his senses and focused his mind. Too often, his business deals felt like mercenary hits. If buying the company outright wasn't an option, he shorted the stock and released his data to the ether. His success depended on a cutthroat approach to competition. Given clues, other players followed the stench of rotten meat and cut their losses. He fought. At the end of the matches, he retired to his hotel hidey-holes and felt like he'd survived a car accident. Other days, he celebrated his conquests with a drink.

A doctor approached carrying a medical bag. She cupped Charon's face. "I heard you were handsome."

"Lies," Charon said.

"After I stitch your face, those lies might be true."

Alessio laughed and slung a towel over his shoulder. As his heart rate decelerated, his field of vision widened. The conference guests milled over cocktails and passed appetizers. Whatever scheduled activities came next would have to wait. He scanned the crowd for his associates. They mingled with executives and did their job. He looked for Nina.

Vivian stood in front of a mist fan.

The siren, Gabby, lounged with a cocktail and a bevy of admirers.

"Where the fuck is she?" he asked.

A server passed by.

Grabbing the man's arm, he gritted his teeth. "Where's Nina?"

"Ugh, sir, I don't know," the server said.

Grunting, he released the man, walked back to the makeshift ring and stood on a chair to leverage the additional height. Scores of people met his gaze, but none of them sported Nina's gold-streaked hair, intelligent eyes or defiant chin. "Nina!"

The crowd glanced from left to right.

"Fuck." He climbed down from the chair and marched toward the resort.

"Great fight."

"I never doubted."

"Vicious," a woman said.

Ignoring every comment, he pushed open the resort's back doors. Making his way to reception, he called the suite, but nobody answered. Slamming down the receiver, he stared at the receptionist. "Get me security, *now*."

"Yes, Mr. Chen! Right away."

Bracing his elbow on the desk, he swore and rubbed his temples. He could feel a headache pressing against his eyes. He needed hydration and he needed it fast.

Charon hobbled across the polished floor holding his shirt. "Are you the savage personified?"

Shrugging into the shirt, he winced. "Nina's not here."

"Did she make a run for it?"

He frowned. "I don't think so." This morning, she had seemed content to explore the limits of their truce and her place in his world. He would consider her preferences, and she would embrace his lifestyle. What was so fucking hard about spending time with a billionaire? He closed his eyes and took calming breaths. If she ran, he would respect her decision. If someone had kidnapped her, woe to the idiot who took his woman. The silence stretched.

Nina was never silent.

He didn't need security footage to know she'd left the premises under duress. He pounded his fist against the desk. "Dammit!"

The receptionist's ornate pencil holder fell to its side, rolled off the desk and clattered to the floor.

He picked up the piece and slammed it down. "Get everyone together. We'll review the security footage and find out what happened. I have Jack's phone number, and Stefano's already tracing the signal. If that wannabe asshole took Nina, he'll join his father in his grave."

Charon leaned close. "Murder's off limits."

He brushed past him. "So's Nina."

The ride to the top floor never took this long. Every floor erased his hope he would find her safe in a bubble bath, drunk on champagne and waiting for him to scratch an itch. Closing his eyes, he took deep breaths. Nina's mob accusations hit home. His mother had refused to return to Italy for three very compelling reasons — inefficiencies plagued Italy, her family would ostracize Eitan and she feared for Alessio's life. How far had Alessio come from his ancestor's sins?

The old Italian families who refused ransom requests received locks of hair, severed appendages and heartfelt, grainy videos to sway their cooperation. When they still refused to pay, they found their loved ones in rubbish dumps, abandoned car trunks and nameless fields.

"Don't pay," the authorities said.

The next families paid. Firms sprang up offering to broker deals between criminals and exhausted family members.

Sometimes the payoffs worked, and sometimes they failed. To stymie ransom payments, the authorities introduced a law blocking the bank accounts of victims' relatives. Families stopped reporting kidnappings.

Alessio understood their willingness to pay, but he wouldn't give authorities a chance to interfere with Nina's abduction. He had offered her his protection, but he should have protected her from himself. No matter how she empathized with Jack, he connected the dots between her and the murderer.

The elevator doors opened.

"Victor." To resolve this mess, he would build an altar to the dog's namesake saint. Given his luck, Saint Victor was probably the saint of sinners and thieves. Why hadn't Nina adopted the patron saint of money?

He scanned the suite and found it empty. "Fucking hell!" Turning, he punched a hole in the wall, but the damage did as much good as punching Charon's face. Picking up his phone from a console table, he called Charon. "She's not here."

"When you're ready, we'll meet you downstairs."

Beating the shit out of Jack wouldn't be enough. "I'm ready."

* * * *

On the lower floor, the men in Alessio's administration kept their gazes on the richly carpeted floor. Each man ran a crew skilled in economic assessment, data analytics and information gathering, but they reported to him. By letting Nina slip away, they'd let him down. He lowered himself into a chair and faced his family.

Charon sported three stitches and a busted nose, but he held his head high.

Jason stepped forward. "I had my eyes on..."

Stefano swallowed. "Couldn't have been over thirty seconds..."

Driver crossed his arms over his chest. "I don't know why she didn't scream."

The three men spoke over each other.

He held up his hand to stop the excuses. Running his investment firm with an iron fist yielded results, but it wouldn't rescue Nina. "Tell me what you know."

"An older woman led her toward the spa," Stefano said. "Ten minutes later, the laundry service arrived. The woman pushed the cart up a ramp, closed the rear doors and climbed into the passenger seat. Presumably, Nina left in a load of towels and robes."

Nick snickered.

Charon pointed toward the door. "Out."

Paling, Nick cleared his throat.

Alessio refocused on Stefano.

"GPS coordinates put the number you gave me in Sawtooth National Forest, outside a town called Stanley. The nearest point on the map is Redfish Inlet Campground." Stefano projected a map on the conference room wall. "Nothing exists out there but ten-thousand-foot mountains, a few rustic cabins and five miles of lakefront."

"Well, we can assume he didn't take her to the travel cabins," Driver said. "Only an idiot would be stupid enough to hide a hostage amid nosy retirees and gossipy maids."

"Jack's stupid, but I won't underestimate desperation." Alessio narrowed his gaze and traced the map's contour lines. He assumed most cell phone carriers would work in 'hot spots' around the lake and cabins, but the topography would distort the signal. Federal legislation required wireless service providers to improve accuracy for emergency response. GPS and satellites in low-Earth orbit didn't care about topography. If Stefano said the Jack's phone was on the shores of Redfish Lake, Alessio believed him. "Has the phone moved?"

"Not since yesterday," Stefano said.

"And only the older woman left with the laundry cart?" he asked.

Driver drummed his fingers on the table. "Someone had to drive the truck to the resort."

Jason turned his laptop screen to reveal the local paper. "Big to-do in town. Local woman found dead behind cleaning service. Residents demand sheriff stop policing high-profile visitors and focus on working-class Idaho residents."

Charon looked out of the window. "We have a big problem."

Stefano stood. "Is the sheriff on site today?"

Driver flexed his fingers. "Who do you think rang the fight bell?"

Alessio ignored the banter and followed the roads leading into the valley around Redfish Lake. He'd fished the Wood River Valley and Big Wood River. The surroundings lakes froze solid during winter and warmed up to sixty-give degree Fahrenheit by late summer. He doubted Jack would choose a place that dropped fifty degrees below zero. The man would hole up in a permanent dwelling situated near a road for easy access, but far from tourists and ambitious fishermen. "Are there roads to the southern half of the lake?"

"No," Stefano said, "but the signal hasn't moved."

"He has access to a boat." Shaking his head, he wondered how to approach. "I don't have time to climb a mountain and come in the back door."

"Use a helicopter," Driver said.

He considered the option and shook his head. Given the noise, Jack might overreact. Standing, he looked at Charon. "We're going fishing."

Charon winced, but he stood.

"I could come and help monitor the cell phone," Stefano said.

"Not a chance." Driver crossed his arms. "We know who runs this show."

"Fuck off," Jason said.

Alessio stepped away from the bickering men, but he paused before he left the room. "I'll be back in a day or two. In the meantime, nobody knows Nina or I left the premises. If they ask, we're loved up and unavailable."

"And if they really ask?"

More than any of his other associates, Driver pushed back against his demands, and he appreciated the man's confidence. "Feed them shit until they balk."

Driver cracked his knuckles.

He turned and looked out over the men and women who'd converged on the resort. They came to Idaho to make deals and expand their companies. Without his approval, their deals would stall out. His bar tab, on the other hand, would balloon. His associates could handle the crowd.

* * * *

Off the Sandy Beach Boat Ramp, kayakers and paddle boarders milled around the lake's clear water. In an hour, the sun would set and daytime activities would conclude. Until that happened, cars and trucks filled the parking lot, children played in the shallows and hikers checked their trail maps. Alessio turned the borrowed white pickup truck toward the parking lot and put the vehicle in park. He watched a ranger directing traffic and facilitating boat checks on behalf of the sheriff's office.

Charon unbuckled his seatbelt. "You have a plan."

Pulling down a baseball hat, he nodded. He'd borrowed one of Nina's hair elastics and shoved his hair under the cap. Without his mane, he looked like any other forty-year-old man headed out onto the water. Charon would get him close to Jack and would keep watch over the boat. "I tried to reason with Jack, but he ignored my text messages."

"He's waiting for you to crack."

He appreciated the warning, but he didn't make it this far in life for some two-bit asshole to get the upper hand. He climbed from the truck and rolled his shoulders.

The ranger walked up to the vehicle. White hair and square glasses belied his age. "Where are you two headed?"

"Fishing," Charon said.

Straightening his glasses, the ranger frowned. "Where's your gear?"

Alessio appreciated the Park Service. He'd heard a west coast ranger celebrated her hundredth birthday while on patrol. The man standing in front of him might not be far off the benchmark, but he didn't have time for geriatric pleasantries. He stepped forward. "Have you seen anyone at the inlet campground?"

"Passes are $14 per day for a single site. With a senior discount, the pass is $7."

He moderated his breathing. "Noted."

The ranger cocked his head. "Where's your camping gear?"

"Why? You want to join us?" he asked.

Charon cleared his throat.

Noting the rebuke, he smiled as if he had all the time in the world. If law enforcement did their job, he wouldn't have to deliver kidnappers and murders trussed and bagged for processing. His arms felt like lead weights, but retrieving Nina demanded everything he had. "Good eye. My buddy's bringing the gear."

"You got a fishing license?" The ranger crossed his arms. "Hate to send you all the way back to Stanley for paperwork."

He pulled out his phone and checked the service. His satellite connection held and no news from the team assured him that Jack had stayed put on the other side of the lake. He turned the phone toward the park's protector. "The Idaho Department of Fishing and Game's website is top-notch."

"Huh." Shaking his head, the ranger walked off.

A faded blue van pulled into the parking lot towing a small motorboat.

The truck's driver slowed.

Charon raised a hand.

The driver waved back, pulled up alongside Alessio's truck and jumped out of the van.

The man looked like a cross between a circus bear and a grunge lumberjack. Plaid flannel hung open over a dingy wife beater and holes in his jeans gaped at the knees. A large, gold cross necklace flashed over the woolen ensemble and a glass vial clattered beside it. Alessio had never seen a man's hairline start at his scalp and continue right past his collarbone. If a west coast hipster fled for Idaho's woods, solar radiation amplified the product.

"Ridley Waltson, pleasure to meet you." The man stuck out his hand and pumped Charon's grip. "Love to see the tourism dollars flowing back into the community. You know, I once rescued the King of Jordan's motorcade? Ran out of gas. Can you believe it? You'd need a dull knife to cut the tension between working-class Idaho and its high-profile visitors, but you guys want a boat and tackle gear?" He slapped his thigh. "You got it!"

Alessio leaned toward Charon. "How much did you pay this guy?"

Charon smiled. "It's your money."

"So, too much."

Charon rolled his shoulders and absorbed Ridley's banter.

Alessio inspected the boat. Every time he lifted his arm, his body ached and his pounding headache would only grow worse. When he was younger, he woke up the day after a fight and went back to training. These days, he stretched and soaked away his aches. Riding a decrepit boat over Redfish Lake to save Nina hadn't been in his game plan, but he would save the impetuous, hard-headed woman.

"Well, we sure appreciate the gear," Charon said. "When we're done, we'll let you know."

"Yep. Sure. Anytime," Ridley said. "I'll swing right by and pick it up. Oh, and don't worry about the fuel. It's on me." He winked and stuck out his thumb.

Charon matched the gesture.

Ridley backed the boat toward the launch, released the restraints and let the vessel bob in the water.

The sheriff sauntered over. "Ridley, that you?"

"I, uh, got a prior engagement." Ridley gunned the truck's engine and fled.

Alessio climbed aboard the boat and inspected the engine. Modern outboards started like a car. All you had to do was tilt them down and turn the key. Ridley obviously prided himself on this vessel, but it wasn't modern. The carbureted, two-stroke engine looked like it ditched maintenance intervals for a grease addiction. Beneath a dusting of mildew, the vessel wore its cold, cantankerous crown with pride. He would be lucky if he could get it to start.

He checked the tank for clear vents, tilted down the engine to send the fuel to the carburetors and squeezed the primer bulb. "Dude, you coming or you leaving the fishing to me?" He shouted loud enough for the sheriff, Charon, Ridley and everyone in sight to hear.

Charon waved, climbed into the boat and lowered himself on top of an ice bucket. "Ready."

Advancing the throttle, Alessio turned the key, pushed the choke and cranked the engine.

The engine sputtered to life.

Releasing the choke, he returned the throttle to neutral and let the boat putter away from the dock. In the latter part of the nineteenth century, prospectors and trappers established Stanley, Ketchum and Sawtooth City. Exhausted by the Civil War, settlers logged the hills for firewood, mineshafts supports and homestead beams. Nature bounced back, but somewhere in the hills, Jack hid out like a two-bit gangster. He'd had enough of Jack's comic book dreams.

Charon opened the ice chest and sank his right arm to the shoulder.

"That bad?" he asked above the engine noise.

"Can barely feel it," Charon said.

He clapped a hand on his back. "I'm sorry. Maybe we need a new sport."

"I know the rules."

He dropped his hand and scanned the lake's southern end. "After we retrieve Nina, we need to talk about the next twenty years."

Charon jerked up his head. "You retiring?"

He shook his head and let the cool, clear breeze open his senses. Black and white granite, tall pine trees and sandy shores reminded him how new and desolate land could feel. Given the right incentive, a man could turn this landscape into a goldmine or drive it into a wasteland. Nobody he worked with would choose the wasteland. Charon had a Patagonian *estancia* waiting for him, but first, he would help retrieve Nina. "You're getting a promotion."

"Next time, let's stick with a performance review," Charon said.

He laughed, revved up the engine and debated whether he would return to the resort in time for a steak dinner. "When you look at what we know, Jack has a pattern. He preys on older women because he doesn't have resources to attract young ones."

"Martha was a tool," Charon said.

He bit back his frustration. "She was a skilled painter."

"I'm sorry."

"Jack won't have another chance to cause harm." Cruising straight down the middle of Redfish Lake, he almost hoped Jack saw through his disguise and met him on the lakeshore. Beneath his vest, he wore a gun, and he would use a clear shot to save Nina. He lived off absolutes, and she respected the letter of the law. Brokering deals for decades had taught him to go for what he wanted, and he wanted her wit, her exhibitionism and her fine ass back in one piece.

"You going to waltz in and grab her?" Charon asked.

"Not a high chance of success." He slowed the motor. "I don't know why he took her. I'll pay to find out."

"He knows you love her. He wants to hurt you."

"Maybe." He swallowed his emotions.

"That bad?"

He cut the motor. "As bad as it could be."

The boat drifted in silence.

He didn't need to define how much Nina meant to him, but if given a choice, Charon should look to her welfare first. "Listen... If things go south..."

Holding up a hand, Charon stopped him. "We're all coming home."

"You don't know what I wanted to say."

Charon barked out a laugh. "Shove it. At heart, you're a romantic asshole."

He laughed. "And you're just an asshole."

"She probably wants kids."

Revving the motor seemed like an appropriate response. Instead, he plucked a pole from Ridley's stockpile and cast a line. "Probably." Shading his eyes, he looked toward the jagged mountains and waited.

Beyond Redfish Lake, the Salmon River flowed north to meet the Snake River, the Columbia River and the Pacific Ocean. Countless sockeye salmon once made the nine-hundred-mile pilgrimage from the ocean to their valley spawning grounds, but fewer and fewer returned. The National Marine Fisheries Service established a local hatchery and stocked the lake with sockeye salmon, but trout, steelhead and Chinook salmon populated the lake as well. Alessio needed a lure, and a shiny fish wouldn't be enough to tempt Jack. He pulled out his phone.

$10 million for Nina, $1 for the dog.

Aren't you clever? $100MM.

Waiting for Stefano to confirm the GPS coordinates, Alessio felt a tug, reeled in his line and found a fat bull trout dancing from the hook. He tossed the fish back into the water.

His phone vibrated.

After pulling it from his pocket, he read the message confirming Jack's location. "All right, let's go."

Charon motored the boat to the shore and tied up next to a small, aluminum canoe.

Brown picnic tables, spacious fire rings and vintage site markers comprised a tiny, backcountry campground. A single tent occupied a campsite. Alessio tied up the boat and climbed onto the shore.

A man, woman and two children stepped from the shadows behind the tent.

The family either had a portable power source for their tablets or they held off watching their downloads until they exhausted the backcountry's towering, jagged beauty. Alessio lifted his had in greeting. "Nice day!"

Meandering toward the shore, the father hooked his thumbs in his pants' belt loops. "I didn't expect to see anyone out here. You guys backpacking up into the high country or claiming a camping spot for the night?"

"Just a spot of fishing," he said.

The man peered into the boat. "Catch anything?"

He looked at Charon. "Not yet."

Charon rolled his eyes.

He turned toward the camper. "Anyone else out here?"

"Nah," the man said.

"That's good. We'll take a site on the other side of the campground. We wouldn't want to disturb you or your family. You guys have a nice afternoon."

The man laughed. "Don't mind us. A trail heads up to Redfish Lake Creek Canyon. It has a few scenic views and side trails. If you're really feeling lazy, take the easy, short trail up to Lily Lake. Even my kids can do it. Bit more trash than I expected" — the man shrugged — "but we'll pack out what we can carry."

Alessio itched to abandon the small talk.

"That your canoe?" Charon asked.

The father wriggled his nose. "Figured a ranger left it and hitched a ride on the resort's pontoon."

Charon tipped the canoe to the side. "Pretty clean to be abandoned."

Alessio stared at the boat. Lazy, short and easy summed up the man wrecking his weekend. "Which way to Lily Lake?"

The father pointed toward the southern end of the campground. "Look for a small sign that points to the 'Lily Pond' and 'Waterfall' trail. Take a right and you'll find a granite bowl filled with lily pads. It's about the cutest thing in the mountains. If you keep going uphill, you'll pass an old log cabin and an overlook directly across from a ledge waterfall."

He moved to follow the trail. He'd bet ten million he'd find Nina and Jack's trash. The man probably ate instant noodles, drank weak beer and figured he was roughing it. Turning, Alessio considered the camper's family. "How're you getting back to the boat launch?"

"Oh! There's a shuttle. The Hiker Boat Shuttle Service comes by once a day and checks on us." He slapped his knee. "Fourteen dollars one-way, nineteen dollars for a round trip and three dollars for dogs. Can you imagine bringing your dog?"

"I can imagine a lot of things," he said. "Why don't you borrow our boat and take the kids out fishing. You know how to run an outboard?"

The father straightened. "Sure."

Charon started the engine. "Wear your life jackets and try not to sink it."

"You sure?" The man scratched his head.

Alessio nodded.

"Kids!" The father turned and beckoned his family toward the boat.

Handing Charon his phone, Alessio patted his gun and the myriad of supplies he'd stashed in his pocketed vest. Ridley's venison jerky didn't make the cut, but a pocketknife, a first-aid kit and a powerful painkiller did. If Nina needed the painkiller, he'd make sure Jack met a quick end. "Keep texting the asshole. Start at ten million and work your way up until he caves or I tell you to stop. Draw it out."

Charon pocketed the phone. "You're not really going to pay him."

He started forward on the trail. "I'll pay him, but whether he lives to collect the money depends on his decision-making skills."

"You're serious," Charon said.

He stepped into the scattered underbrush. "I've never been more serious in my life."

Chapter Twenty-One

In the dilapidated shed, Nina cuddled a sleeping Victor. A rusty, corrugated roof offered peeks of the dazzling Milky Way. A full moon cast shadows, and she imagined soaking up the starry skies under better conditions.

Victor stirred and barked in his sleep.

"Shh." She stroked his matted, white fur. He needed a bath, a bag of dog treats and a soft bed, but given proper care, he would recover. She wondered if she could say the same about herself. She smelled like dried sweat, her tongue swelled from thirst and mosquitos feasted on her exposed skin. "We're going to make it."

A large animal moved through the underbrush.

She froze and reassessed her statement. Chipmunks and squirrels could nibble at the shed's edges without bothering her, but she had no protection against a predator. Peering through a hole in the wall, she caught a glimpse of fur and fangs in the shadows.

Victor raised his head and howled.

"Shh!"

Oblivious to her request, he jumped off her lap.

His furious barking kept the animal at bay.

"Shut the fuck up!" Jack yelled from the cabin.

"Jack! Jack!" Her throat burned. "This is inhumane!" Her screams went unanswered, and she slumped against the shed well. "He's the biggest predator of all, isn't he?" Pulling Victor back to her lap, she stroked his fur. "Don't mind the noises. It was probably a deer or a big, sweet-natured, lumbering moose."

Victor cocked his furry, white head.

A claw raked against the shed.

Jumping, she scrambled toward the shed's center. Something warm, fetid and alive investigated the outbuilding. Something with paws. She pickup up a rusted tool and banged against the wall. "Go away!"

The animal retreated and lumbered into the darkness.

Mosquitos buzzed, but the ensuing silence felt like a reprieve. She'd pick Jack over a bear but leaving her outside to feed the wildlife accomplished none his goals. "Doesn't he need to keep us alive?"

Victor whined.

Shaking her head, she closed her eyes and replayed her journey to the dry shed.

At an empty boat ramp, Jack had unloaded her from a nondescript white van, kept a gun to her back and prodded her into a canoe beneath a blazing mid-afternoon sun.

Her feet and hands had remained bound, but she'd screamed to draw attention to her plight.

He'd jammed the gun into her ribs. *"You do it again and I'll shoot you. You'll bleed out for days and I'll still collect my money to lead him to your body. Your choice."*

Across the lake, families picnicked near a parking lot and kids splashing in the water. If Jack shot her, would the echo travel? She debated risking her life for a Good Samaritan rescue.

Jack tightened his grip.

Resigned, she hoped Alessio had the common sense to call the police. Kidnapping dogs fell short of cross-country intervention, but kidnapping women deserved attention.

Pulling up at a campground, Jack had climbed out of the canoe, lifted her from the aluminum hull and deposited her in the shallow water. Unable to move, she'd sat in the frigid pool and waited. A single tent occupied the campground, but nobody had unzipped the flap to investigate the site's new neighbor. She'd tried another scream.

Jack had pulled the gun from his waistband and backhanded her.

She'd tasted blood. Spitting into the water, she'd flipped her hair out of her eyes. "Do you even know how to shoot a gun?"

He'd paused. "Would you like me to demonstrate?"

"I'd like you to leave me alone and disappear."

Smiling, he'd pulled her to her feet. "I should have known Martha was useless."

She'd hung her head.

"But you? You're golden." Leaning down, he'd cut the ties at her feet, turned her toward the bank and pushed her toward shore. "The hike's not long."

She'd stumbled through the woods and tried to break every twig she'd encountered. Afraid local law enforcement needed an engraved map, she'd kicked rocks, dug her sandals into the mud and spit out the moisture remaining in her mouth. Any scout worth his or her salt could follow her progress up the mountain.

"He doesn't love you," Jack had said.

"Love doesn't matter. He's too stubborn to let you win."

Jack had laughed. "I'm counting on it."

Keeping her mouth closed had seemed like a prudent response. Until she'd found a way out of this mess, antagonizing her captor made little sense. Once she had her freedom, she'd have plenty to say to the idiot who thought he could trade her life for his ease. "I should have confronted you at the masquerade."

"Oh, we all enjoyed your show." He'd laughed. "You should know Alessio only cares about money. My father ran PIN Networks for a decade, and it was a leading-edge telecommunications company. I remember going up to his office as a boy, staring out of the windows at the other high rises and thinking, 'Wow, my old man built this place.' Your new fuck buddy took one look at the balance sheet and decided he'd seen enough. He didn't do my father the courtesy of asking him to explain himself. Two years later, my parents and I shared a rented condo with cockroaches."

She'd crinkled a handful of pine needles and scattered them on the ground. "Sounds like your old man didn't manage his money. Who burns through a nest egg in two years?"

"He put everything he had into that company! A year later, Alessio's goon killed him."

She'd sighed. "And he left nothing for you. Pity."

Jack had raised his gun.

"Go, on, Jack. Hit me again. Keep dragging strangers into your twisted revenge scheme."

Lowering his arm, he'd exhaled. "You're just a woman. I never had a plan. I met Martha at a swanky hotel bar. One of those black and white places with a markup so high you wonder if customers have ever priced a bottle of gin at a grocery store. She sipped her martini and ran her mouth about the man who owned the place. Funny, I realized I knew him too."

"But he didn't know you." She'd wet her lips. "Alessio didn't know Michael had a son."

"Well, he did." Pushing her into motion, he'd followed. "I fucked that bitch and camped out at her condo for a few days. I gave her everything I had and lured her into an introduction, but she'd folded. She couldn't do it, could she?"

Sitting down on the trail had seemed like a reasonable response, but she wouldn't submit. How many women reached for the moon and found themselves pushing fifty with nothing but a midlife crisis to keep them warm? Strong women embraced their community, excelled at work and left their mark in the world. Weak ones waited and prayed for a Hail Mary. Nina didn't blame Martha for taking advantage of Jack, but she regretted missing the weakness beneath Martha's spontaneity and joyous laughter. She could have done more to help her friend. "Martha used you, didn't she?"

"I've never met a woman who could hold her course."

"And your mother?" she'd asked.

"Dead."

She'd recoiled. "By your hand?"

"She drank herself stupid, wandered into the night and drowned in a shallow pond behind the shit condo complex we called home."

Biting her tongue, she'd wondered if he'd told her the truth. She'd scanned his face for a clue to his honesty.

He'd stared back.

His eyes had looked as bleak and forlorn as she could imagine. Growing up under her grandmother's care had saved her life, but Jack had withered and nobody had remained to nurture him. She wasn't about to take up his cause. If she died in this granite wilderness, she'd wanted him to remember her humanity. "I'm sorry."

"Sympathy won't save you," he'd said. "I'll take the lead. If you run, I'll shoot."

"So much for the human race." She'd focused on the rising path. Above the first tree line, jagged rocks jutted from the earth. He'd directed her through a valley of massive rock walls filled with fissures. Piles of crumbled boulders made hillocks, but a thin, dirt trail snaked through the obstacles. She'd hoped the ground would open up and swallow her whole.

Twenty minutes later, he'd stopped at a rustic log cabin.

Weathered, gray plywood had shielded the windows and moss had grown on the old roof, but someone had kept shrubs from encroaching on the abandoned property. She'd put her money on the Park Service.

He'd walked past the cabin and opened the door to a leaning shed.

She'd recognized the corrugated metal and run toward the building.

Standing back, Jack had revealed Victor in a crate.

The dog had yapped and growled.

She'd sunk to her knees next to the snarling animal. Hands behind her back, she'd shoved her face close to the wire cage. "Shh. I'm going to take care of you."

Victor had barked and lunged for the cage wall.

Fearing survival mode had kept him in fight mode, she'd made soft, lullaby sounds and bore his attack behind the rigid wires.

Jack had slammed shut the door and clicked a lock.

Trapped in the darkness, she'd exhaled.

Victor had collapsed to his stomach.

"Hey, I'm still here."

Small holes in the roof let in rays of sunlight, but the dark, oppressive shed felt way too small. Enclosed in the patchy cave, she'd caught the filthy crate's stench and given thanks the structure protected Victor from becoming a tasty, overbred snack. "Hey, pretty boy. We're in this together." Turning, she'd left her tied hands near the crate wall and waited.

The spent animal had raised his head, sniffed and licked her palm.

She'd felt his warm, moist breath and scratched his chin. "You put up a good fight."

Victor had huffed.

Hours later, she wondered if she would be the main course for whatever animal prowled the night. Rising to her knees, she shuffled around the shed and searched again for a tool to free her hands. She hadn't spent a lot of time outside of New York, but pictures of run-down settler shacks had made her history books. At this point, she didn't care if the shack's prior residents had logged for railroad ties or clear-cut the entire national forest. Somewhere in the shed, a rusted tool waited. Small rodents scurried through the shadows and spider webs wisped against her legs like ghostly hands. She kept probing through the patchwork shadows.

When her fingers grazed the coarse, speckled patina of rusted metal, she bit back tears. Rubbing the ties binding her hands against the metal, she hoped the old tool freed her constraints. An hour later, the ties popped and blood dripped down her wrists, but she could roll her shoulders. Climbing over the dusty mess, she pried open Victor's crate and held out her hand.

He sniffed her palm, whined and crept from inside.

The moment he stepped free, she clutching him to her chest and sighed. "I'm sorry. Neither of us deserved this mess." Setting the dog down, she climbed on top of his crate and tried to pry the roof off the shed. Despite the roof's brittle appearance, the material held fast. "Help me!" Her rough, guttural voice added urgency to her cry. "Please!"

Nobody answered.

Victor cowered in the corner.

She retreated from the roof. Slumping to the ground, she wrapped her arms around her knees and hung her head.

Victor edged closer.

His soft, plaintive whines rallied her reserves. Escaping Jack meant more than her freedom. Victor deserved a home, and Martha deserved vindication. If she didn't incriminate the man who abducted her, he would harm someone else. Lifting her head, she rubbed her eyes and held out her hand. "I'm all spent, too. Let's rest."

Victor nestled against her side.

His tight, warm body near her thigh affirmed her obligations. Even if she squeezed him through a hole in the roof, he wouldn't survive the wilderness.

Her body demanded food and water, and Victor needed the same. Jack had as much empathy as a boulder. Taking deep breaths, she listened to the swaying trees, closed her eyes and debated how far she would go. Ideally, Alessio called the police and Jack ended up in a padded cell. If all else failed, she would save her strength, claw out Jack's eyes and leave him to the crows. He would do the same for her.

* * * *

Later that night, Nina awoke, stood and peered through the shed roof. Beyond the confined space, countless stars blazed. She smiled and soaked up the beauty.

Lightning stuck nearby.

Jumping away from the opening, she inhaled the smell of freshly cracked timber and fresh ozone.

Victor whined.

She scooped up the dog and held him against her chest. "We're going to be okay."

Lightning cracked again.

"We're in a fucking Easy-Bake Oven." She heard movement outside the shed. "Jack, you piece of shit, I need water! Stop treating me like a caged animal!"

"Well, I'm glad you haven't given up." Alessio's voice filtered through cracks in the shed's rear wall.

She gasped.

"Go ahead. Keep making demands. At least I know you're alive."

His voice sounded like velvet-clad steel, and she wanted to flee the metal cage and collapse into his arms. Every question in her mind dissipated. He would get her out of this mess and have a plan to deal with Jack. The plan's finale teased her conscious, but he'd come to save her, and she refused to look back.

He slid a water bottle beneath the wall.

She gulped down the water, poured some into a cupped palm and gave Victor a sip. As the dog lapped at her hands, his matted hair brushed her fingers. "He's one of the good guys. Play nice, okay?"

A low scratching sound filtered through the old metal.

Victor scrambled from her side and pawed at the walls.

"What are you doing?" she asked.

331

"Digging," Alessio said.

At this rate, she might die of hunger before he and Victor made contact. Looking for the implement that freed her hands, she prepared to chip in.

The cabin door opened and banged against the log walls with a sickening thud.

"Can't sleep with all this racket!"

She froze and dropped the tool in the near darkness. "Jack."

Victor's frenzied digging increased.

Alessio made a soft, shushing sound.

Terrified the men would harm one another, she tossed the water bottle into the shed's deepest corner and scooted toward the shed door. "Come on, Jack! Let me out so we can find a solution. PIN Networks isn't obsolete. You made your point."

Jack laughed. "You have no idea."

She listened. Somewhere between the cabin and the shed, Jack apparently took a piss. "You know Alessio won't pay. I'm nothing to him."

"You're stupider than I thought. If I sign a non-disclosure agreement, he's offering me twenty million. Either you're good at sucking dick or the man hates to lose."

His backhanded compliment fell flat. "Jack, can I have water? Food? Victor's hungry."

"Fuck off."

The cabin door slammed. Jack had gone back inside.

Edging toward Victor's tiny hole and the memory of Alessio's voice, she gripped the rusted tool and chipped away at the packed earth. "Twenty million?"

"Charon has my phone. By now, I thought he'd be up to fifty," Alessio said.

She clapped her hand over her mouth. "You're not really going to pay Jack."

Alessio's digging paused. "I'll pay him, but I doubt he'll live to retrieve it."

"Alessio…"

Lightning splintered a nearby tree and branches rained down.

Alessio tapped the shed wall. "Keep digging, Nina. We'll get you out of here."

Putting her palm against the shuddering metal, she pictured him crouched on the other side. Despite her fears, she'd never felt alone on this rugged mountain, but Jack had so much to lose. Picking up the old tool, she dug as if her life depended on it.

"You calm me," Alessio said.

She paused. "Say what?"

"The minute I heard your voice and knew you were alive, I felt at peace."

"I usually have the opposite effect on men."

He laughed.

She let his admission sink in, but she dug as if he life depended on it.

An hour later, she had a pile of small rocks, a mound of dry dirt and bloody hands.

Victor pushed past her and fled the shed.

"Traitor," she said.

Alessio reached under the gap. "C'mon. You can squeeze through. I hit granite, so you either escape this way, or I'll have to tear down the shed."

"Is that an option?" She reached through the hole and felt the wind brush her skin. The sensation raised the hair on the back of her hand, and she eased into the shallow depression.

He pulled against the wall's lower edge and created space.

The metal groaned.

She retreated and considered another angle. Every extra inch of space mattered. She'd known that Italian had been a bad idea. Sliding her pry bar through the opening for Alessio to widen the hole, she exhaled, wedged herself into the gap and shifted her hips. The metal scored her back, but pain felt like a small price to pay. As she clawed her way into the night, lightning struck again and thunder rumbled through the valley. Free of the outbuilding, she scrambled to her feet and dirt fell from her body.

He pulled her against his chest and pressed a kiss to her temple. "I have you."

Exhaling, she reveled in the human contact. Despite the moon, the landscape looked eerily dark, but the swirl of stars overhead reminded her to breathe. After Jack's afternoon blow, her face had surely swelled. Now her back hurt and her hands bled. She turned from Alessio and hid her frustrated tears.

He cupped the side of her head and waited.

Hidden beneath a hat, his features remained hidden, but his presence gave her a reason to bury her fears. "Alessio, I'm a mess…"

"I have you, you're beautiful" — dropping his hand, he looked over her shoulder — "and Jack will pay."

Victor barked and yipped at her feet.

Leaning down, she scooped up the dog and cradled him against her elbow.

He quieted.

The storm rustled the trees and small animals moved through the dense shadows. She cleared her throat. "Just remember, he made a mistake." Going to bat for the man who treated her like an animal shouldn't be this easy, but she believed in redemption. "You can't kill him."

He cupped her face. "Another woman died in Stanley."

She squeezed shut her eyes. Escaping felt like her grand finale, but she couldn't ignore Jack's carnage. "I'm sorry."

"Let's find cover." He pulled her deeper into the woods behind the shed.

A wolf howled.

Victor raised his voice in response.

The cabin door slammed open.

"Nina! What the fuck are you doing in that shed?" Jack shone a flashlight over the bare area between the cabin and the shed. His beam swung wide, illuminated the dirt left over from her escape and stopped. "Nina, where are you?"

His singsong call sounded as ominous as the predator's slow scratch.

Alessio dropped her hand in the darkness.

"No!" Her harsh whisper burned her throat. "He can't see us."

A gunshot rang out.

Alessio stayed motionless at her side.

"Did your little pooch help you escape?" Jack asked.

A second bullet whizzed through the trees.

"Come out, come out, wherever you are!"

"He's a terrible shot." Alessio dropped his head and whispered low against her shoulder. A third bullet struck the shed and ricocheted into the darkness. "However, he might get lucky and hit us."

"He could be faking," she said. "He could be a master marksman."

Alessio bit back a laugh. "I doubt it."

Slapping his solid chest would satisfy her, but she feared making a sound.

Kissing her quickly, Alessio stepped out of the trees. He pulled a gun from a shoulder holster, held it pointed toward the ground and walked into the clearing. "Been a while, Jack."

His voice sounded strong and confident against the granite valley. Straining to see through the shadows, she watched him skirt the shed's edge.

Jack fired a shot. "Fuck you!"

Alessio stepped past the shed. "Drop the gun, and I'll add another five million to your collection."

"So you can shoot me?" Jack laughed. "Fuck, no."

Clutching Victor, she moved behind a large pine. "They'll shoot each other, won't they?"

Victor growled.

Scanning the surroundings, she looked for a distraction that would give Alessio time to disarm Jack. He might want to avenge Martha's death and her minor injuries, but her needs mattered, and she needed to bring both men down from the mountain.

Above her, the range's ragged silhouette blocked out the Milky Way. Spires jutted from outcrops weathered by wind and water. Their tall, oblong forms stood like midnight sentinels. If she found a way to light a signal fire, the rangers would come, but she'd never mastered that particular trick. She focused on the nearest outcrop. A pile of small boulders rested at its base. If she could set the stones in motion, they would tear up the underbrush and cause a commotion.

Her hands ached, and she doubted her plan.

A gun fired.

Dropping to a crouch, she stripped off her shirt, wound the fabric around her right hand and gripped the rusted tool. The mountains were an immense mass of intrusive, igneous rock. Faults, glaciers and ice storms broke up the range, but she only needed a piece of the landscape. Standing, she shifted the iron bar, winced at the pain and eased her way up the mountainside. "All right, let's end this mess."

Victor trotted at her heels.

She glanced at her skittering companion and smiled. "Good dog."

Chapter Twenty-Two

Holding the gun in his left hand, Alessio kept his right shoulder pinned to the shed. If Jack's next shot landed, he could absorb the injury and fire in retaliation. If Jack hit his head, well, all bets were off. Any other day, he would tackle the asshole, but his body ached, and he blamed Charon for throwing off his game. He shook his head. The blame wasn't fair. Without Charon at his side, he would never find the peace of mind to sleep.

Pressing the button on the side of the handgrip, Jack ejected the gun's magazine.

He sighed. Hand-to-hand, he could kick Jack's ass without breaking a sweat. If he wanted to kill the man while he fumbled with the magazine, he had an open shot. His fingers itched to pull the trigger, but Nina would never forgive him. Her outrage would temper his satisfaction and stymie whatever relationship their future held. Drawing a deep breath, he waited while Jack fumbled with the 9mm pistol. How long had he owned the piece? A week? The gun shop owner had probably picked out the ammunition, too.

Apparently, target practice was a father–son activity Michael Sanna had missed. He didn't have time to psychoanalyze Jack's daddy issues, but he twisted his watch and gave thanks for his own father's steady hand. Climbing the mountain, he feared his pugilistic tendencies would outweigh his reason. If he went berserk, he could find himself facing down a gun, but Nina's life calmed his impulses and channeled his reason.

A pebble skittered down the slope.

Jack flinched and looked up.

He sighed. A fumbling, grown man bent on revenge might draw his sympathy, but Jack wanted cash. He didn't care if Nina wanted him to mentor his associates. Jack could find mentors in the jailhouse. "Jack, the night's almost over. If we're not down the mountain by dawn, the cavalry's coming up."

Jack jammed the ammunition into the magazine's top. He fumbled a bullet, turned forward the bullet's round side and shoved the piece into place. "I'm getting my money."

"Yep." He sighed. "It's all about the money."

With the butt of his hand, Jack jammed the magazine into the handgrip. The magazine locked into place with a click, and Jack grinned.

Raising his gun, he aimed for Jack's bicep and fired. The shot went wide. "I should have brought Charon."

Jack grinned. "You're not so scary without your friends."

He squinted, slipped his right hand into his pocket, took a deep breath and aimed for Jack's bicep a second time. He pulled the trigger and exhaled.

The bullet found its mark and spun Jack into the log cabin.

Gripping the wound, Jack transferred the pistol to his other hand and gritted his teeth. "You're no better than the rest of us."

"True." He listened for Victor's bark or Nina's tears. Hearing nothing but the fast-moving summer storm, he trusted Nina to keep herself safe and returned to the man holding the gun. "Did Michael tell you how PIN collapsed?"

"Fuck you!" Jack yelled.

He bit back a smile. If the man planned to kill him, he would have staggered to his feet and charged across the clearing. Instead, he cowered behind vengeance and cold steel. "The single largest bankruptcy in American history was a telecommunications firm. PIN followed in its wake. Your father took on too much debt. He owed hundreds of millions of dollars, and he never planned to repay it. When he stopped serving the loans, investors would have to write off the debt. I sounded the alarm."

Jack fired a wild shot. "You can afford it!"

In the morning, a woodchuck would find the bullet, test the metal against his teeth and toss it to the ground as worthless trash. This ridiculous standoff had one ending, and Alessio wearied of the sport. "Long-term growth requires capital to flow to productive purposes. Your father manufactured paper profits, dodged infrastructure maintenance and lied to investors. I don't care how much you idolized him. He was a shit executive. Martin's no better."

"He said you'd say that!" Jack's voice wavered.

He closed his eyes and exhaled. After he'd blacklisted the company, The New York Stock Exchange had delisted PIN Network's stock. Without insurance, creditors had withdrawn and the company contracted. Employees had reported tales of accounting fraud and insider deals. On the other side of the country, he'd sat in peaceful acceptance. He'd honored the terms of his contract and his arbitration policies made him a billionaire, but he'd dismissed the fallout. In retrospect, a softer touch might yield the same effect. He sighed. He didn't have time to play nurse to every corrupt executive wanting to atone for past sins. "What will you do with the money?"

"Start my own firm," Jack said.

Cocking his head, he heard a distant rumbling. "Doing what?"

"Pool rentals. Like, vacation rentals, but your neighbor's pool."

"Already exists," he said.

"Fuck you!" Jack pulled away from the cabin and clutched his bicep. "You think you know everything, don't you?" He staggered toward the shed. "You don't know me!"

He widened his stance and raised his gun. "I know you take out your aggression on women and small animals. Who does that make you?" A growing rumble drowned out Jack's response. Raising his hand, Alessio pitched his head and listened. "Get down!"

"What the hell?" Jack crouched. "Is this a fucking earthquake?"

The ground shook, and he heard an explosion. Looking up, he saw a cloud of dust rising above the horizon. An avalanche of sound grew louder, and the western slope exploded in a dust-filled melee. Trees snapped and great, sickening cracks split granite monoliths into pieces. Shoving his gun in his waistband, he sprinted toward the shadows where he'd left Nina. "Run!"

"Wait!" Jack cried.

Ignoring Jack, he ran for Nina. "Leave the dog and run!" Skidding to a halt in an empty stand of trees, he looked over his shoulder.

Jack scrambled on pebbles and struggled to gain traction.

A bolder the size of a car burst into the clearing.

He hit the ground.

The boulder knocked out the cabin.

A beam caught Jack on the back of the head, and he fell flat on his face.

The shed walls shuttered and collapsed in on themselves.

Smaller rocks followed the boulder's wake. As the monolith crashed toward the lake, the rumbling faded.

Alessio stood. "Nina! Where the hell are you?"

Nobody answered.

He'd told the woman to stay put, but now he had an unconscious assailant, a missing girlfriend and a dog that had probably found its way under the rock fall. Shaking his head, he searched for clues to her departure, but dust choked the air and disoriented his vision. "Nina! Are you okay?" He didn't need her location, but he needed her safety. "Nina!"

Jack moaned.

"Shit." Making his way through the fallen branches and cabin scraps, he kneeled at Jack's side and checked his pulse.

"I didn't..."

He clapped his shoulder. Hard.

Jack passed out.

"Whoops, wrong shoulder."

"Alessio!" Nina cried.

His name echoed in the clearing and his heart trilled. Abandoning Jack, he stood and moved toward the sound of her voice.

She stepped out of the trees. In one hand, she held Victor and in the other hand, she held the metal pole she'd used to dig her way out of the shed.

A rock rolled through the clearing.

He and Nina sprang apart.

She blinked. "Did I do that?"

Shaking his head, he closed the distance and wrapped his arms around her. She smelled like sweat and dust, but she breathed. Burying his face in her hair, he exhaled. "You started a rock slide?"

Lightning cracked over the lake.

She wrinkled her nose. "Just a little one."

Looping his arm over her shoulder, he led her away from the trees and kept one ear tuned to the mountainside in case her investment yielded more results. "Do you ever follow instructions?"

"What instructions?" she asked.

"I told you to find cover."

"You said, '*Let's find cover.*' Well, I covered your ass."

"You obliterated a cabin, nearly squished your kidnapper and sent a tidal wave clear across the lake."

She shrugged. "I was effective."

Jack moaned.

Walking toward him, she looked down.

Alessio came to her side.

"What next?" she asked.

"We leave him."

A wolf howled in the silence.

"I don't think so," she said.

He sighed. If he activated his watch, Charon would send half the military to extract him, and he'd have to explain how Nina had single-handedly cleared a new ski slope. "He's unconscious, but he's breathing. We'll head back to the lakeshore and call for help."

She handed him the dog. "We can't leave him." She crouched at Jack's side. "Can you hear me?"

Jack moaned.

She pulled him to standing and draped his arm around her shoulders. "Come on. Alessio, you take the other side."

He balked. "The man tried to kill me."

"So?" She frowned and adjusted Jack's weight. "You're still alive."

Setting down the agitated, matted dog, he crossed his arms. "This is ridiculous. He's a murderer. He killed Martha and some poor woman in Stanley. Countless others might exist."

Victor growled.

She shrugged and stumbled under Jack's unwieldy weight. "He's still a person."

"Fuck me." Bending at the knees, he pulled Jack out of her arms, lifted him over his shoulder and moved out of the clearing. The man weighed a good amount, but with a gun in his hand, he held all the power in the world. Too bad three sessions at a shooting range didn't make a person an expert marksman. Lumbering down the trail, he exhaled and counted his gains. Nina and Victor walked at his side. As soon as he deposited Jack outside Stanley's police headquarters, he could return to the resort and resume his life.

She paused to tie her shoe and smiled. "Thank you."

He grunted and shifted Jack's weight. "He's going to jail. I'm not giving him the money."

She stood and cupped his face. "I know."

"Then why are you grinning?"

"This trip will make a great story." Dropping her hand, she took the lead down the mountain. "It could have been worse."

It could have been much worse, but the mountains and her anchoring convictions soothed him. Also, her ass looked like heaven.

Victor followed in her wake, and the dog's soiled, matted ass did not look like heaven.

Jack vomited down his back.

Closing his eyes, he swallowed and tried not to let the rancid smell get to him. "I should have shot you when I had the chance."

Jack moaned.

He jostled the man's weight. "Pass the fuck out before I dump you in a lake and watch you drown."

Jack complied.

He settled into his burdened gait. As soon as he cleaned up the fallout, he would sit Nina down in the penthouse and negotiate their relationship. Charon would keep her safe, she would work remotely and he would spend his free time entertaining her.

A pinecone fell out of the tree and smacked his head.

Looking up, he glared at the star-studded cosmos. "Try me."

* * * *

Emergency lights flashing, a Recreation Area boat waited at the lakeshore. A campsite lantern illuminated the single tent and the boulder sat on top of Jack's canoe. Sheets of metal fanned from the massive weight like an aluminum flower blooming over the water.

A woman strode forward from the lone, occupied campsite. "Sir, I'm Deputy Area Ranger Abby Smith. What happened?"

Alessio dumped Jack on the ground near the dock and wiped clean his hands. "This man needs medical attention."

"And you are?"

"Alessio Chen," he said. "The boulder sitting in the lake knocked down an old log cabin where this guy had camped out. Lucky for him, he'd come outside to use the restroom. The cabin's gone, but a board got loose and beaned him. He's still here."

Jack moaned.

Victor walked up to the man, lifted his leg and peed.

Smith checked Jack's vitals and radioed for an airlift evacuation. Straightening, she stared up the mountain. "In this range, rock slides are a fairly common springtime occurrence. The slides happen when melting snow or rainwater seeps into fissures and daytime temperatures cause the rock to expand." She frowned. "We don't get many of them at night."

He made a noncommittal sound. Somewhere up the mountain, a cheap handgun rested in the bushes. If he felt lucky, the gun would rust into ruins for a future archeologist to find. He pulled Nina to his side. "Fascinating."

"You're forgetting details," Nina said.

"Baby, I don't think the good ranger needs specifics."

Smith cleared her throat. "Oh, I need specifics."

Nina toed Jack. "This asshole kidnapped me and demanded a ransom."

Alessio swallowed.

"When Mr. Wonderful came to save me, Jack" — she nodded toward the man's motionless form — "demanded money. Apparently, the two men share history. Here I was, thinking I was the belle of the ball,

346

when doofus and jockstrap wanted to duke out their grievances."

Alessio gave her points for cavalier creativity, but if she wanted skin in the game, he preferred a more descriptive resolution. "What she means is I came to rescue her."

Nina scratched her cheek. "After Jack locked me in a shed."

Smith moved closer. "Ma'am, I'm here for you."

"Aren't you wonderful!" Nina took the ranger's hand and patted it.

Jack moaned.

Smith nudged him with her boot.

Before Alessio ended up on the wrong side of an interrogation room, he stepped forward. "Jack's responsible for a string of murders. The Stanley woman and a woman in New York named Martha Phosphole probably died by his hand. If I hadn't acted, Nina might have been next."

Smith narrowed her gaze. "How exactly did you act?"

He stretched his jaw. "I, uh, had an associate trace Jack's cell, dug a hole and uh" — he swallowed — "well, I didn't do much."

Nina linked her arm through his arm. "You did plenty. I'm the one who triggered the rockslide." She held out her bloodstained hands. "I thought I could climb the hill and set fire to a tree, but the boulder looked precarious, and I needed a distraction."

"You did *what*?" Smith stared. "Do you know we're under a burn ban?"

"I don't do country life." Nina linked her hands behind her back and looked at the ground. Despite her fondness for fried chicken and apple orchards, people changed, and the sooner she returned to New York

City, the sooner she could incorporate Alessio into her life. Looking up, she shrugged. "It was just a little boulder."

Smith kicked the dirt. "Just a little boulder."

Her boots tread left tracks, and her biceps strained her uniform.

Nina stepped back toward Alessio.

"Large rockfalls impact trails." Smith ticked off her points on her fingers. "They disrupt habitats. We can reroute the trail, but rerouting won't be a long-term solution. Do you know how much backlogged trail maintenance bothers me? And a fire? You're out of your mind, lady." She flung wide her hands. "You could have scorched the entire range."

Looking over her shoulder, Nina met Alessio's amused smile.

He wrapped an arm around her waist. "Did you hear the part about the murderer at your feet?"

Smith shook her hands near her head. "This kind of work is grueling. When obstacles wipe out a trail, the area's unsafe until the landscape stabilizes. Where am I going to find people up to that task of remediating your distraction? Moving rocks is hard, hard work. Did you think about the cabin your boulder demolished? The campers could have been next!"

"I, uh, didn't expect the boulder to plow through the cabin. I thought it would" — Nina cleared her throat — "startle Jack and come to rest."

Smith pointed to the new landmark. "In the lake!"

Alessio cleared his throat. "I'll take care of the trail remediation, a new dock and a generous donation to the National Park Service."

"We don't take bribes," Smith said.

"How about able-bodied volunteers?"

She appraised him. "How many?"

"Eight plus me." He jerked his thumb toward Nina. "She'll pitch in, too, to remedy the damage."

Smith glared, but she turned toward the sound of an approaching helicopter.

Floodlights illuminated the campsite and an amphibious helicopter landed on Redfish Lake. The blades kicked up debris and blew off Alessio's hat.

He shielded his eyes.

Nina tugged at the topknot. "What's up with this?"

He glanced at her. "You care how I look?"

"Yes, I care."

Grinning, he claimed a dust-coated kiss. "I care about you, too."

The helicopter door opened, and two paramedics climbed out. The no-nonsense medical staff consulted with Smith, assessed Jack and went to work. Within minutes, the paramedics strapped Jack to a gurney.

Alessio stood beside Nina like a bulwark against life's whims. "Are you cold?"

She shook her head, but she stayed pressed against his side.

The helicopter took off.

Smith watched it depart and strode back to him.

The lantern light softened her stern features.

"You forgot to mention the bullet wound," she said.

His nose twitched. "Minor omission."

Shaking her head, Smith pried free Nina's clasped hands.

Nina exposed her palms and the cuts along her wrist.

"You need medical attention, too?" Smith asked. "I have a first-aid kit in the boat."

"I'll be okay," Nina said.

Smith rubbed the dried blood from her arm. "The sheriff will meet them at the hospital, but you're not to leave the area."

"The campground?" Nina asked.

Rubbing together her fingers, Smith looked at the rust-color debris and wiped her hands along her pants. "Sun Valley. We'll attribute Jack's injuries to the rockslide. The sheriff will investigate your claims. If he killed Lisa, he'll face jurisdiction in Custer County. Your claims about the other woman will follow suit."

Nina exhaled. "Get him."

"Excuse me?" Smith asked.

Nina shifted and looked up the mountain. "He treated people like trash. Animals have more respect for each other than he does." Shaking her head, she looked at the ranger. "I'm fine, but nobody should look a man in the eye and experience fear."

"The wilderness has a certain karma." Smith scratched her throat. "You need a ride back to the boat ramp?"

Alessio pointed to the rented fishing boat. "Just came out for a spot of fishing."

"Right." Smith checked on the campers, climbed into the ranger boat and extinguished the flashing lights. Hand on the wheel, she picked up her radio and cleared her throat. "All good at the Redfish Lake Inlet Campground. A hiker triggered the rockslide." She waited. "No, I can't fucking believe it, either. Some people have no respect."

He stroked Nina's lower back. Explaining Jack's actions felt too neat, and Jack still had a hole in his bicep. "I think the good ranger knows how to reach us. In the meantime, we'll head back to town and wait for further instructions."

Charon walked up and cracked his knuckles. "Good to see you safe and sound."

"No thanks to you," he said. "What have you been doing for the last few hours?"

Charon tossed him his phone and held up a stick with a roasted marshmallow, "Making s'mores."

"Telling ghost stories!" a kid yelled.

A second kid peered around his brother. "Mr. Chen, did you really fight three men at one time?"

He stared at the youth and felt Nina lean against his frame. Unless he missed a few errant details, he could have her back at the resort in an hour, tend her wounds and tell her how he felt. "Now, why would you believe that tale?"

"You did!" The kid danced back to the campfire. "You did!"

He smiled. "Smart kid." Reaching for Nina's elbow, he guided her to the canoe. If she left his side in the next few days, he would lose his shit. "So" — he cleared his throat — "what next?"

Victor wound his way between her legs and sat at the water.

Leaning down, Alessio scooped up the dog and handed him to Charon. "Can you get us back to the dock?"

"No problem, Don."

He absorbed the nickname, handed her onto the boat deck and settled at her side. He'd come so close to losing her that he refused to release her hand.

Even as Charon revved the motor and spend them across the lake, he held fast. Compared to organized fights, casinos, insurance and investment firms, Redfish Lake's appeal relied on colloquial shadows, but the vistas reminded him of the home he remembered. Some nights, his mother took a night off from the restaurant, his father poured a small-batch liquor from Haifa's roughest neighborhood and laughter filled their small, Zürich house. "Can you see yourself living out here?"

"Hell no," she said. "I need people to see and places to go."

He laughed. Fishing, boating, kayaking and swimming in Idaho's crystal-clear lakes sounded like a good way to pass the years, but loving her sounded better. Judging by the way she leaned her head on his shoulder and held her swollen hand to her chest, she couldn't wait to get back to New York's luxuries. He raised their linked hands to his lips. "Fair enough. I have you."

"Alessio" — she sighed — "he never saw me."

"I know."

She turned her face away from the wind.

Lifting her chin, he dropped his head and pressed a kiss to her lips. She tasted of dust and sweat, but her steady breaths fueled his heart. "I see you. I'll keep you safe."

"He could have killed us." She shook against his side.

Gathering her closer, he let her adrenaline crash. The euphoria of winning a fight and the numbing exhaustion of replaying it would occupy her thoughts for days. "But he didn't. You disarmed him, and if I hadn't shown up, you would have freed yourself and Victor."

"Or died in that awful shed."

"No." He swallowed. "You fought, and you moved heaven and earth to disarm him."

"Mostly earth."

He smiled and kissed her matted hair. "Mostly earth."

She looked up. "Alessio?"

"Hmm," he said.

"Why the hell are you dressed like a local? I miss the suits."

Smiling, he lifted her, settled her on his lap and wrapped his arms around her. "If Jack had a vantage point, I didn't want him to see us coming for him. I wanted to look like a guy out catching fish. The hat covered the topknot."

She laid her head against his chest. "Fish."

"Mmm-hmm," he said.

"Well, you caught one."

"And the hair?" He wondered how one woman's opinion could come to mean so much.

"Interesting." She pulled out the elastic. "But I like it better long."

"Give me a year. I'll be a fucking wild man."

She hummed against his chest. "Is that all it would take?"

Give me everything you have. Exhausted, he let Charon navigate the pink, early morning light. The boat skipped over calm water, birds skimmed the surface and a bull moose lowered his head for a drink. "Nina, I'll always be there for you. No matter what you need, tell me. I want to take care of you, but I don't want my bad habits to push you away. I've spent my entire life fighting to prove my worth, but the only thing I want is you."

She shifted in his arms.

"You're asleep. Fuck."

Raising her hand, she traced his jaw. "I heard you."

"And?" he asked.

She burrowed into his shoulder. "Ditto."

"Such eloquence."

Yawning, she rubbed her face against his chest. "Alessio?"

He tightened his grip.

"I wanted to blow off steam, make Martha happy and forget about my workload, but I'm so happy I found you. Even if you came with a shit obstacle course, I'm staking my claim. You belong to me."

Lowering his head, he pressed a kiss against her temple. "I agree."

Approaching the dock, Charon slowed the boat.

Nina stirred and pulled away.

He hated to release her.

"As soon as we leave the Sawtooth Mountains, I want a breakfast sandwich, a hot bath and a king-sized bed," she said.

"That's it?" he asked.

She frowned. "Did I forget something?"

He traced her swollen lips and smiled. "Whatever you want, it's yours."

Charon snorted and let the boat drift to shore.

Alessio jumped onto the rocky shore, held Nina's hand as she climbed over the edge and assisted her into the white pickup truck's bench seat. His bicep twitched, and he wondered when exhaustion would lay him low. Before he rested, he had to make sure she knew how he felt about her, knew how to barricade herself in his room and how to keep her legs crossed so he could wisely choose sleep. Actually, he'd give her a pass on the third condition. If she wanted to affirm her life with a mind-blowing orgasm, he'd happily down an espresso and give her everything he had.

She gazed out of the window. "It's a pretty spot."

He followed her gaze and took in the peaceful view. Day-trippers and eager sportsmen rose at dawn to pack their coolers for the day, but the lake's winding road remained void of flickering headlights. "It's a beautiful spot. You want to spend the day out here?"

Covering a yawn, she shook her head. "Without Jack, I never would have seen this view."

He handed up Victor.

The dog jumped into the foot well and curled up.

Crossing his arms over the bench seat, he looked at Nina. "When I'm worried about you, I have a hard time admiring the scenery."

She patted the seat. "I'm fine. I'm made of tough stuff. Think of all the fried chicken I ate growing up."

He smiled. "I believe you. When we get back to the resort, we'll figure out what to do next."

Scooping up Victor, she settled the dog in her lap, leaned her head against the seat and closed her eyes. "That sounds good."

He turned and looked for ways to accelerate their departure.

Charon finished tying off a line. "Riley will pick up the boat. You want me to drive, boss?"

Turning, he crossed his arms. "Oh, we're back to 'boss' now?" He ticked off his fingers. "I've also been Don, Dick and Diva."

Laughing, Charon shrugged. "Hey, you want to drive? I'm happy to cuddle up to your woman."

He slammed shut the rear door. "Mine."

Chapter Twenty-Three

Sitting in the muffled silence, Nina had kept her eyes closed. She'd unclenched her fist and let it shake against her thigh. Scrambling up the mountain, she'd feared she would hear a gunshot and a cry that would break her heart. Instead, she'd jammed a pry bar under a rock, jumped on the lever and sent the rock rolling down the mountainside. The rock had crashed into a boulder, split in two and transferred its momentum to the larger object. Impact by impact, the stones had increased in size until the largest boulder tore through the clearing, shattered the cabin and came to rest in the lake.

If she could remake a single decision, she would have picked up Alessio's gun and ordered Jack off the mountain, but the men would have laughed in her face. She'd sighed. She hadn't graduated top of her class to play damsel in distress.

Alessio climbed into the cab next to her.

Charon took the driver's seat.

As the truck climbed out of the valley, the sun broke over the ridgeline, and she nested her head against Alessio's shoulder. "We should talk about some things."

"Like what?"

His warmth and dried sweat smelled better than any cologne. "Nude yoga."

"Really?" he asked.

His chest rumbled beneath her cheek. She smiled. "You're used to being the boss."

"I *am* the boss."

She yawned. "You've turned old-school corporate sophistication into a sleek, modern army of ruthless men who accept physical violence is an option. Financial ruin is an option. What does that make you?"

"Powerful."

Rolling her eyes, she tabled the conversation for another day. He came to her aid and his presence warmed her body and soul. "Violence isn't the only way to get what you want. Sometimes, trust works wonders, too."

He snorted.

She smiled. "When we get back to the resort, we can talk about my ideas."

"I had other ideas for our victory lap."

"I'm sure." Tracing the muscles beneath his shirt, she spread her fingers over his chest and felt his heartbeat. "If you're micromanaging an empire, you can't spend your days in bed."

He remained silent.

Imagining his gears turning, she let proximity be enough.

* * * *

Nina woke up in the immense bed anchoring Alessio's suite.

He sat at a small desk typing on his laptop.

"Hey," she said.

He looked up and smiled. "Hey. How're you doing?"

She examined her hands. When they'd returned to the resort, he'd applied ointment, bathed her and bundled her into bed. If she hadn't seen the exhaustion weighing down his limbs, she would have taken care of the tasks herself, but she didn't want to waste his energy on a fight she might lose. He clearly took satisfaction in the skin-to-skin contact, and she enjoyed every touch. "I'll be fine."

He stood and walked over to the side of the bed. "I have a few meetings, but as soon as I'm done, I'll spend the afternoon with you."

Easing back the covers, she stood and stretched her arms over her head. "I have a better idea."

Frowning, he cocked his head.

"I'm coming with you."

"Nina." He rubbed his smooth cheek. "I don't think you'll enjoy the discussion."

She stretched. "Why? Are you plotting hostile takeovers? World domination?"

"Yes."

Staring, she shrugged. "I want to see. Maybe I can help."

He blinked.

"I can't accept half of you, Alessio. You can't coddle me, walk away to arbitrate your ruthless business dealings and come back to me wiped clean. If I don't understand what you do, how can I help you?"

"I don't need help. I have associates I trust. Remember my friends?"

"Well, now you have a woman." She walked toward her luggage. Pulling out a sleeveless red cocktail dress, she dropped the silk-lined material over her head and stepped into her heels.

He crossed his arms. "Aren't you forgetting a few things?"

She zipped up the dress. "Nope."

"Underwear?"

She shrugged.

"Nina…"

Walking into the bathroom, she let the door swing closed.

* * * *

Driver tapped his fingers on the polished wood conference table. "So?"

Nina held a slight smile and kept her head tilted to the side. She adopted the expression in law school when her professors waxed poetic. Driver's facts made sense, and Alessio had filled in relevant details about industry trends. ADC planned a hostile takeover of a British insurance firm. The target company had rejected ADC's initial offer, but Alessio and his associates dismissed their politely worded refusal and considered their next move.

Flexing his fingers on the polished wood, Driver inhaled. "We can fight to replace the management, or we can go straight to the company's shareholders."

"Shareholders." Alessio flipped a page in his handout. "Without clear direction, the stock will drop, and they'll lose value. They know it, too."

She wet her lips. If she were a member of the target company's management team, she would put together a defense strategy to ward off a hostile takeover, label

ADC's offer unattractive, unwanted and undervalued and fight fire with fire. "Does the UK location matter?"

Charon shook his head. "The UK's business secretary mentioned the government would support any offer that improved local rates. ADC's umbrella company offers efficiencies. The rates will drop."

Driver snorted. "For a while."

Alessio looked up.

"What?" Driver shrugged. "We can't guarantee the future."

Narrowing his gaze, Alessio looked at his handout.

"How high are you willing to go?" she asked.

Every man in the room turned and looked at Alessio.

"Nineteen billion," he said.

She swallowed. With that kind of money at his discretion, his hardball tactics made sense. "Why not twenty? Big numbers are scary."

He laughed. "You're very free with my money."

She winked.

Jason shook his head. "Apparently you're sticking around for comic relief."

Turning to look at the man, she smiled. "I plan on it."

Alessio shuffled his papers. "I want the takeover finalized by the end of next year. How do we convince the firm to relent? The rules governing how foreign companies acquire UK companies aren't complex. As long as we're transparent about our offer and our intentions, the stockholders will relent and the sale will go through without a hitch. A smart board manages the takeover from inside the boardroom."

Jason leaned back in his chair. "The CEO's sleeping with his secretary."

Stefano yawned.

Driver made a fist. "The underwriting department targets minorities."

Alessio pointed his finger. "Sold. Make it public. Take the largest shareholders to dinner and explain how much we would appreciate their vote. If they balk, reveal the dirt you've collected. Maybe the shareholders can talk sense into the board."

"How do you know I have dirt?" Driver asked.

Smiling, Alessio laid down his papers. "You always have dirt."

"And you always have cash."

She felt the room's subdued tension.

Alessio maintained eye contact with Driver, but he moved his leg beneath the table.

The contact comforted and reassured her. She felt so out of her league that she wondered if she would drift into space, but nobody at the table directly questioned her presence. They gave her side eye and chose their words, but Alessio anchored the room.

In time, she would add value to the discussions. Contract reviews and internal audits required more than mediation, but she knew enough industry gossip to identify targets for Alessio's review. At her core, she trusted his settlement techniques. Weariness deepened the lines by his eyes, but every time he intervened, he acted with complete confidence.

She recalled the kiss after Charon had pulled her down from Gabby's stage. Sometimes more pressure thrilled her. If her relationship with him continued, she would learn when to push him and when to hold back. He, being a smart man, would learn the same. Pressing back against his leg below the table, she smiled.

He cleared his throat. "The next item on the agenda concerns the management team."

Charon frowned.

Above his reddish-brown beard, Charon's curious blue eyes shone against long lashes. He came from Greece, but history, marksmanship and driving skills couldn't be the only things keeping him at Alessio's side. When he made himself scarce, she wondered what he did to fill his time.

Driver stared.

The man held his phone like a shield. His face bore several raised scars, and she wondered if he wore his hair and his beard the same length for comfort or pride. Given his no-nonsense approach to Alessio, one trimmer might be the limit of his enthusiasm for grooming products. Leave it to these men to forgo fashion for utility. She looked at Alessio. His longer hair hinted at his playfulness. If he went short, she would still love him.

Stefano thumbed through a series of links on his laptop. "Listen to this shit."

The shortest of the associates, Stefano rarely looked up from his computer. His accent marked him as an Italian, but she wondered what mysteries kept his gaze from making contact.

"We are working around the clock to investigate claims that hackers illegally accessed our mobile network data. We determined the unauthorized access occurred, but we have not determined whether the access jeopardized personal customer data. We are confident we closed the entry point and we continue reviewing the situation to identify the nature of any illegally accessed data from our systems. Please protect yourself by changing your mobile password and security PIN." He closed the laptop and leaned back in the chair. "One of the most popular telecommunications companies in the US can't keep its system locked down. Figures." He kissed his fingers and spread them to the room. "Fuck you, mobile ass-wipes."

Jason laughed.

Nick kept silent.

The blond twins narrowed their eyes and growled.

Nina choked back a laugh. The pair looked intense, but she would cast them as Thor's half-breed cousins. Gods, they were beautiful. Alessio had laid down a million-dollar donation to coerce her into the Idaho trip, but one look at his associates would have greased the wheels.

"Look." Jason jammed his finger against the table. "I don't care what mischief you unleashed, but make sure it doesn't trace back to us. We have enough bullshit on our hands."

Stefano flipped off his peer. "After you bailed out of the air force, you stopped being fun."

Jason crossed his arms. "Funny how shattering your spine leads to changes."

Stefano stood.

"Men," Nick said.

Ahh, the peacemaker. Nina resolved to tease out the group's secrets.

Dropping into his chair, Stefano closed his laptop and glared.

Alessio exhaled. "I told you to trace Jack's number, not tear down the nation's entire mobile system."

"I did what you asked." Stefano shrugged and looked out of the window. A slight smile lifted his lips. "Then I left details of the breech on the dark web. It's not my fault someone followed my lead, teased out data from the company's shit servers and sold a hundred million individuals' data for a few crypto tokens."

"Shit, Stefano," Nick said. "Those people didn't need that stress."

"I bought the data, Dimwit." Stefano smiled. "I have plenty of tokens."

Nick offered his peer a slow clap.

"Enough," Alessio said. "I started to say I'm changing the structure of our team and our name." He frowned. "Although the pack of you might make me regret it."

The left twin cracked a smile. Nina tried to remember his name. *Anders? Anderson?* He looked as stealthy as a blond cannonball, but his brother had fifty pounds on him. *Boulder? Wouldn't that be ironic?*

"ADC Associates makes more sense." Standing, Alessio paced the room. "From now on, each of you will have an area of influence and full authority to make decisions. I don't want to hear about the nitty-gritty details of your conquests. I do want to hear about the wins. If I have to bail your asses out of trouble, you'll get my opinion, but otherwise, the profits will speak for themselves. You leverage my capital, I claim my take and we reconvene as friends."

Nina smiled. The probability of Alessio taking vacation time skyrocketed.

"What about the chick?" Jason asked.

The room went silent.

"She's with me," Alessio said.

Nina stood. "And here I thought we came to Idaho for a spa day."

The second twin smiled.

The man's name was 'Fell'! She cleared her throat. To earn respect from these men, she would have to stand on her feet. "I'm a mediator, but I've spent plenty of time around egotistic inventors. Some of them left disgruntled but sated. I kept records. What inventors don't have is cash or free rein. Give the geeks cash but give them a little freedom and TLC, too. It'll pay off and you won't have to fight for your share." She walked up to Alessio and laid her palm on his arm. "Your tactics work, but I can help."

Alessio smiled. "I'm sure you can."

She grinned.

He leaned down. "Exhibitionist. Do you really have a file of disgruntled inventors?"

She pressed a kiss against his cheek. "Yes, but they weren't my problem."

"Now?" he asked.

She scanned the room and grinned. "Now, I have plenty of problems."

Alessio linked their fingers and led her from the room.

* * * *

Nina stood on the intricate footbridge spanning the Great Falls. Water tumbled over the stacked, weathered New Jersey rocks. A cloudless, late-afternoon sky filled the valley with low light. She savored the suburban scenery.

While visitors took pictures, the falls carved a path through the Passaic River Gorge. The weathered brass plaque at the base of the bridge said the waterfall fell nearly eighty feet. Lenape Native Americans settled on the site, Dutch settlers claimed the land and the National Park Service assumed custodianship. A few minutes ago, she'd added Martha's ashes to the tumultuous mix.

The site's unabashed power and beauty made her wish she'd visited the falls while Martha had lived. Today, she wore a light-yellow dress and a resin pendant Martha had made her. Alessio braced his arms and watched the waterfall. She stepped closer. "When Martha gave you my phone number, what did she say?"

He cleared his throat. "She said you were beautiful woman who made her laugh."

"And you bought that line?" She tilted her head. "You're screwed."

Laughing, he shook his head. "Happily."

She patted his shoulder. "You're handsome and rich, but you're not funny. It's okay to not be funny. You have other redeeming assets. You're handsome, good in bed, indulgent..."

He swatted away her arm. "Maybe Martha had a point. You and I both needed a release."

Martha saw too much of other people and too little of her circumstances. If Nina could go back in time, she would spend more time with her friend and find out what had kept her from pursuing her artistic dreams. Without that option, she would spend hours staring at Martha's artwork and remapping her own life. "Let's get back to your redeeming features."

"Such as?" he asked.

She raised an eyebrow. "You seem to like me."

"Like you." He sighed. "I do. Despite my best efforts, your disobedience and your willingness to empathize with sociopaths, I do."

"Like you."

"Yes, I like you," he said.

"No, I meant you're a sociopath. But I'm working on that aspect. You're opening up."

He rolled his eyes.

She stroked the back of his neck where his skin felt more vulnerable. One day, time might weather their love like these rocks, as his power and influence ran through her life like a heady undercurrent. Covering his hand, she watched the water tumble through the gorge. "I miss her."

"Me, too."

Turning her back on the sight, she wiped away a tear and smoothed her dress.

Falling water gave the air a warm intimacy that cocooned her from the decisions awaiting her. Alessio had challenged her to pick a home base. She would relinquish her job and her plant-filled condo, but until she toured the world at his side, she refused to settle. His wry smile had conveyed his approval. They would get to happily ever after.

He straightened and ran a hand along the railing. "I should have done more for Martha."

"Maybe," she said. "Did she ask?"

He shook his head.

He had brought Martha's painting and her letters to her parents. He'd expressed his deep condolences on their loss and spoken about her ability to befriend everyone from gallery patrons to subway strangers. Both of Martha's elderly parents had greeted them warmly, but their gazes had never focused, and he'd brought the painting back to his penthouse.

Nina had picked her favorite from Martha's condo and added it to the collection. She considered the crowd taking in the view. "I should have done more for Jack."

Alessio snorted. "Don't think about that ass wipe." He tucked her against his side. "He didn't deserve your attention. If I could rewrite history, I'd spot him first, beat a confession from him and hope the show impressed you enough to accept me."

"Accept what?" She leaned against him. Her courtroom suits and conservative dresses stood out on a casino floor accustomed to sequins, cleavage and sky-high heels. If Alessio expected her to morph into the show ponies he dated, she'd have to surrender the gold skirt, take a deep breath and cry into her plants.

He tipped up her chin. "Accept me," he said. "Tell me when I'm being a jerk, but love me unconditionally and welcome me with open arms."

The waterfall's roar faded from her awareness. "And if that's not enough? If I'm not enough? You might be the one who turns away."

Dropping his hand, he stepped back. "You are enough. You're more than enough. Why would you doubt me? Why would you doubt yourself?"

She raised her hand and dropped it to her side. "I thought you'd be a fling."

He crossed his arms. "And now?" Holding up his hand, he stepped back from her. "You're right. I coerced you. Solemnity looks good on you, Nina. If you ever need something, I'm a phone call away."

The distance ached like a gnawing hunger. She could stand in the courtroom, represent her clients and come home to her condo, but the effort would never be enough. Slipping off her heels and pouring her love into Victor and her garden-variety projects would ease the loneliness, but when she sat on the fire escape and looked at the stars shining through the city's lights, she would wonder what other paths her life could take.

Alessio's path shone brighter than the brightest star. He wrapped his judgment in contract language and tough love, but she understood him. She also understood the absolute acceptance she needed to stand by his side. Sun Valley felt like a surreal dream, but New Jersey couldn't lie. She refused to be another orbiting planet, wobbling for attention and hoping for his attention.

He turned and straightened his shoulders.

Before he could storm off, she stepped closer and laid her cheek against his back. "I'm not a fan girl, Alessio. I love you. The feeling scares me. I've never needed anyone as much as I need you. How can I put so much faith in you and trust you'll never fail me?"

Slowly, he turned and took her in his arms.

His gaze, so full of intensity, focused on her.

"Nina, when I said I would protect you, I meant every inch of you." He pushed her mist-dampened hair from her face. "I love you. I can't imagine living my life without you by my side. If you want to settle into a little brownstone and raise noisy children, I'm there."

She smiled and leaned into his hand. "That's what you think I want?"

"No." He dropped his hand, leaned down and traced his lips along her cheek. "But that would be enough. Waking up next to you, stealing kisses in public spaces and knowing half the time you're going commando would get a rise out of me." His teeth grazed her earlobe. "You're enough."

"That's not enough, Alessio," she said.

He pulled back.

"When you're struggling with a decision, I want to know why. Command and protect isn't an option. I want a partnership."

He scratched his lip. "Someone has to be in charge."

"But we think alike," she said. "You'll learn to trust me and leverage my opinion."

Gripping the railing with both hands, he looked over the water. "Okay."

His acquiescence felt as hollow as it sounded. Within the year, she guessed she'd be back to attention-grabbing stunts and sidelong glances from ADC associates. She straightened to her full height and prepared to walk away. Whether he followed her would be his decision. "Okay?"

Turning, he leaned his side against the railing.

The man could grace the cover of *GQ*, but she wouldn't let his assets distract her.

"When I was younger, my father told me to be the lion, the arbiter and the protector."

"That's stupid," she said. "The male lions roar and make a fuss, but the lionesses nurture the pride."

He cocked his head. "Is that so?"

Scrambling, she wished she'd spent less time watching dating shows and more time watching the nature channel. She crossed her arms and hoped for the best. "I grew up in the nineties. It must be true."

He smiled. "The pride's social structure depends on specific roles. Without teamwork, the pride doesn't thrive. Lionesses are the primary hunters and caregivers, but dominant males protect the pride's territory."

"By pissing on everything!" She threw up her hands. "By growing stupid manes and making a fuss."

He laughed and ran his hand through his hair. "Point taken."

She took the concession, but the victory felt hollow.

Taking her hand, he traced her fingertips. "My father succumbed to Lewy body dementia. Before he died, he told me how much he depended on my mother. She brought him peace. Without her work at the Italian restaurant, our family would have struggled. They took shifts raising me." He swallowed. "I didn't realize how much effort went into maintaining our family. For a while, I resented them, but I realize how much they loved me."

"You were a kid."

He cleared his throat. "I refused to put myself in that position. I wouldn't let anyone take away my choices." He looked up. "Nina, until I met you, I felt like I would die in a blaze of glory or a crumbling heap."

"Glory." The waterfall drowned out her whisper.

He pulled her hand to his lips. "I choose you. I love you. We can make this thing work, travel the world, and still come home to New York. I will always love you. The question is, will you always love me?"

She considered the question. One day, his hair would turn silver, and she would still see the fierce man who brandished his fists and dared opponents to cross him. Old and gray, he would be the reserved man in a power suit wielding steely authority over matters, big and small. She would still sit by his side, their legs touching beneath the table, urging on his aggression or holding back his wrath. She knew her power lied not in throttling back his ambitions but keeping him on his toes. "I will always love you, Alessio."

"Only when you're scared?"

She shook her head.

"Horny?"

She laughed.

He leaned close. "Are you wearing underwear?"

Rubbing together her smooth legs, she smiled. "Really? We're scattering Martha's ashes."

He rubbed his five o'clock stubble across her cheek. "She would have wanted you to be happy."

Pulling back, she considered the question. She had her job in New York, but she also had Alessio. As long as he didn't want to put down roots in Sun Valley, she could adjust to his jet-setting lifestyle. Victor let the maid, Emily, rub his belly. Secure in Alessio's penthouse, he had free rein of the top floor. If he wanted to scratch his butt on the seventeenth-century antique Persian runner, he could. But really, who would see him? She and Alessio alternated between their bedroom and their office. The times they emerged for social engagements resulted in hedonistic meals and wind-whipped walks through Central Park. Once or twice, Alessio had mentioned foreign cities, but inertia and pleasure kept him homebound. She loved testing his strength, getting a rise out of him and enjoying the slow, ensuing burn, but she wanted more than subdued embers. "I am happy."

"Good."

She pulled free, turned and walked down the footbridge. Weaving through scattered crowds, she let her hips sway.

"Nina..."

The wind blew up her skirt.

Holding her hand across the skirt's front, she let the wind flash her ass.

"Nina..."

She grinned.

"You have a beautiful ass!"

His yell cut through the crowd's noise. Turning, she blew a kiss over her shoulder.

He barreled through a small crowd of teenagers.

"What the fuck, man?" a Goth teenager asked.

Alessio growled.

Stifling a laugh, she slowed and dropped her hand.

He picked up her grip and squeezed it tight. "Forever?"

She squeezed his hand in return, pressed against him to control her skirt and smiled. He was such a stubborn, pugilistic titan, but he was her titan—and she loved him. "Forever."

Want to see more from this author?
Here's a taster for you to enjoy!

Sun Valley Mafia: Remaking a Man
Amy Craig

Coming January 2023

Excerpt

Standing on the marble front step of her family's Miami mansion, Gisella tapped her designer footwear, adjusted her sunglasses and blocked out the bright spring day. She breathed deeply and shuffled the bags hanging from her toned arms.

At the end of the driveway, her brother Antonio revved his red convertible's souped-up engine and pounded the dashboard in time to blaring rock music. Miami traffic streamed past the estate. People stared.

Why can't he just leave? She marveled at his arrogance, but she kept her expression neutral and her phone in her pocket. He was the youngest of her two siblings, and he had the stocky, tan physique her male family members prized. He also had a propensity to wear outlandish suits, a revolving door of girlfriends and a sophomoric sense of humor. If he caught her taking a selfie in front of the house, he would turn it into a meme, but her account depended on dance stills and teasing hints of glamour. The minute he left the estate, she would take the picture while her hair looked good.

Flexing her toes, she rifled through the bags on her arms. One duffle held her ballet kit, another tote functioned as a purse and the bags from her morning shopping spree hiked her credit card bill. Instead of feeling guilty for the extravagance, she admired her long, lean legs.

Her form allowed her to excel as a professional ballerina, but she worried she had the coltish naivety to match her legs. When would she work up the nerve to demand a driver's license and stop relying on Antonio for transportation? Every time she talked about her license, her father pouted and asked what more he could do to ensure her comfort.

If her mother had lived, Gisella's life might be so different.

A car horn honked. A woman blew kisses. "Antonio!!"

He ignored the entreaty, let the engine rumble and scanned the beachside traffic. His muscled forearm hung over the door, and he tapped his fingers against the expensive paint job. Milky fingerprints marred the convertible's finish.

A second Miami driver slowed to gawk at the handsome, moneyed mobster. A trailing car smashed the vehicle's lights. Horns blared and doors flew open.

Releasing the engine's pent-up energy, Antonio took advantage of the distraction and roared across two lanes of traffic.

Gisella rolled her eyes and snapped the picture she needed, but she doubted her high-gloss smile was worth the price of the photograph.

Riding home with her brother from dance rehearsals and a shopping spree, she had stared out of the window and listened to him complain about women and their fickle ways. His problems never changed, but the consistency soothed her. If he spent more time listening to the women, he would have fewer problems with them.

For instance, she had wanted to close her eyes and rest, but Antonio couldn't take a hint. As soon as she made Principal Dancer, she could move out of her father's house and make rent, but she would have to stop shopping like a mafia princess.

Squaring her shoulders, she faced her father's front door. Most Miami residents painted their doors to ward off humidity's warping effects. *Papà* imported Cocobolo heartwood and exposed the precious wood to the elements. His house could grace the cover of *Architectural Digest*, but his acceptance in local society depended on discretion. Biscayne Bay would freeze over before he opened the mansion's doors to gawking strangers.

Every piece of furniture came with a decorator's commission, authenticity papers and a cataloged serial number. The insurance company knew the exact cost of her father's investment, and if the house burned, they'd be wise to pay up.

She appreciated the wealth, but its origins bothered her. Her sweet *Papà*, Gregorio Vitella, ran drugs from South America up the Eastern shoreline. She feared that enjoying the proceeds made her complicit in his crimes.

Pressed by a tipsy ballet friend, she'd admitted the concession that let her sleep at night. Her father's legitimate insurance company probably covered her bills, but how could a person separate good money from bad people — and where did that distinction place her?

Pushing open the door, she scanned the marble foyer and dropped her bags, but a green potted palm, a black concert piano and an excruciatingly expensive console table provided little company. The console table rested on acrobatic loops of brass. Beneath a glass top, python skin gleamed with a subtle sheen, and she wondered if the piece's black crystal pulls would make an interesting jewelry set. Opening a drawer, she checked for mail and flipped through the family correspondence. "*Come stai, Papà?*"

Her question echoed.

Raising her head, she set down the mail and waited.

A hidden white paneled door opened. Martin, the butler, emerged, wearing the formal black suit and crisp white shirt required for his service. He'd perfected the practiced, subservient gaze on his own. She'd grown to like him, but she wondered how long he would last in the household.

"*Signorina* Gisella, your father is in his study."

Keeping a bright smile on her face, she handed Martin her shopping bags and kept her purse on her shoulder. "Thanks. I'll freshen up and join him."

"Yes, *Signorina*."

The man couldn't speak ten words of Italian. As soon as staff members picked up a basic understanding of the language, her father fired them. Smart members played dumb. Gisella found her allies among them, but she'd learned to mind her comments, too.

Ducking into the gilt-papered bathroom off the foyer, she pinched her cheeks, added lipstick and prepared to act like a dutiful daughter. Her life revolved around the Miami Ballet Company, beachside runs and formal dinners, but in her father's house, she would forever be 'Gigi'.

Bracing her hands on the sink, she tilted her head. Her loving father owned Florida's biggest commercial real estate company, Cosmica Insurance Holdings, but he also ran the Florida branch of the Italian mob.

He wore a suit to school functions, but when business soured at home, he rolled up his shirtsleeves, and the gentlemanly look faded. When she had been ten, she'd witnessed the reality of his business dealings through a crack in the study door. She'd never seen his victim again, and she'd kept her observations to herself — but she listened.

When classmates at her parochial school asked what her father did for work, she parroted the company line. "CIH offers property insurance, casualty insurance and value-added insurance services across twenty southeastern states."

They looked impressed.

Why shouldn't they? Every new homeowner in Florida received a direct mailing touting CIH's low rates and friendly staff. The mailings glossed over the company's potential money laundering credentials, but who read the fine print?

Leaving the bathroom, she made her way to the back of the house and to her father's study. The caviar-black masculine room had views of the pool and heavy leather furniture. Despite a sparking oasis waiting beyond the windows, the room looked like a cave.

Last fall, her father's interior designer Lisette had joined the family before Sunday dinner. Wearing a pantsuit, she'd sipped a dirty martini and made vague references to former clients. *"I prefer to create a visual impact by mixing wood species and texture. That movie star I mentioned"* — she sipped her drink — *"had a thing for ebony."*

Gisella had wanted to like the woman, but her influence on the house's décor leaned toward gilt and Hollywood glamour. Having a thing for ebony shocked her as much as Lisette's cosmetic surgery bill. Once a woman immersed herself in wealth, keeping life entertaining required novelty and a steady flow of cash. *"How do you plan to tackle the study?"*

Lisette had wrinkled her surgically enhanced nose. *"The hospitality industry uses black to create glamour, drama and intimacy. Everyone's doing it."*

Gisella had sipped her wine and assumed Lisette was doing her father.

Walking across the room, Gisella admitted the study's black walls created drama, but if her father wanted to scare his minions into compliance, he could pull out the handgun he kept in the desk's top drawer. To keep her in line, he deployed guilt. *'What would your mother think?'*

She wrinkled her nose.

Walking around the polished walnut desk, she leaned down and pressed a kiss to his cheek. He smelled of black tea, Damascus rose, tobacco and leather. At sixty-five years old, he looked ten years younger. Faint silver streaks threaded his black hair. He could wear chinos and he would still smell like old manners and aged wine caves. *"Come è andato il lavoro, Papà?"*

"It is what it is." Continuing in Italian, he set aside his papers. "How was your shopping trip?"

She sat opposite him and crossed her legs. "Fruitful."

He laughed.

Pulling a stack of receipts from her purse, she slid them across the desk. "The rest will come by email."

Shrugging, he leaned back in his chair and left the crumpled slips on the table. "Gigi, you're old enough to drink and old enough to marry."

She picked at her nails. "Is that so?"

"More than old enough. In the home country…"

Looking up, she tilted her head. "We're not in the home country."

He held up a hand. "But if we were, you'd be a bride, and I'd be a grandpa."

"Ursula is older."

"Your sister wants to be a nun."

"So she says." Looking past his full head of hair, she regretted her outburst and second-guessed her decision to come home after rehearsal. If she'd stayed out and shared a drink with Antonio, she'd have to listen to his stories and give up her evening run. She couldn't hide from her father. He financed her life and provided patronage for her art. Looking at him, she softened her expression and recalled the sunlit days he'd spent with her and Ursula. "You're too young to be a grandpa."

"Hear me out," he said.

She exhaled. Drinks with Antonio sounded better. At least he planned to fuck up his own life instead of hers.

When her mother had drowned off the Amalfi Coast, *Papà* had whisked his three children to Miami and begun a new life on the Atlantic's eastern coast. Given how he'd lost his wife, one would think he would have chosen Oklahoma, but he knew how to make money along a coastline. Aunts and nannies had sopped up spilled milk, but when he'd come home at night, he'd kissed her cheek and left his old-world scent against her shoulder.

Some nights, remembering the smell of roses and leather, she recalled how much consistency mattered to children and old men. "Yes, *Papà*."

"I have a series of eligible young men lined up. You will give them each an evening and tell me which man suits you."

"What if I prefer women?"

"Gisella Santa Maria Vitella!" He slammed his palm against the desk.

A vase rattled but resisted gravity's lure.

She rolled her eyes and stood. The dates her father arranged would be insurance agents or mob hit men. She couldn't decide which option she found more appalling. "I can find my own dates, Daddy."

He gripped the leather armrests. "Sit down."

Lowering her frame, she kept her back straight and maintained eye contact. The company's Artistic Director scared her more than her father did, but his familiar expectations could surprise her. Cosseted and pampered, she enjoyed an easy life until she slammed into a glass wall keeping her from enjoying life's stunning vistas. Eventually, she found an exit, and her father acquiesced to her wishes.

He cleared his throat. "You're too old to prance around the stage in a tutu."

She wet her lips. "Too old to dance, and too young to procreate. What's a girl to do? Marriage is a contract, isn't it? Do I get a lawyer?"

He raised an eyebrow.

Outside the mansion's walls, ballet defined her life and gave her predictability. At fifteen, she'd enrolled in the company school and trained for three years. After graduation, she'd joined the ballet as a School Apprentice and spent two years in the trenches before joining the corps de ballet. Three years later, she'd made Soloist, then Principal Soloist. The lure of becoming Principal Dancer kept her focused.

The goal also kept her father off her back. It was like he'd made a deal with his six-year-old daughter, and he refused to back out of his agreement. For the last twenty years, he'd sponsored the company's performances, but rarely attended them.

Last month, she'd celebrated her twenty-fifth birthday. Most dancers stopped dancing professionally between thirty-five and forty years of age. She'd known her father wouldn't give her that much time and would propose an arranged marriage. She might have to accept it, but an IUD would buy her time to achieve her dreams. Crossing her arms, she settled back into the chair.

Sometimes, she lay awake at night and imagined defying her father, but he killed the men who disobeyed him, and she lacked a mother to intercede on her behalf. Caught between ideals and reality, she walked a narrow line and kept her gaze focused on the future. Sometimes, she dreamed of her mother, but she wondered how much time had reshaped the memories.

She remembered holding her breath under water to watch fish, but now she hated to swim. Her inability to trust her memories undermined her faith in herself, and her father's coddling approach undermined her achievements. She could dance across the stage playing a role, but striking out on her own meant vulnerability. Until she knew she could succeed, she would humor his demands. "I hear you, *Papà*. Who's the first victim?"

"You will love Marco."

Tilting her head to the side, she rubbed her scalp. "Doubtful, but tell me where to report."

"You're a good girl, and you'll make me proud. I've tried to raise you the old way, but your aunts can't replace your mother. I'm getting old. You've had leeway to pursue your dancing, but tomorrow evening at eight, you and Marco will dine."

She shook her head. "Not tomorrow, *Papà*. I organized a beach cleanup."

"You hate the water. Find someone else to pick up trash…"

Holding up her hand, she interrupted his mandate. "CIH is sponsoring the event."

His forehead wrinkled.

Maybe he was getting old. "Perhaps Tuesday?" she offered.

His nostrils flared. "Tuesday."

Standing, she rounded the desk, pressed a kiss against his smooth cheek and let his scent calm her frustration. How many times had he threatened her dancing? How many times had he shipped her back to Italy to take in the old country? Here she remained. Marco and the remaining suitors would fizzle out, and she'd continue dancing. "*Ti amo, Papino.*"

He pulled back. "You will go on this date."

"Sure." Picking up the receipts, she dropped them in the trashcan. "I have plenty of new dresses to wear."

"Gigi…"

She winked. Walking out of the office, she let her clicking heels say everything she held back. The marble-backed rhythm sounded so final, like the sound of a bullet fired at close range. Violence hung over her family like a constant threat. If her father understood anything, he understood endings. Keeping him focused on new beginnings remained her job.

Opening the door to her room, she shucked the heels for soft slippers, settled into a stretch and let the music guide her.

Ursula opened the door connecting their rooms and pushed a shoe out of the way. "I thought dancers didn't wear high heels."

"They do when they want salespeople to take them seriously."

Dropping to the floor, Ursula lolled her head. "You'd think a black credit card and a bodyguard would be enough to get their attention."

"You'd think." Gisella deepened her stretch and puzzled through Ursula's recent transformation. Her sister's dark brown hair, olive skin and generous curves could rock a bikini, but lately she'd insisted on dressing like a martyr. If Ursula deviated from her prayers and walked into a boutique, the salespeople might press the panic button. Gisella suppressed a smile.

Her sister had always been serious, but her devotion had deepened in the last six months. After Sunday mass, Gisella had known why. No longer content to hide behind her hymnal, Ursula had stared at Father Pietro, the hot new priest. The man of the cloth must have given Ursula a bit of pious encouragement.

Gisella shrugged and laid her torso along her leg. If Ursula wanted to plan her life around vespers, God love her. "How was your day?"

"Good. Lots of praying, solemnity, hymns and stuff."

Gisella raised her head. "And stuff?"

Ursula swallowed. "Church stuff."

"Maybe you could put the stuff on hold and help me cleanup the beach tomorrow. Every set of hands helps."

"Sure." Ursula stood. "I have a few hours to spare."

Watching her sister slip into the next room, Gisella judged her sister's choices. Dancing made her feel alive. Why would any woman dedicate her life to an organization that spent so much time imagining what came after death?

About the Author

Amy Craig lives in Baton Rouge, Louisiana USA with her family and a small menagerie of pets. She writes women's fiction and contemporary romances with intelligent and empathetic heroines. She can't always vouch for the men. She has worked as an engineer, project manager, and incompetent waitress. In her spare time, she plays tennis and expands her husband's honey-do list.

Amy loves to hear from readers. You can find her contact information, website details and author profile page at https://www.totallybound.com

Home of Erotic Romance

Sign up for our newsletter and find out about all our romance book releases, eBook sales and promotions, sneak peeks and FREE romance books!

Made in the USA
Columbia, SC
14 January 2024

30461796R00231